TOLD BY AN IDIOT

Other Virago Modern Classics published by The Dial Press

ANTONIA WHITE
Frost in May
The Lost Traveller
The Sugar House
Beyond the Glass
Strangers

RADCLYFFE HALL
The Unlit Lamp

REBECCA WEST
Harriet Hume
The Judge
The Return of the Soldier

F. TENNYSON JESSE
The Lacquer Lady

SARAH GRAND
The Beth Book

BARBARA COMYNS
The Vet's Daughter
Our Spoons Came
  from Woolworths

HENRY HANDEL RICHARDSON
The Getting of Wisdom
Maurice Guest

MARY WEBB
Gone to Earth
Precious Bane

EMILY EDEN
The Semi-Attached Couple
  & The Semi-Detached House

MARGARET KENNEDY
The Ladies of Lyndon
Together and Apart

MAY SINCLAIR
Mary Olivier: A Life

ADA LEVERSON
The Little Ottleys

E. ARNOT ROBERTSON
Ordinary Families

ELIZABETH TAYLOR
Mrs. Palfrey at the Claremont
The Sleeping Beauty
In a Summer Season
The Soul of Kindness

Rose Macaulay

TOLD BY AN IDIOT

With a new introduction by
A. N. Wilson

The Dial Press
DOUBLEDAY & COMPANY, INC.
GARDEN CITY, NEW YORK

1983

First published in Great Britain by
William Collins Ltd. 1923

Life's but a walking shadow, a poor player
That struts and frets his hour upon the stage
And then is heard no more ; it is a tale
Told by an idiot, full of sound and fury,
Signifying nothing . . .

(W. SHAKESPEARE.)

L'histoire, comme une idiote, mécaniquement se répète.

(Paul Morand, Fermé la nuit.)

INTRODUCTION

Told by an Idiot is only in part a novel. For, in telling the story of three generations of the Garden family (1879-1920), Rose Macaulay was writing a brilliant essay: about the oddity of religious belief; about clothes and books; above all, about whether human nature changes from decade to decade, and the extent to which it is affected by gender (a word she preferred to *sex*).

To that extent, there are obvious parallels with Virginia Woolf's *Orlando*. Although *Told by an Idiot* is a much less fanciful book (nobody lives through three centuries, nobody changes sex), there are innumerable points at which the two books seem to touch. Rose Macaulay, like Virginia Woolf, was a writer whose natural mode was the essay and whose genius shone most unambiguously when she was making "a casual commentary" on life. As it happened, both women were writing at a period when excuses had to be found *not* to write novels. In the very cadences of the sentences of their two books, moreover, there are similarities. Although the situation between Rome Garden and Mr Jayne is much stronger than anything Virginia Woolf would have attempted (and Mrs Jayne is an absurd figure who has just wandered out of Rose Macaulay's reading of Dostoevsky) it leads to a highly Woolfian passage:

> Drowned she felt, under deep, cold seas of passion and of pain. Wrecked and foundered, at the bottom of grey seas. Something cried, small and weak and hurt within her, and it was the voice of love or (as Mr Jayne would have it) of life.

On the basis of this similarity, between Virginia Woolf and Rose Macaulay, I had decided to begin my consideration of *Told by an Idiot*.

> In 1790, 1690, 1590 and back through every decade of every century, there have been Rome Gardens, fastidious, *mondaine*, urbane, lettered, critical, amused, sceptical and what was called in 1890 *fin de siècle*.

Here was a sentence, I had supposed, which merely showed that Rose Macaulay had been reading Virginia Woolf's *Orlando*. Instead of changing sex, like the protagonist in Virginia Woolf's fantasy, the women in *Told by an Idiot* have sexless names like Rome and Stanley; or else, they are like Imogen, their niece, who "was. . . as sexless as any girl or boy may be. She was still, in all her imaginings, her continuous, unwritten stories about herself, a young man."

Such was the germ of my idea: that Rose Macaulay, delighted by *Orlando* which she later described as "nonsense, of course, but rather lovely and fascinating nonsense, don't you think?"[1] was inspired by reading Virginia Woolf to write an essay, half sentimental and half satirical, on the position of women in society from the closing decades of the Victorian era to the end of the First World War. While not subscribing to Harold Bloom's notion that art in the post-Romantic era is nearly always produced by "the anxiety of influence", I proposed to construct a neat reading of the novel (is not *Told by an Idiot* set in Bloomsbury?) to show that Rose Macaulay, having recently abandoned her Anglo-Catholic faith and discarded the poetic earnestness of her earlier novels, had found, in the last chapter of *Orlando*, the catalyst which enabled her to survey her lost certitudes with a voice appropriate to the moment.

1. Rose Macaulay, *Letters to a Friend* (Collins 1961), p.315.

It is not a bad theory, until one notices that *Orlando* (1928) was published five years after *Told by an Idiot* (1923). If there are similarities between the two books, it was "old stringy Rose Macaulay" (as Mrs Woolf unflatteringly called her[2]) who got there first. It is all a lesson in the fickleness of fortune. Every young "A level" candidate now has the works of Virginia Woolf by heart. But in her lifetime she was read by a tiny public and regarded as "not a Jane Austen: a Felicia Hemans, rather".[3] Rose Macaulay, for her part, is not much read these days. In the decades after the First War, however, she was enormously popular and labelled as "one of the most brilliant of living women writers".[4] It is the kind of reversal which would not have surprised the sardonic narrator of *Told by an Idiot*, who surely speaks through her heroine Rome in the concluding pages:

> Human beings surely tend to overrate their own importance. Funny, hustling, strutting, vain, eager little creatures that we are, so clever and so excited about the business of living, so absorbed and intent about it all, so proud of our achievements, so tragically deploring our disasters, so prone to talk about the wreckage of civilisation, as if it mattered much, as if civilisations had not been wrecked and wrecked all down human history, and it all came to the same thing in the end.

It was surely in so far as she subscribed to this silly view that Rose Macaulay was an inferior novelist. Even if the wreckage of (say) the Babylonian empire was in any way

2. *The Diary of Virginia Woolf*, Vol IV 1931-1935 (Hogarth Press 1982), p.351.

3. Ibid, p.254.

4. Constance Babington Smith, *Rose Macaulay: a biography* (Collins 1972), p.107.

the *same* as the wreckage of the British Empire, we would still be entitled to wonder whether novelists *ought* to think it possible to overrate the importance of human beings. All the greatest novelists, and the best of all the second-rate ones, have surely been consumed by curiosity about these "vain, eager little creatures that we are".

There is, in Rome's case, an explanation for her cynicism. Rome, whose name so obviously is a blend of the Christian name and the first letter in the surname of her author, is, like Rose herself, tall, sardonic and to outward view rather sexless. In fact, she has broken her heart over a married man. It is almost exactly the same story that Rose Macaulay wrote thirty years later in *The Towers of Trebizond*, (where the gender of neither lover is made clear). It is obvious, as her biographer has pointed out, that this theme derives from a love affair which began for the novelist in 1918. The remarkable thing about it is not the affair itself (none of our business) but the way she made it into art. The man in question actually lived on until 1942, and their clandestine affection for one another appears to have been unwavering. Unlike Rome's Mr Jayne or the lost lover, Vere, in *The Towers of Trebizond*, he died in a hospital bed of cancer. Anyone not knowing the immediate biographical details would assume that Laurie's grief for Vere and Rome's grief for Mr Jayne sprang from an identical experience. In fact, Rose Macaulay, like so many authors, wrote her own story before, and not after, she had actually experienced it. In the same way, Tennyson wrote inconsolably sad verse and doubted the existence of an afterlife long before the demise of Arthur Hallam; and Hilaire Belloc's bleak sonnets which appear to reflect the loneliness of his widowerhood were actually penned while his wife was still alive.

Any direct biographical reading of *Told by an Idiot* is

likely, then, to be misleading. But novelists write to allay
their own fears as much as to chronicle experience and in
general terms, this novel reflects Rose Macaulay's character and preoccupations as gaily and vividly as anything she
wrote. The ludicrous opening sentence is part of her own
family lore. Writing years later of G.M. Trevelyan, the
historian and master of Trinity College, Cambridge, she
said:

> He is a cousin. And married to a daughter of that eminent
> Victorian novelist, Mrs Humphry Ward, who wrote so
> earnestly on Doubt. She knew all about that, as her father,
> Tom Arnold (from whom I drew, rather sketchily, the idea
> of my Mr Garden in *Told by an Idiot*) spent his life migrating
> from one church or no church to another and back again.
> My mother was brought up on my grandmother's stories of
> him; she (my grandmother) would come in saying, with
> sympathetic interest, "Poor Tom Arnold has lost his faith
> *again*", and so he had.[5]

The Gardens, like Rose Macaulay's own antecedents,
are one of those intellectual families who were the
backbone of Victorian England. For all the novel's
insistence that human nature and the problems affecting
society are immutable from age to age, we can now see that
such dynasties are gone forever. It is rare, in our own day,
for the intelligentsia (unless they are papist) to breed so
prolifically. When one thinks of the contribution to science
and letters made by such huge families as the Macaulays,
the Arnolds, the Huxleys, the Darwins, the Bensons and
the Sidgwicks (all intermarried) one realises what we have
lost with our financially timid approach to human repro-
duction. Rose Macaulay was only a little older than

5. *Letters to a Friend*, p.111.

Imogen, the younger heroine of the *Tale*, "She looked and felt intelligent. When anyone spoke of theology to her, it was as if the blood of all her clerical ancestors answered to the call."

Rose herself was the second child of George Campbell Macaulay and Grace Mary Conybeare, and a glimpse at her family tree reveals a parson, a don or a schoolmaster on almost every twig. Her father was a distinguished medieval scholar (he edited the works of John Gower) and when Rose was born he was a master at Rugby School under the headmastership of Dr Jex Blake. He had seven children altogether. Like so many clever families of that generation, they were literally a dying breed. None of them married. None of them had issue. On the doctor's advice (those were the days) the family abandoned the English Midlands and moved to Italy when Rose (or Emilie Rose as they called her) was six. Her mother, with incipient tuberculosis, was thought to be dying. (Grace Macaulay lived another thirty-eight years, dying aged seventy in 1925.)

Until she was thirteen, home for Rose was Varazze, then an unspoilt little town some twenty miles west of Genoa. Memories of the place fill her early poems and novels; and her love of the Mediterranean was one of the most constant features of her life. She was an inveterate, rather adventurously dotty traveller, and even during the Second World War managed to get to the Iberian Peninsula to work on her book *They Went to Portugal*. It was at Varazze that she first acquired her delight in Catholic worship (though her hostility to the bigotry and intolerance of the Roman church was always deep). The Mediterranean was also where she developed a lifelong addiction to swimming. (Morning bathes in the Serpentine were part of her daily routine deep into her seventies.) And nostalgia for her Italian childhood always informed her deep love of Latin literature. In many ways, despite the obsession with theology which she inherited from her innumerable clerical ancestors, she would have been happier in the BC era, so long as she could have enjoyed the intelligent patronage of a patrician family. She always used to write of Pliny the Younger, for instance, in affectionate tones ("I like so much all the descriptions of his various villas"[6]) as if he had been some bookish Victorian uncle who had, like her father, decided to settle abroad.

When she was thirteen, the family moved back to England and lived in Oxford, partly so that her father could begin his great work of collating manuscripts of Gower's *Confessio Amantis*, and partly so that she and her siblings could be educated. She attended Oxford High School, and Somerville College, where nerves failed her in her final exams and she was awarded an *aegrotat*. (This, as so often in the lives of otherwise intelligent people, was a fact which always rankled, to the end of her days.) Pretty soon after her undergraduate life was over, she settled in London, sharing a flat with a female friend and starting to write novels.

Religion — which had flitted in and out of her consciousness as a child — returned to her and became important after the murder, (on the North-West frontier) of her beloved brother Aulay in February 1909. She became a thoroughgoing Anglo-Catholic, going to confession and attending retreats, while her literary career went from strength to strength. She had by now returned home to live with her parents, who had retired to Great Shelford near Cambridge. In spite of an active social life (Rupert Brooke was a frequent caller) and an increasingly golden reputation as a novelist (in 1912 her novel *Lee Shore*

6. *Letters to a Friend*, p. 142.

won Hodder and Stoughton's £1,000 prize) she toyed with the idea of becoming a nun or a missionary; and she envied her sister Margaret, who had taken the veil and gone off to Bethnal Green as a deaconess.

During the First World War, Rose continued to write novels (*The Making of a Bigot, Non-Combatants and Others, What Not: A Prophetic Comedy*) and to do voluntary war work. She was a disastrously ineffectual VAD nurse and she was at length persuaded to take clerical work, commuting to work a ten-hour day in the War Office throughout 1917.

It was when she was transferred to the Ministry of Information in 1918 that she met the married man who was to be her lover for the next twenty-three years. She was thirty-seven, and completely "innocent" when the affair began. This love, and the ghastliness of the First War in which so many of her young friends died, contributed to her abandonment of religion. (She retained her love of the Church of England, and was a distinctly high church unbeliever, or Anglo-agnostic, as she preferred to call herself.) In the post-war world, she emerged as a sharp, brittle, satirical writer and in 1920 her novel *Potterism* — an attack on the vulgar newspapers — was her first "best-seller" in England and America. She did not much like being labelled: few writers do. But from now on, her public expected her to be a satirist; and her novels of this post-war period were for the most part light-hearted, intelligently-written skits on contemporary absurdity. In consequence, they all seem a little dated now, fun as they invariably are.

Told by an Idiot, partly because she sets its earlier chapters in the Victorian past, is more approachable, because it deals with more perennial themes, and most of the book's scenes and situations are set up, one feels, so that Rose Macaulay can discuss them as she would in an essay. In 1889, at the age of one, Imogen "neither then nor at any later time, had any clear idea about what women ought or ought not to be. Anything they liked, she probably thought. If, indeed, there were, specifically, any such creatures as women. . . "

This remained, generally, Rose Macaulay's own view of sexual politics, until she died, aged seventy-seven, in 1958. She was fortunate enough, by reason of breeding, intelligence and financial security, to be able to mix on equal terms with men all her life. In early womanhood, she had resented not having the vote. (On that subject, she would have agreed with Stanley in *Told by an Idiot*: "To her the denial of representation in the governing body of her country on grounds of sex was not so much an injustice as a piece of inexplicable lunacy, as if all persons measuring, say, below five foot eight, had been denied votes.") But once the vote was granted to her, there was really nothing which she was prevented from doing on the grounds of gender.

In 1923, when this novel was published, these were more revolutionary notions than they seem today; and it could be said that she fails to take account of the plight of women from less advantaged or liberal backgrounds. The story presents, nevertheless, a fairly pessimistic picture of the complications which ensue when women and men come together without being able to enjoy sexless friendship or companionship. In spite of her rather airy attitude to erotic love ("Who, as Imogen had asked, cared how babies came?") there is here an almost consistently bleak view of marriage.

The novel does not set out to answer any of these problems of the sexual life, but in an elegant way, it highlights them, and points to some of the cruel absurdities which govern marital conventions. Reading it today, one still feels that many of its points stand: for, although we are more tolerant of "free love" and have more liberal divorce laws than obtained in 1923, we still inflict needless misery on ourselves — this is the point of Rome's and Imogen's musings — because of the rigid way in which we consider the roles of the two genders. For all that, family life in some form or another, continues to totter on. *How* babies come might be, as Imogen reflected, a fairly tedious matter. When they come, it probably does them no harm to be born to mothers like Vicky, the least "viewy" of the sisters in the novel. "You couldn't exactly discuss things with her, but she could and did discuss them with you. She would tell you what she thought of the world and its ways in a flow of merry comment." Although so much merrier and more talkative than her own mama, Vicky's marriage has not been appreciably different in style from that of her parents. And it is the warmth of Vicky's family life which prevents *Told by an Idiot* from having a Stracheyesque shrillness.

Rose Macaulay did not herself marry. Her novels taken as a whole present the view that marriage is what Milton called "a drooping and disconsolate household captivity". She dreaded the tedium of it. It was more than a distaste for domestic routines. (When she died, ten unemptied teapots were found in various crannies of her small flat in Hinde Street.) But, more, it was the sense that married people become each other's prisoners. This hazard, represented in Maurice's marriage to Amy, is reflected in novel after novel.

For all that, the novelist herself had come from a happy home, was devoted to her parents, and did not disapprove of marriage as an institution. Although *Told by an Idiot* has much in common with the Bloomsburyite scorn for the Victorians, it is not as scornful of Mr and Mrs Garden as Virginia Woolf or Lytton Strachey would have been. Rose always revered the moral sturdiness of her Victorian forebears and she loved the authors they had loved: Horace and Herrick; Plato and the Cambridge Platonists; Matthew Arnold. And although she mocks Mr Garden's capacity to absorb contradictory religious beliefs, she does so with an obvious affection which is quite different from (say) Strachey's life of Manning.

It has to be said from a purely literary point of view that she is much better at mocking religion than she is at describing it seriously. The purple prose in which Imogen feels herself "full of the Holy Ghost" is probably the most embarrassing passage in the novel. Her satire works best when she is distant from theological conviction, noting with Gibbonian detachment the extraordinary mental somersaults of which the religious mind is capable. And she was a canny enough craftsman to know this fact about herself. When, in old age, she abandoned a thirty-year habit of agnosticism and took to church-going with comic frequency, she yet retained, when her creative intelligence was engaged, some of Rome Garden's distant pose. *The Towers of Trebizond*, her last book and her best, must be one of the churchiest novels ever written. But it achieves its remarkable power because Laurie does not succumb to the browbeating of Father Chantry-Pigg.

> Still the towers of Trebizond, the fabled city, shimmer on a far horizon, gated and walled and held in luminous enchantment. It seems that, for me, and however much I stand outside them, this must for ever be.

The crucial thing is that she remained outside. For, it was outside those walls that her fiction flourished. After *Told by an Idiot*, there were ten novels, all of which deserve to be better known. She had an elegance of mind which lit up everything she wrote; she belonged to the last generation of whom one could use the word *wit* as a high, and not a silly word. She had a considerable range, deep knowledge lightly carried and, for all her natural tendency to scorn, she had something very like warmth of heart. The decision of Virago Press to reprint some fiction by Rose Macaulay is a very cheering one. It implies a confidence that our generation is not too coarse to appreciate her.

A.N. Wilson, London 1982

A FAMILY AT HOME

ONE evening, shortly before Christmas, in the days when our forefathers, being young, possessed the earth,—in brief, in the year 1879,—Mrs. Garden came briskly into the drawing-room from Mr. Garden's study and said in her crisp, even voice to her six children, " Well, my dears, I have to tell you something. Poor papa has lost his faith again."

Poor papa had very often lost his faith during the fifty years of his life. Sometimes he became, from being an Anglican clergyman, a Unitarian minister, sometimes a Roman Catholic layman (he was, by nature, habit and heredity, a priest or minister of religion, but the Roman Catholic church makes trouble about wives and children), sometimes some strange kind of dissenter, sometimes a plain agnostic, who believed that there lived more faith in honest doubt than in half the creeds (and as to this he should know, for on quite half the creeds he was by now an expert). On his last return to Anglicanism, he had accepted a country living.

Victoria, the eldest of the six children, named less for the then regnant queen than for papa's temporary victory over unbelief in the year of her birth, 1856, spoke sharply. She was twenty-three, and very pretty, and saw no reason why papa should be allowed so many more faiths and losses of faith in his career than the papas of others.

" *Really*, mamma . . . it is too bad of papa. I

3

knew it was coming ; I said so, didn't I, Maurice ?
His sermons have been so funny lately, and he's been
reading Comte all day in his study instead of going out
visiting, and getting all kinds of horrid pamphlets
from the Rationalist Press Association, and poring over
an article in the *Examiner* about 'A Clergyman's
Doubts.' And I suppose St. Thomas's Day has brought
it to a head." (Victoria was High Church, so knew
all about saints' days.) "And now we shall have to
leave the vicarage, just when we've made friends with
all sorts of nice people with tennis courts and ball-
rooms. Papa *should* be more careful, and it *is* too bad."

Maurice, the second child (named for Frederick
Denison) who was at Cambridge, and a firm rationalist,
having fought and lost the battle of belief while a
freshman, inquired, cynically, but not undutifully,
and with more patience than his sister, " What is he
going to be this time ? "

"An Ethicist," said Mrs. Garden, in her clear, non-
committal voice. " We are joining the Ethical Society."

" Whatever's that ? " Vicky crossly asked.

" It has no creeds but only conduct " . . . ("And I,"
Vicky interpolated, " have no conduct but only creeds.")
. . . " and a chapel in South Place, Finsbury Pavement, and a magazine which sometimes has a poem
by Robert Browning. It published that one about a
man who strangled a girl he was fond of with her own
hair on a wet evening. I don't know why he thought
it specially suitable for the Ethical Society Magazine.
. . . They meet for worship on Sundays."

" Worship of what, mamma ? "

" Nobility of character, dear. They sing ethical
hymns about it."

Vicky gave a little scream.

Mrs. Garden looked at Stanley, her third daughter
(named less for the explorer than for the Dean, whom

Mr. Garden had always greatly admired) and found, as she had expected, Stanley's solemn blue eyes burning on hers. Stanley was, in fancy, in the South Place Ethical Chapel already, singing the ethical hymns . . .

" Fall, fall, ye ancient litanies and creeds !
    Not prayers nor curses deep
    The power can longer keep
That once ye kept by filling human needs.

Fall, fall, ye mighty temples to the ground !
    Not in their sculptured rise
    Is the real exercise
Of human nature's brightest power found.

'Tis in the lofty hope, the daily toil,
    'Tis in the gifted line,
    In each far thought divine,
That brings down heaven to light our common soil.

'Tis in the great, the lovely and the true,
    'Tis in the generous thought
    Of all that man has wrought,
Of all that yet remains for man to do . . ."

Stanley had read this and other hymns in a little book her papa had.

"Then I suppose," said Rome, the second daughter, who knew of old that papa must always live near a place of worship dedicated to his creed of the moment, "then I suppose we are moving to Finsbury Pavement." Rome had been named less for the city than for the church, of which papa had been a member at the time of her birth, twenty years ago ; and, after all, if Florence, why not Rome ? Rome looked clever. She had a white, thin face, and vivid blue-green eyes, like the sea beneath

rocks; and she thought it very original of papa to believe
so much and so often. Her own mind was sceptical.

Vicky's brow smoothed. Moving to London. There
was something in that. Though, of course, it mustn't
be Finsbury Pavement; she would see to that.

Irving, the youngest but one (named less for the actor
than to commemorate the brief period when papa
had been an Irvingite, and had believed in twelve
living apostles who must all die and then would come
the Last Day), said, " Golly, what a lark ! " Irving
was sixteen, and was all for a move, all for change,
of residence, if not of creed. He was an opportunist
and a realist, and made the best of the vagaries of
circumstance. He was destined to do well in life. He
was not, like Maurice, sicklied o'er with the pale cast
of thought, nor, like Vicky, caught in the mesh of each
passing fashion, nor, like Stanley, an ardent hunter of
the Idea, nor, like Rome, a critic. He was more like
(only he had more enterprise and initiative) his younger
sister, Una, a very calm and jolly schoolgirl, named
less for her who braved the dragon than for the One
Person in whom papa had believed at the time of her
birth (One Person not in the Trinitarian, but in the
Unitarian, sense).

" Three hundred a year less," remarked Rome, from
the couch whereon she lay (for her back was often tired)
and looked ironically at Vicky, to see how she liked the
thought of that.

Vicky's smooth cheek flushed. She had forgotten
about money.

" Oh *really* . . . Oh, I do think papa is too bad.
Mamma, *must* he lose it just this winter—his faith, I
mean ? Can't he wait till next ? "

Mamma's faint (was it also ironic, or merely patient ?)
movement of the eyebrows meant that it was too late :
papa's faith was already lost.

" By next winter he may have found it again," Rome suggested.

" Well, even if so," said Vicky, " who's going to go on giving him livings every time ? . . . Oh, yes, mamma, I know all the bishops love him, but there *is* a limit to the patience of bishops. . . . Does the Ethical Society have clergymen or anything ? "

" I believe they have elders. Papa may become an elder."

" *That's* no use. Elders aren't paid. Don't you remember when he was a Quaker elder, when we were all little ? I'm sure it's not a paid job. We shall be loathsomely poor again, and have to live without any fun or pretty things. And I dare say it's low class, too. Papa never bothers about that, of course. He'd follow General Booth into the Army, if he thought he had a call."

" I trust that I should, Vicky."

Papa had entered the room, and stood looking on them all, with his beautiful, distinguished, melancholy face (framed in small side whiskers), and his deep blue eyes like Stanley's. Vicky's ill-humour melted away, because papa was so gentle and so beautiful and so kind. And, after all, London was London, even with only four hundred a year.

" Mamma has told you our news, I see," said papa, in his sweet, mellow voice. He looked and spoke like a papa out of Charlotte M. Yonge, though his conduct with regard to the Anglican church was so different.

" Yes, Aubrey, I've told them," said mamma.

" I hope you won't mind, papa," said Vicky saucily, " if *I* go to church at St. Albans, Holborn. *I'm* a ritualist, not an ethicist."

" Indeed, Vicky, I should be very sorry if you did not all follow your own lights, wherever they lead you."

Papa's broad-mindedness amounted to a disease,

Vicky sometimes thought. A queer kind of clergyman
he was. What would Father Stanton and Father
Mackonichie of St. Albans think of him? Father
Mackonichie, who was habitually flung into jail
because he would face east when told to face north—
as important as all that, he felt it.

" Well, my darlings," papa went on in his nice voice;
" I must apologise to you all for this—this disturbance
of your lives and mine. I would have spared it you if
I could. But I have been over and over the ground,
and I see no other way compatible with intellectual
honesty. Honesty must come first. . . . Your mother
and I are agreed."

Of course ; they always were. From Anglicanism
to Roman Catholicism, from Catholicism to Quakerism,
from Quakerism to Unitarianism, Postivism, Baptist-
ism (yes, they had once sunk, to Vicky's shame, as
low as that in the social scale, owing chiefly to the
influence of Charles Spurgeon), and back to Anglicanism again—through everything, mamma, silent, resigned and possibly ironic, had followed papa. And
little Stanley had seen the idea behind all papa's
religions and tumbled headlong after him, and Maurice
had grimly decided that it was safer to abjure all
creeds, and Rome had critically looked on, with her
faint, amused smile and her single eyeglass, and Irving
and Una had been led, heedless and incurious, to each
of papa's places of worship in turn, but had understood
none of them. They had not the religious temperament. Nor had Vicky, who attended her ritualistic
churches from æsthetic fancy and a flair for being in
the fashion, for seeing and hearing some new thing.
She didn't care which way priests faced, though she
did enjoy incense. Vicky was a gay soul, and preferred dances and lawn tennis and young men to
religion. Stanley, too, was gay—as merry as a grig,

papa called her—but she had a burning ardour of mind
and temper that made the world for her a place of
exciting experiments. She now thought it worthy and
honourable to be poor, for she had been reading William
Morris and Ruskin and Socialism, as intelligent young
women did in those days, and was all for handicrafts
and the one-man job. She was eighteen, and had
had her first term at Somerville College, Oxford, which
had just been founded and had twelve members.

Irving, always practical, said, " When are we going
to move ? And where to ? "

" In February," said mamma. " Probably we shall
live in Bloomsbury. We have heard of a house there."

" Bloomsbury," said Vicky. " That's not so bad."

Sitting down at the piano, she began softly to play
and sing.

Papa sat by the fire, his thin hand on mamma's, his
thoughtful face pale and uplifted, as if he had made
the Great Sacrifice once more, as indeed he had. Stanley
sat on a cushion at his feet, and leant her dark head
against his knee. She was a small, sturdy girl, and
she wore a frock of blue, hand-embroidered cloth,
plain and tight over the shoulders and breast, high-
necked, with white ruching at the throat, and below
the waist straighter than was the fashion, because Mr.
Morris said that ripples and flounces wasted material
and ruined line. Vicky, sinuous and green, rippled
to the knees like running water. Irving sat on a
Morris-chintz chair, reading *The Moonstone*; Maurice
on a Liberty cretonne sofa, reading a leader in yesterday's *Observer*.

" It is, unfortunately, impossible to conceal from
ourselves that the condition of Ireland, never per-
ceptibly improved by the announcement of the pro-
jected remedy for her distress and discontents, has for

some weeks gone steadily from bad to worse. The state of things which exists there is, for all practical purposes, indistinguishable from civil war. The insurrectionary forces arrayed against law and order are not, indeed, drilled and disciplined bodies ; but what they lack in this respect they make up for in numbers and in recklessness."

Such was the sad state of Ireland in December, 1879, as sometimes before, as sometimes since. Or, anyhow, such was its state according to the *Observer*, a paper with which Maurice seldom, and Stanley never, agreed. Stanley put her faith in Mr. Gladstone, and Maurice in no politicians, though he appreciated Dizzy as a personality. Papa had always voted Liberal and Gladstone, but thought that the latter lacked religious tolerance.

Maurice turned to another leader, which began, " In these troubled times . . ." And certainly they *were* troubled, as times very nearly always, perhaps quite always, are. The *Observer* told news of the Basuto war, the Russian danger in Afghanistan, Land League troubles, danger of war with Spain, trouble in Egypt, trouble in Bulgaria, trouble in Midlothian (where Mr. Gladstone was speaking against the government), trouble of all sorts, everywhere. What a world ! Stanley, an assiduous student of it, sometimes almost gave it up in despair ; but never quite, for she always thought of something one ought to do, or join, or help, which might avert shipwreck. Just now it was handicrafts, and the restoration of beauty to rich and poor.

2

MAMMA AND HER CHILDREN

MAMMA, sitting with papa's hand in hers, watched
them all, with her quiet gray eyes looking through
pince-nez, and her slight smile. Pretty Vicky, singing
" My Queen," with the lamplight shining on her mass
of chestnut hair parted Rossetti-wise in the middle,
her pink cheeks, her long white neck, her graceful,
slim, flowing form, her æsthetic green dress (for Vicky
was bitten with the æsthetic craze). Pretty Vicky.
She loved gaiety and parties and comfort so much, it
was a shame to cut down her dress allowance, as would
be necessary. Perhaps Vicky would get engaged very
soon, though, to one of her æsthetic or worldly young
men. Vicky was not one of those sexless, intellectual
girls, like Rome, with her indifference, or Stanley, with
her funny talk of platonic friendships. To Vicky a
young man *was* a young man, and no platonics about
it. Sometimes mamma was afraid that Vicky, for all
her æstheticism, was a little *fast;* she would go out
for long day expeditions alone with the young man of
the moment, and laugh when her mother said, doubt-
fully, " Vicky, when *I* was young . . ."

" When *you* were young, mamma dear," Vicky would
say, caressing and mocking, " you were an early Victorian. Or even a Williamite. Papa, prunes, prisms !
I'm a late Victorian, and we do what we like."

"A *mid*-Victorian, I hope, dear," mamma would
loyally interpolate, but Vicky would fling back, " Oh,
mamma, H.M. has reigned forty-two years now ! You
don't think she's going to reign for eighty-four ! Late
Victorian, that's what we are. *Fin-de-siècle.* Probably
the world will end very soon, it's gone on so long, so

let's have a good time while we can. We're only young once. I feel, mamma, at the very end of the road, and as if nothing mattered but to live and dance and play while we can, because the time's so short. Clergymen say it's a sign of the world coming to an end, all these wars and disturbances everywhere, and unbelief, and women and trains being so fast in their habits, and young men so effeminate."

Thus Vicky, mocking and gay and absurd. Her mother's keen, near-sighted gray eyes strayed from her round the pretty lamplit room, which was partly Liberty and Morris, with its chintzes and wallpapers and cretonnes, and blue china plates over the door (that was the children) and partly mid-Victorian, with its chiffoniers and papier-maché and red plush chairs, and Dicksee's "Harmony" hanging over the piano. On the table lay the magazines—the *Nineteenth Century*, the *Cornhill*, the *Saturday Review*, the *Spectator*, and the *Examiner*, with the article by Samuel Butler on "A Clergyman's Doubts." They had made the vicarage so pretty, it would be hard to leave it for a dingy London house. It was a pity (though hardly surprising) that the Anglican church could find no place for Aubrey during the intervals when he could not say the creed. Aubrey was so modern. Mrs. Garden's own father, also a clergyman, believed in the Established Church and the Bible, and agreed with the writer of the Book of Genesis (and Bishop Usher, its commentator) that the world had been created in the year 4004 B.C., and that Adam and Eve had been created shortly afterwards, full of virtue, and had fallen ; and so on, through all the Bible books. . . . After all, the scriptures *were* written (and even marginally annotated) for our learning. . . . But Mrs. Garden's papa had begun being a clergyman when religion had been more settled, before Darwin and Huxley and Herbert Spencer

had revolutionised science. You didn't expect an
able modern Oxford man like Aubrey to be an Early
Victorian clergyman.

Maurice on the Liberty sofa snorted suddenly over
what he was reading, and mamma smiled at him.
The dear, perverse, violent boy! He was always
disagreeing with every one. Mamma's eyes rested
gently on her son's small, alert head, with its ruffled
top locks of light, straight hair, like a cock canary's
crest, its sharp, long chin and straight, thin lips.
Maurice was like mamma's brothers had been, in the
fifties, only they had worn peg-top trousers and long,
fair whiskers that stood out like fans. Maurice wore
glasses, and looked pale, as if he had read too much ;
not like young Irving, sprawling in an easy chair with
The Moonstone, beautiful and dark and pleased.
Nor like Stanley, who, though she read and thought and
often talked cleverly like a book, had high spirits and
was full of fun. Little Stanley, with her round, childish face above the white ruching, her big forehead and
blunt little nose, and deep, ardent, grave blue eyes.
What a child she was for enthusiasms and ideas and
headlong plans! And her talk about platonic friendships and women's rights and social revolution and
bringing beauty into common life. The New Girl.
If Vicky was one kind of New Girl (which may be
doubted), Stanley was another, even newer. . . .
There shot into mamma's mind, not for the first time,
a question—had girls always been new ? She remembered in her own youth the older people talking about
the New Girl, the New Woman. Were girls and women
really always newer than boys and men, or was it
only that people noticed it more, and said more about
it ? Elderly people wrote to the papers about it.
"The Girl of the Period," in the *Saturday Review*—
fast, painted, scanty of dress (where are our fair, demure

English girls gone?) with veils less concealing than provocative. . . . What, Mrs. Garden wondered, was a provocative veil? The New Young Woman. Bold, fast, blue-stockinged, self-indulgent, unchaperoned, advanced, undomesticated, reading and talking about things of which their mothers had never, before marriage, heard—in brief, NEW. (To know all that the mid-Victorians said about modern girls, and, indeed, about modern youth of both sexes, you have only to read certain novelists and journalists of the nineteen twenties, who are saying the same things to-day about what they call the Young Generation.)   Had Adam and Eve, Mrs. Garden wondered, commented thus on their daughters—or, more likely, on their daughters-in-law? (According to Mrs. Garden's papa, these had been the same young women, but in the late seventies one wasn't, fortunately, obliged to believe the worst immoralities of the Old Testament.)

"Youth," it was said at this period, as at other periods before and since, "youth in the last quarter of the nineteenth century has broken with tradition. It is no longer willing to accept forms and formulæ only on account of their age," (at what stage in history youth ever did this is never explained).   "It has set out on a voyage of inquiry, and, finding some things which are doubtful and others which are insufficient, is searching for forms of experience more in harmony with the realities of life and knowledge."   (These are the actual words of a writer of the nineteen twenties, but they were used, in effect, also in the eighteen seventies and many other decades.)

And had the young, both men and women, always believed that they alone could save the world, that the last generation, the elderly people, were no good, were, in fact, responsible for the unfortunate state in which the world had always up to now been, and that it was for the young to usher in the New Day ? Well, no doubt they were right. The only hitch seemed to be that the young people always seemed to get elderly before they had had time to bring in the New Day, and then they were no good any more, and the next generation had to take on the job, and still the New Day coyly refused to be ushered in. Except that, of course, in a sense, each day was a new one. But not, alas, much of an improvement on the day before.

" These troubled times. . . ." Had there ever been, would there ever be, a day when the newspapers said, " In these quiet and happy times ? " Stanley, inspired by Mr. William Morris, was sure of it. The millenium was just round the corner, struggling in the womb of time, only it needed workers, workers, and again workers, to deliver it safely. Some lecturer under whom Stanley had sat had put it like that, and she had repeated it to her mother. Well, of course, in these days . . . the New Girl, being so new and so free, could use such metaphors. In the fifties you couldn't ; unmarried girls couldn't, anyhow. Stanley had, indeed, coloured a little when she had said it. Stanley was not only unmarried, but declared that she never would be married, there was too much to be done (which was a way some young women were talking just then). She was going, after Oxford, to work in a settlement, and teach people weaving, dyeing and beauty, after learning them herself at the Morris workshops. It was all very nice, but mamma would rather Stanley had a husband and babies. (Mammas, it may be observed in passing, differ from other women in being very seldom new.)

Then mamma's eyes rested on her chubby, beautiful baby, Una, lolling on the hearthrug, one light brown pigtail over each shoulder, reading, with calm and lovely blue eyes, some dreadful rubbish in the *Boy's*

Own Paper, her cheek bulged out with a lump of toffee.
A nice, good, placid child of fifteen, who never thought,
never read anything but tosh, talked in slang, and took
life as it came, cheerful, unquestioning and serene.
Una was the least clever and the best balanced of the
Gardens. She was going, when she was older, to look
rather like the Sistine Madonna.

How unlike her happy, handsome solidity was to
Rome ! Rome lay back on her couch, her face like a
clear white cameo against deep blue cushions, the
lamplight shining on her fair, silky curls, cut short
in one of the manners of the day. Rome's thin lips
twisted easily into pain and laughter ; her jade-green
eyes mocked and watched. " I'm afraid of your
sister. She looks as if she was going to put us all
into a book," people would sometimes say to the others
of her. But Rome never wrote about anything or
any one ; it was not worth while.

3

SISTERS IN THE GARDEN

MAURICE threw down the second serial part of *Theo-
phrastus Such*, which had just come out.

" The woman's going all to pieces," he said, in his
crisp, quick, disgusted voice. " Sermonising and tosh.
. . . The fact is," said Maurice, " the fact is, the
novel, anyhow in this country, has had its day. Except
for the unpretending thrillers. We should give it a
rest. The poets still have things to say and are saying
them (though not so well as they used to ; *their* palmy
days are over, too) but not the novelists. . . ."

Vicky, to drown his discourse, began to sing loud
and clear :

"When I was a *young* maid, a *young* maid, a
   young maid . . ."

"Of course she's old," went on Maurice, referring to
Mary Anne Evans. "And she's been spoilt. She's
not a teacher, she's a novelist. Or she was. Now
she's dropped being a novelist and become merely a
preacher. That's the end of her. I wish to God
people would know their job and stick to it. She
was a jolly *good* novelist. . . . Sorry, pater "—Mr.
Garden had frowned at the expletive—" but I didn't
think you'd mind—*now*. I suppose you and I are both
agreed, aren't we, as to the non-existence of a Deity."

"All the same, my dear boy . . ."

All the same (this was Rome's thought) papa had so
recently believed in a Deity, and would, no doubt, so
soon again believe in a Deity, that it seemed bad taste
to fill the brief interim with vain oaths. Maurice had
no reverence at all, and no taste. You would think,
as Vicky turned from the piano to say, that, whatever
he did or didn't believe himself, he might remember
that some people were not only Christians but Church,
and High Church at that. But Maurice only grinned
at her. She tweaked his fair crest in passing, and
arranged her own glossy chestnut coiffure at the painted
looking-glass over the chimney-piece. This Rossetti
shape suited her, she thought, better than the high
coils of last year.

The parlourmaid announced the curate, a good-
looking, intelligent, cheerful young man, whom they
all liked. He had hardly shaken hands when Mr.
Garden said to him, " I want a talk with you, Carter,"
and took him off to the study, to break it to him about
the Ethical Society.

"Papa might just as well have told him here," Vicky
petulantly said. " It would only have needed a

sentence, and then we could have had a jolly evening."

" Of course, papa feels he must go into it thoroughly with Mr. Carter," said mamma. " Poor Mr. Carter will be dreadfully hurt by it, I'm afraid. He has always been so fond of papa, and he has never himself seen any reason for doubt."

" There *is* no reason for doubt," muttered Vicky, beneath her breath. Then, louder, impatience conquering respect, " What does papa think the Church is for, except to tell us what we can't know for ourselves about what to believe ? "

Mamma replied, taking up her embroidery, " Papa doesn't know what the Church is for. That is his great difficulty. And, Vicky, it is not for us, who have studied so much less, to protest . . ."

" Well," said Vicky, " I shall go into the garden. It's a night for men and angels. Come on, Stan."

Stanley came, and the sisters paced together, wrapped in shawls, down the gravel path, beneath a deep blue sky full of frosty, twinkling stars and the pale glow which precedes winter moonrise. It was one of those frosty Christmases which our parents (they say) used to have in their youths. Hot summers and frosty winters—that is what they say they used to have : one is not obliged to believe them, but it is a picturesque thought.

" I'll tell you what I'm going to do, Stannie. I shall get married."

" Who to, Vicky ? "

"Ah ! " Vicky's long eyes were mysterious in the starlight. " Perhaps I've not made up my mind yet ; perhaps I have. All I do know is that I'm not going to live round about South Place, Finsbury Pavement, on £400 a year just because papa must needs go to an ethical chapel. I — shall — get — married. And well married, too. Why not ? I can, you know, if I want to."

" Captain Penrose," said Stanley.

" *He's* not the only one, my child. There are others. No, I shan't tell you a word more now. You wait and see. And when I'm married you shall come and stay with me, and meet lots and lots of men."

Lots and lots of men. The kind of men who'd be friends with Vicky and Captain Penrose (or whoever else Mr. Vicky might prove to be).

" I shall be busy, you know," said Stanley, doubtful and conceited. " I shall have very little spare time, if I take up weaving and dyeing."

" Don't take up weaving and dyeing. It's shockingly cranky, anyway, all this Morris craze of yours."

"All the best things are thought cranky at first."

" Don't you believe it. The new princess dress isn't. . . . Now mind, I'm saying this for your good, my dear ; men won't look at you if you go about with dyed hands and talk about manual labour and the one-man job and the return of beauty to the home."

" Vicky, you're *vulgar*. And as I don't mean to marry, what does it matter if they look at me or not ? "

" Oh, tell that to the marines. . . . I'm getting frozen. Come along in, and we'll turn the curate's head, unless papa's still breaking his heart. . . . You're a little prig, Stan., that's your trouble, my child."

It was quite true. Stanley *was* a little prig. She not only read Ruskin and Morris and Karl Marx, but quoted them. There came a day, later on, when she saw through Ruskin, but it is no use pretending that that day was yet. She was a prig, and believed that it was up to such as her to reform the world. She saw herself (at the moment, for her vision of herself varied) as the modern woman, clever, emancipated, high-minded, too intellectually fastidious to take the vulgar view. She took herself seriously, in spite of the childish giggle at the comedy of life which broke like gurgling water through her earnestness.

"The first Nowell the angels did sing," sang Vicky, in her clear, fluting voice, and danced in at the drawing-room window.

4

MAMMA AND ROME

MAMMA sat by Rome's side and embroidered, while papa interviewed his curate in the study. You could see, now these two sat together, that they were alike, not so much in feature or colour as in some underlying, elusive essence of personality. But Rome's mocking, amused, critical self looked ironically out of her blue-green eyes, and mamma's dwelt very still and deep within her.

"Well, mamma." Rome put down her book, which was by Anatole France.

"Well, Rome."

"You don't much mind this." Rome was commenting, not inquiring.

"Oh, no." Mamma was placid. "Not," she added, "that I *want* to live in London particularly. Dirty place. No gardens."

Rome said, definitely, "I prefer London," and mamma nodded. Rome was urbane. Negligent, foppish and cool, she liked to watch life at its games, be flicked by the edges of its flying skirts. And the game of life was more varied and entertaining in London than in the country, and equally absurd. So Rome preferred London. It was like having a better seat at the play. Lack of bodily energy threw her back largely in the country on to the entertainment of her own rather cynical mind. She was often bored, sometimes ill-humoured, sharp and morose. The years might bring her a greater patience, but at twenty she was not patient. The very sharp clarity of her mind, that chafed against muddled thinking, stupidity, humbug and sentimentality, made intercourse difficult for her in the country, where heaven has ordained that even fewer persons shall reside who are free from these things than is the case in large towns.

"How long," inquired Rome negligently, slipping round an old silver ring on her thin white finger, "do you give the Ethical Church, mamma?"

Mamma was feather-stitching, rapidly and correctly. The movement of her head indicated that she declined to prophesy.

"No point in looking ahead," she said practically. "One always sees a change a little while before it comes, in time to be prepared, and that's all we need. Papa is never sudden."

The whimsical smile that twitched at one corner of Rome's thin mouth was unreturned by mamma, whose face was gravely bent over her work. Mamma was a good wife, and never joked about papa's vagaries with her children. No one had ever got behind mamma's guard in the matter of papa—if it was a guard. Who could see into mamma's mind? idly speculated Rome. Mamma had, at forty-five, achieved a kind of delicate impenetrability. Papa, at fifty, was as limpid as the clear water of a running stream, where you may watch the fishes swimming to and fro, round and round.

Papa came back, alone and looking hurt. At the same moment Vicky came in at the long window, pink-cheeked, smelling of frost.

"Where's Mr. Carter, papa?"

"Gone away, Vicky. He—he couldn't stop."

"I suppose he was shocked to death! Oh, well . . ."

But, of them all, only mamma knew *how* shocked

the orthodox people of the eighteen seventies were
about matters of unbelief. The children had been
brought up in the wrong atmosphere really to know it.
Mamma knew that to Mr. Carter papa's action would
seem dreadful, blasphemous, very nearly wicked. . . .

"After all," said Vicky impatiently, "we're living
in the year 1879. We're moderns, after all."

Dashingly modern Vicky looked, in her sinuous art-
green dress, with her massed Rossetti hair and jade
ear-rings. Daringly, brilliantly modern, and all agog
for life. A dashing girl, as they called them in 1879—
if a girl bitten with æstheticism can still dash, and it
may be taken for granted that dashing girls will always
dash, whatever bites them. Catching up slim young
Irving from his chair, Vicky twirled him round the room
in a waltz.

5

BLOOMSBURY AND SOUTH PLACE

In February the Gardens moved to Bloomsbury.
Different people and more people came to the house ;
it was rather like the old days when papa had been a
Unitarian. Mr. Stopford Brooke began coming to
see papa again, and Dr. Martineau, and all his old and
new friends who lived in London, even Father Stanton,
of St. Albans, Holborn, and Mr. Charles Spurgeon.
The circle of papa's friends had swollen and swollen
with the years, from his undergraduate days onwards.
Not only was papa lovable and popular, but he touched
so many circles, fished in so many waters, and his fellow-
fishermen of each particular water usually remained
faithful to him even when he moved on to another
pool. Good-humoured, witty Mr. Spurgeon, for instance,

did not break with papa when he deserted the City
Temple for a second go of Anglicanism, though he
was sadly disappointed in him. Nor were papa's
interests bound by religion ; he had friends, distinguished and indistinguished, among politicians, journalists, poets, professors, and social reformers, besides
his relatives and mamma's. And now, of course, there
was a quite fresh influx, from the South Place Ethical
Chapel. So, one way and another, what with papa's
friends and mamma's and the children's, a good deal
of life flowed into the Bloomsbury Square house. Papa
was, in his quiet way, happy, now that the wrench was
over. He was writing, and had for years been writing,
a very long book on comparative religions, and for
this he worked at the British Museum, which was so
conveniently near. And on Sundays he went to South
Place, and worshipped ethically.

" Do not crouch to-day and worship,"

he would sing, in his sweet tenor voice,

> *" The old past, whose life is fled ;*
> *Hush your voice to tender reverence,*
> *Crowned he lies, but cold and dead.*
> *For the present reigns our monarch,*
> *With an added weight of hours ;*
> *Honour her, for she is mighty !*
> *Honour her, for she is ours ! "*

(The author, Miss Adelaide Proctor, had very rightly,
it will be noted, dethroned a male and enthroned a
female.)
So sang papa and mamma on a Sunday morning in
April. Then some one rose and said a few ethical
words about the desirability of not being fettered by

religious dogma, and the congregation, who all thought
this desirable too, listened attentively.

Papa gazed wistfully in front of him, at the varnished
seats and painted woodwork and the ethical texts in-
scribed round the walls. " Live for Others." " Live
Nobly." " Duty First." . . . He had made the
great sacrifice, and once more dethroned the past, for
honesty's sake, and if it entailed a jarring of literary
and artistic fastidiousness, who was he to rebel ? God
knew, he had been æsthetically happier joining in the
Roman mass (tawdry and vulgar-looking as the churches
where this service is held so usually are) or chanting the
Anglican liturgy in the little fourteenth century church
in Hampshire—though, as to that, some of Hymns
A. & M. were quite as bad as anything in the ethical
hymn-book—but never had he been so utterly honest,
so stripped to the bare bone of all complacency, humbug
and self-deception, as now.   Or so, anyhow, he believed,
but who shall read the human heart ?

Again they sang :

> " Hush the loud cannon's roar,
> The frantic warrior's call !
> Why should the earth be drenched in gore ?
> Are we not brothers all ? "

For, sad to say, the earth was, in the spring of 1880,
drenched (as usual) in gore. The gore of Afghans
and British in Afghanistan, of Basutos in Basutoland,
Chilians and Bolivians in Central America, Liberals
and Conservatives in Great Britain, where the elections
were being fiercely contested, besides such permanently
flowing gore as that of Jews in Russia and Christians
in Turkey. The Ethical Society hoped pathetically
that all these so unlikely persons would enjoy peace
and brotherhood one day.

They trooped out into South Place. Grave, intelligent, ethical men and women clustered and hummed together like bees. They talked about the elections, which were going well, for nearly all the Ethical members were Liberals, and the Liberals were sweeping the country.

"Why are Ethical members Liberals?" Rome inquired in the note-book to which she committed as much of her private commentary on life as ever found its way to paper. "Partly, no doubt, because of the Liberal attitude towards religion, but it must be more than that. *T.C.*" "T.C." meant "trace connection," and was a very frequent entry. Rome looked forward to a time when, by means of prolonged investigation all the connections she had noted should be traced; that, she held, would add to her understanding of this strange, amusing life. What, for instance, was the connection between High Church dogma and ornate ritual; between belief in class distinctions and in the British Empire; between dissent and Little Englandism; art and unconventional morals; the *bourgeoisie* and respectability; socialism and queer clothes? All these pairs and many others were marked T.C., and had a little space under them, in which the connection, when traced, was explained, in concise and lucid language. In another part of the book there were pages assigned to "Curious uses of words." Rome felt a great, perhaps a morbid, interest in investigating life and language. She wrote, "Why are Ethical members Liberals?" when papa and mamma, coming in from chapel, told her how delighted South Place was with the elections. Papa, of course, had always been a Liberal, through all his religious vicissitudes.

Vicky came in, like a graceful whirlwind, from Walworth, S.E., where she had attended church at St. Austin's, the monastery of Brother à Beckett, and flung herself into a chair in an ecstasy.

"A service straight from heaven!" she cried. "Too utterly utter! *Such* incense—perfumes of Araby! And Brother à Beckett preached about the authority of the State over the Church. It simply doesn't exist. The State is *nowhere*, and not to be taken the slightest notice of. . . . And who do you think was there, just in front of us—Mr. Pater and the adorable Oscar in a velveteen coat, looking like the prince of men and talking like the king of wits (yes, mamma, talking, but in quite an undertone). But too utter! I was devastated. I was with Charles. I'd made him come with me, to try if grace would abound—but no, not yet; Charles remains without, with the dogs and the . . ."

" Vicky," mamma interpolated.

" . . . and the sorcerers, mamma, dear," Vicky finished, innocently. " What did you *think* I was going to say ? "

" You must allow Charles his conscience, Vicky," said papa.

Charles was Vicky's half-affianced suitor, but unfortunately an agnostic, or rather a Gallio, and Vicky declared that they should not become regularly engaged until such time as Charles should embrace the Anglican, or some other equally to be respected, church. Unbelief might be fashionable, but Vicky didn't hold with it. Also, and worse, Charles was not yet in the æsthetic push; he was, instead, in the Foreign Office, and took no interest in the New Beauty. Velveteen coats he disliked, and art fabrics, and lilies except in gardens, and languor except in offices, and vice except in the places appointed for it. And all these distastes would, as Vicky complained, make the parties they would give such a difficulty. Vicky told Charles that, unless he conquered them, she might feel compelled to become affianced instead to Mr. Ernest Waller, a young essayist who understood Beauty, though not, indeed, Anglicanism, as he had been a pupil of Mr. Pater's in the days when Mr. Pater had been something of a pagan. But better burn incense before heathen gods, said Vicky, than burn none at all.

So, when papa said, " You must allow Charles his conscience," Vicky returned, firmly, " Dear papa, *no*. Conscience should be our servant, not our master. That's what Brother à Beckett said in his sermon this morning. Or, anyhow, something like it. Conscience is given us to be educated and trained up the way it should go. An unruly conscience is an endless nuisance. He that bridleth not his own conscience . . ."

Papa, sensible of his own so inconveniently unbridled conscience, said mildly, " I think Brother à Beckett was perhaps referring to the tongue," and Vicky lightly admitted that her memory might have got confused.

" But never mind sermons and the conscience, here's grandpapa," she said ; and, sure enough, there was grandpapa, who was staying with them on a visit. Grandpapa was the father of mamma, and a dean, and a very handsome man of seventy-five, and he was one of the last ditchers in the matter of orthodoxy, and had yielded no inch to science or the higher criticism, and believed in the verbal inspiration of the Bible and the divine credentials of the Anglican Establishment, and disliked popery, ritual, dissent and free thought with equal coldness. Papa he had never approved of ; a weak, vacillating fellow, whose reputation was little affected by one disgraceful change more or less. · It did not particularly signify that papa had joined the Ethical Church ; nothing about papa particularly signified ; a weak, wrong-headed, silly fellow, who would certainly, for all his scholarship, never be a Dean. It was far more distressing that

Anne (mamma), who ought to have made a firm stand
and saved her husband from his folly, should thus
abet him and follow him about from church to church.
And the children had been deplorably brought up.
Grandpapa, who thought it blasphemous not to believe
in Noah and his ark, and even in the date assigned
to these by Bishop Usher, and had written to *The Times*
protesting against the use in schools of the arithmetic
book of Bishop Colenso, on account of the modernist
instruction imparted by this bishop to the heathen
in this matter of the date of the ark,—grandpapa
heard these unhappy children of his daughter's discussing the very bases of revealed truth ; grandpapa,
who held that our first parents lost paradise through
disobedience, pride, inquisitiveness and false modesty,
heard Maurice's perverse defiance of law and authority.
Rome's calm contempt and conceited criticism of
accepted standards, Stanley's incessant, eager, " Why,
what for, and why not ? " and Vicky's horror at the
breadth and crudeness of the Prayer Book marriage
service.

Grandpapa, being a conservative and a Disraelian,
was just now not well pleased. He did not think that
the Gladstone government would be able to deal
adequately or rightly with the inheritance of foreign
responsibilities left them by their predecessors. South
Africa, Egypt, Afghanistan,—what would the liberals,
many of them Little Englanders, in fact though not
yet in name, do with all this white man's burden, as
the responsibilities of Empire were so soon, so horribly
soon, to be called ? Had grandpapa thought of it, he
would certainly have called them that. His grandson,
Maurice, called them, on the other hand, " all those
damned little Tory wars," a difference in nomenclature
which indicated a real difference in political attitude.

Grandpapa entered with the *Observer*, which regretted

as he did the way the elections had gone, and with the *Guardian*, which did not. He sat down and patted Vicky on the shoulder, and said that Dean Liddon had preached at St. Paul's, where he had attended morning service.

"A capital defence of the faith," said grandpapa. " Bones to it, and substance. None of your sentimental slop. You've all been running after ethics, or ritual, or this, that and the other, but I've had the pure Word. Liddon's too High, but he's sound. I remember in '55 . . ."

One of grandpapa's familiar stories, told as old people told their stories, with loving rounding of detail.

Vicky's mind reached vainly back towards '55, and could not get there. Crinolines and sweeping whiskers, the Pre-Raphaelites and the Crimea, Bible orthodoxy and the Tractarians, all the great Victorians. A dim, entrancing period, when papa and mamma were getting married, and people were too old-fashioned to see life straight as it was. And to grandpapa, '55 was quite lately, just the other day, and '80 was like an engine got loose from its train and dashing madly in advance, heading precipitately for a crash.

" I remember," said grandpapa, " I remember . . ."

Papa said, " That was the year King's College asked Maurice to retire because of *Theological Essays.*

What dull things elderly people remembered !

" Next Sunday," said Vicky, " I shall take Charles to South Place, papa. I hear Mr. Pater is preaching there. Too sweet and quaint ; he preaches everywhere. And often the divine Oscar sits under him."

6

STANLEY AND ROME

MAURICE and Stanley were back from Cambridge and
Oxford for the Easter vacation, talking, talking, talking.
Stanley, in a crimson stockinette jersey, tight like an
eel's skin, and a tight little brown skirt caught in at
the knees, her chubby face pink with excitement and
health, talked of Oxford, of the river, of lectures, of
Mr. Pater, and of friendship. Friendship was like
dancing flames to Stanley in this her first Oxford year ;
a radiant, painful apocalypse of joy.

"Are they so splendid ? " Rome speculated of these
glorious girls. " *Is* any one so splendid, ever ? "

She sat idly, her hands clasped behind her short,
silky curls, Mallock's *New Republic* open at her side.
Stanley sat on the edge of a table, and swung her
legs. How romantic Stanley was ! What were girls,
what, indeed, were boys either, that such a halo
should encircle their foolish heads ?

There was proceeding at this time a now long-forgotten
campaign called the Woman's Movement, and on to
the gay youthful fringe of this Stanley and her friends
were catching. Women, long suppressed, were emerg-
ing ; women were to be doctors, lawyers, human
beings, everything ; women were to have their share
of the earth, their share of adventure, to flourish in
all the arts, ride perched in handsom cabs, even on
monstrous bicycles, find the North Pole. . . .

" Too energetic for me," Rome commented.

" Oh, but you'll be a great writer, perhaps."

" No. Why ? There's nothing I want to write.
What's the use of writing ? Too much of that already.
. . . Oh, well, go on about Oxford, Stan. You don't

convince me that it's anything but a very ordinary place full of quite ordinary people, but I rather like to hear you being absurd."

Rome's faint, delicately thin voice expressed acquiescent but not scornful irony. Stanley was a bore sometimes, but an intelligent bore.

She went on about Oxford, and Mr. Pater, and some lectures on art by William Morris that she had been to. Stanley was drunk with beauty ; she was plunging deep into the æsthetic movement on whose surface Vicky played.

" You know, Rome," she puckered her forehead over it, " more and more I feel that the *merely* æsthetic people are on the wrong tack. Beauty for ourselves can't be enough ; it's got to be made possible for every one. . . . That's where Vicky and her friends are off it. A lily in a blue vase all to yourself isn't enough. All this . . ." she looked round at the Liberty room, the peacock patterns, the willow pattern china, the oak settle, " all this—it's not fair we should be able to have it when every one can't. It's greedy . . ."

" Every one's greedy."

" No," said Stanley, and her eyes glowed, for she was thinking of her splendid friends. " *No*. Greediness is in every one, but it can be conquered. Socialism is the way. . . . I wish you could meet Evelyn Peters. She's joined the Socialist Democratic Federation. . . . I want to ask her here to stay, in June. She's not just an ordinary person, you know. She's splendid. She's six years older than me, and enormously cleverer, and she's read everything and met every one. . . . I can't tell you how I feel about her. . . ."

Obvious, thought Rome, how Stanley felt, with her shining eyes and flushed cheeks and shy, changing voice. In love ; that was what Stanley was. Stanley was for ever in and out of love ; she had been the same

all through her schooldays. So had Vicky, but with
Vicky it was men, and less romantic and earnest.
Stanley was always flinging her whole being prostrate
in adoring enthusiasm before some one or something,
funny child. She was looking at Rome now in shy,
gleaming hesitation, wondering if Rome were despising
her, laughing at her, but not able to keep Evelyn Peters
to herself. To say, "Evelyn Peters is my friend,"
was an exquisite æsthetic joy, and made their friendship a more real, achieved thing.

Rome felt a little uncomfortable behind her bland
nonchalance ; Stanley's emotions were so strong.

7

GRANDPAPA

WHEN Maurice was there Stanley did not talk about
her friends ; such talk was not suitable for Maurice,
whose own friendships were so different. Often in
these days they talked politics. Maurice was a Radical.

" Chamberlain's the man," he said, " Chamberlain
and Dilke. Whiggery's played out ; dead as mutton.
Mild Liberalism has had its day. Yes, pater, your day
is over. The seventies have been the hey-day of Liberalism. I grant you it's done well—Education Act, Irish
Disestablishment, abolition of tests, and so on. Such
obvious reforms, you see, that every sane person has
had to be a Liberal. That's watered Liberalism down.
Now we've got to go further, and only the extremists
will stick on ; the old gang will desert. Radicalism's
the only thing for England now."

Maurice, pacing the room with his quick little steps,
his hands in his pockets, his chin in the air, would talk
thus in his crisp, rapid, asseverating voice, even to

grandpapa, who had, when he had done the same thing
as a schoolboy, ordered him out of the room for imper-
tinence. Grandpapa and Maurice did not, in fact,
each really like the other—obstinate age and opin-
ionated youth. Because grandpapa was in the room,
Maurice said, "They've returned old Bradlaugh for
Northampton all right. Now we shall see some fun,"
and grandpapa said, "Don't mention that abominable
blasphemer in my presence."

Papa said gently, with his cultured tolerance, "A
good deal, I fancy, has been attributed to Bradlaugh
of which he has not been guilty."

"Are you denying," inquired grandpapa, "that the
fellow is a miserable blaspheming atheist and a Malthusian ? "

"An atheist," papa admitted, discreetly passing over
the last charge, "no doubt he is. And very undesirably
coarse and violent in his methods of controversy and
propaganda. But I am not sure that the charge of
blasphemy is a fair one, on the evidence we have."

"Any man," said grandpapa, sharply, "who denies
his Maker blasphemes."

" In that case," said Maurice moodily, " I blas-
pheme," and left the room.

Papa apologised for him.

" You must forgive the boy ; he is still crude."

Grandpapa shut his firm mouth tightly, and Rome
thought, "He is still cruder."

Vicky asked lightly, "What is a Malthusian, grandpapa ? " and grandpapa, who came of a coarse and
outspoken generation, snapped, "A follower of Malthus."

"And who was Malthus, grandpapa ? "

Grandpapa, catching his daughter's eye, and recollect-
ing that it was the year 1880, not the coarse period of
his own youth, hummed and cleared his throat and said,
"A very ungentlemanly fellow, my dear."

And that was all about Malthus that young misses of 1880 needed to know. Or so their elders believed. But in 1880, as now, young misses often knew more than their parents and grandparents supposed. Rome and Stanley, better read in history than Vicky, could have enlightened both her and grandpapa on the theme of Malthus.

8

DISCUSSING RELIGION

It was a good thing that grandpapa's visit ended next day. Without him, Maurice was better-mannered, less truculent. They could then discuss Radicalism, Bradlaugh, blasphemy, beauty, Malthus and the elections, *en famille*, without prejudice. They were, as a family, immense talkers, inordinate arguers. The only two who did not discuss life at large were Irving and Una ; their conversation was and always would be of the lives they personally led, and those led by such animals as they kept. The lives led by others worried them not at all. They recked not of the Woman's Movement, but Irving amiably held Maurice's high bicycle while Stanley, divested of her tight skirt and clad in a pair of his trousers, mounted it and pedalled round and round the quiet square. It was Irving who knew that a lower kind of bicycle was on its way, had even been seen in embryo.

" But girls'll never ride it," he opined. " That's jolly certain."

" Girls will probably be wearing knickerbockers in a year or two," Stanley, always hopeful, asserted. " For exercise and games and things. Or else a new kind of skirt will come in, short and wide. Our clothes are absurd."

" Women's clothes always are," said Irving, content that this should be so.

Stanley would rush in, happy and bruised, assume again her absurd, caught-in-at-the-knees skirt, and argue desperately with Maurice about Christian socialism. Stanley was a Christian, ardent and practical; that was the effect Oxford was having on her. She privately wondered how papa, having known and loved Oxford, could bear the Ethical Church. But probably the Oxford Anglicanism of papa's day had not been so inspiring.

Vicky told Stanley that socialism, Christian or unchristian, was very crude; religion was an affair of art and beauty, not of economics.

" Religion—oh, I don't know." Stanley wondered, frowning. " What *is* religion, Rome ? "

Rome, looking up from Samuel Butler, merely said, " How should I know ? You'd better ask papa. He should know; he's writing a book about it."

" No ; I don't mean comparative religions. I mean *religion*. . . ."

"A primitive insurance against disaster," Maurice defined it. He always looked up and took notice when religion was mentioned ; to this family the word was like " rats " to a dog, owing, perhaps, to their many clerical ancestors, perhaps to the fact that they were latish Victorians.

" But it *courts* disaster. . . ." Stanley was sure of that. " Look where it leads people. Into all sorts of hardships and dangers and sacrifices. Look at Christianity—in the Gospels, I mean."

" That's a perversion. Originally religion was merely a function of the self-preservative instinct. Offer sacrifices to the gods and save your crops. And even Christianity, after all, insures heavily against the flaws in this life by belief in another."

" What about the Ethical Church ? They don't believe in another."

"A perversion too. A mere sop thrown to the religious instinct by people who don't like to starve it altogether. A morbid absurdity. A house without foundations. If they simply mean, as they appear to, that they think they ought to be good, why meet in South Place and sing about it ? "

" Why," inquired Rome, who never did so, " meet anywhere and sing about anything ? "

" Why," said Maurice, " indeed ?   A morbid instinct inherent in human nature. Mine, I am glad to say, is untainted by it ; so is yours, Rome. Vicky has it badly, and Stanley, who gets everything in turns, has it on and off, but she is but young and may get over it. . . . The queer thing about Stanley is that she's trying to run two quite incompatible things at the same time. Æsthetics and Christian socialism—you might as well be a cricketer and a rowing man, or hang Dicksee and Whistler together on your walls. The æsthetes may go slumming, in the absurd way Vicky does, but they've no use for socialism."

" I'm *not* an æsthete," Stanley cried, finding it out suddenly. " I'm through with that. I'm going in with the socialists all the way. I shall join the Socialist Democratic Federation at once."

That was Stanley's headlong manner of entering into movements. She was a great and impetuous joiner.

But Rome, playing with her monocle on its dangling ribbon, looked at all movements with fastidious rejection. *Cui*, her faintly mocking regard would seem to inquire, *bono ?*

9

DISCUSSING LIFE

1880 pursued its way. Mr Gladstone formed his cabinet
of sober peers and startling commoners, the new parliament met, the Radicals at once began to shock the
Whigs with their unheard-of proposals for so-called
reform, Lord Randolph Churchill and his Fourth Party
mounted guard, brisk and pert, in the offing, Parnell
and his thirty-five Irishmen scowled from another
offing, demanding the three F's, and, for a special
comic turn side-show, Mr. Bradlaugh, the unbeliever,
was hustled in and out of the House, claiming to affirm,
being ejected with violence, returning at a rush, ejected
yet again, and so on and so forth, until gentlemanly
unbelievers said, "A disgraceful business. Why can't
the man behave like other agnostics, without all this
fuss ? " and gentlemanly Christians said, " Why can't
the House let him alone ? " and the dignified Press
said, " It is repugnant to public opinion that one who
openly denies his God should be allowed in a House
representative of a great Christian nation," for, believe
it or not as you choose, that was the way the Press still
talked in the year 1880.

-Maurice Garden and his friends at Cambridge greeted
Mr. Bradlaugh's determined onslaughts with encouraging cheers. Maurice Garden enjoyed battle, and he
rightly thought the cause of liberty of thought served
by this tempestuous affair.

Freedom : that was at this time the obsession of
Maurice Garden and his compeers. Freedom of thought,
freedom of speech (though not, of course, of action), freedom of small nations (such as Armenia, Ireland, Poland,
and the Transvaal Boers), for that was a catchword

among our forefathers of the nineteenth century;
freedom even of large ones, such as India ; freedom of
women, that strange, thin cry raised so far only by
sparse, sporadic groups, freedom of labour (whatever
that may have meant, and Maurice Garden, a clear-
thinking young man, could have told you precisely
and at length what he meant by it) ; freedom even of
Russians, that last word in improbabilities.

" Freedom ? " queried Rome. "A word that wants
defining "—and that was all she had to say of it. While
Maurice and Stanley went, hot heads down, for the
kernel, she was for ever meticulously, aloofly, fingering
the shell, reducing it to absurdity. That seemed, at
times, to be all that Rome cared about, all she had the
humanity, the vital energy, to seek. Stanley, rushing
buoyantly through Oxford, seizing upon this new idea
and that, eagerly mapping out her future, ardently
burning her present candle at both ends, intellectually,
socially and athletically (so far as young women were
allowed to be athletic in those days, when hockey and
bicycling had not come in and lawn tennis consisted in
lobbing a ball gently over a net with a racket weighing
seventeen ounces and shaped like a crooked spoon)—
Stanley seemed to Rome, whom God had saved from
too much love of living, amusingly violent and crude.

They were oddly different, these four sisters ; Vicky
so sprightly, Rome so cool, Stanley so eager, Una
so placid.

" Your languid indifference is tip-top form, my dear,"
Vicky would say to Rome. " You're *fin-de-siècle*—that's
utterly the last word to-day. But I can't emulate you."

" Don't you want to *do* anything, Rome ? " Stanley
home for the long vacation, asked, and Rome's eyebrows went up.

" Do anything ? Jamais de ma vie. What should
I do ? "

" Well, anything. Any of the things women do.
Teaching.   Settlement work.   Doctoring.   Writing.
Painting.   Anything."

" What a list !   What frightful labours !   I do not."

" But aren't you bored ? "

" In moderation.   I survive.   I even amuse myself."

" *I* think, you know, that women *ought* to do things,
just as much as men."

"And just as little.   What's worth doing, after all ? "

" Things *need* doing.   The world is so shocking. . . .
All this time women have been suppressed and kept
under and not allowed to help in putting things right,
and now they're just getting free. . . ."

" There's one thing about freedom " (a word upon
which Rome had of late been speculating), " each generation of people begins by thinking they've got it for
the first time in history, and ends by being sure the
generation younger than themselves have too much
of it.   It can't really always have been increasing at the
rate people suppose, or there would be more of it by now."

" It's only lately begun, for women.   What was there
for mamma to do, when *she* was young ?   Nothing.
Only to marry papa.   But now . . ."

" What is there for Vicky to do, now *she's* young ?
Nothing.   Only to marry Charles—or another."

" Oh, well, Vicky slums.   And she could do any of
the other things if she liked. . . . Anyhow Rome,
you're not supporting *marriage* as the only woman's
job worth doing ! "

" No.   Not even marriage.   Perhaps, in fact, less
than most things marriage.   I only said it is, so far as
one can infer, Vicky's job. . . . The only job worth
doing in this curious fantasia of a world, as I see it, is
to amuse oneself as well as may be and to get through
it with no more trouble than need be.   What else is
there ? "

With all the desperate needs of the certainly curious but as certainly necessitous world crying in her ears, with vistas of adventure and achievement stretching illimitably before her eyes, Stanley found this too immense a question. She could only answer it with another. "Why do you think we were born, then?" and Rome's matter of fact, "Obviously because papa and mamma got married," sent her sulkily away to play cricket on the lawn with Irving and Una. Apathy, languor, selfishness, did very greatly anger her. She was the more troubled in that she knew Rome to be clever—cleverer than herself. Rome could have done anything, and elected to do nothing. Rome would probably not even marry; her caustic tongue and cool indifference kept those who admired her at arm's length; she made them feel that any expression of regard was an error in taste; she shrivelled it up by an amused, inquiring look through the deadly monocle she placed in one blue-green eye for the purpose.

IO

VICKY GETS MARRIED

VICKY, on the contrary, became, during this summer, definitely affianced to Charles, whom she had decided to marry next spring. She had not, as yet, made of Charles either an æsthete or a ritualist, but these things, she hoped, would come after marriage, and anyhow Charles was intelligent, his career promised well, he had sufficient income, and, in fine, she loved him.

"The main thing, after all, Vicky," papa inevitably said.

"No, papa; the *main* thing is that the American

merchant princesses are descending on the land like
locusts, and that if I don't secure Charles they will,
even though he hasn't a title—yet. He's so obviously
a distinguished person in embryo. American merchant
princesses have brains."

Vicky, having surrendered, put on a new tenderness,
even an occasional gravity. It was as if you could
catch glimpses here and there of the gay wife and
mother that was to supersede the flighty girl. Beneath
her chaff and bickerings with her Charles, her love
swelled into that stream so necessary to carry her
through the long and arduous business. She did her
shopping for her new life with taste and gusto, tempering
Morris picturesqueness with Chippendale elegance,
chasing Queen Anne with unflagging energy from
auction to auction, and from one Israelitish shop to
another, tinkling the while with snakish bangles,
swinging golden swine from her ears, as was the bar-
barous and yet graceful custom of our ancestresses in
that year.

II

MAURICE STARTS LIFE

MAURICE left Cambridge, armed with a distinguished
first in his classical tripos.

"And what now ? " inquired papa, indulgently.

" Wilbur has offered me a job on the *New View*.
That will do me, for a bit."

The *New View* was a weekly paper of the early
eighties, started to defeat Whiggery by the spread of
Radicalism. Its gods were Sir Charles Dilke and Mr.
Joseph Chamberlain, its objects to introduce a more
democratic taxation, to reform the suffrage, to free
Ireland, to curtail Empire, and so forth. As its will

was strong, it suffered but it did not suffer long, and is, in fact, now forgotten but by the seekers among the pathetic chronicles of wasted years. All the same, it was, in its brief day, not unfruitful of good ; it was deeply, if not widely, respected, and many of our more intelligent forbears wrote for it for a space, particularly that generation which left the Universities round about the year 1880. It was hoped by some of them (including Maurice Garden) that it would make a good jumping-off ground for a political career. As it turned out, the first thing into which Maurice jumped off from it was love. At dinner at the Wilburs, he met Amy Wilbur, the young daughter of his editor. She was small and ivory-coloured, with long dark eyes under slanting brows, a large, round, shallow dimple in each smooth cheek, a small tilting red mouth (red even in those days, when lip salve was not used except in the half world) a smooth, childlike voice, and a laugh like silver bells. Maurice thought her like a geisha out of the new opera, *The Mikado*, and was enchanted with her lovely gaiety. Such is love and its blindness that Maurice, who detested both silliness and petty malice in male or female, did not see that his Amy was silly and malicious. He saw nothing but her enchanting exterior, and on that and his small salary he got married in haste. None of the Gardens except himself and papa much cared about Amy, and papa liked nearly every one, and certainly nearly all pretty girls. As to mamma's feelings towards her daughter-in-law, who could divine them ?

Vicky said to Rome, " They are both making a horrific mistake. Maurice is a prickly person, who won't suffer fools. In a year he'll be wanting to beat her. She hasn't the wits or the personality to be the least help to him in his career, either. When he's a rising politician and she ought to be holding salons, she won't be able to. Her salons will be mere at homes."

"When," Rome speculated, "does an at home become a salon ? I've often wondered."

They decided that it was a salon when several distinguished people came to it, rather from habit than from accident. Also, the conversation must be reasonably intelligent (or, anyhow, the conversers must believe that it was so, for that is all that can be hoped of any conversation). And people must come, or pretend that they came, mainly for the talk, and not so much for any food there might be, or to show their new clothes.

"Asses they must be," said Una, who was listening. " I shan't go to salons ever."

" No one will ask you, my child. Anything *you'll* find yourself at will be a common party, with food and drink and foolish chit-chat."

" Like *your* parties," Una agreed, amiably content. No teasing worried Una ; she was as placid as a young cow.

12

EIGHTIES

So, with Vicky and Maurice happily wedded (*settled*, as they wittily called it in those days, though, indeed, they knew as well as we do that marriage is liable to be as inconclusive and unsettling an affair as any other, and somewhat more than most), and papa and mamma happily, if impermanently, ethicised, and the three younger children still pursuing, or being pursued by, education, and Rome perfunctorily, amusedly and inactively surveying the foolish world, the Garden family entered on that eager, clever, civilised, earnest decade, the eighteen eighties. Earnest indeed it was, for people still took politics seriously, and creeds, and literature, and life. Over the period still brooded the mighty ones, those who are usually called the Giants (literary and scientific) of the Victorian era. For the nineteenth century was an age of giant-makers, of hero-worshippers.

The eighties were also a great time for women. What was called *emancipation* then occurred to them. Young ladies were getting education, and it went to their heads. No creature was ever more solemn, more earnest, more full of good intentions for the world, than the university-educated young female of the eighties. We shall not look upon her like again ; she has gone, to make place for us, her lighter-minded daughters, surely a lesser generation, without enthusiasm, ardour or aspiration.

It was these ardent good intentions, this burning social conscience, as well as the desire to do the emancipated thing, that drove Stanley, leaving Oxford in 1882, to take up settlement work in Poplar. So Poplarised, so orientalised, did she become, that she took to speaking of her parental home in Bloomsbury as being in the West End. To her, everything west of St. Paul's became the West End. The West End, its locality and its limits, is indeed a debatable land. Where you think it is seems to depend on where you live or work. To those who work in Fleet Street, as do so many journalists, it seems that anything west of the Strand is the West End. "West End Cocaine Orgie," you see on newspaper placards, and find that the orgie occurred in Piccadilly or Soho. Mayfair and its environs are also spoken of by these scribblers of the east as the West End. But to those who live in Mayfair, the West End begins at about Edgware Road, and Mayfair seems about the middle, and to the

denizens of Edgware Road the West End is Bayswater,
Kensington, or Shepherd's Bush. The dwellers in
these outlying lands of the sunset do really acknowledge
that they are the West End ; and to them Mayfair and
Piccadilly are not even the middle, but the east. A
strange, irrational phrase, which bears so fluctuating
and dubious a meaning. But then nearly all phrases
are strange and irrational, like most of those who use
them.

Anyhow, and be that as it may, Stanley went and
worked in Poplar, to ameliorate the lot of the extremely
poor, who lived there then as now. She took up with
Fabians and admired greatly Mr. Bernard Shaw, while
cleaving still to William Morris. She was concerned
about Sweated Women, and served on Women's Labour
Committees. Her good working intelligence caused
people to give her charges and responsibilities beyond
her years. She was now a sturdy, capable, square-set,
brown-faced young woman, attractive, with her thrust-
out under-lip and chin, and her beautiful blue eyes
under heavy black brows. She spoke well on platforms in a deep, girlish voice, was as strong as a pony,
and could work from morning till night without flagging.
There was something candid and lovable about Stanley.
A doctor and a clergyman asked her in wedlock, but
she did not much care about them, and was too busy
and interested to think about marriage.

She had, among other strong and ardent beliefs,
belief in God. She had religion, inherited perhaps from
her papa, but taking in her a more concentrated and
less diffused form. To her the Christian church was
a militant church, the sword of God come to do battle
for the poor and oppressed. To her a church was an
enchanted house, glorious as a child's dream, the Mass
as amazing as a fairy story and as true as sunrise.
She did not much mind at which churches she attended

this miracle, but on the whole preferred those of the Anglican establishment to the Roman variety, finding these latter rather more lacking in beauty than churches need be. Stanley was an optimist. She looked on the shocking, wicked, and ill-constructed universe, and felt that there must certainly be something behind this odd business. There must, she reasoned, be divine spirit and fire somewhere, to account for such flashes of good as were so frequently evident in it. Something gallant, unquenchable, imperishably ardent and brave, must burn at its shoddy heart.

Vicky complained that Stanley thought of God (" in whom, of course," said Vicky, " we all believe ") as a socialist agitator, and Stanley perhaps did. Certainly God, she believed, was fighting sweated industries.

" With signally small success," Maurice said, for the commission on these industries had just concluded.

" God very seldom succeeds," Stanley agreed. " He has very nearly everything against him, of course."

She seldom mentioned God, being, for the most part, as shyly inarticulate as a schoolgirl on this theme so vital to her. But of unemployment, labour troubles, and sweated industries, she and Maurice would talk by the hour. She wrote articles for his paper on the conditions of working women in Poplar. She attended street labour meetings in the east, while Maurice did the same in Trafalgar Square and Hyde Park.

In 1882, the year that Stanley left Oxford, Una left school. It was no use sending her to college, for she had not learning, nor the inclination to acquire it. She had done with lessons.

" You don't want just to slack about for ever, I suppose ? " Stanley put it to her, sternly.

" For ever. . . ." Una looked at her with wide, sleepy blue eyes, trying and failing to think of eternity.

Una lived in to-day, not in yesterday or to-morrow.
She was rather like a puppy.

" I don't much care," she said at length.   " I mean,
I've never thought about it.   I'm never bored, anyhow.   There's theatres, and badminton, and dancing,
and all the shops, and taking the dogs in the parks. . . .
Of course I'd like better to live in the country again.
But London's all right.   *I'm* all right.   I'm not booky
like you, you see."

Stanley said it had nothing to do with being booky ;
there were things that wanted doing.   Doubtless there
were.   But she failed to rouse Una to any thought of
doing them.   Una stayed at home, and went to parties,
and theatres, and played games, and occasionally rode,
and walked the dogs in the parks, and stayed with
friends in the country, and enjoyed life.

" I suppose she'll just marry," Stanley disappointedly
said, for in the eighteen eighties marriage was not well
thought of, though freely practised, by young feminine
highbrows.

As to Irving, another cheery hedonist, he was enjoying himself very much at Cambridge and reading for
a pass.

13

PARENTS

THE eighteen eighties were freely strewn with, among
other things, Vicky's children.   The halcyon period
for children had not yet set in ; did not, in fact, set in
until well on in the twentieth century.   In the eighteen
eighties and nineties children were still thwarted, still
disciplined, still suppressed, though with an abatement
of mid-Victorian savagery.   The idea had not yet
started that they were interesting little creatures to

be encouraged and admired. On the whole, the bringing up of children (at best a poor business) was perhaps less badly done during the last fifteen years of the nineteenth century than before or since. It may safely be said that it is always pretty badly done, since most parents and all children are very stupid and uncivilised, and anyhow to " bring up " (queer phrase !) the unfortunate raw material that human nature is, to bring it up to any semblance of virtue or intelligence (the parents, probably, having but small acquaintance with either) is a gargantuan task, almost beyond human powers. Some children do, indeed, grow up as well as can, in the circumstances, be expected, but this is, as a rule, in spite of, rather than on account of, the misguided efforts of their parents. And most children do not grow up well at all, but quite otherwise, which is why the world is as we see it.

Vicky was, as parents go, not a bad one. She loved her children, but did not unduly spoil them or turn their heads with injudicious attentions. Year by year her nursery filled with nice, pretty, sturdy little Du Maurier boys, and fine, promising active, little Du Maurier girls, in sailor suits, jerseys, tam-o'-shanters, and little frocks sashed about the knees, and year by year, Vicky was to be found again in what newspaper reporters, in their mystic jargon, call, for reasons understood by none but themselves, " a certain condition." " The woman," they will write, " said she was in a certain condition." As if every one, all the time, were not in a certain condition. Whether these journalists think the statement, " she was going to have a baby " indecent, or coarse, will probably never transpire, for they are a strange, instinct-driven, non-analytical race, who can seldom give reasons for their terminology. Who shall see into their hearts ? Perhaps they really do think that the human race should not be mentioned until it is visible to the human eye.

Anyhow Vicky, of a franker breed than these, said year by year, with resignation, *"Again*, my dears, I replenish the earth," and added sometimes, in petulant inquiry, " How long, oh, Lord, how long ? "

But Amy, the wife of Maurice, had, like newspaper men, her pruderies. Of her coming infants she preferred to speak gently, in fretful undertones. When she told Maurice about the first, she did not, like Vicky, sing out, on his return from the office, " What *do* you think ? There's a baby on the way ! " but, drawing her inspiration from fiction, she hid her face against his coat and murmured, " Oh, *Maurice* ! Guess."

Maurice said, " Guess what ? How do you mean, guess, darling ? " to which she replied, " Well, I do think you're slow to-night . . . Oh, Maurice . . ."

And then Maurice, instead of saying, like the young husbands in the fiction she was used to, " Darling, you *can't* mean. . . . What angels women are ! " said instead, " Oh, I say, do you mean we've got a baby coming ? Good business."

A baby. What a coarse, downright word for the little creature. Later, of course, one got used to it, but just at first, at the very, very outset, the dimmest dawn of its tiny being, it was scarcely a baby. And what about her being an angel ? Obviously Maurice did not know the rules of this game.

When the baby, and the subsequent baby (there were only two altogether) arrived, Amy spoiled them. She was a depraved mother. Also she was unjust. She was, of course, the type of mother whose strong sex instinct leads her to prefer boys to girls, and she took no pains to hide this. Maurice said, stubbornly, " The girl shall have as good a chance as the boy, and as good an education. We'll make no difference,"

but Amy said, " Chance ! Fiddlesticks ! What chances
does a girl want, except to marry well ? What does a
girl want with education ? I'm not going to have her
turned into a bluestocking. Girls can't have real
brains, anyhow. They can't *do* anything—only sit
about and look superior."

This referred to Rome, and these were the remarks
that fell like nagging drops of water on Maurice's
sensitive, irritable nerves and mind, slowly teasing love
out of existence, and beating into him (less slowly)
that he had married a fool.

Maurice found outlet from domestic irritation in
political excitement. There was, for instance, the
Home Rule Bill. It seemed to Maurice, as to many
others, immeasurably important that this bill should
go through. Its failure to do so, his own failure to be
elected in the elections of 1886, and the victory of the
Unionists, plunged him into a sharper and more militant
Radicalism. At the age of twenty-nine he was an
ardent, scornful, clear-brained idealist and cynic,
successful on platforms and brilliant with pens. He was
becoming a stand-by of the Radical press, a thorn in
the Tory flesh. His wife, by this time, after four years
of marriage, definitely disliked him, because he had
bad, sharp manners, was often disagreeable to her,
often drank a little too much, and obviously despised
the things she said. She consoled herself with going to
parties, spoiling her babies, and flirting with other
people. He consoled himself with politics, writing,
talking, and drinking. An ill-assorted couple. Maurice
hoped that his children would be more what he desired.
So far, of course, they were fonder of Amy. Even the
boy was fonder of Amy, though sons often have a natural
leaning towards their fathers, and frequently grow up
with no more than a careless affection for their mothers ;
for, contrary to a common belief, the great affection

felt by Œdipus for his mother is most unusual, and, indeed, Œdipus would probably have felt nothing of the sort had he known of the relationship. It is noticeable that sons usually select as a bride a woman as unlike their mothers and sisters as possible. It makes a change.

So Maurice had reason to hope that his son, anyhow, would prefer him as time went on, and therefore be inclined to share his point of view about life. As to the girl, she might grow up a fool or she might not ; impossible to tell, at three years old. Most girls did.

In 1887 the Golden Jubilee of Queen Victoria occurred. Maurice wrote a deplorably unsuitable article for the occasion, called " Gaudeamus," and taking for its theme the subject races of Ireland and India and the less fortunate and less moneyed classes in Great Britain, which brought him into a good deal of disrepute, and made Amy more than ever disgusted with him.

" Hardly the moment," papa commented. " One sympathises with his impatience, but the dear old lady's jubilee is hardly the moment to rub in the flaws of her Empire."

14

PAPA AND THE FAITH

PAPA was now a Roman Catholic again. After three or four years of Ethicism, the absence of a God had begun to tell on him. It had slowly sapped what had always been the very foundation of his life—his belief in absolute standards of righteousness. For, if there were no God, on what indeed did these standards rest ? It was all very well to sing in South Place of " the great, the lovely and the true," but what things *were* great, lovely and true, and how could one be sure of them, if they derived their sanction from nothing but man's own self-interested and fluctuating judgments? Deeply troubled by these thoughts, which were, of course, by no means new to him, papa was driven at last out of his beautiful and noble halfway house to the bleak cross roads. Either he must become a moral nihilist, or he must believe again in a God. Since to become a moral nihilist was to papa unthinkable, so alien was it from all his habits, his traditions and his thoughts, so alien, indeed, from all the thought of his period, the only alternative was to believe in a God. And papa, swung by reaction, determined that this time (was it by way of atonement, or safeguard?) he would do the thing thoroughly. He would enter once more into that great ark of refuge from perplexing thoughts, the Roman branch of the Catholic Church. There (so long as he should remain there) he would be safe. He would rest therein like a folded sheep, and wander no more. So, humbly, in the year 1886, he did allegiance again to this great and consoling Church (which, as he said, he had never left, for you cannot leave it, though you may be unfaithful) and worshipped inconspiciously and devoutly in a small and austere Dominican chapel.

His only grief was that mamma at this point struck. She made the great refusal. She loved papa no less faithfully than ever, but his continuous faiths had worn her out. She said quietly, " I am not going to be a Roman Catholic again, Aubrey."

He bowed his head at her decision. It was perhaps, he admitted, too much to expect that she should. " But not *Roman* Catholic, dearest . . ." was his only protest. " Surely not *Roman*, now."

" I beg your pardon, Aubrey. Catholic. Anyhow, I am too old to join new churches, or even the old ones again."

" You will stay an Ethicist, then," he said, tentatively.

" No. I have never cared very much for that. I don't think I shall attend any place of worship in future."

He looked at her, startled, and placed his hand on hers, impeding the rapidity of her embroidery needle.

"Anne—my dear love. You haven't lost faith in everything, as I have been in danger of doing during the last year ? The South Place chapel hasn't done that to you, dear one ? "

Mamma let her work lie still on her lap, while papa's hand rested on hers. She seemed to consider, looking inwards and backwards, down and down the years.

" No, Aubrey," she said presently. " The South Place chapel hasn't done that to me. It wasn't important enough . . ."

Her faint smile at him was enigmatic.

" I don't," she added, " quite know what I do believe. But I have long ago come to the conclusion that it matters very little. You, you see, have seemed equally happy for a time, equally unhappy after a time, in all the creeds or no-creeds. And equally good, my dear. I suppose I may say that I believe in none of them, or believe in all. In any case, it matters very little. I have come with you always into the churches and out of them, but now I think you will find peace in the Rom—— in the Catholic Church, without me, and I fear that so much ritual, after so much lack of it, would only fuss me. I shall stay at home. There is a good deal to do there always, and I am afraid I am better at doing practical things than at thinking difficult things out. You won't mind, Aubrey ? "

" My darling, no. You must follow your own conscience. Mine has been a sad will o' the wisp to us both—but, God helping me, it has lighted me now into my last home. . . . Yet who knows, who knows . . . ? "

Mamma gently patted his hand and went on with her embroidery, bending over it her patient, near-sighted, spectacled eyes. She was mildly, unenthusiastically relieved to be done with the Ethical Church. She had never really liked those hymns. . . . Dear Aubrey, he would be happier again now. He could take to himself confidently once more those eternal moral values which had threatened him during the past six months with their utter wreckage and collapse. Once more he would be able to give reasons for his faith in virtue, for his belief that lying, theft, selfishness, and adultery were wrong. Once more the world's foundations stood, and papa would not lie wakeful in the night and sigh to watch them shake.

But the solitary, unworthy little thought nagged at mamma's mind, "Amy will sneer. Amy will make foolish, common fun of him . . ."

Dismissing Amy as a silly and vulgar little creature, mamma folded her embroidery and went to speak to the cook.

15

KEEPING HOUSE

Speaking to the cook. What a delightful kind of conversation this must be. For, if you are a proper housewife, you do not just say to the cook, " Kindly provide meals, as usual, for the household to-day. That is, in fact, what you are paid to do. So do it, and let me hear no more about it." Instead, you go to the larder and see what is in it. You find a piece of meat, and try to guess what it is. You say, " We will have that neck of mutton, or loin of beef " (or whatever you think it is) "roasted, boiled, or fricasseed, for lunch. Then, of what is left of it, you will make some nice cutlets for dinner. Now how about sweets ? "

Then you and the cook will settle down happily for a long gossip about sweets—a delightful topic. The cook says, "I had thought of a nice jam roll." You say that you, for your part, had thought of something else, and so it goes on, like a drawing-room game, until you or the cook win, by sheer strength of will. Cooks usually have most of this, so they nearly always win. They can think of more reasons than you can why the thing suggested is impossible. They know there is not enough jam, or cream, or mushrooms, or bread-crumbs—not enough to make it *nice*, as it should be made. Rather would they suggest a nice apple charlotte. ....

"Very well, cook, have it your own way. You have won, as usual. But it has been a good game, and I have Kept House." That is what the good housewife (presumably) reflects as she leaves the kitchen.

Perhaps there is more to it than this ; perhaps bills are also discussed, and butchers, and groceries, and the price of comestibles. No one who has not done it knows precisely what is done, or how. It is the cook's hour, and the housewife's, and no fifth ear overhears. Mrs. Garden, in the year 1887, had done it every day for thirty-one years. Whether as an Anglican, a Unitarian, a Roman Catholic, an Agnostic, a Quaker, an Irvingite, a Seventh-day Adventist, a Baptist, or an Ethicist, still she had daily Kept House. Magic phrase ! What happens to houses unkept, Rome had idly asked. Mamma had shaken a dubious head. No house that she had ever heard of had been unkept.

16

UNA

UNA, staying in Essex with friends, contracted an engagement with a neighbouring young yeoman farmer, whom she used to meet out riding. The friends protested, dismayed at such a mésalliance having been arranged for under, so to speak, their auspices. But Una, now twenty-three, grandly beautiful, alternately lazy and amazingly energetic, looking like Diana or a splendid young Ceres, with no desires, it seemed, but for the healthy pleasures of the moment, held firmly to her decision. She loved her Ted, and loved, too, the life he led. She would wed him without delay. She went home and told her family so.

Papa said, " If you are sure of your love and his, that is all that matters, little Una " (with the faint note of deprecation, even of remorse, with which he was wont to say her name, in these days when he believed once again in the Athanasian creed ; for, though he might have bestowed this name in the most Trinitarian orthodoxy, the fact was that he had not ; it had been a badge of incomplete belief).

Mamma said, " Well, child, you were bound to marry some one in the country. I always knew that. And you won't mind that he and his people eat and talk a little differently from you, so I think you'll be happy. Bless you."

To Rome mamma said, " There's one thing about Una ; she always knows what she wants and goes straight for it. I wish she could have married a gentleman, but this young fellow is a good mate for her, I believe. She won't care about the differences. There's no humbug about Una. She's the modern girl all through. Splendid, direct, capable children they are."

That was in the year 1887, and mamma did not know that in the nineteen twenties there would still be girls like Una, and people would still be calling them the modern girl, and saying how direct, admirable and wonderful, or how independent, reckless and head-strong, they were, and, in either case, how unlike the girls of thirty and forty years ago. For, in popular estimation, girls must be changing all the time—new every morning ; there must be a new fashion in girls, as in hats, every year. But those who have lived on this earth as much as sixty years know (though they never say, for they like, amiably, to keep in with the young by joining in popular cries, and are too elderly to go to the trouble of speaking the truth) that girls, like other persons, have always been much the same, and always will be. Not the same as one another, for the greyhound is not more different from the spaniel than is one girl from the next ; but the same types of girls and of boys, of women and of men, have for ever existed, and will never cease to exist, and there is nothing new under the sun. Yet in the eighteen eighties and nineties, our ancestors were talking blandly of the New Woman, just as to-day people babble of the Modern Girl.

Rome said, " Yes, Una'll be all right. She knows the way to live . . ." and was caught by her own phrase into the question, what *is* the way to live, then ? Mine, Una's, Vicky's, Stanley's, Maurice's, papa's ? Perhaps there is no way to live. Perhaps the thing is just to live, without a way. And that is, actually, what Una will do.

Una's Ted came to stay in Bloomsbury with the Gardens. He was large and silent and beautiful, and ate hugely, and looked awful, said Vicky, in his Sunday clothes, which were the ones he wore all the time in London. Also, his boots creaked. But you could see, through it all, how he would be striding about his native fields in gaiters and breeches and old tweeds,

T.B.I.

sucking a pipe and looking like a young earth-god.
You could see, therefore, why Una loved him ; you
could see it even while he breathed hard at meals in his
tight collar, and sucked his knife. He was physically
glorious ; a young Antæus strayed by mistake to town.
He and Una were a splendid pair.

Una cared not at all what impression he made on her
family. She was not sensitive. The touch of his
hands made her quiver luxuriously, and when he took
her in his arms and turned her face up to his and bruised
her mouth with kisses, the world's walls shivered and
dissolved round her and she was poured out like water.
He was beautiful and splendid and her man, and knew
all about the things she cared for, and she loved him
with a full, happy passion that responded frankly and
generously to his. They chaffed and bickered and
played and caressed, and talked about horses and dogs
and love, and went to the Zoo.

Amy giggled behind the young man's back, and said,
" *Did* you see him stuffing his mouth with bun and
trying to wash it down with tea out of his saucer ? "

" Why not ? " said Rome. "And he did wash it
down ; he didn't only try."

" *Well !* " Amy let out a breath and nodded twice.
" Rather Una than me, that's all."

17

STANLEY

THESE years, '87, '88, '89, were stirring years for
Maurice and Stanley. In them were founded the
Independent Labour Party and the Christian Social
Union, and the *Star* newspaper. And there was the
great dock strike, and " bloody Sunday," when

Maurice disgraced Amy and himself by joining in an unseemly fracas with the police, in which he incurred a sprained wrist and a night in prison. In point of fact, as Amy said, he was rather drunk at the time.

Stanley enjoyed the labour movement. She was not like Maurice, merely up against things; she eagerly swam with the tide, and the tide which carried her during this particular phase of her life was revolutionary labour. She was joyously in the van of the movement. The dock strike stirred her more than the Pigott forgeries, more than the poisoning of Mr. Maybrick by Mrs. Maybrick, more than the death of Robert Browning.

Stirring times indeed. But in '89 something happened which stirred Stanley more profoundly than the times. She fell in love and married. It was bound to occur, to such an ardent claimer of life. The man was a writer of light essays and short stories and clever, unproduced plays. He was thirty, and he had an odd, short white face, and narrow, laughing eyes beneath a clever forehead, and little money, but a sense of irony and of form and of the stage. He was in the most modern literary set in London, and his name was Denman Croft. At first Stanley thought him very affected, and she was right, for the most modern literary set *was* affected just then; but in a month or so she loved him with an acute, painful ecstasy that made her dizzy and blinded her to all the world besides. Her work lost interest; she was alive only in those hours when they were together; love absorbed her body and soul. Why, he protested, did she not live in the more reasonable parts of London, and meet people worth meeting? All sorts of exciting, amusing things were happening in the world of letters and art just now, and she ought to be in it. Stanley began to feel that perhaps she ought. After all, one could be progressive, and fight for labour reform and trades unions as well in the west as in the east. Then, while she was thus reflecting, it became apparent to her that Denman Croft was going immediately to propose marriage to her. She had for some weeks known that he loved her, but was scarcely ready for this crisis when it came. Passionate ecstasy possessed them both ; they sank into it blind and breathless and let its waves break over them.

Life, life, life. Stanley, who had always lived to the uttermost, felt that she had never lived before. Spirit, brain and body interacted and co-operated in the riot of their passion.

They married almost at once, and took a house in Margaretta Street, Chelsea.

Stanley always reflected her time, and it was, people said, a time of transition. For that matter, times always are, and one year is always rather different from the last. In this year, the threshold of the nineties, all things were, it was said, being made new. New forms of art and literature were being experimented with, new ideas aired. New verse was being written, new drama, essays, fiction and journalism. Stanley was so much interested in it all (being, as she now was, in close touch with the latest phase in these matters) that her social and political earnestness flagged, for you cannot have all kinds of earnestness at once. Instead of going in the evenings to committee meetings and mass labour meetings, she now went to plays and literary parties. Instead of writing articles on women's work, she began to write poetry and short sketches. All this, and the social life she now led, and the excitement of love, Denman, and her new home, was so stimulating and absorbing that she had little attention to spare for anything else. Stanley was like that— enthusiastic, headlong, a deep plunger, a whole-hogger.

" They do have the most fantastic beings to dinner,"

Vicky said to her Charles. " Velvet coats and immense ties. . . . It reminds me of ten years ago,
when I was being æsthetic. But these people are
much smarter talkers. Denman says they are really
doing something good, too. He's an attractive creature,
though I think his new play is absurd and he's desperately affected. The way that child adores him!
Stanley does go so head over ears into everything.
None of the rest of us could love like that. It frightens
one for her. . . . But anyhow, I'm glad she's off
that stupid trades' union and sweated labour fuss.
Maurice does more than enough of that for the family,
and I was afraid Stan was going to turn into a female
fanatic, like some of those short-haired friends of hers.
That's not what we women ought to be, is it, my
Imogen ? "

Vicky caught up her Imogen, an infant of one summer,
in her arms, and kissed her. But Imogen, neither
then nor at any later time, had any clear idea about
what women ought or ought not to be. Anything
they liked, she probably thought. If, indeed, there
were, specifically, any such creatures as women. . . .
For Imogen was born to have a doubtful mind, on this
as on other subjects. She might almost have been
called mentally defective in some directions, of so little
was she ever to be sure.

" Stanley," pronounced Vicky, " has more Zeitgeist "
(for that unpleasant word had of late come in) "than
any one I ever met."

I

ROME

THE threshold of the nineties. Decades have a delusive edge to them. They are not, of course, really periods at all, except as any other ten years may be. But we, looking at them, are caught by the different name each bears, and give them different attributes, and tie labels on them, as if they were flowers in a border. The nineties, we say, were gay, tired, *fin-de-siècle*, witty, dilettante, decadent, yellow, and Max Beerbohm was their prophet; or they were noisy, imperial, patriotic, militant, crude, and Kipling was their prophet. And, indeed, you may find attributes to differentiate any period from any other. What people wrote of the nineties at the time was that they were modern, which, of course, at the time they were; that they were hustling. . . . ("In these days of hurry and rapid motion, when there is so little time to rest and reflect," as people say in sermons and elsewhere, as if the greater rapidity of motion did not give one more time to rest and reflect, since one the sooner arrives at one's destination); that they were noisy; that literary output was enormous; that (alternatively) the new writers were very good, or that the good writers had gone from among us. One knows the kind of thing; all discourses on contemporary periods have been full of it, from the earliest times even unto these last.

Rome was thirty-one. She was of middle height, a slight, pale, delicate young woman, with ironic blue-green eyes and mocking lips a little compressed at the corners, and a pointed kind of face, and fair, silky hair, which she wore no longer short, but swept gracefully up and back from her small head, defining its shape and showing the fine line from nape to crown. She was a woman of the world, a known diner out, a good talker, something of a wit, so that her presence was sought by hostesses as that of an amusing bachelor is sought. She had elegance, distinction, brain, a light and cool touch on the topics of her world, a calm, mocking, sceptical detachment, a fastidious taste in letters and in persons. She knew her way about, as the phrase goes, and could be relied on to be socially adequate, in spite of a dangerous distaste for fools, and in spite of the " dancing and destructive eye " (to use a phrase long afterwards applied to one whose mentality perhaps a little resembled hers) which she turned on all aspects of the life around her. People called her intensely modern—whatever that might mean. In 1890 it presumably meant that you would have been surprised to find her type in 1880. But as a matter of fact, you would not, had you been endowed with a little perspicacity, been in the least surprised ; you would have found it, had you looked, all down the ages (though always as a rare growth). In 1790, 1690, 1590, and back through every decade of every century, there have been Rome Gardens, fastidious, *mondaine*, urbane, lettered, critical, amused, sceptical, and what was called in 1890 *fin-de-siècle*. It is not a type which, so to speak, makes the world go round ; it does not assist movements nor join in crusades ; it coolly distrusts enthusiasm and eschews the heat and ardour of the day. It is to be found among both sexes equally, and is the stuff of which the urbane bachelor and spinster, rather than the spouse and parent, are made. For mating and producing (as a career, not as an occasional encounter) are apt to destroy the type, by forcing it

to too continuous and ardent intercourse with life ;
that graceful and dilettante aloofness can scarcely
survive such prolonged heat. To be cool, sceptical
and passionate at one and the same time—it has been
done, but it remains difficult. To love ardently such
absurdities as infants, and yet to retain unmarred the
sense of the absurdity of all life—this, too, has been
done, but the best parents do not do it. Something
has to go, as a sacrifice to the juggernaut Life, which
rebels against being regarded as merely absurd (and
rightly, for, in truth, it is not merely absurd, and this
is one of the things which should always be remembered
about it).

The literary persons of the early nineties wanted
Rome to join them in their pursuits.

Why so, Rome questioned. Money ? Very certainly
I have not enough, but I should not have appreciably
more if I wrote and published essays, or even books.
Notoriety ? It might well be of the wrong kind ;
and anyhow, does it add to one's pleasure ? Miss
Rome Garden, the author of those clever critical essays.
. . . Or perhaps of those dull critical essays. . . .
Either way, what did one gain ? Why write ? Why
this craze for transmitting ideas by means of marks on
paper ? Why not, if one must transmit ideas, use the
tongue, that unruly member given us for the purpose ?
Better still, why not retain the ideas for one's own
private edification, untransmitted ? Writing. There
was this about writing—or rather about publishing—it
showed that some one had thought it worth while to
pay for having one's ideas printed. For printers were
paid, and binders, even if not oneself. So it conferred
a kind of cachet. Most literary persons sorely needed
such a cachet, for you would never guess from meeting
them that any one would pay them for their ideas. On
the other hand, publishing one's folly gave it away ;

one was then known for a fool, whereas previously
people might have only suspected it. . . . In brief
and in fine, writing was not worth while. Wise men
and women would derive such pleasure as they could
from the writings of others, without putting themselves
to the trouble of providing reading matter in their turn.
Reading matter was not like dinners, concerning which
there must be give and take.

Thus the do-nothing Miss Rome Garden to the eager
literary young men and women about her, who all
thought that literature was having a new birth and that
they were its brilliant midwives, as, indeed, it is not
unusual to think. And possibly it was the case.
Literature has so many new births ; it is a hardy annual.
The younger literary people of 1890 had a titillating
feeling of standing a-tiptoe to welcome a new day.
"A great creative period is at hand," they said. The
old and famous still brooded over the land like giant
trees. Such a brooding, indeed, has scarcely since
been known, for in these later days we allow no trees
to become giants. But in their shadow the rebellious
young shoots sprang up, sharp and green and alive.
The mid-Victorians were passing ; the Edwardians
were in the schoolroom or the nursery, the Georgians
in the cradle or not yet anywhere ; here was a clear
decade in which the late Victorian stars might dance.
It was a period of experiment ; new forms were being
tried, new ideas would have been aired were any ideas
ever new ; new franknesses, so-called, were permitted,
or anyhow practised—the mild beginnings of the
returning tide which was to break against the reticence
of fifty years.

" I don't," said Mrs. Garden to Rome, " care about
all these sex novels people have taken to writing now."

But Rome rejected the phrase.

" Sex novels, mamma ? What are they ? Novels

have always been about sex, or rather sexes. There's nothing new in that ; it's the oldest story in the world. People must have a sex in this life ; it's inevitable. Novels must be about people ; that's inevitable too. So novels must be partly about sex, and they're nearly always about two sexes, and usually largely about the relations of the two sexes to one another. They always have been. . . ."

All the same, mamma did *not* care about these sex novels that people had taken to writing now. *Problem* novels, she called them, for reasons of her own. Rome thought sex no problem ; the least problematic affair, perhaps, in this world. Of course, there were problems connected with it, as with everything else, but in itself sex was no problem. Rather the contrary. *The Moonstone*, now—*that* was a problem novel.

" I don't like indecency," said mamma, in her delicate, clipped voice. " These modern writers will say anything. It's ill-bred."

Mamma could not be expected to know that these libertines of 1890 would be regarded as quaint Victorian prudes in 1920.

"As to that book Mr. Jayne gave you, I call it merely silly," mamma murmured, with raised brows, and so settled *Dorian Grey*.

" Silly it is," Rome agreed. " But here and there, though too seldom, it has a wit."

But mamma was not listening. Her mamma-like mind was straying after Mr. Jayne. . . .

2

MR. JAYNE

MR. JAYNE and Rome. Both brilliant, both elegant,
both urbane, both so gracefully of the world worldly,
yet both scholars too. Mr. Jayne wrote memoirs and
enchanting historical and political essays. An amusing
yet erudite Oxford man, who had been at the British
Legation at St. Petersburg. Hostesses desired him for
their more sophisticated parties, because he had a wit,
and knew Russia, which was at once more unusual and
more fashionable then than now. It was at one of
Vicky's dinner parties that he and Rome had first met.
If Vicky thought, how suitable, it was only what any
one in the world must think about these two. Afterwards they met continually, and became friends. Rome
thought him conceited, clever, entertaining, attractive,
and disarming, and the most companionable man of
her wide acquaintance. By June, 1890, they were in
love ; a state of mind unusual in both. They did not
mention it, but in July he mentioned to her, what he
mentioned to few people, that he had a Russian wife
living with her parents, a revolutionary professor and
his wife, in the country outside Moscow.

They were spending Sunday on the Thames, rowing
up from Bourne End to Marlow. They spoke of this
matter of Mr. Jayne's wife after their lunch, which they
ate on the bank, in the shade of willows.

" How delightful," said Rome, taking a Gentleman's
Relish sandwich.

Delightful to have a wife in Russia ; to have a reason,
and such a reason, for visiting that interesting land.
Delightful for Mr. Jayne to have waiting for him,
among steppes and woods, a handsome Russian female

and two fair Slav infants . . . or perhaps they were
English, these little Jaynes, with beautiful mouths and
long, thrust-out chins. . . . Delightful, anyhow. The
Russian country in the summer, all corn and oil and
moujiks. Moscow in the autumn, all churches and
revolutionaries and plots and secret police. And in
the winter . . . but one cannot think about Russia
in the winter at all ; it does not bear contemplation,
and one does not visit it. . . . What a romance !
Mr. Jayne was indeed fortunate.

So Miss Garden conveyed.

" I am not there very much," said Mr. Jayne. " Only
on and off. Olga prefers to live there, with her parents
and our two children. She has many friends there,
all very busy plotting. They are of the intelligentsia.
Life is very interesting to her."

" I can imagine that it must be."

So cool and well-bred were Miss Garden and Mr.
Jayne that you never would have divined that the
latter, eating sandwiches, was crying within his soul,
" My dearest Rome. I dislike my wife. We make
each other sick with *ennui* when we meet. We married
in a moment's mania. It is you I want. Don't you
know it ? Won't you let me tell you ? " or that the
former, sipping cider, was saying silently, " You have
told me this at last because you know that we have
fallen in love. Why not months ago ? And what
now ? "

Nothing of this they showed, but lounged in the
green shade, and drank and ate, Miss Garden, clear-cut
and cool, in a striped cotton boating-dress, with a
conically-shaped straw hat tipped over her eyes, Mr.
Jayne in flannels, long and slim, his palish face shaved
smooth in the new fashion, so that you saw the lines of
his clever mouth and long, thrust-out chin. Mr. Jayne's
eyes were deep-set and gray, and he wore pince-nez,

and he was at this time thirty-six years old. At what age, Rome wondered, had he married Mrs. Jayne of the Russian intelligentsia ?

However, they did not enter into this, but began to discuss the plays of Mr. Bernard Shaw, a well-known socialist writer, and Mr. Rudyard Kipling, a young man in India who was making some stir.

" We can still be friends," thought Rome, on their way home. " Nothing need be changed between us. This Olga of his is his wife ; I am his friend. It would be very bourgeois to be less his friend because he has a wife. That is a view of life I dislike. We are civilised people, Mr. Jayne and I."

3

CIVILISED PEOPLE

AND civilised they were, for the rest of the summer of 1890. In November, Rome asked Mr. Jayne, who was having tea with her alone, whether he was visiting Russia shortly. He replied in the negative, for he was, he said, too busy working on his new book to get abroad.

"And further," he added, in the same composed tone, " I prefer to remain in the same country with you. I can't, you see, do without you at hand. You know how often I consult you, and talk things over with you. . . . And further still," continued Mr. Jayne quietly, " I love you."

So saying, he rose and stood over her, bending down with his hands on her shoulders and his pale face close to hers.

" My dearest," he said, " let us stop pretending. *Shall* we stop pretending ? Does our pretence do us or any one else any good ? I love you more than any

words I've got can say. You know it, you know
it . . . dear heart. . . ."

He drew her up from her chair and looked into her
face, and that was the defeat of their civilisation, for
at their mutual touch it broke in disorder and fled. He
kissed her mouth and face and hands, and passion rose
about them like a sea in which they drowned.

Five minutes later they talked it out, sitting with a
space between them, for " While you hold me I can't
think," Rome said. She passed her hand over her face,
which felt hot and stung from the hard pressing of
his mouth, and tried to assemble her thoughts, shaken
by the first passion of her thirty-one agreeable and
intelligent years.

" I'm not," she said, " going to take you away from
your wife. Not in any way. What we have must
make no difference to what *she* has. . . ."

It will be seen, therefore, that their conversation
was as old as the world, and scarcely worth recording.
It pursued the normal lines. That is to say, Mr. Jayne
replied, " She has nothing of me that matters," rather
inaccurately classing under the head of what did not
matter his children, his name, and the right to his bed
and board. As is the habit in these situations, Mr.
Jayne meant that what mattered, and what Mrs. Jayne
had not got, was his love, his passion, his spirit and
his soul. These, he indicated, were Rome's alone, as
Rome's were his.

What to do about it was the question. One must,
said Rome, holding herself in, continue to be civilised.
And what, inquired Mr. Jayne, is civilisation—this
arbitrary civilisation of society's making, that binds
the spirit's freedom in chains? It was all founded
on social expediency, on primitive laws to protect
inheritance, to safeguard property. . . . Had Rome
read Professor Westermark's great work on the history

of human marriage ? Rome had. What of it ? The
point was : there was Mrs. Jayne in Russia, and Mr. and
Mrs. Jayne's two children.   These were Mr. Jayne's
obligations, and nothing he and she did must come
between him and them.   That laid firmly down, she and
Mr. Jayne could do what they liked ; that was how
Rome saw it. One must keep one's contracts, and
behave as persons of honour and breeding should
behave.

"As I see it," said Rome, " the fact that we love each
other needn't prevent our being friends. We are not
babies. . . ."

" Friends," said Mr. Jayne, in agreement, doubt,
scepticism, contempt, hope, or bitter derision, as the
case might be.

And more they said, until they were interrupted by
the entrance of Mrs. Garden's papa, the Dean, who had
called in his brougham to see mamma, but, mamma
being out at Vicky's, he sat down between these two
white, disturbed, hot-eyed and shaken persons and
began to talk of Mr. Parnell and his disgrace.

Grandpapa opined that Mr. Parnell had no more
place in public life.

Mr. Jayne replied that anyhow it appeared that he
would be hounded out of it.

" Cant," he said. " Truckling to Nonconformist
cant and humbug and Catholic bigotry. A man's
private affairs have nothing to do with his public life.
It's contemptible, the way the Nationalists have caved
in to that old humbug, Gladstone."

Grandpapa had always thought Gladstone a humbug
(though not so old as all that came to ; he himself was
eighty-five and going strong), but with the rest of Mr.
Jayne's thesis he was in disagreement. Our political
leaders must not be men of notoriously loose lives.
The sanctity of the home must, at all costs, be upheld.

" O'Shea's home," said Mr. Jayne, " never had much of that. Neither O'Shea nor Mrs. O'Shea was great on it."

" For that matter," Rome joined in, crisp and bland, as if civilisation had not met its débacle in the drawing-room but a half hour since, " for that matter, what homes *have* sanctity ? Why do people think that sanctity is particularly to be found in homes, of all places ? And can a bachelor's or spinster's home have it, or do the people in the home need to be married ? What is it, this curious *sanctity*, that bishops write to the papers about, and that is, they say, being attacked all the time, and is so easily destroyed ? In what homes is it to be found ? I have often wondered."

" Whom God hath joined together," replied grand-papa readily, " that is the answer to your question, my dear child, is it not."

" Oh, God," muttered Mr. Jayne, but probably rather as an ejaculation than as a sceptical comment on the authority behind matrimony.

Whichever it was, grandpapa did not care about the phrase, and looked at him sharply. He believed Mr. Jayne to be an unbeliever, and did not greatly care for the tone of his writings. However, they conversed intelligently for a while about the future of the Irish party before Mr. Jayne rose to go.

" Come into the hall," his eyes said. But Rome did not go into the hall.

He was gone. Rome sat still in the shadow of the window. His steps echoed down the square.

" Do you see much of that young fellow, my dear ? " grandpapa asked, in his old, rumbling voice.

" Oh, yes," said Rome, feeling exalted and light in the head, and as if she had drunk alcohol. " Oh, yes, grandpapa. We are great friends."

" Do your parents like him, my child ? "

" Oh, yes, grandpapa. Very much. Oh, I think every one likes him. He is a great success, you know."

She was talking foolishly, and at random, straying about the room, taking up books, wishing grandpapa would go.

Grandpapa grunted. Rather queer goings on, he thought, for Rome to be entertaining young men by herself when her papa and mamma were out. What were unmarried young women coming to ? If mamma had gone on like that thirty years ago. . . . But this, of course, was 1890—desperately modern. Grandpapa, though he not infrequently wrote to the *Times*, the *Spectator*, and the *Guardian*, to say how modern the current year was (for, of course, current years always were and are), did not always remember it. The untramelled (it seemed to him untramelled) freedom of intercourse enjoyed by modern young men and women (especially young women) continually shocked him. Grandpapa had enjoyed much free and untramelled intercourse in his own distant youth, during the Regency, but fifty years of Victorianism had since intervened, and he believed that intercourse should not now be free. He could not understand his granddaughter Stanley, who was continually abusing what she called the conventional prudery of the age ; what further liberties, in heaven's name, did young women want ? To do her justice, Rome did not join in this cry for further emancipation ; Rome accepted the conventions, with an acquiescent, ironic smile. There they were : why make oneself hot with kicking over the traces ? One accepted the social follies and codes. . . .

(" On the contrary," Maurice would say, " I refuse them."

" It will make no difference to them either way," said Rome).

Rome, a good *raconteuse* and mimic, proceeded to

entertain grandpapa with an account of a dinner party at which she had been taken in by that curious and noisy member of Parliament, Mr. Augustus Conybeare, whom grandpapa disliked exceedingly.

Then mamma and papa came home, and Rome went upstairs to dress for another dinner party. Thus do social life and the storm-tossed journey of the human soul run on concurrently, and neither makes way for the other.

4

ON THE PINCIO

THROUGH that winter civilisation fought its losing battle with more primitive forces over the souls and bodies of Miss Garden and Mr. Jayne.

" There is only one way in which we can meet and be together," said Rome, " and that is as friends. There is no other relation possible in the circumstances. I will be party to no scandal, my best. If we can't meet one another with self-control, then we mustn't meet at all. What is the use of tilting at the laws of society ? There they are, and thus it is. . . ."

" You make a fetish of society," said Mr. Jayne, with gloom. " For a woman of your brains, it is queer."

" Perhaps," said Rome.

Then, it becoming apparent that she and Mr. Jayne were not at present going to meet one another with self-control, Rome went for the winter to the city of that name, with her papa, whose spiritual home it, of course, now was. Mrs. Garden did not go, because she desired to be in at the birth of Stanley's baby.

But civilisation had not reckoned sufficiently with the forces of emotion. These led Mr. Jayne, but a few

weeks after Miss Garden had departed, to follow her to
Italy, and, in fact, to Rome.

So, one bright February morning, he called at the
Gardens' hotel pension in the Via Babuino, and found
Rome and her papa in act to set forth for a walk on the
Pincio. Miss Garden, looking pale, fair and elegant in
a long, fur-edged, high-shouldered cape coat and a tall
pointed, blue velvet hat beneath which her hair gleamed
gold, received him as urbanely, as coolly, as detachedly
as ever; she seemed to have got her emotions well
under control in the month since they had parted. Mr.
Jayne responded to her tone, and all the morning, as
they strolled about with Mr. Garden, they were bland
and cool and amusing; well-bred English visitors,
turning interested and satirical eyes on the fashionable
crowds about them, stopping now and then to exchange
amenities with fellow-strollers, for Mr. Jayne knew
Roman society well, and Mr. Garden had come armed
with introductions from his co-religionists, though,
indeed, he was little disposed for much society, wishing
to spend such time as he did not devote to seeing Rome
in studious research at the Vatican library. His daughter
was a little afraid that the Eternal City might seriously
disturb his faith, and that papa might fall under the
undeniably fascinating influence of paganism, which
makes such a far finer and nobler show in Rome than
mediæval Christianity. And, indeed, with St. Peter's
papa was not pleased; he scarcely liked to say so,
even to himself, but it did seem to him to be of a garish
hugeness that smacked almost of vulgarity, and pained
his fastidious taste. On the other hand, there were
many old churches of a more pleasing style, and in
these his soul found rest when disturbed by the massive
splendours of classical Rome. No; papa would not
become a pagan; he knew too much of pagan corruptions and cruelties for that. Corruptions and

cruelties he admitted, of course, in the history of Christianity also ; corruption and cruelty are, indeed, properties of the unfortunate and paradoxical human race ; but papa was persuaded that only defective Christians (after all, Christians always are and have been defective) were corrupt and cruel, whereas the most completely pagan of pagans had been so, and paganism is, indeed, rather an incentive than a discouragement to vice. In fact, papa was, by this time, thoroughly biased in this matter, and so was probably safe. Or, anyhow, so his daughter hoped. For it would, there was no denying it, be exceedingly awkward were papa to become a pagan, quite apart from the preliminary anguish with which his soul would be torn were he to be shaken from his present faith. Were there pagan places of worship in London ? Probably papa would have to build a private chapel, and in it erect images of his new gods. . . . For pagans had never been happy without much worship ; they had been the most religious of believers. Except, of course, the lax and broad-church pagan, and probably papa, if he got paganism at all, would get it strong.

So Rome was quite pleased that papa should be walking on the Pincio with her, getting a good view of the dome of St. Peter's, which is the finest and most impressive part of that cathedral, rather than wandering about the Forum and peering into the new excavations, murmuring scraps of Latin as he peered.

In the warm, sunlit air, with the band playing Verdi, and the gay crowds promenading, and the enchanted city spread all a-glitter beneath them, Rome was caught into a deep and intoxicated joy. The bitter, restless struggling of the last months gave way to peace ; the happy peace that looks not ahead, but rejoices in the moment. The tall and gay companion strolling at her side, so fluent in several languages, so apt to catch a half-worded meaning, to smile at an unuttered jest, so informed, so polished, so of the world worldly . . . take Mr. Jayne as merely that, and she had her friend and companion back again, which was deeply restful and vastly stimulating. And beneath that was her lover, whom she loved ; beneath his urbane exterior his passion throbbed and leaped, and his deep need of her cried, and in her the answering need cried back.

5

IN THE CAMPAGNA

TOGETHER they walked in the Campagna, in the bright, soft wash of the February sun. Mr Jayne had been in Rome a week, and they had gone out to Tivoli together, without papa, who was reading in the Vatican library. They lunched at the restaurant by the waterfalls, then explored Hadrian's Villa with the plan in Murray, and quarrelled about which were the different rooms. Failing to agree on this problem, they sat down in the Trichinium and looked at the view, and discussed the more urgent problem of their lives.

" You must," said Mr. Jayne, " come to me. It is the only right and reasonable way out. We'll live in no half-way house, with secrecy and concealment. We should both hate that. But Olga will not divorce me ; it's no use thinking of that. In her view, and that of all her countrywomen, husbands are never faithful. The infidelity of a husband is no reason to a Russian woman for divorce. Unless she herself wants to marry another man, and that is likely enough, in Olga's case, to happen. We are nothing to each other, she and I. Such love as we had—and it was never love—is dead long ago. We don't even like each other."

"Curious," mused Rome, "not to foresee these developments at the outset, before taking the serious step of marriage. Marriage is an action too freely practised and too seldom adequately considered."

"That is so," Mr. Jayne agreed. "But, and however that may be, what is done is done. What we now have to consider, however inadequately, is the future. It is very plain that you and I must be together. Yes, yes, yes. Nothing else is plain, but that is. The one light in chaos. . . . My dearest love, you can't be denying that. It is the only conceivable thing—the only thinkable way out."

"Way out," said Rome. "I think, rather, a way in. . . . Which way do we take—out or in?" Musingly she looked over the Campagna to blue hills, and Mr. Jayne, his eyes on her white profile, on the gleam of gold hair beneath her dark fur cap, and on her slender hands that clasped her knees, leant closer to her and replied, with neither hesitation nor doubt, "In."

"Indeed," said Miss Garden, "these questions can't be decided in this rough and ready, impetuous manner. The mind must have its share in deciding these important matters, not merely the emotions and desires. Or else what is the good of education, or of having learnt to think clearly at all?"

"Very little," said Mr. Jayne. "However, in this case the more clearly one thinks the more plain the way to take becomes. It is confused and muddled thinking that would lead us to conform to convention and give one another up, merely because of a social code."

"The social code," said Miss Garden, "though as a rule I prefer to observe it, is in this case neither here nor there. I have ruled that out ; cleared the field, so to speak, for the essentials. Now, what *are* the

essentials ?   Your wife, whom you have undertaken to
live with. . . ."

" By mutual agreement, we have given that up long
since," said Mr. Jayne, not for the first time.

". . . and your children, whom you have brought
into the world and are responsible for."

" They are their mother's. She lets me see nothing
of them. She is determined to bring them up as
Russian patriots."

" Still, they are half yours, and it is a question
whether you should not claim your share. In fact, I
think it is certain that you should. If you broke off
completely from your wife and lived with me, your
right in them would be gone. . . .   Then, of course,
there is the ethical point as to your contract, the vow
you made to your wife on marriage, which positively
excludes similar relations with any one else while she
remains your wife."

" I ought never to have made them. I was a fool.
The wrong was in the vows, not in their breach."

" Granted that they were wrong, that does not settle
the further point of whether, having been made, with
every circumstance of deliberation, they should not be
kept."

" Oh, God," said Mr. Jayne.   " You talk, my dearest
dear, like a pedant, a prig, or a book of logic. Don't
you *care*, Rome ? "

" You know," said Miss Garden, " that I do. . . .
No, don't touch me. I must think it out. I *am* a
pedant and a prig, if you like, and I *must* think it out,
not only feel. But now I will think of the other side.
Oh, yes, I know there is another side. We love one
another, and we can neither of us be happy, or fully
ourselves, without being together. Without one another we shall be incomplete, unhappy, and perhaps
(not certainly) morally and mentally stunted and

warped. Indeed, I see that as clearly as you can. Further, our being together may, as you say, not hurt your wife ; she may not care in the least. As to that, I simply don't know. How could I ? She may even let you still have a share in your children. Russian points of view are so different from ours. But one should be certain of that before taking any step. . . . Then there are still points on the other side, that we have to think of. Any children we might have would be illegitimate. That would be hard on them."

" In point of fact," said Mr. Jayne, " it is largely illusory, that hardship. And in this case they (if they should ever exist) needn't even know. You would take my name. Who is to go on remembering that I have a Russian wife ? Very few people in England even know it. We should soon live down any talk there might be."

"And then," went on Rome, ticking off another point on her fingers, " there are my papa and mamma, whom we should hurt very badly. In their eyes what we are discussing isn't a thing to be discussed at all ; it is a deadly sin, and there's an end of it. They are very fond of me, and they would be terribly unhappy. That, too, is a point to be considered."

" Perhaps. But not to be given much weight to. It's damnable to have to hurt the people we love—but, after all, we can't let our parents rule our lives. We're living in the eighteen nineties ; we're not mid-Victorians. And we have to make up our own minds what to do with our lives. We can't be tied up by any one else's views, either those of our relations or of society in general. We have to make our own judgments and choices, all along. And parents shouldn't be hurt by their children's choices, even if they do think them wrong ; they should live and let live. All this judging for other people, and being hurt, is poisonous. It's a relic of the patriarchal system,—or the matriarchal."

Miss Garden smiled.

" Possibly. I should say, rather, that it was in-cidental to parental affection, and always will be. Anyhow, there it is. . . . They don't, of course, even believe that divorce is right, let alone adultery." Her cool, thoughtful enunciation of the last word gave it its uttermost value. Miss Garden never slurred or shirked either words or facts.

" But that," she added, " doesn't, of course, dispose of our lives. That's only one point out of many. The question is, what is, now and ultimately, the right and best thing for me and you to do. You've decided. Well, I haven't—yet. Give me a week, Francis. I promise I won't take more."

" You are so beautiful," said Mr. Jayne, changing the subject and speaking inaccurately, and lifted her hands to his face. " You are so beautiful. There is no one like you. You are like the golden sickle moon riding over the world. You hold my life in your two hands. Be kind to it, Rome. *I love you, I love you, I love you.* If we deny our love we shall be blasphem-ing. Love like ours transcends all barriers, and well you know it. Take your week, if you must, only decide rightly at the end of it, my heart's glory. The fine thing we shall make of life together, you and I, the fine, precious, lovely thing. It's been so poor and common—full of bickerings and jars and commonness and discontents. . . .

" *Oh, Rome. . . .*"

6

RUSSIAN TRAGEDY

THE Russian woman, with her two beautiful children
and her stout, dazed, unhappy mamma, waited in
the hall of the flat of Mr. Jayne. They were weary,
having travelled across Russia and from Russia to
London, to find Mr. Jayne, and then, having learnt
that he was in Rome, straight from London thither,
spending two nights in the train and arriving this
morning, more alive than dead (for who, this side of the
grave, is not?) but very tired. The two children
were so tired that they whimpered disagreeably, and
their mother often wiped their noses with her
travel-grimed handkerchief, but not so often as they
required it.

Olga Petrushka was a beautiful woman, square-
headed, with a fair, northern skin and large, deep blue
eyes, black-lashed, and massive plaits of flaxen hair.
Her eyes looked wild and haunted, for Russians have
such dreadful experiences, and her cheeks were hollowed ;
she looked like a woman who has seen death and worse
too close, and indeed she had. She was shabbily
dressed in an old fur dolman over a scarlet dress, and
a fur cap. The two children were bundled up in bear-
skin coats, like little animals. Her little dancing
bears, she would call them in lighter moments. Ever
and anon she would fling them sweet cakes out of her
reticule, and they would gobble them greedily.

But Nina Naryshkin, their grandmother, sat and
rocked to and fro, to and fro, and said nothing but,
" Aie, aie, aie."

The hall porter turned on the little family a beaming
and kindly eye. They were, in all probability, thieves,

and not, as the Russian lady asserted, the family of Signor Jayne, so he would not admit them into Signor Jayne's room, but he liked to see their gambols.

Every now and then the younger lady would say in Russian, " Cheer up, then, little children. Your father will soon be here, and he will give you more sweet cakes. Aha, how your dirty little mouths water to hear it ! Boris, you rascal, don't pull your sister's pig-tail. What children ! They drive me to despair."

And then Mr. Jayne arrived. He came in at the open hall door, with a tall, fair, English lady, and he was saying to her, " If you don't mind coming in for a moment, I will get you the book."

The hall porter stepped forward with a bow, and indicated in the background Mrs. Jayne and the little Jaynes.

What a moment for Mr. Jayne ! What a moment for Mrs. Jayne, her mamma, and the little Jaynes. What a moment for Miss Garden ! What a moment for the hall porter, who loved both domestic re-unions and quarrels, and was as yet uncertain which this would be (it might even be both), but, above all, loved moments, and that it would certainly be.

And so it proved. Where Russians are, there, one may say, moments are, for these live in moments.

Olga Petrushka stepped forward with a loud cry and outstretched arms, and exclaimed in Russian, "Ah, Franya Stefanovitch " (one of the names she had for him, for Russians give one another hundreds of names each, and this accounts in part for the curious, confused state in which this nation is often to be found), " I have found you at last."

Mr. Jayne, always composed, retained his calm. He shook hands with his wife and mother-in-law, and addressed them in French.

" How are you, my dear Olga ? Why did you not

tell me you wanted to see me ? I would have come to Moscow. It is a long way to have come, with your mother and the children too. How are you, my little villains ? "

"Ah, my God," said Mrs. Jayne, also now in French, which she spoke with rapidity and violence, " how could I stay another day in Russia ? The misery I have been through ! Poor little papa—Nicolai Nicolaivitch—they have arrested him for revolutionary propaganda and sent him to Siberia, with my brother, Feodor. They had evidence also against mamma and myself, and would have arrested us, and only barely we escaped in time, with the little bears. The poor cherubs—kiss them, Franya. They have been crying for their little father and the love and good food and warm house he will give them. For now they and we have no one but you. ' Go to England, Olga,' papa said as they took him. It is the one safe country. The English are good to Russian exiles, and your husband will take care of you and mamma and the little ones. . . .' But you are with a lady, Franya. Introduce us."

" I beg your pardon. Miss Garden, my wife, and Mme Naryskhin, her mother. Miss Garden and her father are great friends of mine. . . . If you will go into my rooms and wait for me for a moment, Olga, I will see Miss Garden to her pension and return."

" No," said Miss Garden, in her fluent and exquisite French. " No, I beg of you. I will go home alone ; indeed, it is no way. Good-evening, Madame Jayne and Madame Naryskhin."

Mr. Jayne went out into the street with her. His unhappy eyes met hers.

" To-morrow morning," he muttered, " I shall call. . . . This alters nothing. . . . I will come to-morrow morning, and we will talk."

" Yes," said Miss Garden.   " We must talk."

Mr. Jayne went back into the hall, and escorted his family upstairs to his rooms.

"Aie, aie, aie," shuddered Olga Petrushka, flinging off her fur coat and cap, and leaping round the room in her red dress, like a Russian in a novel.   " Let's get warm.   Come, little bears "—she spoke German now— " to your papa's arms.   Kiss him, Katya ; hug him, Boris.   Tell him we have come across Europe to be with him, now that all else is gone.   Forgive and forget, eh, Franya Maryavitch ?   You and I must keep one another warm. . . .   Aie, aie, aie, my poor papa," she wailed in Russian.   " I keep seeing his face as they took him, and my poor Feodor's.   As to mamma, she is dazed ; she will never get over it.   We must keep her always with us, poor little mamma. . . . Tea at once, Franya.   I am going to be sick," she added in Magyar, and was.

Mr. Jayne laid his wife on his bed and took off her shoes and bathed her forehead, while she moaned in Polish.   Then he made tea for her and the children and his mother-in-law, who sat heavily in a chair and drank five cups, and looked at him with drowsy, inimical eyes, saying never a word.   He felt like a dead man, in a world full of ghosts.   Who were these, who had this claim upon him ?   Their clinging hands were pulling him down, out of life into a tomb.   The February evening shadows lay coldly on his heart.   These poor, distraught women, these little children—he must take infinite care of them, and let them lack for nothing, but he must not let them come close into his life ; they would throttle it.   His life, his true life, was with Rome.   Rome, the gallant, fastidious dandy, with her delicate poise, her pride, her cool wit and grace. Not with this violent, unhappy, inconsequent Slav, chattering in several tongues upon his bed.

To-morrow he would go and talk to Rome . . .
explain to Rome. . . .

7

ENGLISH TRAGEDY

MISS GARDEN received Mr. Jayne. Neither had slept
much, for Mr. Jayne had given his bed to his family
and lain himself on a horsehair couch, and Miss Garden
had been troubled by her thoughts. Their faces
were pale and shadowed and heavy-eyed.

Miss Garden said, " This is the end, of course. I
shan't need a week now. Fate has intervened very
opportunely."

" No," said Mr. Jayne, with passion. " No. Nothing
is changed. For God's sake, don't think that our
situation is changed. It is not. She wants protection
and security and a home, and I will provide all those
for her and her mother and the children. Me she does
not want. They shall have everything they want.
But I shall not live with them."

" You still think that you and I can live together ? "
Miss Garden was sceptical of his optimism. " I don't
think your wife would tolerate that. No, Frank, it's
no use. They belong to you. They need you. I
can't come between you. It would be heartless and
selfish. Imagine the situation for a moment . . . it
is impossible."

They both imagined it. Mr. Jayne shuddered, like
a man very cold.

" You don't want to be involved in such a—such a
melodrama," he said, bitterly.

" Put it at that if you like. I take it we are neither
of us fond of melodrama. But, apart from that, I

said all along, and meant it, that if your wife wants you I can't take you. She has first claim."

" I shall not live with Olga Petrushka and her mother."

" That's your own affair, of course. You are very likely right, since you don't get on well together. But you must see that you and I can't . . ."

Miss Garden stopped, for her voice began to shake. How she loved him ! She pressed her hands together in her lap till the rings bruised her fingers.

Mr. Jayne gazed at her gloomily, observing her lightly poised body, slim and elegant in a dark blue taffeta dress which stood out behind below the waist in a kind of shelf, and made her shape rather like that of a swan. He saw her slight, anguished hands that hurt each other, and the pale tremor of her face.

" She's been through hell, and she wants you," said Miss Garden, trying to keep control.

" I tell you I can't live with her, nor she with me. Do you want to turn my life into a tragi-comic opera ? "

" Most life is a tragi-comic opera," said Rome, trying to smile. " Perhaps all."

" But you're resolved anyhow to keep yours clear of *my* tragi-comedies," he flung at her.

Then he apologised.

" I don't mean that ; I don't know what I'm saying. . . . Oh, I won't press you now to decide. We'll wait, Rome. You'll see, in a month or so, how things have arranged themselves—how easy it will all be. Olga will have recovered her balance by then ; she changes from hour to hour, like all Russians. In a few weeks she will be tired of me and want to be in Paris, or back in Russia. She doesn't really want me ; it's only that she is unstrung by trouble. Upset ; that's what she is. All I ask you to do is to wait."

" No, Frank. It can never be, unless she goes, sometime, to live with some one else, some other man.

Otherwise she would be liable, even if she left you for a time, to want you again at intervals. I can't make a third. . . . You see, whatever happens now, your family must always be a real fact to me, not an abstraction. I've seen them . . . Katya is just like you—your chin and eyes. . . . The children love you very much ; I saw that. . . . And she loves you too. . . ."

" She does not. That's not love—not as I know love."

" As to that, we all know love in different ways, I suppose. . . . Truly, Francis, I have quite decided. I can't live with you. . . . No, no, don't . . ."

He was holding her in his arms and kissing her face, her lips, her eyes, muttering entreaties.

" If you loved me you'd do it."

" I do love you, and I shan't do it."

" I'm asking nothing dishonourable of you. You don't think it wrong on general principles ; yesterday you were willing to consider it. You're just refusing life for a quixotic whim . . . refusing, denying life. . . . Rome, you can't do it. Don't you know, now you're in my arms, that you can't, that it would be to deny the best in us ? "

" What's the best, what's the worst ? I don't know, and nor do you. I'm not an ethicist. All I know is that your wife, while she wants you, or thinks she wants you, has first claim. . . . It's a question of fairness and decent feeling . . . or bring it down, if you like, to a question of taste. Perhaps that is the only basis there really is for decisions of this sort for people like us."

" Taste. That's a fine cry to mess up two lives by. I'd almost rather you were religious, and talked of the will of God. One could respect that, at least."

" I can't do that, as I happen not to be sure whether

God exists. And it would make nothing simpler really, since one would then have to discover what one believed the will of God to be. Don't do religious people the injustice of believing that anything is simpler or easier for them ; it's more difficult, since life is more exacting. . . . But it comes to the same thing ; all these processes of thought lead to the same result if applied by the same mind. It depends on the individual outlook. And this is mine. . . . Oh, don't make it so damnably difficult for us both, my dearest. . . ."

Miss Garden, who never swore and never wept, here collapsed into tears, all her urbane breeding broken at last. He consoled her so tenderly, so pitifully, so mournfully, that she wept the more for love of him.

"Go now," she said at last. "We mustn't meet again till we can both do it quietly, without such pain. Papa and I are going back to London next week. Write to me sometimes and let me know how you do and where you are. My dearest Frank . . ."

8

FOUNDERED

ROME was alone. She sat in a hard Italian chair, quite still, and felt cold and numb, and as if she had died. Drowned she felt, under deep, cold seas of passion and of pain. Wrecked and foundered and drowned, at the bottom of gray seas. Something cried, small and weak and hurt within her, and it was the voice of love, or (as Mr. Jayne would have it) of life ; life which she had denied and slain. Never had she greatly loved before ; never would she greatly love again ; and the great love she now had she was slaying. That was what the hurt voice cried in her as she sat alone in the great, bare, chilly room, the sad little scaldino on the floor at her feet.

She was dry-eyed now that she was alone, and had no more to face Mr. Jayne's love and pain. Her own she could bear. Harder and harder, and cooler and more cynical she would grow, as she walked the world alone, leaving love behind. Was that the choice? Did one either do the decent, difficult thing, and wither to bitterness in doing it, or take the easy road, the road of joy and fulfilment, and be thereby enriched and fulfilled? And what was fulfilment, and what enrichment? What, ah, what, was this strange tale that life is; what its meaning, what its purpose, what its end?

Rome did not know. She knew one thing only. Frustration, renunciation, death—whether you called your criterion the will of God, or social ethics, or a quixotic whim, or your own private standards of decency and taste, it led you to these; led you to the same sad place, where you lay drowned dead beneath bitter seas.

Midday chimed over the city. Miss Garden rose, and put on her out-door things, and went forth to meet her papa for lunch. Life moves on, through whatever deserts, and one must compose oneself to meet it, never betraying one's soul.

9

VICKY ON THE WORLD

" It's good to have you back again, my Rome," Vicky said. " I miss you at my parties. There are lots of new people I want you to meet. An adorable Oxford youth, whom you'll find after your own heart. Already he writes essays like a polished gentleman of the world, and he a round-faced cherub barely out of school. A coming man, my dear, mark my words. Such brilliance, such style, such absurd urbanity! Denman introduced him. I prefer him enormously to Denman's other cronies—that affected Mr. Le Gallienne, for instance, and that conceited young Beardsley. Not but that young Beardsley, too, has a wit. I'll say that for Denman—he keeps a witty table. . . . Well, have you brought papa back still a good Roman? Father Stanton says, by the way, we're to call the Pope's church in this country the Italian Mission. It's quite time papa had a change of creed, anyhow; I begin to fear for his health since he read *Robert Elsmere* and wasn't driven by it to honest doubt."

"Neither," said Rome, "was he driven by the Forum to the pagan gods. One begins to think that papa is settling down."

"Oh, I trust not. Dear papa, he's not old yet. . . . What a country you have come back to, though, my dear. Strikes everywhere—dockers, railwaymen, miners, even tailors. . . . Maurice is perfectly happy, encouraging them all. But, darling Maurice, I'm *seriously* afraid he may cut Amy's throat one day. Serve her right, the little cat. If I were Maurice I'd beat her. Perhaps he will one day, when he's not quite sober. I wish she'd run off with one of the vulgar men she flirts with, and leave him in peace. *He'll* never run off, because he won't leave the children to her. Poor old boy, he's so desperately up against things the whole time. Mamma's miserable about him, I know, though she never says a word. However, she's consoled by all her nice grandchildren. Even grandpapa, you know, admits that the deplorable modern generation is doing its duty as regards multiplication. Why *do* old Bibly clergymen like grandpapa

think it so important to produce more life ? One would
think, one really *would* think, that there was plenty of
that already. But no. Be fruitful, they say : multiply:
replenish the earth. It says so in Genesis, and clergymen of grandpapa's generation can't get away from
Genesis. Poor grandpapa. He's writing to the *Guardian*, as usual, about the Modern Woman. She's dreadfully on his mind. Latchkeys. He doesn't think
women ought to have them. Why not ? He doesn't
explain. Man may open their front doors with keys,
but women must, he thinks, always ring up the unfortunate maids. He can think of no reasons why ;
he is past reasons, but not past convictions. What,
he asked, in Stanley's drawing-room the other day, is
to take the place for women, of the old sanctities and
safeties ? ' The new safeties, I imagine, sir,' Denman
replied. Grandpapa grunted and frowned. He thinks
women on bicycles really indecent, poor old dear. As
a matter of fact, Denman does too—at least, ungrace-
ful—which to him is the same thing. But Rome, my
dear, you simply must get one. We're all doing it
now. It's glorious ; the nearest approach to wings
permitted to men and women here below. Intoxicat-
ing ! Stanley lives on hers, now her son has safely
arrived. And it's transforming clothes. Short jackets
and cloth caps are coming in. Bustles are no more.
And, my dear—*bloomers* are seen in the land ! Yes,
actually. Stanley cycles in them ; she looks delightful,
whatever Denman says. No, I don't. Charles doesn't
approve. Conspicuous, he thinks. And, of course, so
it is. Well, men will be men. They'll never be civilised
where women are concerned, most of them. But the
poor silly old world really does march a little. We're
all getting most thrillingly *fin-de-siècle*. I wonder if
all times have been as deliriously modern, while they
lasted, as our times."

" Probably," said Rome. " It's one of the more certain, though more ephemeral, qualities that times have. I wonder at what age grandpapa began deploring it. Not during the Regency or under William the Fourth, I imagine. I suppose *his* grandpapa was deploring it then."

" Oh, and there's another shocking female modernism become quite common this winter, my dear. *Cigarettes!* I haven't perpetrated that myself yet, as Charles thinks that unfeminine too, and I'm sure the children would steal them and be sick. Besides, I don't think it really becoming to an elegant female. But Stanley does. That literary set of hers is a funny mixture of forwardness and reaction. Forward women and reactionary men, I think. Grandpapa hasn't tumbled to Stanley's cigarettes yet. My hat, when he does! Well, it's a funny world. I suppose my daughters will grow up smoking like their brothers, without thinking twice about it. . . . The darlings, they're all so troublesome just now. That kindergarten can't or won't teach Imogen to speak properly. If she gabbles like this at three, what will she do at thirty? And Hughie drawls and contradicts . . ."

Their talk then ran along family lines.

10

STANLEY AND DENMAN

STANLEY pedalled swiftly, a sturdy, attractive figure in serge knickerbockers (" bloomers," they were called while that graceful and sensible fashion of our ancestresses endured) along a smooth, sandy road between pine woods. The April sunlight flickered on the pale brown, needle-strewn road ; the light wind sang in the

pines and blew dark curls of hair from under Stanley's
sailor hat-brim. Her bicycle basket was full of
primroses. Her round, brown cheeks glowed pink ;
her lips were parted in a low, tuneless song (tuneless
because Stanley could never get a tune right). It
expressed her happiness, relieved the pressure of her
joy at being alive. Such a day ! Such a bicycle !
Such sweet and merry air !

She stopped, got off her bicycle, leant it against a
gate, and lay down flat on her back in the wood, staring
up into the green gloom. London, Denman, her baby,
were far off. She was alone with beauty. She was
passionately realising the moment, its fleeting ex-
quisiteness, its still, fragile beauty. So exquisite it
was, so frail and so transitory, that she could have
wept, even as she clasped it close. To savour the
loveliness of moments, to bathe in them as in a wine-
gold, sun-warmed sea, and then to pass on to the next
—that was life.

Then, presently, the moment lost its keenness, and
she was no longer alone with beauty. Her husband
and her baby broke the charmed circle, looking in.
How she loved them ! But they took from her something ; her loneliness, that queer, eerie separateness,
that only bachelors and spinsters know. They need
not, to know it, be unattached, virgin bachelors and
spinsters ; love does not spoil separateness, but house-
holds do.

Stanley rose to her feet, brushed the pine-needles
from her neat clothes and untidy hair, put on her sailor
hat, and got on her bicycle again. Before her there
was a long slope down. To take it, brakeless, feet up
on the rest, was like flying. Stanley was no longer a
mystic, a wife, or a mother ; she was a hoydenish
little girl out for a holiday.

She reached Weybridge station, and entrained for

London in one of the halting, smoke-palled, crawling
trains of the period. In it she read Ibsen's *Dolls'
House*, for she and Denman were going to see it
next week at the Independent Theatre. What a play!
What moralising! What *purpose*! What deplorable
solemnity! There seemed, to the set of light-hearted
and cynical æsthetes among whom Stanley moved,
nothing to do about the *Dolls' House* but to laugh at it.
These strange, solemn Scandinavians! Yet numbers
of cultured readers in England took it seriously, as
cultured English readers love to take foreign plays.
They found it impressive and fine, almost a gospel.
Further, the bourgeois, the Philistines, the people who
are inaccurately said to spend more time than the
elect *in the street* (why is this believed of them?),
mocked at it, so that there must be something in it,
for, as has been well said (or if it has not it should have
been) majorities are always wrong.

" The fact is," said Stanley to herself, " the fact is,
cultivated people like tracts. Especially cultivated
women like tracts about their own emancipation.
And of course, in a way, they're right. . . . But
plays with purposes . . ."

It will be observed that Stanley, whom nature had
made to welcome purposes wherever found, had well
assimilated the spirit of her literary group, which preferred art to be for the sake of art only. She had, as
Vicky said of her, so much Zeitgeist. What seemed
to her and her friends the good drama of the moment
was light social comedy, full of gay, sparkling nonsense
and epigrams for the sake of epigrams. Or the more
profound and mordaunt wit of Mr. George Bernard
Shaw, who had lately begun to write plays. Mr. Shaw
had, indeed, purpose, but his wit carried it off.

Waterloo. Even the trains of 1891 got there at last.
Stanley went to look for her bicycle. Finding it and

wheeling it off, she felt herself to be one of the happiest persons in the station. She had everything. A bicycle, a husband, a baby, a house, freedom, love, literary and social opportunity, charming friends. Life was indeed felicitous to such as she.

" Progress of Royal Labour Commission," the newspaper placards shouted. " More L.C.C. scandals. Free brass bands for the poor ! "

Stanley frowned. It was a damnable world, after all. A vulgar, grudging, grabbing world. The voice of the press was as the shrill voice of Amy the wife of Maurice. " Free brass bands for the poor ! " That was how Amy would say it, with her silly, gibing laugh. Even, a little, how Irving would say it. But Irving, though he despised the democratic ways of the London County Council, and free brass bands for the poor, was not silly or spiteful. He was merely a delightful, philistine young gentleman on the Stock Exchange.

Stanley bicycled (amid perils less great, less numerous, in the year 1891 than now) to Margaretta Street, Chelsea. There was the house, small, dingy, white, with a green door and a tiny square of front garden. Stanley found her latch-key, flung open the green door with a kind of impetuous, happy eagerness, and came face to face with her husband in the little hall.

" Hallo," he said, and quizzically surveyed her, up and down, from her blown hair and flushed cheeks to her neat, roomy knickerbockers and stout brogues. " Hallo."

" Hallo, Den. I've had the *rippingest* ride. How's baby ? And yourself ? "

" Both flourish, I believe. . . . You know we've people to dinner to-night ? You've not left yourself a great deal of time, have you. . . . You don't look your best, my dear girl, if I may say so."

" No, I expect not ; I'm blown to bits. What's it matter ? Come on, Den, we must both hurry."

She ran upstairs, turned hot water into the bath, tiptoed into the nursery where her son slept, and back to her room. Denman was in his dressing-room, beyond the open door.

" I've had a lovely ride, Den. Weybridge way."

" Glad you enjoyed it. But lovely's the wrong word. Anything less lovely than a woman in those unspeakable garments I never saw. I detest them. Women ought to wear graceful, trailing things always. . . . I can't think why you *do* it. Your sense of beauty must be sadly defective."

" Beauty—oh, well, it's convenience that matters most, surely. For that matter, very few modern clothes, male or female, are beautiful. But I don't think these are ugly. One can't trail all the time ; it's a dirty trick on foot and dangerous on a bicycle."

" It's better to be elegant, dirty and dangerous than frumpish, clean and safe. That's an epigram. The fact is, women ought never to indulge in activities, either of body or mind ; it's not their rôle. They can't do it gracefully."

" What do you want them to do, then, poor things ? Just sit about ? "

" Precisely that. You've expressed it accurately, if not very beautifully. An elegant inertia is what is required of women . . . what on earth has that girl done with my black socks ? . . . Any activity necessary to the human race can be performed by such men as are prepared to sacrifice themselves. All this feminine pedalling about and playing ridiculous games, and speaking on platforms, and writing books, and serving on committees—Lord save us."

" They'd get awfully fat, your sitting-about females ;

they wouldn't be graceful long. Hurry up, Den, or you'll be late, not I."

"We shall both be late. It matters very little. If any of our guests have the bad taste to be punctual it will serve them right. Crackanthorpe won't be punctual, anyhow; he never is. . . . Make yourself lovely to-night, Stan; I want to forget those awful bloomers. They make you look like a horrible joke in *Punch* about the New Woman."

"Well, I'd rather look like the New Woman than like the 'Woman (not new)' in the same pictures—sanctimonious idiots. . . . Really, Den, you're silly about women . . ."

"Oh, for God's sake," said Denman, smothered in his shirt.

Stanley went to the bathroom with a touch of ill-humour, which she sang away, like a kettle, in clouds of steam.

Denman, hearing the tuneless song, winced in amused distaste. As a matter of fact, he would have liked a bath himself.

II

A YOUNG MASHER

How agreeable, how elegant, and how fastidious were the young mashers of the early nineties! We shall not look upon their like again. Du Maurier has immortalised them, beautiful creatures with slim waists and swallow-tailed evening coats, and clear-cut patrician features, chatting to magnificent women with curled mouths, straight brows, and noble, sweeping figures. The women of those days, if we are to believe Du Maurier, were nobly built as goddesses, classical-featured, generous of stature and of bosom, but roped

in straitly between ribs and hips, so as to produce
waists that nature never planned. Because of this
compression, they would often suffer greatly, and
sometimes fall ill with anæmia, or cancer, or both,
and die in great anguish. But, while they yet lived
and breathed, they were noble and elegant objects,
and their gentlemen friends matched them for grace.

Irving Arthur Penrhyn Garden, aged twenty-eight,
earning a comfortable and honest livelihood on the
Stock Exchange, was a masher. He lived in bachelor
chambers in Bruton Street, and was a popular diner-
out and dance-goer, for, though he had not brilliance
or fame, he had dark and slim good looks, cheerfulness,
savoir faire, and was that creature so sought of hostesses,
an agreeable young bachelor. His tastes were healthy,
his wit sound, his political and religious views gentlemanly, and his prospects satisfactory. Present cor-
rectness and future prosperity were stamped on Irving
Garden ; so unlike that queer fish, his brother Maurice,
the Radical journalist, who was stamped with present
incorrectness and future failure. Irving would, no
doubt, make a good marriage some time. Meanwhile,
he was enjoying life. He had no part with the highbrows, the cranks, the fops, the æsthetes, or any other
extreme persons ; he took no interest in foreign literature, Home Rule for Ireland, the women's movement,
the Independent Theatre, labour agitations, the new
art, George Meredith, or Russian exiles, finding them
(respectively) uninteresting, impracticable, unattractive,
depressing, paid-by-anarchist-gold, queer, unintelligible,
and a damned nuisance. He considered his brother
Maurice to be playing the wrong game ; Stanley's
friends he thought an affected, conceited crew, both
the men and the women being unsexed, and for ever
writing things one didn't want to read. Rome fell too
easily into superfluous irony, so that people never knew

when she was pulling their legs, and if she didn't marry soon, now that she was over thirty, people would begin thinking her an old maid. Una was all right, but shouldn't have married down. And, though Irving was an affectionate youth and loved his parents, he did think it a little comic of the pater to change his religion *quite* so often ; it made people smile. There should be limits to the number of religions allowed to each man in his life. Anyhow, what was wrong with the C. of E. ? On the whole, Vicky was the member of his family of whom Irving most approved. Vicky seemed to him what a woman should be. She looked pretty, dressed and danced well, was amusing, lived in the right part of London, and gave very decent, lively little dinners, at which people weren't always trying to be clever. Or anyhow, *he* wasn't asked to the ones at which they tried to be clever.

And with all this, Irving was no fool. He was doing very well at his job, had a good, sound head, quite well stocked with ideas, and knew his way about.

Such was Irving Arthur Penrhyn Garden, walking cheerfully, gracefully and competently through the year of grace 1891.

12

RUSSIAN INTERLUDE

THAT summer Russian refugees were greatly the mode. They would flee to Great Britain in shoals, from the fearful atrocities of their government. Those who came were mostly of the intellectual classes (the less intellectual being too stupid to flee) who had been plotting, or writing, or speaking, or otherwise expressing their distaste for their country's constitution, and thus incurring the displeasure of the authorities. Some of them had been sent to Siberia and had escaped; others had served their time there and returned; others again had not yet visited that land, but feared that they might. Once in London, they found kind English intellectuals eager to take an interest in them, and plenty of their own countrymen with whom to meet and continue to plot. It was quite the fashion, in the nineties, to have a few exiled Russians at your parties. They introduced a new way of taking tea, very nasty, with lemon and no milk. Vicky's youngest daughter, Imogen, as an infant, was once given a sip of this tea, from the cup of a hairy Russian professor, and was sent up to the nursery for spewing it out. Imogen developed thus an early and unjust distaste for Russians, which did not leave her through life.

In the May of 1891, some new Russian refugees suddenly broke on London—the unexpected and hitherto little mentioned wife, mother-in-law, and children of Mr. Jayne, the brilliant writer of essays and memoirs. It had been vaguely rumoured before that Mr. Jayne had some kind of Russian wife, but no one had expected her to make an appearance; it had been supposed that Mr. Jayne, being a man of some *savoir faire*, would have seen to that. However, here she was, a large and handsome Russian woman with two large and handsome children, a stout, tragic, yet conversational mamma, an inconsequent manner of speech, like that of Russians in novels, and a wide acquaintance with other Russian refugees, with whom she plotted on Sunday afternoons and all through Thursday nights. She settled, with her mother and children, in Mr. Jayne's flat. Mr. Jayne left the flat to them and took rooms of his own some way off; he probably thought he would be in the way if he lived in the flat, where Mrs. Jayne entertained her fellow-countrymen a good deal. Mrs. Jayne accused him bitterly of neglecting her in her loneliness and grief. He replied that experience had proved that they were not happy together, and that, therefore, he would provide for the support of her, her mother, and his two children, but would not share a dwelling with them, which would be both foolish and immoral. He added that, as she knew, he wished she and her mother would sometime see her way to living abroad, where they would be much happier. Mrs. Jayne replied that they intended to live in London until the Day of Deliverance, by which she meant the day when they could with safety return to Russia. She then went into hysterics and said that doubtless he wished her dead.

Mr. Jayne said, " These scenes make life impossible. You drive me to leave London. I shall live in Italy for the present. My bank will pay you an allowance, and I will visit you from time to time."

" Why do you hate me so, Franya Stefanovitch ? " she cried.

" I don't hate you. But you know as well as I do what a poor business we make of living together. It is one of the worst and most unintelligent forms of immorality for two people who irritate each other to expose themselves to misery and anger by living together. Therefore, with no malice, we will live apart."

" There's another woman. You wish to live with a mistress. I know it."

" If you think so, get a divorce."

" Never. I will never divorce you. You are my husband, and the father of my poor little bears. Who ever heard of a faithful husband ? We say in Russia that they are like the golden bear—a fabulous creature. No, I must put up with your infidelities. But if you leave me for too long I shall come and find you, and stick a knife into you and your mistress. I am not patient, Franya."

"I never supposed that you were, Olga. And I may tell you, though I do not expect you to believe me, that I have no mistress, and never have had."

She laughed at him.

"Ha ha! Are you the golden bear, then, found at last? Go away with you, you and your lies. You make me sick. . . . I wish that you were dead."

The last part of this conversation took place at the hall door, and, as Mr. Jayne went out, a young Russian came in. He was Sergius Dmitri, a cousin of Mrs. Jayne's, a student, who had also fled from Russia during the recent troubles. He was a passionate admirer of his cousin, and wished very much that she would get rid of this cold, unloving English husband of hers, and come to live with him. He heard her last words to Mr. Jayne.

"Sergius," she said, seeing him, "I want you to do me a service. Follow my husband this afternoon and see where he goes and whom he sees. I suspect him of having a mistress, and I wish to be certain. If he has, he will go straight to her now . . . I'll be revenged on him, the villain. After him, Sergius."

The young Russian saw Mr. Jayne disappearing round the corner, and hurried after him.

Mr. Jayne went to call on the Gardens. He took Rome out with him, and they sat on a bench in the garden in Bloomsbury Square.

"You must come away with me," he said. "We will live in Italy. She hates me. So does her mother. I can't live in the same town with them, let alone the same house. I have told her so. I am going to live in Italy, and work there at my books. Am I to go alone, or will you come?"

Rome saw across the square the windows of the house of her papa and mamma. She considered them ; she considered also life, in many of its aspects. She considered international marriages, and unhappy family life. Love she considered, and hate, the enduringness and the moral and spiritual consequences of each. She thought of her own happiness, of Mr. Jayne's, of Mrs. Jayne's, of that of their two children. Of social ethics, she thought, and of personal joy, and of human laws, which of them stand merely on expediency, which on some ultimate virtue. She thought also of vows, of contracts, and of honour. Having considered these things, and considering also her very great love for Mr. Jayne and his for her, she turned to him and opened her lips to reply.

But the words, whatever they were, which she would have uttered—and neither Mr. Jayne nor any one else was ever to know—were checked before her tongue formed them. For some one jumped out of the trees behind the bench on which they sat, and jabbed a long knife into Mr. Jayne's back, between the shoulders, and rushed away.

Other people near ran up. Mr. Jayne had fallen choking, forwards. They did not dare to remove the knife, but carried him out into the square and into the Gardens' house, where he lay on his side on a couch, unconscious, choking and bleeding at the lungs. The doctor was in attendance in ten minutes, but could do little, and in twenty Mr. Jayne was dead.

The assassin had, meanwhile, been captured. He proved to be a Russian, one Sergius Dmitri, described as a student, living in London. The only account of his action he gave was that he had known Mr. Jayne in Russia and disliked him, and that Mr. Jayne had not done his duty by his wife, who was Sergius Dmitri's cousin. So Sergius Dmitri had, in a moment of impulse, knifed Mr. Jayne. No, he could not say that he regretted his action.

His record showed him to be of the anarchist persuasion, and a thrower of several bombs in his native land, some of which had reached their marks. Human life was not, it was apparent, sacred to him. Mrs. Jayne, prostrated with grief, cursed him for murdering her husband, the father of her children, who had devotedly loved her and whom she had devotedly loved. He had never neglected her; that was a fancy of her cousin's, who had been a prey to jealousy.

Sergius Dmitri was hanged. Mrs. Jayne continued for a time to live in her husband's flat, supported by his money, but, soon tiring of widowhood, married a fellow-countryman and went, with her mother and children, to live in Paris.

Miss Garden, who had been so close a witness of the horrid event, and who was known besides as an intimate friend of Mr. Jayne's, never afterwards referred to the affair, even to her relatives. Miss Garden was no giver of confidences; no one ever learnt how she had felt about the business or about Mr. Jayne. There were not wanting, of course, those who said that these two had loved too well, had, in fact, been involved in an affair. But, in view of Miss Garden's reputation for cool inviolability, and of her calm manner after the tragedy, such rumours obtained little credence. Miss Garden did, indeed, leave London shortly after the inquest, and spent the rest of the summer in the country, but she returned in the autumn as apparently bland, cool and composed as always.

13

NINETY-TWO

EIGHTEEN ninety-two. Mr. Garden was troubled by
the death, in January, of Cardinal Manning, and by
the disputes conducted in the Press between Professor
Huxley, Mr. Gladstone, and the Duke of Argyll, concerning the Book of Genesis and the existence of God,
which had, in the eyes of all these eminent persons,
some strange connection one with another. Mrs.
Garden's father, the Dean, was, on the contrary,
troubled by neither of these events, since he did not
care for the Cardinal, knew that the professor had not,
theologically, a leg to stand on, and the duke at most
one. Grandpapa was more stirred, in the early part
of 1892, by the untimely death of the Duke of Clarence,
by the alarming increase of female bicyclists, and by
the prevalent nuisance of that popular song, " Ta-ra-ra-
boomdeay."

Vicky was stirred by Paderewski, by the influenza
epidemic, which all her children got, and by the new
high-shouldered sleeve. Maurice by the doings of the
L.C.C. Progressives, the imminence of the parliamentary
elections, the just claims but ignorant utterances of the
Labour Party, woman's suffrage, the birth of the *Morning Leader*, and Mr. Charles Booth's *Life and Labour in
London* ; Stanley by woman's suffrage, *Tess of the
D'Urbevilles*, the comedies of Mr. Oscar Wilde and Mr.
J. M. Barrie, *The Light that Failed*, and Mr. H. G. Wells.
Irving by golf, Mr. Arthur Roberts, Miss Marie Lloyd,
and *Sherlock Holmes* ; and Una by the arrival of a
new baby and the purchase of a new hunter.

Rome was not very greatly stirred by any of these
things. Into her old detached amusement at the

queer pageant of life had come a faint weariness, as if
nothing were very much worth while. If she thought
anything worth serious comment, she did not reveal
it. Life was to her at this time more than ever a tale
told by an idiot, signifying nothing. She went on her
way as usual, reading, seeing pictures, hearing music,
meeting people, talking, smoking, bicycling, leading the
life led by intelligent dilettanti in the small, cultivated
nucleus of a great city. There was nothing to show
that she endured the world with difficulty; that in the
early mornings she would wake and lie helpless, without
armour, waiting the onslaught of the new day, and in
the evenings would slip from her armour with a shivering sigh, to drown engulfed by darkness and the hopeless passion of the night. "Some day," she would
say to herself, "I shall not mind so much. The edge
will get blunt. Some day . . . some day . . ."

But the black night mocked her, and she could not
see that day on the furthermost dip of the horizon;
she could only see Mr. Jayne's dear, pale face turned to
her with wistful hoping in his gray eyes behind their
glasses, and he was saying, "Am I to go alone, or will
you come?" and then, even as, having considered life,
she opened her lips to reply, there was Mr. Jayne
lurching forward, choked with blood, his question
answered, for he was to go alone.

"My dear," whispered Rome, in tears, to the
unanswering, endless night. "My dear. Come back
to me, and I will give you anything and everything.
. . . But you will never come back, and I can give
you nothing any more."

And thus she could not see, however far off, that
day when she should not mind so much, that day when
the edge should get blunt.

Maurice, in 1892, was against very nearly everything. He was against the Conservative party, for

the usual reasons. He was against the Liberal party,
because Mr. Gladstone opposed woman's suffrage
and the Labour party and the Eight Hours' Day. He
was against the Woman's Suffrage Bill because it was
a class bill. He was against Mr. Keir Hardie and the
new Labour party because they talked what he considered sentimental tosh, damaging their own cause,
and because Amy, his wife, echoed it parrot-like. He
was against the Social Democratic Federation for the
same reasons, and because it did not prevent its members
from making bombs. He was against the socialist
meetings in Hyde Park and Trafalgar Square which
he had been used to approve, because they, too, talked
tosh. More and more, as Maurice advanced from the
heat of youth into the clear-sighted unsentimentality of
middle life (he was now thirty-five) he disliked tosh,
and more and more most of the world seemed to him to
be for ever talking it. The people, the parliamentarians,
the press, the governing classes, the imperialists, the
democrats, the middle classes, rivalled one another
in the flow of cant and nonsense they emitted. Oh,
God, for clear heads and hard facts, unmuddled by
humbug and romanticism! Almost, Maurice was
impelled to vote for Lord Salisbury, whose cool, cynical
hardness was a relief ; but, after all, deeper than his
hatred of sentimentalism, lay his hatred of injustice
and economic cruelty and class privilege. He was a
democrat impatient with democracy, a journalist
despising journalism, the product of an expensive
education at war with educational inequality, a politician loathing politics, a husband chafing at his wife, a
child of his age in rebellion against it, an agnostic
irritated by the thoughtful, loquacious agnosticism of
his day.

" There seems," as his mother said of him, " to be no
hole into which Maurice fits. Whereas Stanley fits

into them all.   They are both too extreme, dear children.
It is neither necessary, surely, to be fighting everything
all one's time, nor to chase after every wind that blows.
. . .   I sometimes think that the best balanced and
the most *solid* of you all is Una."

"Oh, yes, dear mamma," Vicky replied.   "Una is
fast-rooted in the soil.   Country people are always
the best balanced.   The only new things Una takes up
are bicycles and golf ;   the only old things she drops
are her g's.   Una is eternal and sublime ;   there's
nothing of the new woman about her, and nothing of
the reactionary either.   There never was any one less
self-conscious, or less conscious of her period.   All the
rest of us think we're moderns, but Una knows not
times ;   she merely swings along, her dogs at her heels,
her children at her skirts, her golf clubs over her shoulder,
and always another baby on the way.   And the beauty
of the child !   She'd make a sensation in London—
though she's not the type of the moment, not elegant or
artificial, too much the unsophisticated child of nature.
Oh, yes, Una is on the grand scale."

"Well, your grandfather thinks even Una is too
modern.   It's the golf and bicycling and g's, I suppose.
I expect the fact is that it's difficult, in these days, to
avoid being new.   You children and your friends all
are.   In fact, the whole world seems to be."

"The world is always new, mamma darling, and
always old.   It's no newer than it was in 1880, or 1870
—in fact, not so new, by some years.   The only year
in which it was really new was, according to grandpapa and the annotators of the Book of Genesis,
4004 B.C."

"Yes, I dare say it was sadly new then, and no doubt
grandpapa would have found it so.   But somehow
one hears the *word* a good deal just now, used by young
people as well as old.   What with new women, and

new art, and new literature, and new humour, and the new hedonism that Denman and Stanley talk about, and that seems to mean making your drawing-room like an old curiosity shop and burning incense in it and lighting it with darkened crimson lamps and lying on divans with black and gold cushions and smoking scented cigarettes and reading improper plays aloud . . . Only Rome says that isn't new in the least, but thousands of years old."

" Oh, Rome. Rome thinks nothing new. She was born blasée. She hasn't got grandpapa's or Stanley's fresh mind. She always expects the unexpected. Oscar Wilde says that to do that shows a thoroughly modern mind. If Rome had been Eve, she'd have looked at the new world through a monocle (she'd have worn that, even if nothing else) and seen that it was stale, and said with a yawn, 'All this is very *vieux jeu.*' "

"And very possibly," said mamma, " it was."

14

FIN-DE-SIÈCLE

'NINETY-THREE passed. In it grandpapa died, others said of influenza following on old age, but he himself would have it that it was of a shock he received one day when driving, convalescent, in Hyde Park; for his horses, very respectable and old-fashioned animals, shied at a lady bicyclist, and grandpapa's heart jolted, and when he got home he took to his bed and never rose again. So much, he whispered, hoarsely and somewhat sardonically, to his daughter, for the New Woman and her pranks. But what did it signify, he added. If he was not to get well of this attack, he was ready to go.   He trusted (though a worm) in his Maker, and was not unprepared.   So grandpapa, dignified to the last, departed from this life, one of the last of the Regency bucks and the Tory clerics, perhaps the last of all to condemn on theological grounds the arithmetic book of Bishop Colenso.

Fantastic observers might have imagined that, with the departure of this firm old Victorian, who had so disapproved of novelty, life span still more giddily on its rapid way.   Certainly the years 1893 and 1894 do, for some reason, appear to have struck both those who gloried in novelty, and those whom it shocked, as more than usually new.   The audacious experimentalism which is always with us was even more self-conscious then than is customary.   Such are time's revenges that the so daring social, literary and intellectual cleavages made by our forefathers in those years are now regarded as quaintly old-fashioned compromises with freedom, even as our own audacities will doubtless be regarded thirty years hence.   But the people of the nineties, even as the people of the eighties, seventies, sixties, and so back, and even as the people of the twentieth century, thought they were emancipating themselves from tradition, saw themselves as bold buccaneers sailing uncharted seas, and found it great fun.   The illusion of advance is sustaining, to all right-minded persons, and should by all means be cultivated. It gives self-confidence and poise.   It even seems to please elderly persons to mark or fancy changes of habit, which they have no wish to emulate, among their juniors, and it certainly pleases their juniors to be thus remarked upon, for they, too, believe that they are something new—the new young, as they have always delighted to call themselves—so all are pleased and no harm is done.   The eighteen nineties were no different, in this respect, from the nineteen twenties.

But 1894 does actually seem to have been a more amusing year than most that we have now. What with the New Humour, and the New Earnestness, and the New Writers, and the New Remorse, and the New Woman, and the New Drama, and the New Journalism, and the New Child, and the New Parent, and the New Conversation, and the telephone, and the gramophone, and the new enormous sleeves, there was a great deal of novelty about.

It is a curious time to look back upon to-day. Curious to read the newspapers, reviews, and comic papers of the time ; to find, for instance, in the *Observer* a leading article on the last novel of Mrs. Humphry Ward, as if it were a European event, and one the next Sunday on, " What is the modern girl coming to, for she opens her front door with a key ? " To come, too, on reviews of Mr. Hall Caine's *Manxman*, such as that by Mr. Edmund Gosse in the *St. James's Gazette,*—"A contribution to literature ; and the most fastidious critic would give in exchange for it a wilderness of that deciduous trash which our publishers call fiction. It is not possible to part from it without a warm tribute of approval." But how possible it has now become ! Indeed, in our times it has been known that a certain author, having in an unguarded hour committed to print an appreciation of Sir Hall Caine, and then having learnt his mistake, has changed his name and started life again, unable otherwise to support his disgrace. *Autre temps, autres mœurs.* Certainly the nineties were a long time ago. Strange, too, to read some of the contemporary press comments on that innocent, well-produced, extremely well illustrated, and, on the whole, capable periodical, the *Yellow Book* —" the outcry," as Mr. Arthur Symons put it later, when the publication of the *Savoy* was greeted with much the same noise, " the outcry for no reason in

the world but the human necessity for making a noise."
You would think that the worst that could be said of
the *Yellow Book* was that it was not eclectic, that it
opened its hospitable doors to the worse writers as
well as to the better, and that its intellectually lowest
contributions were too widely sundered from its highest ;
and the best that could be said of it (and how much
this is !) is that Aubrey Beardsley drew for it, Henry
James and Max Beerbohm wrote prose for it, and
W. B. Yeats poetry, and that it had, on the whole, some
of the more capable writers of the day as contributors.
But, in point of fact, the best that was said of it was
that it was brilliant, daring, courageous, new, and
intensely modern, and the worst that it was bizarre,
revolting, affected, new, and decadent. It appears to
a later generation to have been none of these things ;
that is, it was brilliant in patches only, and commonplace in patches ; it was not daring except in that it is
greatly daring to publish any periodical ever ; it was
not more intensely modern than everything always is,
and most of its contributors were middle-aged ; its
weak and trite contributions (though, indeed, it did
at times sink pretty low) were too few to allow of the
word revolting being properly applied to the whole
magazine, even by him whom Mr. Gosse called, in
another context, the most fastidious critic ; and as
for decadent, this it may, indeed, have been, as no one
has ever discovered what, if anything, this word, as
generally used at this time, meant. Exhibiting those
qualities which mark the decline of a great period, it
should mean ; whereas many of those who survive
from the nineties maintain that, on the other hand,
they marked the beginning of a good period. Or it
may mean merely less good than its predecessors, and
this the *Yellow Book* was assuredly not, but quite the
contrary. It was, in fact, not unlike various capable,

well-produced periodicals of our own day. Many of its surviving contributors contribute now to these newer journals. But how seldom does one now hear them or their writings or the periodicals to which they contribute called ultra-modern, daring, shocking, decadent, or bizarre. Rather, in fact, the contrary. Thus, it will be observed, do the moderns of one day become the safe establishments of the next. In ten years the public will be saying of our present moderns, "They are safe. They are *vieux jeu*. They resemble cathedrals." What a death's head at the feast of life is this fearful fate which is suspended before even the newest of us, and which, if we survive long enough, we shall by no means avoid. Happy, possibly, were those moderns of the nineties who died with their modernity still enveloping them, so that no one shall ever call them cathedrals. Gloriously decadent, though no longer new, they shall for ever remain, and no man shall call Aubrey Beardsley respectable, established or dull, for he belonged to the Beardsley period, and, though he may be outmoded, he shall never be outrun.

15

SUNDAY EVENING AT THE CROFTS

THE Denman Crofts thought it was delightfully new of them to have to one of their Sunday evenings a good-looking young pickpocket and a handsome woman whose profession it was to ply for hire on the streets. The pickpocket had been captured with his hand in Stanley's pocket, and brought home to supper as an alternative to being delivered to the constabulary, for three reasons : first, he was good-looking, and masculine beauty was in fashion that year ; secondly, he was

a sinner, and sins were talked of with approbation just
then by the most modern literary set, particularly
strange sins of divers colours, and as no one knew which
sins were strange or coloured and which were plain,
it might be that picking pockets was as strange and
as coloured as any ; thirdly, to have a pickpocket at
a Sunday evening party was New, and the other guests
would be pleased and envious. The lady was there for
reasons very similar, and both were a great success.
Every one treated them with friendliness and tact, so
that they soon ceased to be shy, though remaining to
the end a trifle puzzled and suspicious, and not very
fluent in conversation. Possibly, their host suggested
to Rome, they were suffering from an embarrassing
attack of the New Remorse.

" Strange sinners certainly seem a little *difficile*,"
agreed Rome, who had been making exhausting efforts
with the pickpocket, " and loose livers sometimes
appear to be rather tight talkers. Your protegés
cannot be said precisely to birrell."

"Anyhow, dear Denman," added a graceful young
gentleman at her side, " picking pockets is a banal
vice. I should scarcely call it a vice at all ; it is nearly
as innocent as picking cowslips on a May morning. I
wish I could have procured you a lady who knelt in
front of me in church yesterday afternoon while I was
waiting to make my confession. She was improving
the time by extracting the contents of the reticule
left in the seat next her by the penitent who had gone
up to her duties before her. A piquant idea, for she
would get absolution almost in the moment of sinning."

" Well," said Denman, " we did the best we could at
short notice. I would prefer to have obtained a bomb-
fiend. The latest vice, you know, is secreting bombs
in Hyde Park. We shall all be doing it soon. It is
reported to be even more stimulating than secreting

cocaine. There is no need, unless desired, ever to find the bombs again, still less to use them ; that is an extension of the vice, only practised by those who wish to qualify as extremists, or bomb-fiends. The ordinary victims of the bomb habit merely secrete ; they make a cache, and store away bombs as squirrels nuts. A pretty habit, but ceasing by now even to be strange. It is deplorable how the best vices become vulgarised. Rome, will you join me in a bomb-secreting orgie to-morrow at dusk ? "

" By all means, Denman. It would restore my spirits. I have been sadly depressed lately by reading in one week Sarah Grand, *A Yellow Astor*, *Marcella*, *The Manxman*, and Mr. Zangwill and Mrs. Lynn-Lynton in the *New Review* on ' What Women Should Know.' There is no more spirit in me. Though I was a little revived by *The Green Carnation*. An entrancing work, about all of us. But really entertaining."

" Why such a desperate orgie of literature ? I thought you were of a more fastidious habit—not like Stanley, who insists on reading everything, even *Discords* and the Dreyfus case. I can seldom read any novels. I find their reviews enough, if not too much. I read of *The Manxman* that it would be read and re-read by many thousands with human tears and human laughter, and that settled *The Manxman*. Where do reviewers get their inimitably delicious phrases from ? And if one asked them with the tears and laughter of what animal other than the human animal could human beings read, or even re-read, a book, how would they reply ? Perhaps in the same way that old Meredith did the other day when Dick Le Gallienne asked him to give the public a few words to explain his peculiar style. ' Posterity will still be explaining me, long after I am dead. Why, then, should I forestall their labours ? ' "

" I wonder," Rome mused, " if posterity will really be so diligent and so intelligent as their ancestors seem to think. People always say they write for posterity when they are not appreciated at the moment. They seem to imagine posterity as a smug and spectacled best scholar, spending its time delving among the chronicles of wasted years in the reading-room of the British Museum, and hailing with rapture the literary efforts of their ancestors."

" Whereas I," said Denman, " see posterity as a leaping savage, enjoying nameless orgies among the ruins of our civilisation, but not enjoying literature. Possibly, even, there will be no posterity. The débacle of our civilisation—and it's obviously too good to last—may mean the débacle of the world itself. I hope so. *A bas le* Posterity, I say. Who wants it ? I scorn to write for it, or to plant horrible little baby trees for it, or to suck up to it in any way whatsoever. Crude and uncultured savage. *Vive l'aujourd'hui !* "

"And I," said Rome, " see posterity as a being precisely like ourselves. It will read every morning in its newspapers, just as we do, that our relations with France are strained, that so many people have been murdered, born, divorced, married, that such and such a war is in progress, that such and such a law has been passed, or speech made, or book published, and it will know, just as we do, that none of it matters in the least. . . . I've no grudge against posterity. Let it have its little day."

" It will," said the graceful young man, with gloom. " I can't share Denman's faith in the approaching annihilation of humanity. Humanity in general is much too bourgeois and uninteresting to do anything but increase greatly and keep the earth replenished. It is impossible to imagine that the gods love it. *We* shall perish ; we, the fine exotic flower of an effete civilisation—(by the way, how exquisitely lovely and innocently wicked Lady Pember looks to-night ; she, not the cow-like young woman talking to Mrs. Crofts, ought to be the strange scarlet—or is it mauve—sinner) —but we are a small minority. The majority, which hasn't even the art of gracefully fading out, will heavily continue. It is thus that I picture posterity—a ponderous suburban bourgeois in mutton-chop whiskers or tight stays, sniffing at our poetry, our wit and our *Yellow Book*, and saying, ' How decadent they were in the nineties.' By the way, what does decadent mean ? I always understood that man fell once and for all, long ago, and could not therefore be falling still. I prefer deciduous. How deliciously it slides round the tongue, like an over-ripe peach. I wonder it is not more used in verse. To me it suggests a creamy, green absinthe, or a long, close kiss on moist, coral-pink lips. Disgusting. I detest moist lips, and absinthe makes me feel sick, though I try and pretend it doesn't."

Stanley, charming and smiling, with her pleasant, round, brown face, lively, deep blue eye, and enormous box sleeve, darted across the room to them.

" Den, we *must* remove our strange sinners now. I'm worn out with them. They'll neither of them say more than yes, no, and eh, and they've both drunk too much already, and keeping one eye on Mr. Sykes lest he get too near people's pockets and the other on the lady lest she get hold of more whisky, is too heavy a responsibility. You must take them away. And then Lady Pember wants to talk to you, darling."

Denman gave her a queer, quick look out of his narrow, smiling eyes, as he turned away.

"And Rome, love, I want to bring Aubrey Beardsley to you. He is being assaulted by Miss Carruthers, who has been reading *Marcella, Our Manifold Life* by Sarah Grand, and the newspapers, and wants to know what he thinks of the Emancipation of Women, the Double Standard of Morality, and the approaching death of Mr. Froude. Poor Aubrey has never thought of any of them ; he takes no interest in emancipations, and his taste in women is most reactionary—any one could tell that, from the ladies he draws, he thinks any other kind most unwholesome ; he never reads Protestant historians ; and he has never thought about even a single standard of morality. Double standard, indeed ! As if there weren't as many standards as there are people."

" Not nearly, Mrs. Croft, fortunately. I'm sure Aubrey himself can't contribute one ; nor can I. But it is stupid of Aubrey not to read poor Mr. Froude. He is such a noble and happy liar. He really does practise lying for lying's sake—not like Macaulay, mere utilitarian lying for principle's sake, though he does some of that too. Froude is an artist. He will be missed, even though he is a Protestant. He hates accuracy with as much passion as the good popes hated thought, as Oscar Wilde says somewhere apropos of something else. (Oscar's grammar is so aften loose.) How right both Mr. Froude and the good popes are ! Look at Denman being firm with the sinners ; how delightfully he does it ; he would make a good prison warder."

" The sinners," said Miss Garden, regarding them through her monocle, " certainly *are* rather strange. I am afraid they have both drunk to excess. There, now he has piloted them safely to the door ; that is a relief. Yes, Stanley, do fetch me Mr. Beardsley. Will he shock me to-night ? I was told that the other evening he shocked his table at the Café Royal to death by his talk. John Lane had to remove him. It is possible to go too far even for the Café Royal, and he did it. I suppose that is why he is looking so elated to-night, like Alexander seeking fresh worlds to conquer. ' He shocked the Café Royal.' What an epitaph ! On the other hand, I hear that he was shocked himself the other day. Mr. Henley did it, in bluff mood, at a party at the Pennells. How do you do, Mr. Beardsley ? "

16

DIVORCE AT THE CROFTS

IT did not last, the Crofts' marriage. In the spring of '95, Stanley wearied of her husband's infidelities, and could not bear them any more. As to Denman, he felt often, though he loved her, that he had married a young woman who had her tiresome aspects ; she was a feminist, a prig, she tried to write, and badly at that, she was still over-much concerned with public affairs, with committees, with the emancipation (save the mark !) of women. And she was for ever fussing over the children, who should be treated as amusing toys. He loved her, but she tried him often. She was strident, obstinate, stupidly in earnest about things that seemed to him to demand a light indifference ; then, cumbrously, she would try to adopt his tone, and fail. Marriage. Well, it presented great difficulties. He sighed sometimes for the freedom of his bachelor days. Meanwhile, life had its moments, exquisite, fleeting, frail. And at these Stanley, who was not really stupid, guessed quite accurately, and was stabbed by each afresh until her very life-blood seemed to drain away. leaving her, so she felt, a helpless ghost of a woman, without assurance, heart or power to go on, but with only her stabbed love and a proud, burning rage. And, in the spring of '95, she broached this matter of divorce.

He asked her forgiveness.

"I can't help it, Stanley. I suppose it's the way I'm made. . . . The queer thing is, I've loved you all the time. You can't understand that. Women are so—so monogamous."

"That old cliché, Den! It isn't clever enough for you. Some men are monogamous. Some men couldn't love several women at the same time. And some women can . . . I'm dead sick of it, anyhow. All this beastly philandering. It's merely trivial. It *means* nothing. It's turning life and love into a parlour game. Do you take nothing seriously, Denman— not your relations with people, or with love, or with life—not even your fatherhood?"

"Oh, don't preach at me. I'm a waster, and let's leave it at that. . . . I'm damnably sorry for everything, of course. . . . But you're not altogether and always easy to live with, you know. All this stuff about women, for instance . . . you know how I hate it . . ."

"You know how I hate *your* stuff about women, if we are to drag in that now. . . . Oh, Den, don't let's be childish. What does all that matter now? We're up against a much bigger thing than a difference of opinion about the suffrage."

"You can't forgive me, of course. And I suppose you're justified."

"Oh, I suppose I could forgive you. I could forgive you anything, perhaps. I have before, after all. But I think I had better not, for all our sakes. You'd rather be free, wouldn't you? Oh, you needn't answer. I know you'd rather be free. I don't suspect you of wanting to live permanently with Alice Pember, or with any one else; you just want to be free and irresponsible, and make love to whom you like. Well, you shall. I shan't keep you. You're not meant for a husband and father, and you've tired yourself long enough trying to be one. You can drop it now."

" I suppose you're right, from your point of view. You'd better divorce me . . . I'm terribly sorry, Stan. We were so tremendously happy once."

" Don't." Stanley caught her breath and sharply bit her lip. " You've no right to talk of that. That's all past. We've not been happy for a long time now. . . . And you know you despise me and think me a fool. . . . Oh, what's the use of talking. . . ."

Three days later, Stanley, with her son and daughter, aged four and two, left her husband's house and took up her temporary abode with her parents, while her divorce suit slowly prepared itself.

" Divorce is damnable," Stanley said to Rome. " Why should people be penalised by having to go through this ghastly business, with all its loathsome publicity, merely because they wish to annul a private contract which only concerns themselves ? Why shouldn't they be able to go to a lawyer together and say, "Annul this contract," as with any other contract ? Instead of which, if it's even suspected that they *both* want it annulled, they're not allowed to do it at all ; and if it's the wife who wants it, they have to fake up this ridiculous cruelty-or-desertion business. And, above all, why should we be gibbeted in the news-papers for doing a purely private piece of legal business ? Why, in the name of decency and common sense, should a thing become public news merely because it occurs in a law court ? And is our whole English constitution and system so rotten because we are rotten, or aren't our laws a long way behind public opinion ? . . . Some-times I think I can't go through with it, it's all so beastly, and that we'll just live apart without a divorce. But I know that wouldn't do. There's got to be some-thing desperately final between Denman and me, or

we might be coming together again, when he's tired of
Alice Pember. I love him so much, beneath everything, that if he wanted to I probably should. And I
know it would be no use. We should make nothing
of it now. It would be bad for both of us, and worse
for Bill, and Molly. And it would all happen over
again. No, it's got to be a clean cut, even if the imbecile
state only allows us to have it on these disgusting terms.
. . . Sometimes, Rome, I think the whole world and
its laws and systems and conventions is just a lunatic
asylum."

"I've always known that, my dear. What else
should it be?"

"*Rome, how does one bear it?*"

Stanley, whose way it was to express her joys and
griefs—she was not self-contained, like Rome—was
pacing up and down the room, her hands clenched
behind her, her cheeks flushed with feverish, waking
nights, her eyes heavy under sullen brows.

"I hardly know," Rome answered her gently. "I
hardly know. But, somehow, one goes on, and one
learns to be amused again. . . . I am hoping that
when one is elderly one will mind less. You *will* mind
less, Stanley, in a few years. Life's so strong, it carries
one on all the time to new things. Particularly, I
think, you, because you are so alive. You'll come
even through this desperate business."

Stanley said, "Life's broken to bits. I was so happy
once . . . broken to jagged bits," and left the room
to cry. For, contrary to a common belief, those who
feel most usually cry most too. Stanley was afraid
that she was contracting a tearful habit such as she
might never outgrow, but she did not much care. She
did not much care for anything in these days.

She missed Denman. Missing him was like the
continual sharp ache of a gathered tooth. She missed

his charm, his brilliance, his love, his careless, casual ways, his intense life, his soft, husky voice, the smile on his queer, white face and narrow eyes. She missed his gay, youthful talk, the parties and plays they had been used to go to together, his constant presence in the house. She would wake in the nights, thinking he lay beside her, and that his arm would be thrown, in a half-waking caress, across her; but he was not there. She would wake in the mornings, thinking to see his rumpled brown head sunk in the pillow beside hers; but there was no head, and no pillow but her own. When her son and daughter entered her room in the morning and climbed upon her bed, after the irritating manner of infants, and woke her by pulling at her two dark plaits, she would open drowsy eyes that looked for her husband's short, delightful face smiling above her; but there were only the two young children, with their restless antics and imbecile prattlings. Fatuous beings! One day she would enjoy them again, antics, fatuity and all, even as she had enjoyed them before, but in these days her love for them lay frozen and almost lifeless, with all other love but that one love that tore at her heart with fierce, clawing fingers. It seemed that this love and this anguish consumed her wholly, leaving nothing over. She had never been first a mother; she had been first an individual, a human creature sensitively reacting to all the contacts of the engrossing world, and secondly she had been a wife, a woman who loved a man. A mother, perhaps, third. And now the secondary function, in its death agony, had taken entire possession, and she was no longer either an individual creature or a mother, but only a lover who had lost all.

To tear him out of her heart—that was her constant object. And if the heart (since we are, by foolish custom, so impelled to call the seat of the affections)

had been alone involved, she might have done so.   **But**
who should tear the beloved from the roots he had in
her whole daily life for five years, from his place in her
mind, her brain, her body, her whole being ?   She knew
him for a philanderer, a trivial taster in love and life,
selfish, spoilt, vain, with idiotic opinions about one half
of the human race.   It was, indeed, her knowledge of
all this in him that informed her brain that their separa-
tion must be final and complete.   But, with it all, she
could not tear him from her heart, her soul, her body,
her entire and constant life.   He was herself, and she
herself was being torn in two.

Life was a continual anguish.   She saw that she must
leave her parents' home and live alone.   She was
bringing misery into Bloomsbury Square.   And daily,
night and morning, her parents kissed her, and their
kisses were to her, who craved so bitterly those kisses
that she might no longer have, a continual reminder
and torment.   She was trying to shut off that side of
life, but they did not understand, and kissed her.
Rome, who understood too well, did not kiss her.   She
knew that she must be alone with her children, that
she was no fit housemate for a loving family or friends.
So, presently, she went into rooms, and this was a more
bearable loneliness.

But it left more time on her hands ; more time in
which to brood on life, on love, on illusion, on women,
and on men.   How had she failed in this job of marriage,
of constructing an enduring life with a man she had
loved, who had loved her ?   How had they both failed ?
How frequent was this failure ?   It seemed that love
was not enough.   Such deep misunderstandings pre-
vail, between any two human beings.   Sex bridges
many of them, but not all.   Stanley began, at this
time, to generalise dangerously and inaccurately
(since all such generalisations are inaccurate) about

women and about men. She saw women as eager, restless, nervous children, chattering, discussing, joking, turning the world upside down together while they smoked or brushed their hair, and all to so little purpose. Meanwhile there were men ; the sex ; sphinx-like, placid, inscrutable, practical, doing the next thing, gently smiling at the fuss women made about ideas. Men knew that they did not matter, these excitements and fusses of women, any more than the toys children play with matter. They dismissed them with that serene smile of theirs, and busied themselves with the elemental, enduring things ; sex, fatherhood, work. They knew what mattered ; they went for the essentials. They didn't waste their time frothing about with words and ideas. Men were somehow admirable, in their strong stability. Their nervous systems were so magnificent. They could kill animals without feeling sick, break the necks of fishes, put worms on hooks, shoot rabbits and birds, jab bayonets into bodies. Women would never amount to much in this world, because they nearly all have a nervous disease ; they are strung on wires ; they are like children frightened of the dark and excited by the day. It seems fundamental, this difference between the nerves of most women and most men. You see it among little girls and boys ; most little boys, but how few little girls, can squash insects and kill rabbits without a qualm. It is this difference which gives even a stupid man often a greater mastery over life than a clever woman. He is not frightened by life. Women, for the most part, are. Life may be a joke to them, but it is often also a nightmare. To the average man it is neither. Men are marvellously restful. Eternal symbols of parenthood and the stability of life, to which women come back, as to strong towers of refuge, after their excursions and alarms.

This was the kind of nonsense which Stanley wove to herself during these unbalanced days of her life. Nonsense, because all generalities about human beings are nonsense. But many people, including Stanley, find interest in making them up, and it is a harmless game.

17

PANTA REI

It seemed to Stanley, through this spring and summer of 1895, that a phase was over, not only in her own life, which was apt so faithfully to mirror the fleeting times, but in the world at large. That literary, artistic, and social movement so vaguely described as " decadent " by those who could scarcely define that or any other word, nor would greatly care to if they could, seemed to be on the wane. The trial and conviction of Mr. Oscar Wilde did it no good, and the many who had been unjust towards the movement before became un-juster still, adopting an " I told you so " air, which mattered as little as any other air adopted by those of like mentality, but which had, nevertheless, its effect on strengthening the forces of so-called healthy philis-tinism in the land. As a contemporary poet sang—

" If these be artists, then may Philistines
    Arise, plain sturdy Britons as of yore,
    And sweep them off, and purge away the signs
    That England e'er such noxious offspring bore."

Even the anti-Philistines, the so-called decadents themselves, were disconcerted and shaken by this public dèbacle of one of the most prominent of their number. " Those who write, draw and talk in this

clever new manner that we have never liked," said
the Philistines, firmly assured, "are obviously as
unpleasant as, even more unpleasant than, we have
believed." "They might as well say," said the prac-
tisers of the elegant, clever new manner, "that because
Ladas, owned by a Liberal leader, won the Derby last
year, all Liberals are as intelligent about horses as,
even more intelligent about horses than, they have
believed. They might as well say . . ." But it is of
no use to tell people of this mentality what they might
as well say. They will as likely as not proceed to say
it, and it is very certain that they will not therefrom
see the absurdity of that which they have already said.
There is, in fact, no way of dealing with these persons ;
they are the world's masters, laying the ponderous
weight of their foolish and heavy minds upon all sub-
tleties, delicacies and discriminations to flatten them,
talking very loudly, firmly and fatuously the while
through their hats, and through their mouthpiece, the
press. There is no dealing with them ; it is they who
make England, and indeed the world, what it is. "This
nation believes . . ." "The people of this country
have always held . . ." says the press, grandly, as if
indeed *that* made it any more likely to be true, instead
of far less. "This asylum has always believed that
the best form of government is a party system," the
newspapers published in asylums no doubt continually
remark. "The inhabitants of this asylum have always
said . . ."

And so much for public opinion.

Anyhow, from whatever cause, there began at this
time, to put it briefly, a slump in decadence. Max
Nordau wrote this year, with his customary exaggera-
tion, his essay on *Fin-de-siècle*.

"An epoch of history is unmistakably in its decline,
and another is approaching its birth. There is a sound

of rending in every tradition, and it is as though the morrow could not link itself with to-day. Things as they are totter and plunge, and they are suffered to reel and fall because man is weary, and there is no faith that it is worth an effort to uphold them. Views that have hitherto governed minds are dead or driven hence like disenthroned kings. Meanwhile interregnum, in all its terror, prevails. . . . Such is the spectacle presented by the doings of men in the reddened light of the Dusk of the Nations."

Max Nordau was a man of imagination, and had an excessive way of putting things, and seems to have been hypnotised by the arbitrary divisions into which man has chopped time ; but, whatever he may have meant, it is quite true that no period is precisely like another, and that life is, as has been well said, a flux. In brief, *panta rei*, and no less in the middle eighteen nineties than at other times.

18

RELIGION

Of the many impulsions that drive human beings to one form or another of religion, the strongest, perhaps, is pain. The other impulsions—conscience, the mystic sense, personal influence, conviction, experimentalism, loneliness, boredom, remorse, and so forth—all work powerfully on their respective subjects. But pain, mental anguish so great that human nature is driven by it from cover to cover, seeking refuge and finding none, is the most powerful and the most frequent agent for the churches. "There is no help for me in this world," tortured human creatures cry, and are often driven by that cry to questioning whether there may not, perhaps, be help in some other. Anyhow, they think, it is worth the experiment, and the experiment proves an anodyne and a gate of escape from what would scarcely, otherwise, be borne.

Such was Stanley Croft's method of approach to a closer contact with religion than any she had had before; though, before her marriage, she had had a mystical belief in God, which had, during the last five years, all but died out in an atmosphere not well suited to it. Now it returned to her again, touched with just enough remorse for past neglect as might serve for a temperate shadow of that hectic and enjoyable repentance which drove, then and later, so many of her literary contemporaries into the fold of the Catholic church. In reality, perhaps, though it seemed that pain was her immediate impeller, it was ultimately, as usual, the spirit of her age which seized her and drove her to prayer.

She would turn into dark and silent churches, seeking desperately the relief from herself that life denied her and fall on her knees and there stay, numb and helpless, her forehead dropped on her arms, till the sweet, often incense-laden atmosphere (for that was the kind of church she preferred) enveloped her like a warm and healing garment, and she whispered into the dim silence, "God! God! If you are there, speak to me and help me! God, God, God!"

From that cry, for long the only prayer she could utter, other prayers at last grew. The silence melted round her and became a living thing; the red sanctuary lamp was as the light of God flaming in a dim world, a light shining in darkness, and the darkness encompassed it not. The undefeated life of God, burning like a brave star in a stormy night, by which broken, all but foundered ships might steer. It was so that Stanley saw it, and slowly it did actually guide her to a kind of painful peace.

" I wish the poor child would join the true Church,"
Mr. Garden said to Mrs. Garden, for he was still, though
now a little dubiously, a member of that church. " I
think it would help her."

Mamma looked sceptical.

" I think not, Aubrey. She doesn't want to be
bothered with joining churches just now, and she
certainly has no energy to give to it. Besides, she likes
English Catholicism. It has, you must admit, rather
more liberty of thought than your branch." (Mamma
knew, having tried both more than once). " Besides,"
she added quickly, to change the subject from liberty
of thought, which always in these days made papa
look sad—in fact, she had mentioned it in a moment of
carelessness which she immediately regretted—" besides,
there is the divorce."

Papa sighed, and looked sadder than ever.

" Yes. This horrid, this distressing business. I
wish she may give it up before it is too late. Even
High Anglicanism does not allow divorce."

" On that point," said mamma, " and, I fancy, on a
good many others, Stanley does not agree with High
Anglicanism. Fortunately that does not prevent her
from finding comfort in its forms of worship. I am
only thankful that she can. It is hard for those in
trouble who have no faith in another world." Possibly
her mind had turned to Rome, whose faith in worlds,
either this we live in or any other, was negligible.

But papa's mind had turned inward, upon his own
torn soul. Mamma watched him with experienced
anxiety. She knew the signs, and feared that the
Mother of the Churches would not for long hold papa
in her firm arms. Dear Aubrey ; he was so restless.
And he had lately been reading a lot of odd, mystic
books. . . .

19

CELTIC TWILIGHT

IT was very certain that Stanley would not join the
Roman Church. She had too mystic an imagination
to enter any body so definite and sharp of doctrine.
She was more at one at this time with the Celtic poets,
with their opening of strange gates onto dim, magic
lands. The loveliness, like the wavering, lovely rhythms
of the sea, of W. B. Yeats, took her, as it took her whole
generation, by storm; the tired twilight sadness of
Fiona Macleod was balm to her.

> " O years with tears, and tears through weary years,
>   How weary I, who in your arms have lain :
> Now I am tired : the sound of slipping spears
>   Moves soft, and tears fall in a bloody rain,
>   And the chill footless years go over me, who am
>   slain.
>
> I hear, as in a wood dim with old light, the rain
>   Slow falling ; old, old weary human tears,
> And in the deepening dusk my comfort is my
>   pain,
>   Sole comfort left of all my hopes and fears,
>   Pain that alone survives, gaunt hound of the
>   shadowy years."

And,

> " Between the gray pastures and the dark wood
>   A valley of white poppies is lit by the low
>   moon.
> It is the grave of dreams, a holy rood.

It is quiet there : no wind doth ever fall.
  Long, long ago a wind sang once a heart-sweet
    rune.
Now the white poppies grow, silent and tall.

A white bird floats there like a drifting leaf :
  It feeds upon faint sweet hopes and perishing
    dreams,
And the still breath of unremembering grief.

And as a silent leaf the white bird passes,
  Winnowing the dusk by dim, forgetful streams.
I am alone now among the silent grasses."

In such soft and melancholy enchantment as this,
Stanley's desolation found, for a time, comfort.

(Vicky's Imogen, aged seven, found this book at her
grandparents' house one day, opened it, read, breathing
noisily for excitement, and tucked it furtively away in
the pouch of her sailor frock, where she often kept
rabbits, or eggs for hatching. She bore it home un-
discovered, and spent the evening lying on her stomach
and elbows beneath the nursery table reading it, with
moving lips and fingers in her ears, deaf to the clamour
and summons of her brethren, until at last she was
haled to bed, hot-cheeked and wet-eyed, silent upon a
peak in Darien. She had found a new enchantment ;
it was better than Mowgli, even. But, since she was
not really a dishonest little girl, when next she went
to Bloomsbury Square she slipped the book unob-
trusively back into the shelf from which she had stolen
it, and took *The Manxman* instead, thinking, with the
fatuity of her years, to find that it concerned a tail-
less cat ; but with regard to this book she was disappointed, and unable to agree with Mr. Gosse).

20

THE STAR IN THE EAST

STRANGE books and pamphlets littered papa's study table. He met and dined with Mr. George Russell (the Irish poet, not the English churchman). He admired and liked Mr. Russell so much that for his sake he attended the lectures of Madame Blavatsky, and perused the works of Colonel Olcott, Mr. W. Q. Judge, and Mrs. Besant. A feeling of expansion took him, as if the bonds of rigid orthodoxy, which had restrained him for the last nine years, were being forced asunder. . . . It was, with papa, the eternally recurrent spring-time of his soul's re-birth ; he was in travail with a new set of ideas, and their pressure rent him cruelly. Then one day, " I have seen his star in the east," cried papa, and became a Theosophist.

He wanted Stanley to do the same (mamma said firmly that she herself was too old), but Stanley would have none of it. To change your religion you need a certain vitality, an energy of mind and will, an alert-ness towards fresh ideas, and Stanley at this time had little of these things. She clung to a desperate and passionate faith, as a drowning man to a raft ; gradually she even came to take pleasure in services, and would find at the early mass at St. Albans, Holborn, an exalted, mystic, half-sensuous joy. But she was in no mood to choose and investigate a new creed. Besides, Theosophy. . . .

However, papa enjoyed it. Papa was now sixty-five years of age, but his feeling for religions had not waned. Mamma, who had been a little afraid that papa might next be a Jew (for he had been writing a monograph on the Hebrew prophets, whom he greatly admired, and also seeing a good deal of Mr. Zangwill) was, on the whole, relieved. For a long time papa had not been happy in the Roman Catholic Church, finding many of the papal bulls difficult of digestion, and the doctrines of hell-fire and transubstantiation (as interpreted by most of the priesthood) painfully materialistic ; neither was he happy about the attitude of the Church towards M. Loisy and other modernists.

So, when he saw the star in the east, he set out for it with a sigh of relief.

21

IRVING

WHILE papa followed the star, and Stanley doggedly and bitterly sued her husband for restitution of conjugal rights, and Rome urbanely surveyed the world through a monocle and drove elegantly in hansoms, often with an enormous wolf-hound or a couple of poms, and Maurice fired squibs of angry eloquence at everything that came into his line of vision, their brother Irving made a fortune by speculating in South African gold mine shares. Irving, as has been said earlier, was a lucky young man, whom God had fashioned for prosperity. Having made his fortune, he married a handsome, agreeable, and healthy young woman, one Lady Marjorie Banister, the daughter of an obscure north-country earl, and settled down to make more.

It was an epoch of fortune-making. Mr. Cecil Rhodes loomed in the south, an encouraging and stimulating figure to those who had enterprise and a little capital. The new rich were filling Mayfair, making it hum with prosperity. Irving, too, hummed with prosperity, and took a house in Cumberland Place.

He found life an excellent affair, though he had his grievances, one of which was that motor-cars were not allowed on English roads without a man walking with a flag before them. " We are a backward nation," Irving grumbled, after visits to Paris, as so many have grumbled before and since. But, on the whole, Irving approved of modern life. He thought Maurice, who did not, a bear with a sore head.

Maurice was now the editor of an intelligent but acid weekly paper, which carried on a running fight with the government, the opposition, all foreign govern· ments, the British public, most current literature, nearly all current ideas, and the bulk of the press, particularly Henley's *New Review*, which boomed against him monthly. Having a combatant spirit, he found life not unenjoyable, now that he had become so used to and so indifferent to his wife as to have acquired armour against the bitter chafing she had caused him of yore, and to find some domestic pleasure in annoying her. He considered it a low and imbecile world, but to that, too, one gets used, and a weekly paper is, as many have found, a gratifying vent for scorn. Saturday after Saturday, through 1895, the *Gadfly* railed at the unsatisfactory attitude of our Colonial Secretary towards South Africa, the existence of Mr. Cecil Rhodes and the British South Africa Company, the tepid and *laissez-faire* temperament of Lord Rosebery, the shocking weather, the absurd inhibitions against motor-cars, the vulgarity of the cheaper press, the futility of the controversies on education, the slowness of progress in developing Röntgen rays and flying machines, the immense wealth made by the undeserving in cycle companies and gold mines, the smugness of Liberals, the inanity of Tories, the ignorance of the Labour Party, the blatancy of current forms of patriotism, the arrogance of the victory-swollen Japanese,

the bad manners of France, the aggressiveness of
Germany, the feebleness of current literature, and so
on and so forth.

"That's right, old smiler, keep it up. That's the
stuff to give them," Irving amiably encouraged him,
as he and his wife ate at the dinner table of his brother.
"*They* don't mind, and it makes you happy. But
what's bitten you to set you against company pro-
moters? I didn't care for your column about them
last week. They've done you no harm, have they?
The fact is, I was going to ask you if you'd care to come
into a small affair I'm helping to float. Bicycle bolts
are a back number, and that's a fact. In November
next year the red flag comes off, and motor-cars begin
in earnest all over the roads. Amberley and I are
specialising in tyres. We've got Lord Mortlake in, too.
It's a sure thing. We shall be coining thousands in
a couple of years. You'd better come in early. Am I
right?"

Amy's mirth chimed like sweet bells.

"Motor-cars! Oh, I do like that! Why not flying
machines, at once?"

Irving regarded her with tolerant scorn.

"Why not indeed? You may well ask. But for
the moment, motor-cars will do us. I dare say it will
be fliers in ten years or so. And moving photographs,
too. I'm not, you see, a pessimist, like poor dear
Maurice. I believe in Progress. And in Capital.
And in the Future of the Race. And in getting rich
quick. Maurice, am I right?"

"Probably," said Maurice. "You're certainly not
bad at getting rich quick; I'll say that for you. But
I am. So, on the whole . . ."

"Motor-car tyres!" Amy still jeered, being of those
who obtain one idea at a time and grapple it to their
souls with hoops of steel. "Motor-car tyres! They

won't wear out many tyres trundling away behind those old chaps with the flags."

Maurice finished his sentence otherwise than he had intended.

" On the whole, I'm inclined to take shares in this company of yours. Send me along the details as soon as you can."

Amy's utterances often had this subversive effect on his own. He threw her a malevolent glance, and poured himself out some more claret.

Amy put up her pretty, dark eyebrows. She pursed her mouth. She nodded.

" That's right. Throw our money away. Don't bother a bit about me or the children."

" Now, Amy, don't nag him. I'm answerable for this little show, and I can tell you I'm right. Remember I told him to put his shirt on Persimmon. Well, he didn't. You know the results. I don't want to brag, but—well, there it is. Maurice, I think better of your wits than I have for the last ten years."

Maurice, sipping his claret, still kept his sardonic gaze on his wife, who rose and took Irving's wife to another room. Often Amy wished that she had chanced to marry Irving instead of Maurice, though he was too young for her. Oftener Maurice wished that he had married no one, for marriage was oppressive.

22

RULE BRITANNIA

'95 swept on, and speeded up to a riotous finish, with the British South African troops, under the imprudent Dr. Jameson, galloping over the Transvaal border to protect the British of the Rand. Loud applause from the British Isles. In the legal language of the Bow Street trial that followed, " Certain persons, in the month of December, 1895, in South Africa, within Her Majesty's dominions, and without license of Her Majesty, did unlawfully prepare a military expedition to proceed against the dominions of a certain friendly State, to wit, the South African Republic, contrary to the provisions of the Foreign Enlistment Act." In the more poetic language of the Laureate,—

> " Wrong, is it wrong ?   Well, maybe,
> But I'm going, boys, all the same :
> Do they think me a burgher's baby,
> To be scared by a prating name ? "

In the episcopal language of the Bishop of Mashona-land, " Whether the English people liked the exploits of Dr. Jameson or not, the Empire had been built up by such men. They had a Colonial Secretary with his eyes open, who could see farther than most people thought. Africa must take a foremost place in the Empire, and the Church should go hand in hand with its development."

And, in the journalistic language of the *Daily Mail* (born early in '96, and, like other new-born infants, both noisy and pink), " It is well known in official circles that England and the Transvaal must eventually come into collision."

Vicky's children, in a fever of martial jingoism, tem-porarily abandoned the Sherlock Holmes crime-tracking exploits which were engaging their attention those Christ-mas holidays, for the Jameson Raid, riding bestridden chairs furiously round the schoolroom, chanting,

> " Then over the Transvaal border,
> And a gallop for life or death "—

until two chairs broke into pieces, and Imogen, thrown, cut her head on the fender, and the game was forbidden by authority.

The adventure of the raid tickled up British imperialism, which, like the imperialism in Vicky's schoolroom, began to ride merrily for a fall. '96 dawned on a country growing drunk with pride of race and possessions, working up, in fact, for the Diamond Jubilee. Dr. Jameson and his confederates were received with the cheers of the populace and the adoration of the *Daily Mail*, and sentenced to short terms of imprisonment.

Soon after the birth of the *Daily Mail* came the *Savoy*, the last stand of eclectic æstheticism. Stanley Croft had, for a while, an odd feeling of standing hesitant between two forces, one of which was loosening its grasp on her, the other taking hold. The newer force conquered, and she was carried, step by step, from æstheticism to imperialism, from belief in art and intellect to belief in the dominance of the British race over the world. She read Henley and Kipling. She found pride in—

> " Out of the night that covers me,
> Black as the pit from pole to pole,
> I thank whatever gods may be
> For my unconquerable soul . . ."

Her religion ceased to be a mystic, twilight passion. A renascence of sturdy courage took her back into the common ways, where, her divorce now accomplished, she pursued her old aims. She took up life, and became alert to the world again, responsive, like a ship in full sail, to every wind that blew. And the wind that blew on her was a wind of reaction from her recent past, and it drove her out on the seas of ambitious

imperialism, so that love of country became in her, as
in so many, a kind of swaggering tribal pride. The
romance of Greater Britain took her by storm. Not
the infant Imogen, stirred to tears by the swinging by
of red-coated troops to a band, seethed with a more
exalted jingoism. Glory, adventure, pride of race
and the clash of arms—what stimulating dreams were
these, and how primeval their claim upon the soul!
While Stanley's friends shrugged cynical shoulders
over Dr. Jim's exploit and the attitude towards it of
the great British public, while her papa gravely mis-
doubted such militant aggression, while Maurice
sneered and tilted at it in a weekly column, while
Rome contemplated the spectacle with the detached,
intelligent amusement of the blasée but interested
theatre-goer, while Irving, cynically approving, said,
" That's good," thinking of the Rand gold, and Mr.
Cecil Rhodes observed that his friend the doctor had
upset the apple cart—while all these made the comments natural to their tastes, temperaments and points
of view, Stanley, like a martial little girl, flew high the
flag of " Britain for ever ! Up the Rand ! " and her
spirit marched as to a military band.

Vicky also, in her more careless and casual way, was
a supporter of Empire. " Whatever Charles and
Maurice and all those informed people may say, my
dear, this Dr. Jim is a gallant creature, dashing off
to the rescue of his fellow-countrymen and countrywomen like that. For, even if they weren't in actual
danger, they *were* inconvenienced, those poor, tiresome
Uitlanders. And how dreadful to be governed by
Boers ! What people ! Canting, Old Testament hum-
bugs. One dislikes them so excessively, even from here,
that one can imagine the feelings of those who live
among them. Even Maurice isn't so perverse as to
maintain that Boers are tolerable. Oh, I'm all for

Dr. Jim. I insist on taking in that cheery pink new daily that pets him as if he were a Newfoundland dog that has saved a boat-load of drowning people. Such a bright, pleased tone it has. ' The British Public know a good man when they see one,' it says. Such a much more amiable and pleasant attitude towards us than Maurice's ' The public be damned. All it knows about anything that matters would go into a walnut shell and then rattle.' Maurice gets so terribly contemptuous and conceited. I tremble to think what he will be like at sixty, should nature keep him alive, if he finds the world so silly when he is but thirty-eight. Perhaps, however, he will have mellowed."

23

MAURICE, ROME, STANLEY AND THE QUEEN

NINETY-SIX ran out. Irving's tyre company began to make money, and Maurice grew richer. He sent Amy to the Riviera for the winter, and Rome kept his house for him. He was sweeter-tempered than usual. Rome was, in his eyes, a flâneuse and a dilettante of life, but her clear, cynical mind was agreeable to him. Her intelligent mockery was, after Amy's primitive jeering, as caviare after rotten eggs. God ! If only Amy need never come back. But she would inevitably come back. And the children loved her. Children are like that ; no discrimination. They loved Maurice too, but more mildly. And, very temperately, they liked their aunt Rome, whom they often suspected of making fun of them, and, even oftener, of being completely bored. In point of fact, Rome was apt to be bored by persons under sixteen or so. She allowed childhood to be a necessary stage in the growth of human beings, but she found it a tiresome one, and saw no reason why children should consort with adults. Stanley, on the other hand, being by now partially restored to her general goodwill towards humanity, threw herself ardently into the society and interests of her own children and those of others. She taught them imperialism, and about the English flag, and told them adventure stories, and played with them the games suitable to their years. She told them about the Diamond Jubilee, the great event of '97, and how our good, wise and aged queen would, by next June, have reigned for sixty years. Victoria was in fashion just then. She was well thought of, both morally and intellectually. " To the ripe sagacity of the politician," said the loyal press, " she adds the wide knowledge acquired by sixty years of statesmanship. Many a strained international situation has been saved by her personal tact." That was the way the late nineteenth century press spoke of Victoria, the English being a loyal people, with a strong sense of royalty. So the Diamond Jubilee would be a great day for the queen. Since the last Jubilee, in '87, the Empire, or anyhow, the sense of Empire, had grown and developed. Imperialism was now a very heady wine, to those who liked that tipple. To others, such as Maurice Garden, it was more of an emetic.

24

NANSEN IN THE ALBERT HALL

Dr. Nansen came to London, early in '97. Whatever else you thought of anything or any one, you had to admire Dr. Nansen. He addressed thousands of people in the Albert Hall. Vicky took her children to hear him. Already they had read *Farthest North*. Imogen, at eight years old, had read it, absorbed, breathless, intent, tongue clenched between teeth. The man who had sailed through ice, and all but got to the Pole. He was better than soldiers. As good, almost, as sailors. What a man! And there he stood, a giant dwarfed to smallness on the platform of the vast hall, a Scandinavian god, blonde and grave and calm, waiting to begin his lecture, but unable to because the crowd roared and clapped and stamped their feet, and would not stop.

At that huge explosion of welcome, Imogen's skin pringled and pricked all over, as if soldiers were swinging by to music, or a fire engine to the sound of bells, or as if the sun were setting in a glory of gold and green, or as if she were reading " The Revenge " or " The Charge of the Light Brigade," or " I will arise and go now and go to Inisfree." Imogen wept. She did not know that she wept, until the applause was at last over, and Nansen began to speak. Then her brother Hugh poked her in the back and said, " What's up ? Wipe your nose and don't snivel," and she was ashamed, and though she retorted, " Wipe your own. Snivel yourself," it was no satisfaction, because Hughie was not snivelling. Boys didn't, she had learnt, except when there was something to snivel about. They did not understand the female weakness which wept at fire engines, poetry and clapping, and was sick at squashed insects. Imogen wanted (even still half hoped) to be a boy, so she tried to hide her weaknesses.

Nansen began to speak.

" They're all quiet now. A pin might drop," said Imogen to herself, having lately learnt that phrase, but not getting it quite right.

But disappointment took her. Strain as she would, she could not hear what the god said. She could not

make it into words, except now and then. It boomed
along, sonorous, fluent English, above her plane of
listening. A sentence here and there she got, entrancing and teasing, then away the voice soared, booming
in another dimension. . . . Imogen had never learnt
to listen ; now for the first time she knew remorse for
sermon-times spent in day-dreams, lessons at school
during which her mind had drifted away on seas of
fancy like a rudderless boat, to be sharply recalled by
" Imogen Carrington, what have I just said ? " Seldom,
indeed, did Imogen Carrington know. She would
blush and stammer and get an inattention mark. No
one in the second form had so many inattention marks
as she. Perhaps if she had fewer she could have
understood Nansen now.

" Hughie, can you hear ? "

" Most of the time. Don't interrupt."

Yes, Hughie could hear. Hughie was two years
older ; Hughie was ten, and into his square, solid,
intelligent head the sounds emitted by Nansen were
penetrating as words. Hughie could listen, when he
had a mind to. Hughie was more clever than Imogen.
Phyllis and Nancy could hear too, of course ; they were
older. Not Tony ; but then Tony, who was only
seven, wouldn't be trying. He didn't really care.

" Mother, *I can't hear*."

" Don't talk, darling. I'll tell you afterwards. . . ."

But what was the good of that ?

Imogen's straining attention flagged. If she couldn't
hear, she couldn't. She sighed and gave up. She stared,
fascinated, at the splendid figure on the platform, and
imagined him on the Fram, sailing along through
chunks of floating ice, and on each chunk a great white
bear. Floes, they were, not chunks. . . . She and
the boys meant, when they should be grown up, to fit
out a Fram for themselves, and find the Pole. Hughie

had some idea of going for the South Pole. The sort of unusual, intelligent idea Hughie did get. But to Imogen the North was the Pole that called. Away they sailed, away and away . . . Tony was attacked, as he fished from a floe, by a huge mother bear, with three cubs. Imogen got there just in time ; she slew the bear with her long knife, at imminent personal risk ; it toppled backwards into the ice-cold water and died. The green sea reddened hijjously. But the three little cubs Imogen kept. She took them back to the Fram, and there was one for each of them, and they were called Mowgli, Marcus and Mercia, and Marcus was hers (the children had been taken to " The Sign of the Cross " last summer. There was a play indeed !), and the cubs slept in their bunks with them, and ate from their plates at meals. . . .

Another storm of clapping. It was over.

" Did you like it, Jennie ? How much did you follow ? "

" I liked it very much. I followed it a lot . . . Mother, do you think, when I'm big, I shall ever *speak* to him ? I mean, when Hughie and Tony and I have got our ship, and have been to the Pole ? "

" Oh, yes, darling. I should think when that happens, certainly. Only Dr. Nansen may be dead by that time, I'm afraid."

" Is he old, mother ? Is he very old ? Will he die before we grow up ? Will he, mother ? "

" Children, be careful crossing the road. . . . What's the matter, Imogen ? "

" Will he die, mother, before we're grown up ? "

" Who ? Dr. Nansen ? Oh, no, I hope not, why should he ? Tony, don't dawdle. We'll go home by the park. Keep together, children, there's such a crowd. . . . Imogen, *don't* play with strange dogs—I keep telling you."

" Mother, he's such a weeny one . . . all white, with
a black nose and a red tongue. . . . Mother, when *can*
I have a puppy ? "

25

JUBILEE

JUBILEE DAY. Sweltering heat, after a gray beginning ;
baked streets. Irving, out of his wealth and generosity,
had bought a block of seats in the Mall for the procession, and there the family sat. Papa, mamma, Vicky,
and Charles and their daughter Imogen (their other
children were away at school), Rome, Stanley, Irving
and his wife, and Una and Ted up from the country
with two stout and handsome children. The ladies
wore beflowered, rakish, fly-away hats, and dresses
with high collars and hunched sleeves and small waists.
They look absurd now, in old pictures of the period,
but they did not look absurd to one another at the time ;
they looked natural, and *comme-il-faut*, and smart.
The boys wore their Eton suits, and the girls light
frocks. Imogen had a blue smock, gathered across the
yoke, so that when she ran her fingers across the smock-
ing it made a little soft, crisp noise. She sat next her
little cousins from the country. But she was shy of
them and turned her face away, and would say nothing
to them after she had asked, " How is Rover ? How
is Lassie ? Are the puppies born yet ? " Fits of shy-
ness seized upon Imogen like toothache, even now that
she had been ever so long at school, and she would
hang her head and mutter monosyllabic answers, and
wish she were Prince Prigio, with his cap of darkness,
and when, in church, it came to the psalm about,
" Deliver me from the hands of strange children,"

she would pray it ardently, feeling how right David (if that psalm were one of his) had been. She was not shy of her cousins when she stayed at the farm with them, for the farm was like paradise, full of calves, puppies, pigs, and joy, and Katie, Dick, Martin, and Dolly were its hierophants, and, though they weren't much good at being pirates or Red Indians, it was, no doubt, because they were always employed to better purpose. But in the Mall, seated in a tidy row waiting for the procession, it was different. Imogen wished that two of her brothers and sisters could have been there, instead of Katie and Dick. She held a fold of her mother's soft foulard dress tightly between her hot fingers. She whispered.

" Mother. Suppose some one felt sick and couldn't get out ? "

" *Jean*—you don't feel sick, do you, child ? " Vicky was alarmed, knowing the weakness of her daughter's stomach.

" Oh, no, *I* don't feel sick. But if some one did ? What *would* they do, mother ? Suppose the lady just above *you* felt sick, mother ? Suppose she *was* sick ? What would you do, mother ? "

" Don't be silly, Imogen. If you talk like that you'll feel sick yourself. Talk to Katie. Don't you see you're interrupting grandmamma and me ? "

But Imogen's grandmamma smiled across at her small, pink, freckled face.

" Are you enjoying yourself, Jennie ? "

" Yes, grandmamma. . . . Is the queen older than you, grandmamma ? "

" Yes. The Queen is seventy-eight. I am sixty-three. When I was only three years old, the Queen was crowned."

" Did you see her crowned ? "

" No. I was too young."

" Is it a very big crown ? Will she have it on ?
. . . *Mother* "—Imogen had a terrible thought and
whispered it—" suppose *the Queen* was sick, in her
carriage, just opposite here ? What *would* happen,
mother ? Would the procession wait or go on ? "

" Now, Jennie, that will do. You're being tiresome
and silly. Talk to Katie and Dick. I'm talking to
grandmamma ; I told you before."

(For that was the way in which children were kept
under in the last century. Things have changed.)

Gold and purple and crimson. Silver and scarlet
and gold. Fluttering pennons on tall Venetian masts.
The Mall was a street in fairyland, or the New Jerusalem.
And thronged with those who would never see either
more nearly, being neither fantastic nor good. Never
would most of these enter through the strait gate and
see the gates of pearl and the city of golden streets.
But was not this as good ? Silver and violet and
crimson and gold ; gay streamers flying on the wind.
Beautiful as an army with banners, the Mall was. . . .

" Let's count the flags," said Imogen to Katie and
Dick.

" I remember the coronation," said Mr. Garden, half
to Irving, half to any one sitting about who might be
interested, after the way of elderly persons. " I was
a very small boy, but my father took me to see the
procession. I remember he put me up on his shoulder
while it passed. . . . There wasn't quite such a
crowd then as to-day, I think."

" People have increased," said Rome. " Particularly
in London. There are now too many, that is certain."

" The crowd," said Mr. Garden, his memory straying
over that day sixty years ago, " was *prettier* then. I
am nearly sure it was prettier. Costumes were better."

" They could hardly," said Rome, " have been
worse."

" I remember my mother, in a violet pelisse, that I think she had got new for the occasion, and a crinoline . . . Crinolines hadn't grown large in '37—they were very graceful, I think . . . and a pretty poke bonnet. And my father in a cravat, with close whiskers (whiskers hadn't grown large, either) and a tall, gray hat. . . . And myself done up tight in blue nankeen with brass buttons, and your aunt Selina with white, frilled garments showing below her frock. Little girls weren't so pretty," he added, looking across at Imogen's straight blue smock. " Well, well, sixty years ago. A great deal has happened since then. A great reign and a great time."

" They're pretty nearly due now," said Irving, consulting his watch. " Sure to be late, though."

" Who'll come first, mother ? " Imogen asked.

" Captain Ames, on a horse. And behind him Life Guards and dragoons and that kind of person. . . . So I said to her, mamma, that really unless she could undertake to . . . Oh, listen, they really *are* coming now. Listen to the cheering, Jennie."

The noise of loyalty beat and broke like a sea from west to east. The sound shivered down Imogen's spine like music, and, as usual in such moments, her eyes pringled with hot tears, which she squeezed away. Then came the blaring of the trumpets and the rolling of the drums, and, singing high above them like a kettle on the boil, the faint, keen skirling of the pipes.

Imogen's hot hand clutched Vicky's dress.

" Now, Jean, don't get too excited, darling. Try to be quiet and sensible, like Katie and Dick."

" Mother, I *am* too excited, already. *Look*, mother— is that Captain Ames on a horse ? "

Captain Ames on a horse (and what a horse !) it was. And behind him Life Guards, dragoons, lancers, and that kind of person, in noble profusion. Very gallant and

proud and lovely, prancing, curveting, gay as bright
flowers in a wind. . . . Oh, God, what military
men !

A little, white-moustached general rode by, and
great cheers crashed. " That's Lord Roberts, Imogen."
Imogen, who knew her Kipling, had a lump in her
throat for Bobs of Kandahar.

" And that's Lord Charles Beresford—with the
cocked hat, do you see ? "

Then came the great guns, running on their carriages.

And then the cheering broke to a mighty storm, as
it always does when sailors go by.

The sailors, too, had guns. Bluejackets and smart,
neat officers, Britannia's pets, Britannia's pride. . . .

Imogen, who had always meant to be a sailor, and
who even now blindly hoped that somehow, before she
reached the age for Osborne, a way would be made for
her (either she would become a boy, or dress up as a
boy, or the rule excluding girls from the senior service
would be relaxed) gasped and screwed her hands tightly
together against her palpitating breast. Here were
sailors. Straight from the tossing blue sea ; straight
from pacing the quarter-deck, spy-glass in hand,
spying for enemy craft, climbing the rigging, setting her
hard-a-port, manning the guns, raking the enemy
amidships, holding up slavers, receiving surrendered
swords. . . . Here, in brief, were sailors ; and the
junior service faded from the stage. Rule, Britannia,
Britannia rules the waves. The moment was almost
too excessive for a budding sailor, with wet eyes and
lips pressed tight together to keep the face steady.
Fortunately it passed, and was succeeded by the First
Prussian Dragoon Guards, great men with golden
helmets, who could be admired without passion, and
by strange, brown men, with turbans and big beards.

" Indians," Vicky said, and Indians, too, one knew

from Kipling. And, "Sir Partab Singh," added the informing voice.

"Is he the chief of the Indians, mother?"

"Some kind of chief, yes."

Other brown men followed the Indians—little, coppery, fuzzy Maoris; and with them rode splendid white men from New Zealand, and slouch-hatted Rhodesian horse.

"From South Africa. . . . You remember Dr. Jim and his raid, and Cecil Rhodes . . . the Christmas holidays before last . . ."

"When the chair broke and I cut my head." Yes, Imogen remembered, though she had been only seven then. Over the Transvaal border, then a gallop for life or death. . . . The chair was still broken. . . . Every one seemed to remember Dr. Jim and his raid and Cecil Rhodes, for the slouch-hatted riders were cheered and cheered. Hurrah for South Africa! "Political trouble, much less war, cannot now be apprehended," the *Times* had said that morning, in a pæan of Jubilee satisfaction with sixty years of progress abroad and at home.

The best was over, for now began carriages—landaus and pairs. Foreign envoys. The Papal Nuncio sharing a landau with a gentleman from China, who cooled himself with a painted fan. Landau after landau bearing royal gentlemen, royal ladies. What a pity for them to be borne tamely in landaus instead of a-horseback!

A Colonial escort; an Indian escort; Lord Wolseley.

And then the procession's meaning and climax. "The Queen, Jennie."

Eight cream horses soberly drawing an open carriage, surrounded by postilions and red-coated running footmen; and in the carriage the little stout old lady, black-dressed, with black and white bonnet, and with her the beautiful Princess in heliotrope, dressed in the then current fashion, which royal ladies have adhered to ever since, never allowing themselves to be unsettled by the modes of the new century.

The Queen, God save her. The noise was monstrous, louder than any real noise could be.

"Dear old soul," cried Vicky's clear voice as she lustily clapped white kid hands.

Papa's blue eyes looked kindly down on the old lady whose coronation he remembered.

"A record to be proud of," said papa.

"Oh, yes, she's seen some life these sixty years, the old lady," Irving admitted.

"I expect she's feeling the heat a bit," said Una. "Well, I hope she's happy."

Behind them people were saying loyal Victorian things to one another about the dear old Queen.

"She's got the hearts of the Empire all right," they were saying, "whether they're under white skins or brown," and "God bless our dear Queen," and "How well she looks to-day," and "She's an Empress, but she's a woman first. That's why we all love her so," and so on and so forth.

And "There goes the Prince," they said, applauding now the burly middle-aged gentleman riding his horse by his mother's carriage.

"He must be gettin' pretty impatient, poor man," said Amy. "Nearly sixty himself, and mamma still going strong. I expect he thinks this ought to be his silver jubilee, not mamma's diamond one."

Mr. Garden looked pained. He often looked and was pained at the wife of Maurice.

Imogen's heart swelled for the Empress-Queen and the crash of loyalty, but not to bursting point; for here was only a little old lady in a carriage (though drawn by eight cream horses like a fairy godmother's), and it is the swagger of gallantry that stirs. Sailors, soldiers, explorers, martyrs, firemen, circus-riders, Blondin on his rope, Christ on His cross, Joan of Arc on her white steed or her red pile—these are they that shake the soul to tears. Not old ladies, however mighty, who have sat on a throne for sixty years.

" The prince, Jennie. The Prince of Wales."

" *Oh, mother, where ?* "

The Prince of Wales. Gallant figure of legend. Young, noble, princely, with caracolling charger and a triple white plume in a silver helm. The bravest and the most chivalrous of the knights. Where was the Prince of Wales—" *Oh, mother, where ?* "

" There—don't you see him ? The big man in uniform with a gray beard, riding by the Queen's carriage."

The big man. . . . Oh, no, that must be a mistake.

" *That's* not the Prince of Wales, mother. Not *that* one. . . ."

" Of course. Why shouldn't it be ? "

A thousand reasons why it shouldn't be. A hundred thousand reasons. . . . But in vain their legions beat against the hard little fact that it *was.* Imogen's soaring heart sank like a stone in water. Fearful doubts whispered. Had all the Princes of Wales been like that—fat, elderly men with gray beards ? The Black Prince. . . . Oh, no, not the Black Prince. . . .

" The Black Prince wasn't like that, mother, was he ? "

" It must be nearly the end now. Here's the music. . . . What, Jean ? What's bothering you now ? "

" The Black Prince . . ."

" Forget him, my precious. Don't let any prince weigh on your little mind. Here comes the music. Do you hear the pipes, children ? "

So the great procession passed eastward, to rejoice

Trafalgar Square, the Strand, Fleet Street, and the lands across the river.

"It'll be a job getting out of this. Hold on to me, Imogen. Did you enjoy it, darling?"

"Yes." Imogen nodded, with the sun in her screwed-up eyes. "I wish we could run very fast down the streets to where they haven't passed yet, and see them all again. Do you think you could, mother?"

"I'm quite sure we couldn't. . . . You're not over tired, mamma dear?"

"Oh, no. I feel very well. . . . But that child has turned green . . ."

Vicky looked down, startled, at her daughter.

"*Imogen.* Aren't you well?"

"Mother, I think I may be going to be sick."

"Well, sit down till it's over. . . . Bless the child. It's the heat and the excitement. She gets taken like that sometimes, by way of reaction after her treats—most tiresome."

"Poor little mite."

"How are you feeling now, Jennie?"

Imogen said nothing. Yellow as cream cheese, she sat in her seat and asked God not to disgrace her by letting her be sick in public, in the grand stand, on Jubilee Day, with all London looking on.

But, "I'm not sure, mother, that I do very much believe in prayers," she said to Vicky that evening.

26

RECESSIONAL

TRIUMPHANT patriotism is all very well. Proud imperialism is all very well. But these things should be carried with a swagger, like a panache, with a hint of the gay and the absurd, marching, as it were, to the wild, conceited noise of skirling pipes. People of all nations, but more particularly the English, are apt to forget this, and bear their patriotism heavily, unctuously, speak solemnly of the white man's burden, and introduce religion into the gay and worldly affair.

Rudyard Kipling did this, on July 17th of Jubilee year, when he published in the *Times*, "Recessional," beginning,—

> "God of our fathers, known of old,
> Lord of our far-flung battle line,
> Beneath whose awful Hand we hold
> Dominion over palm and pine—
> Lord God of Hosts, be with us yet,
> Lest we forget, lest we forget."

Stanley read it at breakfast, and shuddered. It was such a poem as the Jews might have made, in the days of Israel's glory—terribly godly and solemn. It was addressed to Jehovah, the Jewish Lord of Hosts. Those Jews! How their influence lasts! Beneath whose awful Hand we hold. . . . Awful is a bad word, and hand should never, whosoever hand it is, have a capital h—(but that might have been the printer's fault, as any one who knows printers must, in fairness, admit)—and dominion over palm and pine is much too delightful and romantic a thing to be spoilt by being held thus. And, further down, it was worse.

> "If, drunk with sight of power, we loose
> Wild tongues that have not Thee in awe,
> Such boasting as the Gentiles use,
> Or lesser breeds without the Law . . ."

Are we, then, Jews, and not Gentiles? And what Law? And lesser breeds—that was worst of all.

The whole poem seemed to Stanley so heavily ruinous of a jolly thing, so terribly expressive of the solemn pomposity into which national pride is ever ready to stumble, that it tarnished for her something young and buoyant and absurd into which she had flung herself of late. As Miss Edith Cavell remarked twenty years later, patriotism is not enough. It needs to be as the cherishing love a man has for the soil of his home; or as the bitter, desperate striving unto death of the oppressed race, the damned desperation of the rebel; or as the gay and gallant flying of gaudy banners. Successful, smug, solemn, conquering patriotism is not nearly enough—or perhaps it is a good deal too much. Anyhow, it is all wrong.

"What a man," Stanley muttered, meaning Mr. Rudyard Kipling, who did, if any one, know all about the adventure of empire-building, its swagger, glitter and romance, and must needs turn himself into a preacher.

To Stanley's niece, Imogen, it happened to have "Recessional" read aloud to her form at school, by one whom she greatly loved (for it must be owned that this unbalanced child only too readily adored those who taught her), and shyly she wriggled her mind away from the sense of the sounding lines. She liked,—

> "Far-called, our navies melt away;
> O'er dune and headland sinks the fire;
> Lo, all our pomp of yesterday
> Is one with Nineveh and Tyre . . ."

and,

> "The tumult and the shouting dies,
> The captains and the kings depart . . ."

and,

"All valiant dust that builds on dust . . ."

but disliked the rest. If Miss Treherne liked it, it must, she knew, be somehow good ; further, it was by Kipling, who had made Mowgli, and,—

"It's north you may run to the rime-ringed sun,
     Or south to the blind Horn's hate ;
  Or east all the way into Mississippi Bay,
     Or west to the Golden Gate . . ."

But all the same, Imogen had no use for it. In the foolish jargon of school, it was " pi."

But newspapers said at the time, and history books have said since, that this poem sounded a fine and needed note ; and, in fact, it was a good deal liked. Mr. Garden liked it. Mr. Garden was afraid that Britain was getting a little above itself with empire. As, indeed, it doubtless was, said Stanley, and why not ? Empires, like life, only endure for a brief period, and we may as well enjoy them while we may. They are wasted on those who do not enjoy them. Time bears us off, as lightly as the wind lifts up the smoke and carries it away. . . . The grave's a fine and private place, but in it there are no empires, only the valiant dust that builds on dust, and has come to dust at the last. So let us by all means be above ourselves while we may, and if we can, in the brief space that is ours before we must be below ourselves for ever.

Mr. Garden replied that there were many brief spaces to come, for all of us, and we should be training ourselves for these. . . . For papa was still a Theosophist, and believed in infinitely numerous reincarnations. He did not desire them, for he had had troubles enough,

for one ; but he knew that they would occur. He
looked with apprehension down a vista of lives. To-
morrow and to-morrow and to-morrow, to the last
syllable of recorded time—or, anyhow, until papa
should be made perfect—and that, papa humbly felt,
was a very long time ahead.

27

BOND STREET

LONDON glittered sweetly, washed by the May sun.
The streets were bland and gay, like a lady of fashion
taking the air. Miss Garden walked abroad, bland
and gay too, slim and erect in neat coatee and skirt
(skirt touching the pavement as she walked—disgusting,
but skirts did), lace jabot at the high stock collar, and
large, beribbonned hat, tipped a little forward so that
the sunshine caught the fair hair sweeping upward
from the nape. She led a huge borzoi on a leash, and
as she walked she surveyed London, its people, its
streets, its shops. In a gold net purse bag she carried
notes and clinking sovereigns. She had gambled to
good purpose last night at bridge, the new card game.
She was a great gambler. Bridge, whist, baccarat,
poker, roulette at Monte Carlo—at all these she won
and lost, with the same equable sangfroid. Her
parents did not like it, though Rome's income, left her
by her grandfather, was her own. They did not, in
many ways, approve of their clever Rome, so unlike
themselves. But on such disapprovals, so Rome assured
them, family life is based. Mutual disapproval, mutual
toleration ; that is family, as, indeed, so much other,
life.

Anyhow, Rome gambled. The older she grew the

more greatly and intelligently she gambled. She had
her systems, ingeniously worked out, for Monte Carlo.
She had been there this Easter, together with her friend
and ally, Guy Donkin, a cheerful barrister three years
her junior, who had been used to ask her to marry
him, but had now settled down to a sporting friendship
and confided to her his fleeting affairs of the heart.
Here again, Mr. and Mrs. Garden disapproved. Going
to Monte Carlo to meet a man : staying at the same
hotel with him : seen everywhere with him : even in
the late, the very late thirties, was this right or wise ?
It set people talking. . . .

"As to that," Rome carelessly dismissed it, " be sure
people will always talk.   You may be sure, too, mamma,
that Guy and I do nothing not *comme-il-faut*. We are
both too worldly-wise for that. We may *épater* the
bourgeois possibly, but we shan't *épater* our own world.
We know its foolish rules, and we both find it more
comfortable to keep them."

Entirely of the world Miss Garden looked, this May
morning, strolling down Bond Street, a little cynical,
a little · blasée, very well-dressed, intensely civilised,
exquisitely poised, delicately, cleanly fair. She would
soon be thirty-nine, and looked just that, neither more
nor less.

A window full of jade caught her roving eye. She
went in ; she bought a clear jade elephant, and a dull
jade lump that swung on a fine platinum chain. She
also got a tortoise-shell cigarette case.

She stopped next at a window full of little dogs.
Big-headed Sealyham pups ; Poltalloch terriers. These
she looked at critically.   She meant to have a Poltalloch,
but to order one from their home in the West High-
lands when next she stayed there. Adorable puppies.
The Borzoi sniffed at them through plate glass, and
grunted.

Irish lace. Jabots of pointe de Venise, and deep collars of Honiton and point de Flandres, and hand-herchiefs edged with Chantilly. Miss Garden entered the shop; came out with a jabot for herself, hand-kerchiefs for Vicky's birthday. Then ivory opera glasses, and an amber cigarette holder caught her fancy. Soon her free hand was slung with neat paper packages. That was a bore; she wished she had had them all sent.

She strolled on, turned into Stewart's, ordered a box of chocolates for Stanley's children, and met Mr. Guy Donkin for lunch. They were going to a picture show together.

" I am not," said Miss Garden, " fit for a respectable picture gallery, as you see." She indicated the packages and the Borzoi. " But, nevertheless, we will go. Jeremy shall wait in the street while we criticise the art of our friends. I was overtaken this morning by the lust of possession. I often get in on fine mornings after fortunate nights. I find that the gambler's life works out, on the whole, pretty evenly—what one makes at the dice one loses in the shops. And what one loses at play one saves off the shops. One walk abroad, looking at everything and buying nothing, will save one some hundreds of pounds. It is the easiest way of gaining, though not the most amusing. . . . I see you have a lunch edition. How go the wars ? "

The most noticeable wars at the moment were those between America and Spain, and between Great Britain and the Soudanese.

" Dewey's occupied Manila. The Fuzzies have lost another zareba. It must be warm for fighting out there to-day. . . . Here's an article by some Dean on the vulgarity of modern extravagance. Meant for you, Rome, with all your packages. . . . *Are* we specially extravagant just now ? I suppose there's a lot of money going about, one way and another. Business is so good. And all these gold mines and companies. . . . The Dean is worrying about the growing habit of entertaining in restaurants instead of in the home. Why not ? And about women taking to cosmetics again, after a century of abstinence. Again, why not ? I agree with Max about that. The clergy do worry so, poor dears ; if it isn't one thing it's another. Oh, and on Tuesday we're all to wear a white rose, for the Old Man's funeral day."

" How touching. It will please papa. He's really distressed about the Old Man ; he thinks politics on the grand scale are over, and that the giants are dead. Politics and politicians are certainly intensely dull in these days ; but then, except for an occasional gleam, they probably always were. Partly because people insist on taking them so solemnly, instead of as a farce. . . . There's my ex-brother-in-law, lunching with a quite new and lovely young woman. He always smiles at me, blandly and without shame. I can't forgive him for spoiling Stanley's life, but I can't help rather liking him still. He always sends us tickets for his first nights, and they're very amusing. A shameless reactionary, but so witty. Maurice and Irving cut him, which I think crude. Men are so intolerant. I cut no one, except when I'm afraid of being bored by them. Thank you, yes ; Turkish."

They strolled off through the pleasant city to look at pictures, which they could both criticise with as much intelligence as was necessary, and Miss Garden with rather more. Then Mr. Donkin returned to the Bar, and Miss Garden drove home in a hansom with the Borzoi and the gleanings from Bond Street. At five she was going to an at home somewhere ; later she was dining out and going to the opera. Life was full ; life was amusing ; life hung a brilliant curtain over the

abyss. From the abyss Miss Garden turned her eyes ;
in it lay love and death, locked bitterly together for
evermore.

28

LAST LAP

1898 swaggered by under a hot summer sun. The
century swaggered death-wards, gay with gold and
fatness, unsteady, dark and confused. The *Belle of
New York* at the theatres, the Simple Life on the land,
free-wheel bicycles on the road, motor-cars, coming
first in single spies, then in batallions, the victory of
Omdurman, Kitchener occupying Khartoum and the
French Fashoda, unpleasant international incidents
(for international incidents are always unpleasant),
millionaires rising like stars, fortunes made and spent,
business booming, companies floated and burst, names of
drinks, provender and medicines flaming from the skies,
Swinburne publishing *Rosamund, Queen of the Lombards*,
Mr. Yeats *The Wind among the Reeds*, Mr. Kipling
Stalky & Co. and the *Day's Work*, Mr. Conrad *Tales
of Unrest*, Mr. Stephen Phillips *Paolo and Francesca*,
Mr. Thomas Hardy *Wessex Poems*, Mr. H. G. Wells
The War of the Worlds, Miss Mary Cholmondeley *Red
Pottage*, Mrs. Humphry Ward *Helbeck of Bannisdale*,
Mr. Maurice Hewlett *The Forest Lovers*, Mr. Kenneth
Grahame *Dream Days*, Mr. Hall Caine *The Christian*,
George Meredith greeted by literary England on his seven-
tieth birthday, bad novels pouring into the libraries
with terrifying increase of speed, wireless telegraphy
used at sea, flying machines experimented with, liberals
sickening with Imperialism or Little Englandism,
conservatives with jingoism run mad, the *Speaker*
started, the Encyclopædia Britannica sold by the

Times, anti-ritualist agitations, armament limitation conference convened by Russia and attended by the Powers, all of whom were as busy as bees at home increasing their armies and navies and hatching military plots.

And then the South African Uitlanders sent complaints and petitions from the Rand, and despatches began to pass between Her Majesty's Government and President Kruger's. Despatches are most unfortunate and unwise means of communication ; they always make trouble.

There was bound to be war, people began saying. Mr. Chamberlain and Mr. Rhodes intended it, and would not be happy till they got it. Probably President Kruger and his Burghers also intended it. Certainly the Uitlanders hoped for it. The British public were not averse. They hated the Boers, and wanted excitement and more Empire. It was a hopeless business. War was bound to come, and came, in October, 1899.

Mr. Garden said, "A bad business. Gladstone would never have let it come to this. One doesn't trust Chamberlain. A bad, dishonest business."

Mrs. Garden said, " Those poor lads going out just before the winter. . . ."

Vicky said, " Charles says it won't be long. We shall have them asking for terms in a month."

Maurice said, " That damned jingo, Chamberlain," and filled his fountain pen with more vitriol.

Amy said, " Those canting, snuffling old farmers. *They* won't keep us long."

Rome said, " Unfortunate. But it's a way in which centuries often end."

Stanley said, " Right or wrong, we've got to win now."

Irving said, " I shall take the opportunity to run out

and see to my mining interests. Up the Rand," and
he enlisted in the C.I.V. and went.

Una said, " War ! How silly. If it isn't one thing
it's another. Why not leave the poor farmers alone ? "
For she sympathised with farmers, and was all for
leaving people alone.

The children of all of them shouted for the soldiers
and the flag, and sang " Soldiers of the Queen."

> " And when we say we've always won,
>   And when they ask us how it's done . . ."

A very bright song. That was the right, amusing
spirit of patriotism, not the " Recessional," and not
prayers sent forth for the people's use by Bishops.

Vicky's children got up early one morning in the
Christmas holidays without leave, and saw a detachment
of the C.I.V. go off from Victoria. There was a raw,
yellow fog, and the khaki figures loomed oddly through
it. The press of the swaying, shouting crowd was
terrifying, exhilarating. Imogen, linked up between
Phyllis and Hugh, was crushed, swung, caught off her
feet. Persons of eleven had no business in that crowd.
Phyllis and Nancy had not wanted her and Tony to
come, but they had firmly done so. Imogen could
scarcely see the soldiers, only the broad backs her face
was pressed against. Herd enthusiasm caught and
held them all, and they shouted and sang with the
rest, hoarsely, choking in the fog.

" They'll be killed," sobbed a woman close to them.
" We'll never see their brave faces again. . . ."

At that Imogen's eyes brimmed over, but she could
not put up her hands to wipe them, for her arms
were tight wedged. She could only snuffle and blink.
Splendid heroes ! They would be killed by the Boers,
sure enough, every one of them. . . .   Horrible Boers,

with great Bibles and sjamboks and guns. Hateful, hateful Boers. If only one were allowed to go and fight them, as uncle Irving was going. Thank heaven, it was rather age than sex that kept one from doing that; the boys couldn't go any more than Imogen could. If the boys had been old enough and had gone, Imogen would somehow, she felt sure, have gone too. To be left out was too awful.

But these were grown men. Splendid men. Lucky men, for they would soon be roving the veldt with guns and bayonets under the African sun; they would lurk in ambush behind kopjes and arise and slay their brother Boer, the canting, bearded foe, with great slaughter. Even if they did never come back, how could man die better?

The crowd swayed and shoved, lifting the children from their feet. Imogen's chest was crushed against the back in front of her; she fought for breath. There was an acrid, musty smell; the raw air was close with breathing.

A crowd is queer. A number of individuals gather together for one purpose, and you get not a number of individuals, but a crowd. It is like a new, strange animal, sub-human. It may do anything. Go crazy with panic, or rage, or excitement, or delight. Now it was enthusiasm that gripped and swayed it, and caused it to shout and sing. Songs rippled over it, starting somewhere, caught from mouth to mouth.

"Cook's son, duke's son, son of a belted earl . . .
 Fifty thousand horse and foot going to Table
    Bay . . ."

And then again the constant chorus, "God bless you, Tommy Atkins, here's your country's love to you!"

It was over at last. The heroes had gone. The

crowd broke and pushed out from the station gates, flooding the choked yellow streets.

" There's our bus," said Phyllis, a good organiser. " Come on. Stick together."

They besieged and rushed the bus as troops rush a fort. Being vigorous and athletic children, they stormed it successfully.

" We shall catch it from mother," said Phyllis, now that they had leisure to look ahead. " But it's been worth it."

29

OF CENTURIES

THE sad, disappointing, disillusioning, silly war crawled through that bitter winter of defeat, until, by sheer force of numbers, the undefeatable Boers were a little checked in the spring of 1900.

Life was disappointing. Imogen, along with many others, thought and hoped that 1900 would be a new century. It was not a new century. There was quite a case for its being so. When you turned twelve, you began your thirteenth year. When you had counted up to 100 you had completed that hundred and were good for the next. It all depended on whether you numbered the completion of a year from the first day when you began saying 1900, or not till its last day, when you stopped saying it. The Astronomer Royal adjudicated that it was on its last day, and that they had, in fact, said 1900 prematurely, saying it before the last second of December the 31st. He may have been right. He probably was right. But the disappointment of the young, to whom a year is very long, its end hidden in mists, like mountain tops which you perhaps shall never reach,—the disappointment of the young at the opening of the year 1900 was very great.

"At all events," said Imogen, " we can write 1900. We can say, ' It's 1900.' " But what one could not say was, " I remember, last century, going to the seaside for the holidays. . . ." " Last century, bicycles and steam engines came in . . ." or, " We, of the twentieth century." That would have to wait.

The funny thing was that you could not, however hard you thought, lay your finger on the moment when the new century would be born. Imogen used to try, lying in bed before she went to sleep. One second you said, " We of the nineteenth century "; the next second you said, " We of the twentieth century." But there must be a moment in between, when it was neither; surely there must. A queer little isolated point of time, with no magnitude, but only position. . . . The same point must be between one day and the next, one hour and the next . . . all points in time were such points . . . but you could never find them . . . always you either looked forward or looked back . . . you said " now—now—now," trying to catch now, but you never could . . . and such vain communings with time lead one drowsily into sleep.

30

PRO-BOER

In Stanley the Boer war slew the jingo spirit, turned back on itself the cresting wave of imperialism. Not because it was an ill-fought, stupidly managed, for long unsuccessful war, but because it was war, and war was, when seen functioning, senseless and horrible. It

was nearly as bad when Great Britain at last began
to defeat the too clever farmers. It was almost worst
in the summer of 1900, when the news of the relief of
Mafeking caused so much more tempestuous a hysteria
than other reliefs had caused, and when Lord Roberts
occupied Johannesburg and proclaimed the annexation
of the Orange Free State, and when Pretoria was
taken, and yet the war went on and on and on.

" Is this the way," asked Liberals, " to secure in
the end any kind of working reconciliation between
ourselves and the conquered enemy ? If Great Britain
wishes to be burdened for ever with a sullen, hostile,
exasperated people, embittered with the memory of
burnt farms, useless slaughter and destruction, she is
taking the right course." And so forth. Liberals
always talk like that. Those who disagreed merely
retorted " Pro-Boer," which took less time. The
Latin word " pro " has been found always very useful
and insulting.

Stanley became a pro-Boer. She disliked all she
knew of Boers very much, but that had nothing to do
with it. A pro-Boer, like a pro-German much later,
was one who was in favour of making terms with the
enemy on the victories already gained. The Con-
ciliation Committee were pro-Boer. The Liberal newspapers were pro-Boer, except the *Chronicle*, which
threw Mr. Massingham overboard to be pro-Boer by
himself. Maurice Garden was, of course, pro-Boer.
He loathed Boers, the heavy-witted, brutal Bible-men,
with their unctuous Cromwellian cant. But fiercely
and contemptuously he was pro-Boer. Rome, too,
was pro-Boer ; had been from the first.

"A most unpleasant people," she had said. " What
a mistake not to leave them to themselves. If the
Uitlanders disliked them as much as I should, they
wouldn't go on living there and sending complaints to

us ; they would come away. All this imperialism is so very unbalanced."

"Worse than unbalanced, Rome," her papa sadly said. "One hesitates to speak harshly, but it must be called unchristian. The Churches have gone terribly astray over it. The unhappy Churches. . . ."

Unhappy because terribly astray on so many topics, papa meant. Even now he was mourning the death of his friend, Dr. Mivart, who had been deprived of the sacraments of his Church because he had, in the *Nineteenth Century* and the *Fortnightly Review*, written articles, however reverent, on "The Continuity of Catholicism," and in them seemed to give to the infallible authority of the Church a lower place than to human reason. Alas for the Catholic Church, which so treated its best sons ! Never, papa knew, could he join that great Church again. Religion, too, had suffered a heavy blow in the death, in January, of Dr. Martineau. And Ruskin also went that month. . . . Like leaves the great Victorians were falling. Papa, brooding over a great epoch so soon to close, could not but be a pro-Boer and hope that this horrid war, which jarred and confused its last years, would soon end.

As for Maurice, his newspaper office was raided and smashed on Mafeking night, and he himself carried out and ducked in Trafalgar Square basin. No one hurt him. No one wanted, on this happy, good humoured night, to hurt this small, frail, scornful, slightly intoxicated, obviously courageous, editor, who brightly insulted them to their faces as they tied him up.

Vicky's children were not pro-Boer. No one could have called them that. They were all for a good whacking victory. Imogen, it must be owned, did once, in a moment of seeing the point of view of the foe (Imogen usually saw all the points of view there

were to see ; her eye was not single, which made life
a very dizzy business for her), write a poem beginning :

" Across the great Vaal river we northward trekked
          and came,
    Set up our own dominion, and men acknowledged
          the same ;
    And close behind us followed the Alien whom we
          scorn,
    With his eager, clutching fingers and his lust for
          gold new-born.

            " There is wealth," he cried,
            " I will dig," he cried :
        Between him and us may the Lord decide !
            Through the Lord's good might,
            By the sword's good right,
        Let us up and smite our enemies and put our
              foes to flight ! "

Imogen was not ill-pleased with that poem, which
had ten verses, and which she wrote for a school com-
position.   It seemed to her a fine expression of sturdy
Boer patriotism, however misguided.
    " I can see their point of view," she said to herself,
righteously, and pleased with the phrase.   " Most
people " (which meant, it need scarcely be said, most of
the other girls at school) " can't see it, but I can.
They're beastly, and I'm glad they're beaten, but I
see their point of view."   She said so to some other
little girls in the Third Remove.   But the other little
girls, who didn't see the Boers' point of view, said,
" Oh !   Are you a pro-Boer ?   I say, Imogen Carrington's a pro-Boer."
    " Your uncle was ducked in Trafalgar Square, wasn't
he," said some one else, curiously but not unkindly,

and in the diffident voice suitable to family scandals, "for being a pro-Boer. Do you think the same as him?"

Imogen, blushing, disclaimed this.

"Daddy and mother think uncle Maurice awfully wrong, and so do I. He's a *real* pro-Boer."

"Well, what are you? Are you only shamming pro-Boer?"

"I'm not a pro-Boer at all. I'm pro-us. I only said I could see their point of view. . . ."

"Oh, you do talk tosh. Point of view. No one but grown-up people uses words like that. Imogen's getting awfully cocky now Miss Cradock always says her compositions are good. Come and play tig."

And, since little girls at school are very seldom unkind, they included Imogen in the game and bore no malice.

Irving was no pro-Boer. He wrote home, in the autumn of 1900, "We're getting on, but we've not near finished with brother Boer yet. Maurice is talking through his hat, as usual. Any fool out here knows that if we're to suck any advantage out of this war (and there's no small advantage to be sucked, I can tell you) we've got to *win* it. Those Radical gas-bags at home don't know the first thing about it."

It is an eternal and familiar dispute, and which side one takes in it really seems to depend more on temperament than on the amount one knows about it.

31

END OF VICTORIANISM

THE nineteenth century did actually end at last. Probably every one over twelve and under seventy sat up to see it out, to see the twentieth in, to catch that elusive, dramatic moment and savour it.

The twentieth century. Imogen, when she woke on New Year's Day, could scarcely believe it. It was perhaps, she thought, a drunken dream. For the Carringtons, like all right-thinking persons, always kept Hogmanay in punch. But the twentieth century it was, and a clear frosty morning. Imogen shouted to Nancy, lying in intoxicated slumbers in the other bed, " Happy new century," lest Nancy should say it first, then looked at the new century out of the window. What a jolly century it looked ; what a jolly century it was going to be ! A hundred happy years. At the end of it she would be 112. A snowy-haired but still active old lady, living in a white house on a South Sea island, bathing every morning (but not too early), and then getting back into bed and eating her breakfast of mangoes, bread-fruit, delicious home-grown coffee, and honey. Then a little roller skating on the shining parquet floor of the hall ; a lovely hall, hung with the trophies of her bow—reindeer, sand-bok, polar bear, grizzly, lion, tiger, cheetah, wombat and wolf. No birds. Shooting birds was no fun. Imogen knew, for she had shot her first and only sparrow last week, with her new catapult. The boys had been delighted, but she had nearly cried. It had been beastly. Hereafter she meant only to use the catapult on cows, brothers and sisters, and still life. That old lady of the year 2000 should only have one bird to her score.

The question was, what to do till getting-up time.
Wake Nancy—but this was next to impossible. Nancy
was a remarkably fast sleeper. One might go and try
to wake the boys, and get them to come out catapult-
ing in the garden, or roller skating in the square. Or
one might snuggle down in bed again and read *Treasure
Island*. Or not read, but lie and think about the new
century; perhaps make a poem about it. Imogen
extracted from the pocket of her frock, that hung on
a chair, a stubby pencil, a notebook, and a stick of
barley sugar. With these she curled up among the
bedclothes. Happily she sucked and pondered. Holidays; breakfast time not for ages; Christmas presents
with the gloss still on (among them a pair of roller
skates, *Brassey's Naval Annual*, and a new bow and
arrows), and a brand new century to explore. Sing
joy, sing joy.

"Roland lay in his bunk," murmured Imogen,
drowsily, "and heard the prow of the ship grinding
through icefloes as she pursued her way. Eight bells
sounded. With a hideous shock he remembered the
events of last night. He put his hand to his head; it
was caked with dried blood where the pirates had
struck him with the crow-bar. A faint moan of
anguish was wrung from his white lips. . . ."

Roland was Imogen, and his adventures had mean-
dered on in serial form in her mind for several months.
She had always, ever since she remembered, imperson-
ated some boy or youth as she went about. "Lithe
as a panther," she would murmur within herself, as
she climbed a tree, "Wilfred swarmed up the bare
trunk. He scanned the horizon. In the distance he
saw a puff of smoke, and heard, far away, faint shrieks.
'Indians,' he said, 'at their howwid work. The question for me is, can I warn the settlers in time? If
the Redskins catch me, I shall wish I had never

been born. No; I will escape now and save my-self.'"

It was characteristic of Wilfred, or Roland, or Dennis, or whatever he was at the moment called, that he usually did a cowardly thing at first, then repented and acted like a hero, suffering thereby both the condemnation of his friends for his cowardice and the tortures of his foes for his courage. He was a rather morbid youth, who enjoyed repentance and heroic amendment; no simple, stalwart soul. Usually he was in the navy.

Thus, in idle, barley-sugared dreamings, this representative of the young generation began the new century.

"What," mused her grandfather, watching from his bed the winter morning grow, "will the new age be?"

"Much like the old ages, I shouldn't wonder," Mrs. Garden murmured, drowsily. "People and things stay much the same . . . much the same. . . ."

"The eternal wheel," papa speculated, still adhering to his latest faith, but with a note of question. "The eternal, turning wheel. I wonder . . ."

But what mamma wondered, catching the familiar note of doubt in his voice, was where the eternal, turning wheel would next land papa.

"What a world we'll make it, won't we, my son and daughter," Stanley hopefully exclaimed to her children as they rioted about her room. "What a century we'll have! It belongs to the people of your age, you know. You've got to see it's a good one. . . . Now take yourselves off and let me get up. Run and turn on the cold tap for me, and put the warm at a trickle."

Stanley whistled as she dressed.

"Yet another century," her sister Rome commented, with languid amusement, as her early tea was brought to her. "How many we have, to be sure! I wonder if, perhaps, it is not even too many?"

"*Maurice,*" shrilly called Maurice's wife, entering his room at nine o'clock. " Well, I declare ! "

Maurice lay heavily sleeping, and whisky exhaled from his breath. He had come home at three o'clock this morning.

"A nice way to begin the new year," said Amy ; she did not say " new century," because she was of those who could not see but that the century had been new in 1900. She shook her husband's shoulder, looking down with distaste at his thin, sharp-featured, sleeping face, its usual pallor heavily flushed.

"A nice example to the children. And you always writing rubbish about social reform. . . . You make me sick."

" Go away," said Maurice, half opening hot eyes. " Le' me alone. My head's bad. . . ."

" So I should imagine," said Amy. " I'm sick and tired of you, Maurice."

" Go away, then. Right away. We'd both be happier. Why don't you ? "

" Oh, I dare say I'm old-fashioned," said Amy. " I was brought up to think a wife's place was with her husband. Of course, I'm probably *wrong*. I'm always surprised *you* don't leave *me*, feeling as you do."

Maurice, waking a little more, surveyed her with morose, heavy, aching eyes, and moistened his dry lips.

" You're not surprised. You know it's because of the children. It's my job to see they grow up decently, with decent ideas and a chance."

At that Amy's mirth overcame her.

" Decent ideas ! You're a nice educator of children, aren't you ? *Look* at yourself lying there. . . ."

She pointed to the looking-glass opposite his bed.

" Get out, please," said Maurice, coldly. " I've got to write my leader."

Meanwhile, the most august representative of the Victorian age wavered wearily between her own century and this strange new one, peering blindly down the coming road as into a grave. It did not belong to her, the new century. She had had her day. A few days of the new young era, and she would slip into the night, giving place to the rough young forces knocking at the door.

The great Victorian century was dead.

DISCURSIVE

THE Edwardians were, as we now think, a brief generation to themselves, set between Victorianism and neo-
Georgianism (it is a pity that we should have no better
name for the present reign, for " Georgian " belongs
by right to a period quite other, royalty having ever
been sadly unimaginative in its choice of Christian
names). Set between the nineteenth century and the
full swing of the twentieth, those brief ten years we
call Edwardian seem now like a short spring day.
They were a gay and yet an earnest time. A time of
social reform on the one hand, and social brilliance on
the other. The hey-day at once of intellectual Fabianism and of extravagant dissipation. The hour of the
repertory theatres, the Irish players, Bernard Shaw
and Granville Barker at the Court, Miss Horniman in
the provinces, absurd musical comedies that bloomed
like gay flowers of a day and died. The onrush of
motor-cars and the decline of bicycles and the horse ;
extravagant country house parties at which royalty
consented to be entertained, with royal bonhomie and
royal exactions of etiquette. . . . " Mr. Blank, have we
not seen that suit rather often before ? " " Lady Dash,
surely we remember this wall-paper. . . ." " Lord
Somebody, this is a very abominable dinner. . . ."
What standards to live up to ! There was nothing
dowdy about our King Edward. He set the stakes
high, and all who could afford it played. Pageants
and processions passed in regal splendour. Money

nobly flowed. Ideals changed. The sanctity and domesticity of the Heim was no more a royal fetish. " Respectability," that good old word, degraded and ill-used for so long, sank into discredit, sank lower in the social scale. No more were unfortunate ladies who had had marital troubles coldly banned from court, for a larger charity (except as to suits, dinners, and wall-papers) obtained. Victorian sternness, Victorian prudery and intolerance, still prevailed among some of the older aristocracy, among many of the smaller squirearchy, the professional classes, and the petty *bourgeoisie* ; but among most of the wealthy, most of the titled, most of the gay and extravagant classes, a wider liberty grew.

In the intervals of social pleasures, Edward the Peacemaker was busy about the Balance of Power in Europe. He did not care about his cousin Wilhelm. He made an Entente with France, and came to an understanding with Russia, so that when the Trouble should come—and experienced royalty knows that, from time to time, the Trouble is bound to come—we should not meet it singly. The weak point about ententes is that when the Trouble comes to one's fellow-members, they do not meet it singly either. Considering this, and considering also the annoyance and alarm they inspire in those not in them, and taking them all round, ententes seem, on the whole, a pity. But at the time English people were pleased with this one, and Edward was hopefully called the Peacemaker, just as Victoria had been called Good, and Elizabeth Virgin, and Mary Bloody. We love to name our royalties, and we much prefer to name them kindly. Mary must have been, and doubtless was, very bloody indeed before her people bestowed on her that opprobrious title. Other sovereigns—most other sovereigns—have been pretty bloody too, but none of them bloody enough to be so called.

A queer time ! Perhaps a transition time ; for that matter, this is one of the things times always are. The world of fashion, led by an elderly royal gentleman bred at the Victorian court of his mother, and retaining queer Victorian traditions that younger gentlemen and ladies did not observe. King Edward, for instance, observed Sunday with some strictness. He thought it right ; he felt it should be done. The British Sunday was an institution, and King Edward was all for institutions. A generation was growing up, had already grown up, who did not understand about Sunday in that sense. But you may observe about elderly Victorian persons that, however loosely they may sit to Sunday, they usually have a sense of it. They play or work on it consciously, with a feeling that they are breaking a foolish rule, possibly offending an imaginary public opinion. They seldom quite realise that the rule and the opinion they are thinking of are nearly obsolete. They seldom regard Sunday (with reference to the occupations practised on it) precisely as if it were a weekday. Institutions die hard. They linger long after their informing spirit has died.

Anyhow, King Edward VII. was a Victorian gentleman long before he was an Edwardian. So he observed Sunday and the lesser proprieties, without self-consciousness. He was like his mother, with a difference. Both had a sense of royal dignity and of the Proper Thing. His subjects, too, had a sense of the Proper Thing ; people always have. But the Proper Thing, revered as ever, gradually changed its face, or rather turned a somersault and alighted on its head.

Well, the Edwardians, like the Elizabethans, the Jacobeans, the Carolines, the Georgians, the Victorians,

and the neo-Georgians, were a mixed lot. This attempt
to class them, to stigmatise them with adjectives, is
unscientific, sentimental, and wildly incorrect. But,
because it is rather more interesting than to admit
frankly that they were merely a set of individuals, it
will always be done.

2

VIVE LE ROI

LA reine est morte. Vive le roi. King Edward was
proclaimed by heralds, by trumpeters, and with the
rolling of drums ; and God Save the King. Then they
buried the late queen with royal pomp, and kings,
emperors, archdukes, and crown princes rode with her
to the tomb.

King Edward opened Parliament in state. A great
king he was for pageantry and for state. He read the
Accession Declaration. It was a tactlessly worded
declaration in some ways, for it was drawn up in days
when Roman Catholicism was not well thought of by
the Head of the Church and Defender of the Faith,
King Edward did not like reading it, " His Majesty,"
wrote the outraged Catholic Press, " would willingly
have been relieved from the necessity of branding with
contumelious epithets the religious tenets of any of
his subjects." There were protests, not only from
Roman Catholics, but from protestants and agnostics,
who both, in the main, thought it rude. But some there
were who, though they knew it was rude, knew also
that it was right to be rude to Roman Catholics. " They
are the king's subjects as much as others, and belong
to a distinguished old church," the protesters declared.
" The thing is an antediluvian piece of ill-breeding."

" Bloody Mary. The Inquisition. No Popery," was the crude reply. "And are not Roman Catholics always rude to our religion ? Why, then, should we not be rude to theirs ? "

" Roman Catholics," replied the more polite and sophisticated, " cannot help being a little rude—if you call it so—to other faiths. They are not to blame. It is an article of their faith that theirs is the only true and good church. There is no such article in other faiths. We are not obliged by our religion to believe them wrong, as they are, unfortunately, obliged to believe us wrong. Obviously, then, we should practise the courtesy forbidden to them. It is more generous and more dignified. Also, they are as good as we are. All religions are doubtless, in the main, inaccurate, and one does not differ appreciably from another. And His Majesty ought to preserve a strict impartiality concerning the many and various faiths of his people. The Declaration is ignorant, unstatemanlike, and obscurantist, and smacks of vulgar seventeenth century Protestantism. It is a worse scandal than the Thirty-nine Articles."

But " No Popery " was still the cry of the noisy few, and the scandal remained. Reluctantly protesting his firm intention to give no countenance to the religion of some millions of his subjects, and solemnly in the presence of God professing, testifying, and declaring that he did make this declaration on the plaine and ordinary sense of the words as they were commonly understood by English Protestants, without any evasion, equivocation, or mentall reservation whatso-ever, and without any dispensation from the Pope, either already granted or to be sought later, the King opened his khaki-elected Parliament, which proved as ineffective as parliaments always do. It is of no importance which side is in office in Parliament ; any

study of the subject must convince the earnest student
that all parties are about equally stupid. By some
fluke, useful Acts may from time to time get passed by
any Government that happens to be in power. More
often, foolish and injurious Acts get passed. Personality and intelligence in ministers do certainly make
some difference ; but party, it seems, makes none.
The stupid, the inert, the dishonest, and the ill-in-
tentioned flourish like bay trees impartially on both
sides of the avenue. Only the very *naïf* can believe
that party matters, in the long run. This first Parliament of the twentieth century proved, perhaps, even
more than usually inept, as parliaments elected during
war excitement are apt to be. It could deal neither
with education, defences, labour, finance, or poisoned
beer.

3

PAPA'S NEW FAITH

THE war scrambled on : a tedious, ineffective guerrilla
business. The Concentration Camp trouble began, and
over its rights and wrongs England was split.

Mr. Garden hated the thought of these camps, where
Boer women and children, driven from their homes,
dwelt in discomfort (so said Miss Emily Hobhouse and
others), and fell ill and died. They might be, as their
defenders maintained, kindly meant, but it was all
very disagreeable. In fact, the whole war preyed on
papa's mind and nerves. More and more it seemed to
him a hideous defiance of any possible Christian order
of society, a thing wholly outside the sphere of God's
scheme for the world. But, then, of course, nearly
everything was that, and always had been. So
utterly outside that sphere were most of the world's

happenings that it sometimes seemed to papa as if they could scarcely *be* happenings, as if they must be evil illusions of our own, outside the great Reality. The more papa brooded over this Reality, the more he became persuaded that it must be absolute and all pervasive, that nothing else really existed. " We make evil by our thought," said papa. " God knows no evil. . . . God does not know about the war. Nor about the Concentration Camps. . . ."

It will be seen that papa was ripe for the acceptance of a new creed which had recently come across the Atlantic and was becoming fashionable in this country. Christian Science fastened on papa like a mosquito, and bit him hard. It comforted him very much to think that God did not know about the war. He told his grandchildren about this ignorance on the part of the Deity. Imogen pondered it. She had a meta-physical and inquiring mind, and was always interested in God.

" What *does* God think all those soldiers are doing out in Africa, grandpapa ? " she asked, after a considering pause. " Or doesn't he know they're soldiers ? "

" He knows they are unhappy people following an evil illusion, my child," her grandpapa told her. " You see, there is no war really—not on God's plane. There couldn't be."

Imogen pondered it again, corrugating her forehead. She dearly liked to understand things.

" Will God know about the peace, when it comes ? "

" He will know his children have stopped imagining the evil of war. And he will be very glad."

" Doesn't he know about the soldiers who are killed ? What does he think they've died of ? "

" He knows they are slain by their evil imaginings and those of their enemies. You see, God knows his children *believe* themselves to be at war, and that as long as they go on believing it they will hurt each other and themselves."

It seemed to Imogen that, in that case, God knew all that was really necessary about the war.

"Are you the only person, besides God, who doesn't believe in the war, grandpapa ? " she presently inquired.

" No, my child. There are others. . . . Perhaps one day, when you are older, you will understand more about it, and try to think all evil and all pain out of existence."

" P'raps." Imogen was dubious. She did not quite get the idea. " Of course, I'd *like* it, grandpapa, because then I shouldn't get hurt any more." She rubbed the back of her head, on to which she had fallen that afternoon while roller skating round the square. Her grandfather had told her God didn't know she had fallen and hurt herself, and, in fact, that she was not really hurt at all. God didn't know a great deal about roller skates, Imogen concluded, if he didn't know that people who used them very frequently did fall. But perhaps he didn't know there were any roller skates ; perhaps roller skates were another evil illusion of ours, like the war. Not a bad illusion ; one we had better keep, bruises and all. But perhaps, thought Imogen, who liked to think things out thoroughly, it was really that God didn't know that the contact of the human head with another hard substance caused pain. After all, people who have never tried *don't* know that. Babies don't. . . .

Imogen began to be afraid she was blaspheming. She put the problem later to her mother, but Vicky was less interested than her youngest daughter in meta-physical problems, and merely said, " Oh, Jennie darling, you needn't puzzle your head about what grandpapa tells you. Things that suit learned old gentlemen like him don't always do for little girls like you. Anyhow, don't ever you get thinking that it won't hurt you when you tumble on your head, because it always will. *You'll* never get rid of that illusion, you may be sure. What *you've* got to learn is not to be so careless, and not to spend all your time climbing and racketing about. So long as you'll do that, you'll get tumbles, and they'll hurt, and don't you forget it."

Imogen sighed a little. Her mother was so practical. You asked her for doctrine and she gave you advice. Being married, and particularly being a mother, often makes women like that. They know that doctrine is no use, and cherish the illusion that advice is.

"Papa is very happy in this new no-evil religion of his," mamma said to Rome. "It suits him very well. Better than theosophy did, I think."

Papa's new religion might, from her placid, casual, considering tone, have been a new suit of clothes.

Papa's daughter-in-law, Amy, screamed with mirth over it. Christian Science seemed to her an excellent joke.

"Oh, you're not really hurt," she would say if her daughter Iris came in from hockey with a black eye. "It's all an illusion! What do you want embrocation for? I'll tell your grandpapa of you. . . ."

"Christian Science," Maurice said to her at last, gloomily contemptuous, "is not much more absurd than other religions. Suppose you were to take another for your hourly jokes to-day, just for the sake of a change. It makes no difference which; you don't begin to understand any of them, and you can, no doubt, get a good laugh out of them all, if you try."

Amy said, "There you go, as usual! I suppose you'll be saying *you're* a Christian Science crank next. Anyway, I don't know what you want to speak to me in that way for, just because I like a little fun."

"I don't want to speak to you in any way," replied Maurice.

4

ON EDUCATION

STANLEY, turning forty this year, was sturdier than of old, softer and broader of face, blunt-nosed, chubby, maternal, her deep blue eyes more ardent and intent. Now that her children, who were ten and eight, both went to day schools, she had taken up her old jobs, and was working for Women's Trades' Unions, going every day to an office, sitting on committees, speaking on platforms. Phases come and phases go, and particularly with Stanley, who inherited much from her papa. Stanley was in these days a stop-the-war, pacificist Little Englander, anti-militarist, anti-Chamberlain, anti-Concentration Camp. She would shortly be a Fabian, but had not quite got there yet. She was, of course, a suffragist, but suffragists in 1901 were still a very forlorn outpost ; they were considered crankish and unpractical dreamers. She also spoke and wrote on Prison Reform, Democratic Education, Divorce Reform, Clean Milk, and Health Food. She was an admirer of Mr. Eustace Miles's views on food, Mr. G. B. Shaw's drama and social ethics, Mr. G. K. Chesterton's romantic Christianity, and no one's political opinions. She believed in the future of the world, which was to be splendidly managed by the children now growing up, who were to be splendidly educated for that purpose.

" But how improbable," Rome mildly expostulated, " that they should manage it any better or any worse than every one else has. Your maternal pride carries you away, my dear. Parents can never be clear-sighted ; often have I observed it. Blessed, as the Bible says somewhere, are the barren and they that have not brought forth, for they are the only people with any chance of looking at the world with clear and detached eyes. And even they haven't much. . . . But why do you think the present young will do so unusually well with the future ? "

" Of course," Stanley replied, " they won't do it of themselves. Only so far as they are educated up to it."

" Well, I can't see that educational methods are improving noticeably. Obviously, democratic education is not at present to be encouraged by our governing classes. Look at the Cockerton case. . . ."

" It will come," said Stanley. " This new bill won't go far, but it will do something. Meanwhile, those parents who have thought it out at all are doing rather better by their children than parents used to do. At least we can tell them the truth."

" So far as you see it yourselves. Is that, in most cases, saying much ? "

" No ; very little. But—to take a trivial thing— we can, at least, for instance, tell them the truth about such things as the birth of life. That's something. Billy and Molly already know as much as they need about that."

" Well, they don't actually need very much yet, do they ? I'm sure it won't hurt them to know anything of that sort, but I don't see exactly how it's going to help them to manage the world any better. Because, when the time for doing that comes, they'll know about the birth of life in any case. Boys always seem to pick it up at school, whatever else they don't learn. However, I admit that I think you bring up Billy and Molly very well."

" It's facing facts," said Stanley, " that I want to teach them. The art of not being afraid of life. They've go to do their share in cleaning up the world, and before they can do that they've got to face it squarely. One wants to do away with muffling things up, whatever they are. That's why I tell them everything they ask, so far as I know it, and a lot they don't. The knowledge doesn't matter either way, but the atmosphere of daylight does. I want them to feel there are no facts that can't be talked about."

"But, my dear, what a social training! Because, you know, there *are*. Anyhow, in drawing-rooms, and places where they chat."

"They'll learn all that soon enough," Stanley placidly said. "The world is as vulgar as it is mainly because of its prudery. I'm giving my children weapons against that."

She had given them also a weapon against their cousins, the children of Vicky, who had not been told Facts. Anyhow, Imogen hadn't. Her sisters were older, and boys, as Rome had said, do seem to pick things up at school. But Imogen at thirteen was still in the ignorance thought by Vicky suitable to her years. So, when she exasperated her cousin Billy by her superior proficiency in climbing, running, gymnastics, and all active games—a proficiency natural to her three years' seniority, but growing tiresome during a whole afternoon spent in trials of skill—Billy could at least retort, "I know something you don't. I know how babies come."

"Don't care how they come," Imogen returned, astride on a higher bough of the aspen tree than her cousin could attain to. "They're no use anyhow, the little fools. Who wants babies?"

Billy, having meditated on this unanswerable question, amended his vaunt. "Well, I know how puppies come, too. So there."

Imogen was stumped. You can't say that puppies are no use. She could think of no retort but the ancient one of sex insult.

" Boys are always bothering about stupid things like how babies come. As if it mattered. *I'd* rather know the displacement and horsepower and knots of all the battleships and first-class cruisers."

" You don't."

" I do."

" Bet you a bulls-eye you don't."

" Done. A pink one. Ask any one you like."

" Well, what's the *Terrible* ? "

" 14,200 tons ; 25,000 horsepower ; 22.4 knots. That's an easy one."

" The *Powerful.*"

" Same, of course. No, she only makes 22.1 knots. Stupid to ask me twins."

Billy considered. He did not like to own it, but he could not remember at the moment any other ships of His Majesty's fleet.

" Well, what's the biggest, anyhow ? "

" The *Dominion* and the *King Edward VII.* 16,350 tons ; 18,000 horsepower ; 18.5 knots."

" I don't know that any of that's true."

" You can look in Brassey and find out, then."

" I don't care. Any one can mug up Brassey. Anyhow, girls can't go into the navy."

Imogen jogged up and down on the light swinging branch, whistling through her teeth, pretending not to hear.

"And anyhow," added the taunter below, "*you'd* be no use on a ship, 'cause you'd be sick."

" I wouldn't."

" You would "

" I wouldn't."

" You would."

" You're sick yourself if you smoke a woodbine."

" So are you. *You're* sick if you squash a fly. Girls are. They can't dissect a rabbit. I can."

The sex war was in full swing.

" Boys crib at their lessons. Boys don't wash their necks."

" Nor do girls. You're dirty now. Girls don't play footer at school."

" Hockey's as good. Boys are greedy pigs; they spend their pennies on tuck."

" Who bought eight bulls-eyes this afternoon and sucked six ? "

" Oh, well." Imogen collapsed into sudden good temper. " Don't let's rot. Why did the gooseberry fool ? "

To change the subject further, she swung herself backwards and hung from the branch by her knees, her short mop of curls swinging upside down, the blood singing in her head. Billy, a nice but not very clever little boy, said, " Because the raspberry syrup," and truce was signed. Who, as Imogen had asked, cared how babies came ?

5

PING-PONG

EVERYWHERE people ping-ponged. One would have thought there was no war on. Instead of doing their bits, as we did in a more recent and a more serious war, they all ping-ponged, and, when not ping-ponging, asked, " Why did the razor-bill raise her bill ? Why did the coal scuttle ? What did Anthony Hope ? " And answered, " Because the woodpecker would peck her. Because the table had cedar legs. To see the salad dressing," and anything else of that kind they could think of. Some people, mostly elderly people, could only answer vaguely to everything, " Because the razor-bill razor-bill," and change the subject, thinking how stupid riddles in these days were. Some people excelled at riddles, others at ping-pong, others again at pit, which meant shouting, "oats, oats, oats," or something similar, until they were hoarse. No one would have thought there was a war on.

Indeed, there scarcely was a war on, now. Not a war to matter. Only rounding up, and blockhouses, and cordons, and guerrilla fighting. Irving Garden had had enteric, and was invalided home. He meant to return to South Africa directly peace should be signed, to investigate a good thing he had heard of in the Rand. His nephews and nieces, with whom he was always popular, worshipped at his shrine. He had wonderfully funny stories of the war to tell them. But he preferred to ask them such questions as, "What made Charing Cross?" and to supply them with such answers as "Teaching London Bridge. Am I right?" Such questions, such answers, they found so funny as to be almost painful. Imogen and Tony would giggle until tears came into their eyes. Certainly uncle Irving was amusing. And clever. He drove himself and other people about in a gray car that travelled like the wind and was cursed like the devil by pedestrians and horse drivers on the roads. His brother Maurice cursed him, but good-temperedly, for he liked Irving, and, further, he despised the unenterprising Public for fools. That was why no section of the community gave Maurice and his paper their entire confidence; he attacked what he and those who agreed with him held for evils, but would round, with a contemptuous gesture, on those whose grievances he voiced. He ridiculed the present inefficiency, and ridiculed also the ideals of those who cried for improvement. He threw himself into the struggle for educational reform, and sneered at all reforms proposed as inadequate, pedestrian or absurd. He condemned employers as greedy and Trades Unions as retrograde. He jeered at the inefficiency of the conduct of what remained of the war, at the stupid brutality of concentration camps, at the sentimentality of the pro-Boer party (as they were still called), at the militarism of the Tory militants, the imperialism of the Liberals, and the sentimental radical humanitarianism of Mr. Lloyd George and his party. He addressed stop-the-war meetings until they were broken up with violence by earnest representatives of the continue-the-war party, and suffered much physical damage in the ensuing conflicts ; yet the stop-the-war party did not really trust him. They suspected him of desiring, though without hope, to stop not only the war, but all human activities, and, indeed, the very universe itself ; and this is to go further than is generally approved. The continue-the-war party has risen and fallen with every war ; but the continue-the-world party has a kind of solid permanency, and something of the universal in its ideals. Not to be of it is to be out of sympathy with the great majority of one's fellows. At any time and in any country, but perhaps particularly in England in the early years of the twentieth century, when there was a good deal of enthusiasm for continuance and progress. The early Edwardians were not, as we are to-day, dispirited and discouraged with the course of the world, though they were vexed about the Boer war and the consequent economic depression of the country. They did not, for the most part, feel that life was a bad business and the future outlook too dark and menacing to be worth encouraging. On the contrary, they believed in Life with a large L. The young were bitten by the dry, reforming zeal of Mr. and Mrs. Sidney Webb, or the gay faith in life of Mr. G. K. Chesterton, or the bounding scientific hopefulness of

Mr. H. G. Wells, or the sharp social and ethical criticism of Mr. George Bernard Shaw.

Stanley Croft, young for ever in mind, was bitten by all these and much more. Imperialism left slain behind, she embraced with ardour the fantastic ideal of the cleaning up of England. After the war then; indeed they would proceed furiously with the building of Jerusalem in England's green and pleasant land.

And meanwhile the war went on, and times were bad, and everywhere people ping-ponged. A lack of seriousness was complained of. It always is complained of in this country, which is not, indeed, a very serious one, but always contains some serious persons to complain of the others. "The ping-pong spirit," the graver Press called the national lightness; and clergymen took up the phrase and preached about it.

The public, they said, were like street gamins, loafing about on the watch for any new distraction.

6

GAMIN

IMOGEN and Tony slipped out into the street. It was the first Sunday of the summer holidays, and the first day of August. The sun beat hotly on the asphalt, making it soft, so that one could dent it with one's heels. The children sauntered down Sloane Street, loitering at the closed shop windows, clinking their shillings in their pockets. They enjoyed the streets with the zest of street Arabs. They were a happy and untidy pair; the girl in a short butcher-blue cotton frock, grubby with a week's wear, a hole in the knee of one black-stockinged leg, a soiled white linen cricket hat slouched over her short mop of brown curls, her small, pink face freckled and tanned ; the boy, a year younger, grimy, dark-eyed and beautiful, like his uncle Irving in face, clad in a gray flannel knicker-bocker suit. Neither had dressed for the street in the way that they should have ; they had slipped out, unseen, in their garden clothes and garden grime, to make the most of the last day before they went away for the holidays.

They knew what they meant to do. They were going to have their money's worth, and far more than their money's worth, of underground travelling. Round and round and round, and all for a penny fare. . . . This was a favourite occupation of theirs, a secret, morbid vice. They indulged in it at least twice every holidays. The whole family had been used to do it, but all but these two had now outgrown it. Phyllis, now at Girton, had outgrown it long ago. "The twopenny tube for me," she said. "It's cleaner." "But it doesn't go *round*," said Imogen. "Who wants to go round, you little donkey ? It takes you where you want to get to ; that's the object of a train." It was obvious that Phyllis had grown up. She would not even track people in the streets now. It must happen, soon or late, to all of us. Even Hughie, fifteen and at Rugby, found this underground game rather weak.

But Imogen and Tony still sneaked out, a little shamefaced and secretive, to practise their vice.

Sloane Square. Two penny fares. Down the stairs, into the delicious, romantic, cool valley. The train thundered in, Inner Circle its style. A half empty compartment ; there was small run on the underground this lovely August Sunday. Into it dashed the children ; they had a corner seat each, next the open door. They bumped up and down on the seats, opposite each other. The train speeded off, rushing like a mighty wind. South Kensington station. More people coming in, getting out. Off again. Gloucester Road, High Street, Notting Hill Gate, Queen's Road. . . . The penny fare was well over. Still they travelled, and jogged up and down on the straw seats, and chanted softly, monotonously, so that they could scarcely be heard above the roaring of the train.

> " Sand-strewn caverns, cool and deep,
> Where the winds are all asleep ;
> Where the spent lights quiver and gleam,
> Where the salt weed sways in the stream,
> Where the sea-beasts, ranged all round,
> Feed in the ooze of their pasture-ground ;
> Where the sea-snakes coil and twine,
> Dry their mail and bask in the brine ;
> Where great whales come sailing by,
> Sail and sail with unshut eye,
> Round the world for ever and aye,
> ROUND THE WORLD FOR EVER AND
> AYE. . . ."

Then again,

> " Sand-strewn caverns cool and deep. . . ."

At Paddington they saw the conductor eyeing them, and changed their compartment. This should be done from time to time.

And so on, past King's Cross and Farringdon Street, towards the wild, romantic stations of the east : Liverpool Street, Aldgate, and so round the bend, sweeping west like the sun. Blackfriars, Temple, Charing Cross, Westminster, St. James's Park, Victoria, SLOANE SQUARE. Oh, joy ! Sing for the circle completed, the new circle begun.

" Where great whales come sailing by,
    Sail and sail with unshut eye,
    Round the world for ever and aye.
    ROUND THE WORLD FOR EVER AND
        AYE. . . ."

Imogen changed her chant, and dreamily crooned :

" The world is round, so travellers tell,
        And straight though reach the track ;
    Trudge on, trudge on, 'twill all be well,
        The way will guide one back.
    But ere the circle homeward hies
        Far, far must it remove :
    White in the moon the long road lies
        That leads me from my love."

Round the merry world again. Put a girdle round
the earth in forty minutes. Round and round and
round. What a pennyworth ! You can't buy much
on an English Sunday, but if you can buy eternal
travel, Sunday is justified.

But two inner circles and a bit are really enough. If
you had three whole ones you might begin to feel bored,
or even sick. Sloane Square again : the second circle
completed. South Kensington. The two globe-trotters
emerged from their circling, handed in their penny
tickets, reached the upper air, hot and elated.

Now what ? For a moment they loitered at the
station exit, debating in expert minds the next move.
Money was short ; no luxurious joys could be considered.

Imogen suddenly gripped Tony by the arm.

" Hist, Watson. You see that man in front ? "

Watson, well-trained, nodded.

" We're going to track him. I have a very shrewd
suspicion that he is connected with the Sloane Square

murder mystery. Now mind, we must keep ten paces behind him wherever he goes ; not less, or he'll notice. Like the woman in Church Street did. He's off ; come on. . . . Do you observe anything peculiar about him, Watson ? "

" He's a jolly lean old bird. I expect he's hungry."

" My good Watson, look at his clothes. They're a jolly sight better than ours. He's a millionaire, as it happens. If you want to know a few facts about him, I'll tell you. He moved his washstand this morning from the left side of his bed to the right ; he forgot to wind up his watch last night ; he went to church before breakfast ; he had kidneys when he came in ; and he's now on his way to meet a confederate at lunch."

" Piffle. You can't prove any of it."

" I certainly can, my good Watson. . . ."

" Golly, he's calling a hansom. Shall we hang on behind ? "

Watson's beautiful brown eyes beamed with hope ; Holmes's small green gray ones held for a moment an answering gleam. But only for a moment. Holmes knew by now, having learnt from much sad experience, what adventures could be profitably undertaken and what couldn't.

" No use. We'd be pulled off at once. . . ."

Morosely they watched their victim escape.

Then, " Look, Watson. The fat lady in purple. She must have been to church. . . . Oh, quite simple, Watson, I assure you ; she has a prayer book. . . . Come on. It won't matter how late we get back, because they're having a lunch party and we're feeding in the schoolroom. We'll sleuth her to hell."

In this manner Sunday morning passed very pleasantly and profitably for Vicky's two youngest children.

7

AUTUMN, 1901

1901 drew to its close. An odd, restless, gay, unhappy
year, sad with war and poverty, bitter with quarrels
about inefficiency, concentration camps, Ahmednagar
(the home of the Boers in India, and a name much
thrown about by the pro-Boers in their " ignorant
and perverse outcry "), education, religion, finance,
politics, prisons, motor-cars, and stopping the war ;
gay with new drama (Mr. Bernard Shaw was being
produced, and many musical comedies), new art (at
the New English Art Club), new jokes, new books
(Mr. Conrad had published *Lord Jim*, Mr. Henry James
The Sacred Fount, Mr. Hardy *Poems New and Old*,
Mr. Wells *Love and Mr. Lewisham*, Mr. Yeats *The
Shadowy Waters*, Mr. Chesterton *The Wild Knight*,
Mr. Kipling *Kim*, Mr. Belloc *The Path to Rome*,
Lady Russell *The Benefactress*, Mr. Laurence Hous-
man *A Modern Antæus*, Mr. Anthony Hope *Tristram
of Blent*, Mrs. Humphry Ward *Eleanor*, Mr. Arnold
Bennett *The Grand Babylon Hotel*, Mr. Charles Mar-
riott *The Column*, Mr. George Moore *Sister Teresa*,
Mr. Max Beerbohm *And Yet Again*), new clothes, and
new games.

Popular we were not. That prevalent disease,
Anglophobia, raged impartially in every country, except,
possibly, Japan. Even as far as the remote Bermudas,
continental slanders against us roared. We are a
maligned race ; there is no doubt of it. All races are,
in their degree, maligned, but none so greatly as we—
unless it should be the Children of Israel. It is sad to
think it, but there must be something about us that is
not attractive to foreigners, They have always grieved

at our triumphs and rejoiced at our sorrows. By the
end of 1901 our friendlessness was such (in November
Lord Salisbury said at the Guildhall, " It is a matter
for congratulation that we have found such a friendly
feeling and such a correct attitude on the part of all
the great powers,") that we thought we had better
enter into an alliance with the Japanese, who were
still pleased with us for admiring them about their war
with China.

In the autumn of this year, Stanley published her
small book, *Conditions of Women's Work*, and Mr.
Garden, after years of labour, his mighty work, *Comparative Religions*.

Mrs. Garden had influenza and pneumonia in December, and Mr. Garden, in an anguish of anxiety, called
in three doctors and admitted that his faith had failed.
God's disapproving ignorance of mamma's pneumonia
made intolerable a burden of anxiety which would
have been heavy even with divine sympathy ; and if,
by some awful chance, mamma were to pass on, papa's
grief, guilty and unrecognised, would have been too
bitter to be borne. Christian Science had had but a
brief day, but it was over. In a fit of reaction, papa
became an Evangelical, and took to profound meditation, on the suffering, human and divine, which he had
for so long ignored. He now found the love of God
in suffering, not in its absence.

Always honourable, he recanted the instructions on
the limitations of divine knowledge which he had given
to his grandchildren.

" You perhaps remember, Jennie my child, what I
said to you last year about God's not knowing of the
war. Well, I have come to the conclusion that I was
mistaken. I believe now that God knows all about
His children's griefs and pains. He knows more
about them than we do. Possibly—who knows—

suffering is a necessary part of the scheme of redemption. . . ."

Imogen looked and felt intelligent. When any one spoke of theology to her, is was as if the blood of all her clerical ancestors mounted to the call. She had recently become an agnostic, owing to having perused Renan and John Stuart Mill. She was at the stage in life when she read, with impartial ardour, such writers as these : Mrs. Nesbit's *Wouldbegoods*, Max Pemberton's *Iron Pirate*, and other juvenile works (particularly school stories), Rudyard Kipling, Marryat, the Brontës, and any poetry she could lay hands on, but especially that of W. B. Yeats, Robert Browning, Algernon Swinburne, William Morris, Lewis Carroll, and Walter Ramal.

She said to her grandfather, casually, but a little wistfully too, " I'm not sure, Grandpapa, that I believe in God at all. The arguments against him seem very strong, don't they ? "

Mr. Garden looked a little startled. Possibly he thought that Imogen was beginning too young.

"Ah, Jennie my child—' If my doubt's strong, my faith's still stronger. . . .' That's what Browning said about it, you know."

Imogen nodded.

" I know. I've read that. I s'pose his faith was. Mine isn't. My *doubt's* stronger, Grandpapa."

" Well, my child. . . ." Mr. Garden, gathering together his resources, gave this strayed lamb (that was how, in his new terminology he thought of her) a little evangelical homily on the love of God. Unfortunately Imogen had, then and through life, an intemperate distaste for evangelical language ; it made her feel shy and hot, and, though she loved her grandfather, she was further alienated from faith. She wrote a poem that evening about the dark, terrifying and

Godless world, which she found very good. She would
have liked to show it to others, that they, too, might
find it good, but the tradition of her family and her
school was that this wasn't done.   One wrote anything
one liked, if one suffered from that itch, but to show
it about was swank. " Making a donkey of yourself."
The Carringtons, shy, vain and reserved, did not care
to do that.

"Some day," thought Imogen, " I'll write *books*.
Then people can read them without my showing them.
I'll write a book full of poems."   The new poet.   Even
—might one dare to imagine it—the new *great* poet,
Imogen Carrington.   Or should one be anonymous ?
Anon.   That was a good old poet's name.

"Few people knew," said Imogen, within herself,
" that this slender book of verse, *Questionings*, bound
in green, with gold edges, which had made such a stir
in lit'ry London, was by a wiry, brown-faced, blue-eyed
young lieutenant-commander, composed while he navi-
gated his first-class gunboat, the *Thrush* (805 tons,
1200 h.p., 13 knots, 6 four-inch guns, 2 quick-firers,
2 machine), among the Pacific Islands, taking soundings.
The whole service knew Denis Carton as a brilliant
young officer, but only two or three—or perhaps a
dozen—knew he was a poet too and had written that
green book with gold edges that lay on every drawing-
room table, and was stacked by hundreds in every good
bookshop."   (I cannot account for the confused work-
ings of this poor child's mind ; I can only record the
fact that she still, and for many years to come, thought
of herself, with hope growing faint and ever fainter,
as a brown-skinned, blue-eyed, young naval man.)

As to her religious difficulties, they were, after the
first flush of unbelief, driven into the background of
her mind by school, hockey, the Christmas holidays,
and missing word competitions, and did not obtrude

themselves aggressively again until the time came when her mother decided that she should be confirmed. She then said to her brother Hugh, now in the fifth at Rugby : what did one do about confirmation if one believed Nothing ? Hugh did not think it mattered particularly what one believed. One was confirmed ; it did no harm ; it was done ; it saved argument. Himself, he believed very little of All That, but he had suffered confirmation, saying nothing. No good making fusses, and worrying mother. Jennie had much better go through with it, like other people.

" Well . . . of course *I* don't care . . . if it's not cheating. . . ."

" Course it isn't. Cheating who ? *They* don't care what we believe, they're not such sops. They only want us to do the ordinary things, like other people, and save bother. And, of course "—Hugh was a very fair-minded boy and no bigot—" there may be something in it, after all. Lots of people, quite brainy, sensible chaps, think there is. Anyhow, it can't hurt."

So Imogen was confirmed.

" Perhaps I shall be full of the Holy Ghost," she thought. " Perhaps there really *is* a Holy Ghost. Perhaps my life will be made all new, with tongues of fire upon my head and me telling in strange languages the wonderful works of God. . . . Perhaps . . . but more prob'ly not. . . ."

8

1902

1902 was a great year, for in it the British Empire ceased its tedious fighting with the Boer Republics, and made a meal of them. So the Empire was the richer by so many miles of Africa, with the gold mines, black persons, and sulky Dutchmen appertaining thereto, and the poorer by so many thousand soldiers' lives, so many million pounds, and a good deal of self-confidence and prestige. Anyhow, however you worked out the gain and loss, here was peace, and people shouted and danced for joy, and made bonfires in college courts. Thank God, *that* was over.

A wave of genial friendliness flowed from the warm, silly hearts of Britons towards the conquered foe. Four surly enemy generals were brought to London; asked if they would like to see the Naval Review; declined with grave thanks; were escorted through the streets amid a cheering populace. "Our friends, the enemy," cried the silly crowd, and "Brave soldiers all," and surrounded them with hearty British demonstration and appeals for "a message for England." There was no message for England; no smiles; no words. The warm, silly Britons were a little hurt. The psychology of conquered nations was a riddle to them, it seemed. . . . "God, what an exhibition!" said Maurice Garden in his paper next day.

Meanwhile King Edward VII. had, after some un-avoidable procrastination, been crowned, Mr. Horatio Bottomley had won a thousand pounds from the editor of the *Critic*, in that this editor had impugned his financial probity, and the Man with the Beflowered Buttonhole whose Besotted Pride had caused to flow for three years so much Gold and Tears and Blood (as they called him in the French Press) had received the Freedom of London for his services to his country. This year, also, Mr. Rudyard Kipling delighted athletes by his allusions to flannelled fools and muddied oafs, that ineffectual body the National Service League was formed, Germany and Great Britain began to eye each other's land and sea forces with an increase of hostile

emulation which was bound to end in sorrow, and there
was much trouble over bad trade and wages, unemployment, taxation, and the Education Bill. Passive
Resisters rose violently to the foray over this last,
their Puritan blood hot within them, and would not
pay rates for schools managed by the Church of England
in which their Nonconformist children were given
Church teaching. It made a pretty squabble, and a
good cry for Liberals, and why it was not settled by
representatives of every sect which so desired being
allowed access to the schools alternately is not now clear.
The parliamentary mind moves in a mysterious way ;
it seldom adopts the simple solutions of problems which
commend themselves to the more ingenuous laity.
Anything to make contention and trouble, it seems to
feel.

In such disputations, 1902 wore itself away. And
starving ex-soldiers played accordions or sold matches
by the pavements, their breasts decorated with larger
nosegays of war medals than any one man-at-arms
could conceivably have won by his own prowess in
the field. " Fought for my country," ran their sad,
proud legends about themselves, " and am now
starving. Have a wife and nine small children. . . ."
The families of ex-soldiers were terrific, then as now.
A wretched business altogether.

9

EXIT MAMMA

EDWARDIANISM was in full swing. People began to
recover from the war. They became rich again, and
very gay, and the arts flourished. Irving Garden, his
fortune made in Rand mines, could really afford almost

anything he liked. He bought and drove two motor-cars, a gray one and a navy blue, and presented to Rome, on her forty fourth birthday, a very graceful little scarlet three-seater, in which she drove every-where. Sometimes she drove her parents out, but the traffic made her papa nervous. Mamma was of calmer stuff, and sat placid and unmoved while her daughter ran skilfully like a flame between the monsters of the highway. She did not think that Rome had accidents ; she believed in Rome.

Unfortunately, mamma developed cancer in the spring of 1903, and died, after the usual sufferings and operations, in the autumn.

" It doesn't matter much," she said to Rome, hearing that her death was certain and soon. "A little more or a little less. . . . After all, I am sixty-nine. My only real worry about it is papa. We both hoped that I might be the survivor. I could have managed better."

Mamma's faint sigh flickered. Dear papa. Poor papa. Indeed, thought Rome, he will not manage at all. . . .

No charge was laid on Rome to look after poor papa. Mamma did not do such things : dying, she left the living free. That ultimate belief in the inalienable freedom of the human being looked unconquered out of her tired, still eyes. Mamma had never believed in coercion, even the coercion of love. Modern writers say that Victorian parents did believe in parental tyranny. There is seldom any need to believe modern, or any other, writers. What they seem sometimes to to forget is that Victorian parents were like any other parents in being individuals first, and that the sovereign who happened to reign over them did not reduce all Victorians to a norm, some good, some bad, as the Poet Laureate of the day had put it, but all stamped

with the image of the Queen. You would think, to
hear some persons talk, that Victoria had called into
existence little images of herself all over England,
instead of being merely one very singular and characteristic old lady, who might just as well have occurred
to-day.   In short, the Victorians were not like Queen
Victoria, any more than the Edwardians were like
King Edward, or the Georgians are like King George,
for all creatures are merely themselves.

Mamma, being merely herself, left her family free
of all behests, and drew to her end with an admirable
stoic gentleness.   Dying was to her no great matter or
disturbance.

> " *Time bears us off, as lightly as the wind*
>   *Lifts up the smoke and carries it away,*
>   *And all we know is that a longer life*
>   *Gives but more time to think of our decay.*
>
> *We live till Beauty fails and Passion dies,*
>   *And sleep's our one desire in every breath,*
>   *And in that strong desire, our old love, Life,*
>   *Gives place to that new love whose name is Death.*"

Mamma would sometimes murmur these lines by
Mr. W. H. Davies, a poet (formerly Victorian, now
Edwardian, later to become Georgian) of whom she
was very fond, because he noticed all the charming
things in the countryside that she always observed
herself, such as wet grass, and rainbows, and cuckoos,
and birds' eggs, and coughing sheep (who had always
stirred her to pity).

" My beloved," papa would say, quietly, restraining
his anguish that he might not distress her, " my best
beloved, I shall join you before long, where there is no
more parting. . . ." (Thank God, thank God, he

was at this time a believer in that reunion, and could say it from his heart. Supposing he had still been a Theosophist, believing that mamma would merely go on to another spoke of the Eternal Wheel, and that he would never, try as he might, catch her up. . . . Or even a Roman Catholic, believing that mamma and he would both have to suffer a long expiation, presumably not together, in purgatory. Thank God, evangelicals believed in an immediate heaven for the redeemed, and surely papa and mamma would be found numbered among the redeemed. . . .).

Mamma's hand would gently stroke his.

"Yes, dear. Of course you will join me soon."

Who should see, who had ever seen, into mamma's mind, that lay so deep and still beneath veils?

"Yes, Aubrey. Of course, of course. Quite soon, dear."

They spoke often of that further life; but of papa's life between now and then they did not dare to speak much.

Mamma loved papa, her lover and friend for half a century, and she loved all her children, and all her grandchildren too, the dear, happy boys and girls. But, at the last—or rather, just before the last, for the end was dark silence—it was only her eldest son, Maurice, on whose name she cried in anguish.

"Maurice—Maurice—my boy, my boy! Oh, God, have pity on my boy!"

Maurice was there, sitting at her side, holding her wet, shaking hand in his.

"Mother, mother. It's all right, dear mother. I'm here, close to you."

But still she moaned, "Have pity—have pity on my boy. . . . Maurice, my darling. . . . Have pity . . ." as if her own pain, cutting her in two, were his, not hers.

They had not known—not one of them had wholly known—of those storms that had beaten her through the long years because of Maurice, her eldest boy.

His tears burned in his hot eyes; the easy tears of the constant drinker.

They put her under an anæsthetic; the pain was too great; and she died at dawn.

10

SPIRITUALISM

PAPA could not bear it. It was all very well to talk of joining mamma before long, but papa was not more than seventy-three years of age, and how should he live without mamma for perhaps ten, fifteen, even twenty long years? That unfailing comfort, sympathy and love that had been hers; that patient, silent understanding, that strength and pity for his weakness, that wifely regard for his scholar's mind, that dear companionship that had never failed—having had these for close on fifty years, how should he live without them? He could not live without them. Somehow, he must find them again—reach across the grave to where mamma's love awaited him in the land of the redeemed. . . . The redeemed. Already this evangelistic phraseology did not wholly suit his needs. He wanted mamma nearer than that. . . .

In 1904 there was, as usual, much talk of spiritualism, of establishing connection with the dead. The Psychical Research Society had been flourishing for many years, but papa had never, until now, taken much interest in it. There had been periods in his career when he had believed, with his Church, that God did not smile on such researches, or wish the Veil drawn from the unseen world, and that the researchers, if they too inquisitively drew it, got into shocking company, got, in fact, into touch with those evil spirits who were always waiting ready to pose as the deceased relatives and friends of inquirers. Other periods there had been when papa had believed that the thing was all pathetic buncombe (that was how papa spelt it) since there was, unfortunately, nothing to get into touch with. But now he was sure that he had, in both these beliefs, erred. God could not frown on his bereaved children's efforts to communicate with the beloved who had made life for them. And beyond the Veil waited not the great nothingness, but God and the dear dead. God and mamma. He must and would get into touch with mamma.

Papa attended séances, with what are called Results. Mamma came and talked with him, through the voice of a table and of a medium; she said all kinds of things that only she could have said; she even told him where a lost thimble of hers was, and, sure enough, there it was, dropped behind the sofa cushions. And once materialisation occurred, and mamma, like a luminous wraith, floated about the room. It made papa very happy. He asked her how she did, and what it was like where she now was, and she told him that she did, on the whole, very well, but, as to what it was like, that he would never understand, did she tell him for a year.

" They can't tell us. It's too difficult, too different," the lady who managed the séances explained to papa afterwards. Papa did not greatly care for this lady, and he always winced a little at the thought that mamma had become "They." But he only said, " Yes, I suppose it is."

The séances exhausted him a good deal, but it was worth while.

" So long as it makes him happier," said Rome. " Poor *darling*."

II

THE HAPPY LIBERALS

1905 was a year of great happiness, intelligence and virtue for the Liberal party in the State. It was to be their last happy, intelligent, or virtuous year for many a long day ; indeed, they have not as yet known another, for such a gracious state is only possible to oppositions, and the next time that the Liberals were the Opposition it was too late, for by then oppositions were, like other persons, too tired, war-spoilt, disillusioned and dispirited to practise anything but an unidealistic and unhopeful nagging. But in 1905, with the Tories executing, to the satisfaction of their opponents, the ungracious task of performance, which is, one may roughly say, never a success, the Liberals were very jolly, united, optimistic, and full of energy and plans. What would they not do when they should come, in their turn, into power ? What Tory iniquities were there not for them now to oppose, for them in that rosy future to reverse ? What Aunt Sallies did not the governing party erect for them to shy at ? Chinese Labour, that yellow slavery which was degrading (were that possible) South Africa, the Licensing Act, the Education Act, the Little Loaf, which could be made so pitiable a morsel on posters—against all these they tilted. As to what they would do, once in power, it included the setting of trade again upon its legs, the enriching of the country, the reform of the suffrage, the relief of unemployment, the issue of an education bill which should distress no one. Ardent progressives hoped much from this party ; they even hoped, without grounds, for the removal of sex disabilities in the laws relating to the suffrage, which unlikely matter was part of the programme drawn up in 1905 by the National Liberal Federation. Life was very glorious to any party, in those Edwardian days, before it got in. Liberals in opposition were democratic idealists, in office makeshift opportunists, backing out and climbing down.

Stanley Garden, in 1905, was ardent in Liberal hope. She hoped for everything, even for a vote. This sex disability in the matter of votes oppressed her very seriously. She saw no sense or reason in it, and resented the way the question, whenever it was raised in Parliament, was treated as a joke, like mothers-in-law, or drunkenness, or twins. Were women really a funny topic ? Or rather, were they funnier than men ? And if so, why ? In vain her female sense of humour sought to probe this subject, but no female sense of humour, however acute, has ever done so. Women may and often do regard all humanity as a joke, good or bad, but they can seldom see that they themselves are more of a joke than men, or that the fact of their wanting rights as citizens is more amusing than men wanting similar rights. They can no more see it than they can see that they are touching, or that it is more shocking that women should be killed than that men should, which men see so plainly. Women, in fact, cannot see why they should not be treated like other persons. Stanley could not see it. To her the denial of representation in the governing body of her country on grounds of sex was not so much an injustice as a piece of inexplicable lunacy, as if all persons measuring, say, below five foot eight, had been denied votes.

She saw no more to it than that, in spite of all the anti-suffrage speakers whom she heard say very much more. She became embittered on this subject, with a touch of the feminist bitterness that marked many of the early strugglers for votes. She admitted that men were, taking them in the main, considerably the wiser, the more capable and the more intelligent sex; that is to say that, though most people were ignorant fools, there were even more numerous and more ignorant fools among women than among men; but there it was, and there was no reason why the female fools should have less say than the male fools as to which of the other fools represented their interests in Parliament, and what measures were passed affecting their foolish lives. No; on the face of it it was lunatic and irrational, and no excuse was possible, and that was that.

It certainly was, Rome agreed, but then, in a lunatic and irrational world, was any one extra piece of lunacy worth a fuss? Was, in fact, anything worth a fuss? In the answer to these questions, the sisters fundamentally differed, for Stanley believed very many things to be worth a fuss, and made it accordingly. She was busy now making fusses from most mornings to most evenings, sitting on committees for the improvement of the world, even of the Congo, and so forth. She was what is called a useful and public-spirited woman. Rome, on the other hand, grew with the years more and more the dilettante idler. At forty-six she found very few things worth bothering about. She strolled, drove, or motored round the town, erect, slim, and debonair, increasingly distinguished as gray streaked her fair hair and time chiselled delicate lines in her fine clear skin. Rome cared neither for the happy Liberals nor for the unhappy Tories; she regarded both parties as equally undistinguished.

Fabianism became increasingly the fashion for young intellectuals. Girl and boy undergraduates flung themselves with ardour into this movement, sitting at the feet of Mr. Bernard Shaw and ⸜he Sidney Webbs. Stanley was a keen Fabian, and even attended summer schools. They were not attractive, but yet she hoped that somehow good would be the final goal of ill. She was sorry that none of her nephews and nieces joined her in this movement, though several had attained the natural age for it.

12

THE HAPPY YOUNG

MAURICE's Roger was a gay youth now at Cambridge, who had not intellect and meant to be a novelist. His sister Iris had even less intellect, and meant to be a wife. Nature had not fitted her for learning, and when she left school she merely came (as the phrase goes) out. Parties; these were what Iris liked. Society, not societies. Stanley, aunt-like, thought it a great pity that Maurice's offspring were thus, and blamed Maurice for leaving them too much to Amy. As to Vicky's children, Phyllis, who had done quite adequately at Girton, now lived at home and helped her mother with entertaining and drawing-room meetings, and was, in politics, on the whole a Tory; Nancy, at twenty-one, was at the Slade, learning, so every one but her teachers believed, to draw and paint; Hugh was at Cambridge, a lad of good intelligence, which he devoted to the study of engineering; Tony was still at school; and Imogen was to leave it next year. Imogen was not for college; she would, it was generally believed by her teachers and relatives, not make much of that.

Imogen was quite content; she was, as always, busy writing stories and sunk deep in her own imaginings, which were still of a very puerile sort. Imogen read a great deal, but was not really intelligent; it was as if she had not yet grown up. She knew and cared little about politics or progress. Bernard Shaw was to her merely the most enchanting of playwrights. She was happy, drugged with poetry (her own and that of others), and adventurous dreams. She was a lanky slip of an undeveloped girl, light-footed, active as a cat, but more awkward with her hands than any creature before her; at once a romantic dreamer and a tomboyish child, loving school, her friends, active games, bathing, climbing, reading and writing, animals, W. B. Yeats, Conrad, Kipling, Henry Seton Merriman, Shelley, William Morris, Stevenson, "A Shropshire Lad," meringues, battleships, marzipan, Irene Vanbrugh, Granville Barker, and practically all drama; hating strangers, society, drawing-room meetings, needlework, love stories, people who talked about clothes, sentimentalists, and her aunt Amy. She was at this time as sexless as any girl or boy may be. She was still, in all her imaginings, her continuous, unwritten stories about herself, a young man.

As to Stanley's children, and Irving's, and even Una's, they were still at school. Stanley watched her son and daughter with hope and joy; they were such delightful, exciting creatures, and one day they would take their place in the world and help to upset it and build it up again. *They*, at least, should certainly join the Fabians when they were old enough. Billy and Molly should be neither slack, uninterested, nor Tory. They should join in the game of life as eagerly as now they joined in treasure hunts, that curious rage of this year which caused young and old to fall to digging up the earth, seeking for discs.

13

THE YEAR

THE year and the government petered towards their end. In the east the Japanese were beating the Russians, hands down. In the Dogger Bank, the Russians fired on a fishing fleet from Hull, and there was trouble. In European politics, the Anglo-French *entente* throve, and Anglo-German rivalry swelled the navies. In Scotland the Wee Frees split from the U.P.'s, and fought successfully for the lion's share of the loot. In Wales, Evan Roberts's odd religious revival swept the country, throwing strong men and women into hysteria and bad men and women into virtue, reforming the sinners and seriously annoying the publicans. In the Congo, rubber was grown and collected amid scenes of distressing cruelty, and reports of the horrid business were published in this country by Mr. Roger Casement and Mr. E. D. Morel. In India, Lord Curzon quarrelled with Lord Kitchener. In Thibet, the British Expedition got to Lhassa. In Tangier, the Kaiser Wilhelm of Germany made a speech. In Ireland, Mr. Wyndham resigned. In London, the government apathetically stayed in office, the Tariff Reform campaign raged, treasure discs were dug for, bridge was much played, the Vedrenne-Barker company acted at the Court Theatre, many books were published and pictures painted, and money brightly changed hands. And in the provinces, by-election after by-election was lost to the government, until at last, in November, Mr. Balfour resigned.

14

ROCKETS

THEY stood in the new open space at Aldwych, watching the election results proclaimed by magic lanterns on great screens and flung to the sky in coloured rockets. They had made up a family election party—Maurice, Vicky, Charles, Rome, Stanley and Irving, and many of their young. Stanley had brought Billy and Molly, that they might rejoice in the great Liberal victory and always remember it. She had bought them each, at their request, a little clacker, with which to signal the triumph of right to the world. For to-night was to be a triumph indeed ; Liberalism was to sweep the country. Though even Stanley did not guess to what extent, or how far the inevitable pendulum had swung.

Imogen was entranced by the dark, clear night, the coloured lights, the crowd, the excitement, and little thrills ran up and down her as names and figures and rockets were greeted with cheers and hoots. She cared nothing for the results ; to her the thing was a sporting event on which she had no money. Aunt Stanley, she knew, had her shirt on the Liberals. So had uncle Maurice. But aunt Rome had nothing either way. Imogen's own parents were Conservatives. So, on the whole, was Phyllis, and Phyllis's young man. So was uncle Irving, who was for tariff reform. Probably, on the whole, Liberals were the more right, thought Imogen. But probably no party was particularly right. How excited they all got, anyhow, right or wrong !

The Liberals were forging ahead. There was another Manchester division going up on the screen. Three Manchester seats had already been lost to the Tories.

"Bet you an even twopence it's a Lib." Tony was saying.

"Right you are. Oh, it's Balfour's. . . ."

"Well, he's lost it. Hand over."

The crowd roared with laughter, distress and joy. Balfour out. . . . What next?

"Very badly managed," Irving was complaining all the time, to no one in particular. "Shockingly mismanaged. The most comic election I ever saw. There'll be no front bench left."

"And a jolly good thing." That was Stanley, getting more and more triumphant. "There goes Brodrick. . . ."

Imogen felt dazed and happy, and as if she were in a fairy palace, all blue and red lights. Her upstrained face was stiff and cold, her mouth open with joy, so that the cold air flowed in. She wasn't betting any more, for neither she nor Tony would bet on the Tories now. The Tories were a dead horse. One was sorry for them, but one couldn't bet on them. Did the poor men who lost their seats mind much? Perhaps some of them were pleased. After all, they had none of them sought or desired office. . . . Statesmen always said that of themselves; they only wanted to get in because they thought they were the ones who would do most good; always they said that. Divine guidance, they said, had laid this heavy burden on them, though it was a most frightful bore, and though the thing they wanted to do was to live in the country and keep pigs.

"If I was in office," thought Imogen, "I wouldn't say that. I'd say, 'I sought and wanted office, and I'm jolly glad I've got it, though I expect I'll be rotten at it. I simply love being in power, and thank you awfully for putting me in, and I hope I'll stop in for ages.'"

How shocked every one would be. That wasn't the

way public men ever talked. Would women, if ever
they got into Parliament, like aunt Stanley wanted
them to ? Perhaps they would at first, not being used
to proper public manners, but they would soon learn
that it wasn't nice to talk like that and would begin
on the I-never-wanted-it stunt.

More rockets ; more blue flares. Lovely. Like a
great garden of coloured flowers. *Night is a garden gay
with flowers.* . . . Hours. Showers. Dowers. Bowers.
Cowers. . . .

Their flaring blinds the sleepy hours. . . . No. *The
small dim hours are lit, are starred.* Better. The
rhymes alternately in the middle and end of the lines,
all through. That made it chime, like bells beneath
the sea. . . .

" *Lord,* what a bungle ! " Irving grunted. " It's
all up now. Nothing can save it now. We may as
well go home and get warm. What ? "

His fine, dark, clean-cut face was beautiful in the
coloured flares, as he stared up, a cigar in the corner
of his mouth. How interesting people were, thought
Imogen, the way they all wanted different things, in
different ways. There was uncle Maurice now, smiling
over his briar, as pleased as anything. . . . And
Billy and Molly, silly little goats, twirling away with
their clackers and shouting with Liberal joy because
aunt Stanley told them to. . . . Anyhow, it couldn't
really *matter* who got in. Not matter, like the night,
and the lights, and poetry, and the lovely thrill of it all.
Results didn't matter, only the thing itself.

" Brrr ! " said Vicky, hunching herself together and
hugging her muff. " It's too cold to watch the wrong
side winning any more. Charles, I'm going home to
bed. Come along, all of you, or you'll catch your
deaths."

" Oh, mother. Mayn't I stay as long as father does ? "

" If you like. Very silly of you, Jennie, you're blue
and shivering already. Stanley, aren't you going to
take those noisy and misguided children of yours home ?
It's nearly midnight."

" I suppose I must. But what a night for them to
remember always ! "

What a night, thought Imogen, huddling up in her
coat with a happy shiver, to remember always. Indeed,
yes. Ecstasy and gaudy blossoms of the night. *The
gaudy blossoms of the night. . . . Sharp swords of light.*
. . . Bloss, moss, doss, toss . . . toss ought to do. . .

" There goes Lyttleton. So much for those beastly
Chinamen," cried Maurice.

15

ON PARTIES

So much for the beastly Chinamen, and so much for
the beastly little loaf and the tax on the people's food,
so much for class legislation and sectarian education
bills. So much, in fact, for Toryism, for the happy
Liberals were in, and would be in, growing ever less
and less happy, for close on ten years.

" *Now* we'll show the world," said Stanley.

Maurice cynically grinned at her.

" If you mean you think you're going to get a vote,
my dear, you're off it. This Cabinet hasn't the faintest
intention of accommodating you. Not the very faintest.
And if ever they did put up a bill, they'd never get it
through the Lords. You may send all the deputations
you like, but you won't move them. Women's suffrage
is merely the House joke."

" We'll see," said Stanley, who was of a hopeful
colour.

"All you can say of Liberals," said Maurice, who was not, " is that they're possibly (not certainly) one better than Conservatives. However, I'm not crabbing them. They've got their chance, and let's hope they take it. First they've got to undo all the follies the last government perpetrated. Every government ought to begin with that, always. Then they've got to concentrate on Home Rule. As you say, we shall see."

"Anyhow," said Stanley, " we've got our chance. . . . And there's the *Tribune*. Penny Liberalism at last."

" I give it a year," said Maurice. " If it takes longer dying, Thomasson is an even more stubborn lunatic than I think him. They've started all right ; quite a good first number, only how any Liberal paper can publish a polite message from that damned Tsar beats me. I believe my paper is really the only one that insults the Russian government as it ought to be insulted. All the others either make up to the Tsar for his armies or butter him up because the Hague Conference and his silly prattle about a world peace. It makes one sick. Liberals are as bad as the rest."

It was edifying, during the election days, to learn from various authorities the reasons for the Liberal victory. The *Times* said it was the effect, long delayed, of the suffrage reform bills ; the working classes, at last articulate, had determined to dictate their own policy ; no triumph for Liberalism, no humiliation for Conservatism, but an experiment on the part of Labour. The *Morning Post* said the victory was due to the misrepresentation of Chinese labour by Liberals, false promises, and the inevitable swing of the pendulum. The *Daily Mail* said it was the swing of the pendulum, Chinese labour, the over continuance in office of the last government, the Education Act, taxation, unfair food tax cries, and a liking for antiquated methods of commerce. The *Daily News* said it was a rebellion against reaction, protection, and the Little Loaf. The *Tribune* said it was a rebellion also against poverty, the direction of companies by ministers, and the undoing of the great Victorian reforms ; it was, in fact, the protest of Right against Force, of the common good against class interest, of the ideal element in political life against merely mechanical efficiency. (" Mechanical efficiency ! " Maurice jeered. " Much there was of that in the last government. As to the ideal element, the Liberal ideal is a large loaf and low taxes. Quite a sound one, but nothing to be smug about.") However, the whole press was smug, as always, and so were nearly all statesmen in public speeches ; their cynicism they kept for private life. Mr. Asquith, for instance, said that this uprising of the people was due to moral reprobation of the double dealing of the late government ; plain dealing was what the nation wanted. And Mr. Lloyd George, in his best vein, spoke of a fearful reckoning. A tornado, he called it, of righteous indignation with the trifling that had been going on in high places for years with all that was sacred to the national heart. The oppression of Nonconformists at home, the staining of the British flag abroad with slavery, the riveting of the chains of the drink traffic on the people of this country—against all these had the people risen in wrath. It was a warning to ministers not to trifle with conscience, or to menace liberty in a free land. The people meant to save themselves ; the dykes had been opened, and reaction in all its forms would be swept away by the deluge.

Mr. Balfour, less excited and more philosophic, observed, at his own defeat at Manchester, that, after all, the Tories had been in office ten years, and would doubtless before long be in office again, and that these oscillations of fortune would and did always occur.

He was probably nearer the truth about the elections than most of those who pronounced upon them. It is a safe assertion that no government is popular for long ; get rid of it and let's try another, for anyhow another can't be sillier, is the voter's very natural and proper feeling. The sophisticated voter knows that it will almost certainly be as silly, but, after all, it seems only fair to let each side have its innings.

Anyhow, and whatever the reasons that brought Liberalism into power, there it was. It was expressed by a House which was at present, and before its enthusiasms were whittled away in action, composed largely of political and social theorists, men new to politics and brimming with plans. Mr. H. W. Massingham said it was the ablest parliament he had ever known, but not the most distinguished.

16

DREADNOUGHT

IMOGEN saved up her pocket money for the cheap excursion fare to Portsmouth, and slipped off there alone, on a raw February morning, by the special early train, to see the King launch the *Dreadnought*. The *Dreadnought* was a tremendous naval event. She displaced 19,900 tons, beating the *Dominion* and the *King Edward VII.* by 1200 tons, and she would make 21 knots to their 16.5, and had turbine engines, and carried ten 12-inch guns, and her outline was smooth and lovely and unbroken by casemates, for she was built for speed. Imogen had to go. She slipped off without a word at home, for she had a cough and objections would have been raised. She stood wedged for hours in a crowd on the docks in cold rain that pitted the heaving, green harbour sea, and coughed. She did not command a view of the actual launching, but would see the splendid creature as she left the slip and took the water. Before that there was a service, the service appointed to be used at the launching of the ships of His Majesty's Navy.

"They that go down to the sea in ships, and occupy their business in great waters. These men see the works of the Lord: and His wonders in the deep. For at His word the stormy wind ariseth: which lifteth up the waves thereof. They are carried up to the heaven, and down again to the deep: their soul melteth away because of the trouble. They reel to and fro and stagger like a drunken man: and are at their wit's end. . . ."

After this, Hymn 592 (A. & M.) was irritating and silly, but hymns cannot be helped, bishops will have them.

Then the King smashed the bottle of wine on her and, christened, she took the water. She left the slip and came into the view of the crowd, and a great shout went up, "She's moving!"

Imogen, thrilled, gazed at the lovely, the amazing creature, the giant of the navy. What a battleship! With professional interest Imogen examined her points through her father's field glasses. No openings in the bulkheads—it was that which gave her her smooth, fleet look. She was made for a running fight. She was glorious.

Imogen travelled home, wet through, shivering, her cough tearing at her chest, and went to bed for a month with bronchitis. So much for the navy, said Vicky, crossly. But the amazing gray ship was a comfort to Imogen through her fevered, waking dreams.

17

AT THE FARM

IMOGEN, bow and arrows in hand, crawled through
the wood, beneath overhanging boughs of oaks
and elders and beeches and the deep green arms
of pines, that shut the little copse from the July
sun into a fragrant gloom. Every now and then
she stopped, listened, and laid her ear to the mossy
ground.

" Three miles off and making a beeline south," she
observed, frowning. " My God."

" Michael crawled on," she continued, crawling,
" keeping his head low, so as not to afford a target for
any stray arrow. Who knew what sinister shadows
lurked in the forest, to right and to left ? . . . Hist !
What was that sound ? Something cracked in the
tangle of scrub near him. . . . A Cherokee on a lone
trail, possibly. . . . A Cherokee : the most deadly of
the Red Tribes. . . . Cold sweat stood out on Michael's
brow. Could he reach the camp in time ? Again he
laid his ear to the ground and listened. They were
only two miles now, and still that swift, terrible travelling. . . . The sun beat upon his head and neck ;
he felt dizzy and sick. Suppose he fainted before he
reached his goal. . . . That damned cracking in the
bushes again. . . . Good God ! . . . Out of the
thicket sprang a huge Redskin, uttering the horrid
war-whoop of the Cherokees, which, once heard, is
never forgotten. Michael leaped to his feet, pulled
his bow-string to his ear, let fly. . . ."

Imogen, too, let fly.

" Missed him," she muttered, and swarmed nimbly
up the gnarled trunk of an oak until she reached the

lower boughs, from whence she looked down into a fierce red face, eagle-nosed, feather-crowned.

"Oh, Big Buffalo," she softly called, "Will you parley?"

Big Buffalo grunted, and they parleyed. If Michael would betray the whereabouts of his friends, Big Buffalo would grant him his life. If not, no such easy death as the arrow awaited him, "for we Cherokees well understand the art of killing. . . ." Michael, sick with fear, betrayed his friends, and Big Buffalo left him, primed with information. (In common with other heroes of fiction, Michael never thought of giving incorrect or misleading information.)

"Michael lay in the forest, his head upon his arms. What had he done? There was no undoing it now. Why didn't I choose the stake? Oh, damn, why didn't I? . . ."

It was too warm, sweet and drowsy for prolonged remorse. Michael forgot his shame. The breeze in the pine trees sang like low harps. . . . The shadowy copse was soaked in piney sweetness, golden and dim. Michael, with his bow, his Redskins, and his broken honour, faded out in the loveliness of the hour.

Ecstasy descended on the wood; enchantment held it, saturating it with golden magic. Ants and little wood-beetles scuttled over Imogen's outstretched hands and bare, rough head. Rabbits bobbed and darted close to her. She was part of the woods, caught breathless into that fairy circle like a stolen, enchanted child.

"I am full of the Holy Ghost," said Imogen. "This is the Holy Ghost" . . . and loveliness shook her, as a wind shakes a leaf. These strange, dizzy moments lurked hidden in the world like fairies in a wood, and at any hour they sprang forth and seized her, and the emotion, however often repeated, was each time as keen. They would spring forth and grip her, turning the dædal earth to magic, at any lovely hour, in wood or lane or street, or among the wavering candles and the bread and wine. She was stabbed through and through with beauty sweet as honey and sharp as a sword, and it was as if her heart must break in her at its turning. After this brief intensity of joy or pain, whichever it was, it was as if something in her actually did break, scattering loose a drift of pent-up words. That was how poems came. After the anguished joy, the breaking loose of the words, then the careful stringing of them together on a chain, the fastidious, conscious arranging. Then the setting them down, and reading them over, and the happy, dizzy (however erroneous) belief that they were good. . . . That was how poems came, and that was life at its sharpest, its highest intensity. Afterwards, one sent them to papers, and it was pleasant and gratifying if other people saw them and liked them too. But all that was a side-issue. Vanity is pleasant, gratified ambition is pleasant, earning money is very pleasant, but these are not life at its highest power. You might at once burn every poem you wrote, but you would still have known life.

The song the pines hummed became words, half formed, drifting, sweet. . . . Imogen listened, agape, like an imbecile. It was a lovely, jolly, woody thing that was being sung to her . . . she murmured it over. . . .

A bell rang, far away. Sharply time's voice shivered eternity to fragments. Imogen yawned, got up, brushed pine needles out of her hair and clothes, took up her bow, and strolled out of fairyland. It was tea-time at the farm.

As she sauntered through the little wood, she shot arrows at the trees and stopped to retrieve them.

Then she found a long, sharp stick, pointed, like a spear, and became a knight in a Norman forest. She encountered another knight, a hated foe. There was a fight *à outrance*. They fenced, parried, lunged. . . .

" Swerve to the right, son Roger, he said,
    When you catch his eye through the helmet's slit ;
Swerve to the right, then out at his head,
    And the Lord God give you joy of it. . . ."

A swinging thrust. . . .
" Got him, pardie ! "
" Hullo."
Imogen faced about, and there, on the cart track between the wood and the home field, stood her uncle Ted, large and red, in breeches and gaiters, his pipe between his teeth.
" Oh, hallo, uncle Ted."
Imogen had turned red. She had been seen making an ass of herself alone in the wood. Behaving like a maniac. Damn.
"Anything the matter ? Got the staggers, have you ? " said uncle Ted, as if she were a cow.
" No, I'm all right. Looking for arrows and things, that's all."
" Oh, I see. . . . Comin' up to tea ? "
They walked across the home field together. Imogen was sulky and ashamed. She was emptied of enchantment and the Holy Ghost, and was nothing but an abrupt, slangy, laconic girl, going sullenly into tea, feeling an ass. Uncle Ted was thinking farmer's thoughts, of crops and the like, not of Imogen.
But afterwards he said to Una, " Not quite all there, eh, that girl of Vicky's ? Flings herself about in the wood when she's alone, like some one not right, and talks to herself, too. Eighteen, is she ? It'd be

right enough if she was twelve. But at eighteen or nineteen. . . ."

" Oh, Imogen's all right. She's childish for her age, that's all." Una took every one for granted.

" Childish, yes. That's what I say. They ought to have her seen to. Gabbles, too. I can't make out half she's saying. . . . Katie may do her good, I dare say. Katie's got sense. . . . It's against a girl, going on like that. No sensible young fellow would like it. They ought to have her seen to. What ? "

" Oh, she's all right," said Una again. " There she is in the field playing rounders with the others quite sensibly, you see."

" I dare say. She may be all right at games, but she oughtn't to be let loose alone in woods. She'll get herself talked about. . . ."

Katie, too, thought Imogen mad. But quite nicely mad. Harmless. Like a kid. Katie was a few months younger, but she felt that Imogen was a kid. She said and did such mad things. And she lacked the most elementary knowledge ; she didn't know the first thing, for instance, about clothes, what they were made of, and how they should be made. She was like an imbecile about them ; didn't care, either. She would stare, pleased and admiring, at Katie, who had beauty, as if Katie were a lovely picture, but she never said the right things about her clothes. You'd think, almost, she didn't know one material from another.

When they had done playing rounders, and when Imogen and Tony, who was staying at the farm too, had done damming the brook at the bottom of the field, and when Tony had gone off rook shooting with his cousin Dick, Imogen sat by the brook, her bare muddy legs in a pool, scaring minnows, and brooded over life. Rotten it was, being grown up. Simply rotten. Because you weren't really grown up. You hadn't changed at all. You knew some more, and you cared for a lot of fresh books, but you liked doing all the things you had liked doing before you grew up. Climbing, and playing Red Indians, and playing with soldiers, and walking on stilts. But when you put your hair up, you had to hide all sorts of things away, like a guilty secret. You could play real games, like tennis and cricket and hockey and rounders, and even football, and you could perhaps do the other things with some one else, but not alone. If people found you alone up a tree, or climbing a roof, or listening with your ear to the ground, or astride on a wall, or pretending with a sword, they put up their eyebrows and thought you an ass. Your mother told people you were a tomboy. A tomboy. Imbecile word. As if girls didn't like doing nice things as much as boys. Who started the idea that they didn't, or shouldn't ? . . . Oh, it was rotten, being grown up. Grown up people had a hideous time. They became so queer, talking so much, wanting to go to parties, and even meetings, and all kinds of rotten shows. Mother held meetings in the drawing-room, for good objects. So did aunt Stanley. Different objects, but equally good, no doubt. People came to the meetings and jabbered away, and sometimes you were made to be there, " to learn to take an interest." Votes, cruelty to animals or children, sweated labour, bazaars, white slaves, the Conservative party, the Liberal party. . . . What did any of them matter ? Phyllis was good at them. But now Phyllis was going to be married. And Nancy was at the Slade, and wouldn't attend the meetings, she was too busy drawing and going to dances and parties. The modern girl, mother said, independent, selfish, dashing about with young men and no chaperon. The Edwardian young woman, so different from the Victorian young woman. . . . Only aunt Rome

said she was not different, but just the same. . . .
Anyhow, Nancy wouldn't take her turn at the meetings. So Imogen, younger and more docile, was being
trained up. But she would never be any good. She
hated them. Why shouldn't the boys take their turn?
No one made them. It wasn't fair.

Imogen kicked viciously at the minnows. Rotten,
being a girl. . . . Perhaps she would run away
to sea . . . round the world . . . the South Sea
Islands. . . .

It was getting chilly. Imogen drew her legs out of
the brook and dried them on her handkerchief. Filthy
they were, with mud. She put on her stockings and
old tennis shoes, and wondered what next. Tony was
still rooking. One might go and catch the colt in the
meadow and ride him. . . .

Katie appeared over the hunched shoulder of the
field.

"Imogen, do you want to come and milk? It's
time. . . . Oh, I say, you *are* in a mess. You ass,
what've you been up to?"

"Only damming the brook, and wading. Yes, I
want to milk; rather."

"Hurry up, then."

Katie was beautiful as a June morning. As beautiful
as Una. Pale as milk, with eyes like violets, and dark,
clustering curls. And clever. She could do nearly
everything. Imogen, six months older, was as nought
beside her. But Katie liked her, and was very kind to
her. Katie had just left Roedean; she had been
captain of the school hockey team, and was going now
to play for Essex. A splendid girl. Imogen believed
that Katie had none of the dark and cold forebodings,
the hot excitements, the black nightmares, the sharp,
sweet ecstasies, the mean and base feelings, that as-
sailed herself, any more than Katie would be found

making an ass of herself playing in a wood. Katie, like her mother, was balanced. This tendency to believe that others are balanced, and are not rent by the sad and glad storms which one's own soul knows, is common to many. One supposes it to be because human beings put such a calm face on things, so that the heart alone knows its own turbulence.

Imogen grinned at Katie, and went with her to the milking.

18

HIGHER THOUGHT

PAPA had aged very much in the last two years since mamma had died. He had had wonderful experiences ; he had constantly spoken with, even seen, mamma ; it had made him very happy. But he was aware that the *séances* greatly strained and fatigued him. He slept badly ; his nerves seemed continually on edge. Further, he could not by any means overcome the distaste he felt for the medium who made it her special business to open the door between him and mamma. A common little person, he could not help, even in his charity, thinking her. And Flossie, the spirit on the Other Side, who spoke for mamma (except on those rare occasions when mamma spoke for herself) was, to judge from her manner, voice, and choice of language, even commoner. And silly. Papa scarcely liked to admit to himself *how* silly Flossie seemed to him to be. Mamma must dislike Flossie a good deal, he sometimes thought, but then recollected that, where mamma had gone to dwell, dislike was no more felt, only compassion. He would have liked to ask mamma, on the rare occasions when she spoke for herself, what she thought of Flossie, and of Miss Smythe, the medium on this side. But he did not do so, for Flossie would certainly, and Miss Smythe possibly, through her trance, hear his question and mamma's reply. How he longed for a little private talk, of the kind that mamma and he used to have of old ! But he was not ungrateful. He was in touch with mamma ; he knew her to be extant as a personality, and accessible to him, and that was surely enough. As to the fatigue, that was a small price to pay.

Then, one tragic day, in the autumn of 1906, came one of those great exposures which dog the steps of psychical men and women. Some of the sharp, inquisitive persons who make it their business to nose out frauds and write to *Truth* about them, turned their attention to Miss Smythe and her *séances*. In a few weeks—these things are very easy, and do not take long—Miss Smythe was pilloried in the press as a complete and accomplished fraud. She had, it was made clear except to the most obstinate believers, never been in a trance, never called spirits from the vasty deep, never opened any spiritual doors. The mechanism of the materialisations was once more discovered and exposed. . . . ("What a stale old story," said Rome. "As if we didn't know all about it long ago. These heavy-footed creatures, trampling over children's fairylands. Why can't they let things be ?) . . . and even Flossie, that bright, silly, chatty spirit, was discredited. Florrie was a quack, and had known about the thimble behind the sofa and the other things in some cheap, sly way, or else just guessed.

Alas for papa ! The gates of paradise clanged in his face ; he might believe by faith that paradise was there, and mamma in it, but the door between him and it was shut. Great and bitter sorrow shook him, and shame, for that he had so made cheap his love and mamma's for the benefit of common frauds. He sank into inert grief, from which he was roused, in March, 1907, by the call of Higher Thought. The name, in the first instance, appealed to him. Thought should be higher; it was usually lower, and very certainly much too low.

"Higher than what, papa dear?" Rome inquired. "These comparatives, in the air, are so unfinished. Higher education, higher criticism, the larger hope, the younger generation. . . . Higher, I mean, than what other thought?"

Than the thought customary on similar subjects, papa supposed.

"These geometrical metaphors," Rome murmured. "Well, papa, I am sure it must be very interesting."

It was very interesting. Papa was introduced to a little temple near High Street, Kensington, which, when you stepped on the entrance mat, broke into "God is Love" in electric light over the altar. Here he worshipped and thought highly, in company with a small but ardent band of other high thinkers, who were led in prayer by a Guru of immense power—the power of thought which was not merely higher but highest— over mind and matter. So great was the power of this Guru that he could cure not only diseased bodies and souls, but could correct physical malformations, merely by absent treatment. A lame young man was brought to him, one of whose legs was shorter than its fellow. Certainly, said the Guru, this defect would yield to absent treatment. Further, the treatment would in this case be doubly effective, as he happened to be about to make a journey to Thibet, to visit the Llama, the very centre of fervent prayer, absent treatment, and higher thought. The nearer the Guru got to Thibet, the more powerful would become, he said, the action of his treatment on the leg of the young man. And, sure enough, so it proved. The shorter leg began, as the Guru receded towards Asia, to grow. It grew, and it grew, and it grew. There came a joyful day when the two legs were of identical length. The power of absent treatment was triumphantly justified. But it proved to be a power even greater than the young man and his family had desired or deserved. For the short leg did not stop when it had caught up its companion ; on the contrary, it seemed to be growing with greater velocity than before. And, indeed, it was ; for the Guru, now far beyond reach of communication by letter or telegram, was journeying ever deeper and deeper into the great heart of prayer, Holy Thibet, and as he penetrated it his prayer intensified and multiplied in power, like the impetus of a ball rolling down hill. The short leg surpassed its brother, shot on, and on, and on. . . .

It was still shooting on when papa was told of the curious phenomenon.

" Strange," said papa. " Strange, indeed."

But it was not these portents, however strange, that papa valued in his new faith. It was the freedom, the prayerfulness, the rarefied spiritual atmosphere ; in brief, the height. After Miss Smythe, after the darkened room and the rapping table, and the lower thinking of poor Flossie, it was like a mountain top, where the soul was purged of commonness.

Mamma, papa sometimes thought, would have approved of Higher Thought ; might even, had she been spared, have become a Higher Thinker herself. (It should be remembered, in this connection, that papa, since the exposure of poor Flossie, was no longer in touch with mamma.)

19

LIBERALS IN ACTION

IT is a pity to crab all governments and everything they do. For occasionally it occurs that some government or other (its political colour is an even chance) passes some measure or other which is not so bad as the majority of measures. The Liberal government elected in 1906 composed tolerable bills more than once. It even succeeded, though more rarely, in getting them, in some slightly warped form, tolerated by the Upper House. The Trades Disputes Bill, for instance, got through. Either the Lords were caught napping, or they felt they had to let something through, just to show that things *could* get through, as at hoop-la the owner of the booth has, here and there, among hundreds of objects too large to be ringed by the hoop, one of trifling value which can be fairly ringed and won, just to show that the thing can be done. Anyhow, the Trades Disputes Bill did get through, before the game began of chucking all bills mechanically back, or amending them out of all meaning so that the Commons disowned them and threw them away.

Mr. Birrell had no luck with his Education Bill. It was a good, rational bill, as education bills (a sad theme) go, and no party liked it much, and the Upper House saw that it would not do at all, and sent it back plastered all over with amendments that gave it a new and silly face, like a lady over much made up. So the Commons would have none of it, and that was the end, for the moment, of attempts to improve the management of our elementary schools.

The Lords were now getting into their form, and threw out the Plural Voting Bill with no nonsense about amendments, and no trouble at all. After all, what were they there for, if not to throw out? What indeed, asked the Lower House, many members of whom had for long wondered. As to any kind of women's suffrage bill, the Commons, as firmly as the Lords, would have none of it. It was when this was made clear that the Women's Social and Political Union, that new, vigorous, and vulgar body, began to bestir itself, and to send bodies of women to waylay members on their way to the House; in fact, the militant suffragist nuisance began. There were processions, demonstrations, riots, arrests and imprisonments. Stanley threw herself into these things at first with dogged fervour; she did not like them, but held them advantageous to the Cause. Her niece, Vicky's Nancy, a very wild young woman, who enjoyed fighting and making a disturbance on any pretext, threw herself also into the Cause, fought policemen with vigour, and was dragged off to prison with joy. Imogen wouldn't participate in these public-spirited orgies; she was too shy. And she couldn't see that it was any use, either. She had a hampering and rather pedantic sense of logic, that prevented her from flinging herself into movements with sentimental ardour; she preferred to know exactly how the methods adopted were supposed to work, and to see clearly cause and effect, and no one ever made it precisely clear to her how making rows in the street was going to get a suffrage bill passed. It seemed, in fact, to be working the other way, and alienating some of the few hitherto sympathetic. Her aunt Stanley told her, " It's to show the public and the government how much we care. They're crude weapons, but the only ones we have. Constitutional methods have failed, so far."

" But, aunt Stanley, how do you know these are weapons at all? " Imogen argued.

" We can but try them," Stanley answered, herself a little doubtful on the point.

"Anyhow," she added, " anyhow, no woman who cares about citizenship can be happy sitting still and doing nothing while we're denied it. You do care about the suffrage, don't you, Imogen ? "

" Oh, rather, aunt Stanley, of course I do. I think it's awful cheek not giving it us. There's no *sense* in it, is there ; no meaning. Anti-suffragists do talk a lot of rot. . . . Only don't you think suffragists do too, sometimes ? I mean, aunt Stanley, people do so, when they talk, get off the *point*, don't they. It would be a lot easier to be keen if people didn't talk so much. They talk *round*, not along. Really, there's hardly anything to say about anything. I mean, you could say it all, all that mattered, in a few sentences. But people go on talking about things for hours, saying the same things twice, and a lot of other things that don't really apply, and everything in hundreds of words when quite a few would do. I noticed it in the House the other day when we were there. Two-thirds of what they all said was just flapping about. And they say, " I have said before, Mr. Speaker, and I say again. . . . But *why* do they say it again ? It isn't awfully good even the first time. I do wonder why people are like that, don't you."

" Soft heads and long tongues, my dear, that's why. Can't be helped. One's got to bear it and go ahead. . . . I wish Molly was five years older ; she'll be so tremendously keen. . . ."

Imogen said nothing to that. She knew Molly, her small, elfish cousin of fourteen, pretty well. Molly, with her short, white face and merry, narrow eyes, and quick wits, and easy selfishness and charm, was, though Imogen couldn't know that, her father over again, without his abilities. Imogen was afraid that

Molly, when she left school and grew up, was not going to take that place among the world's workers that aunt Stanley hoped.

As to Billy, a cheerful, stocky Rugby boy of sixteen, he had no views on the suffrage. He didn't care. Politics bored him.

Poor aunt Stanley. Aunt Stanley was a great dear ; treated one always as a friend, not as a niece ; explained things, and discussed, and said what she meant. She was easy to talk to. Easier than Vicky, whom one loved, but couldn't discuss things with ; one couldn't formulate and express one's ideas and project them into that spate of charming, inconsequent talk, that swept on gaily over anything one said. Imogen tried to please aunt Stanley by seeming really keen about suffrage, but it was difficult, because the things she actually was keen on were so many and so absorbing that they didn't leave much time over. Imogen felt that she was no good at these large, unselfish causes that aunt Stanley had at heart ; she hadn't soul enough, or brain enough, or imagination enough, or something. And she did hate meetings. If one had to do anything so tiresome as sitting indoors in the afternoon, were there not the galleries of theatres, her point of view was. She decided that Nancy, who enjoyed it, could do the votes-for-women business for the family.

Meanwhile, Mr. W. H. Dickinson's suffrage bill failed to come to anything, and it became obvious that the Liberal government, in this matter, was to be no use at all.

It was quite a question whether it was going to be much use in any other matter. Poor Law reform it had postponed ; likewise Old Age Pensions. Licensing Reform was dropped ; so was Mr. McKenna's new Education Bill, the Land Valuation Bill, and Irish

Home Rule. It looked as if the Liberal programme was running away like wax in the heat and trouble of the day. How few party programmes, for that matter, ever do become accomplished achievements! They are frail plants, and cannot easily come to fruit in the rough air of office. What with one thing, what with another, they wilt away in flower and die.

To make up for the stagnation of home politics, there was, in 1906 and 1907, plenty of international activity. The nations of Europe were ostensibly drawing together, a happy family. British journalists were entertained in Berlin, German journalists in London, amid some mutual execration and dislike. A *rapprochement* took place between ourselves and Russia, for it was quite the fashion in Europe to fraternise with Russia, her armies were so huge, even if not, apparently, very good at what armies should be good at. There were those in this country who held that it was not quite nice to fraternise with Russia, disapproving of her governmental system, and of the Tsar's very natural suppression of the Duma that had for a few days and by an oversight so strangely existed and actually dared to demand constitutional reform. There were those in Great Britain who said that we should not be at all friendly with a government so little liberal in mentality. But, after all, you must take nations as you find them, and their domestic affairs are quite their own concern, and one should not be provincial in one's judgments, but should make friends even with the mammon of unrighteousness for the sake of the peace of Europe, which was a good deal talked of just then by the Powers, though it is doubtful whether any of them really believed in it. It is certain that the nations by no means neglected the steady increase and building up of armaments by land and sea. They hurried away from the Hague Conference to lay down new battleships at a reckless pace ; even Mr. W. T. Stead said, " Let us strengthen our navy, for on its fighting power the peace of Europe depends." Strengthen our navy we did ; but as to the peace of Europe, that lovely, insubstantial wraith, she was perhaps frightened by all those armoured ships, all those noisy guns, all those fluent statesmen talking, for she never put on much flesh and bones.

20

1907

OUTSIDE politics, 1907 was a gay year enough. There was a severe outbreak of pageantitis, which many people enjoyed very much, and others found vastly disagreeable. Drama was noticeably good ; the Vedrenne-Barker company moved from the Court to the Savoy, and the intelligent playgoer moved after it. Miss Horniman's Repertory Theatre toured the provinces ; and the Abbey Theatre players took English audiences by storm. Acting was good, literature and the arts were much encouraged, dancing and social entertainments were more than ever the fashion. Society, it was said, was getting rowdier. For that matter, society has always been getting rowdier, since the dawn of time. How rowdy it will end, in what nameless orgies it will be found at the Last Day, is a solemn thought indeed.

As to the young, they were thought of and written of much as ever, much as now. The New Young were discovered afresh, and the Edwardian variety was much like the Victorian and the Georgian. They were wild, people said ; they went their own way ; they were hard, reckless, independent, inquiring, impatient of control, and yet rather noble.

" Youth in the new century has broken with tradition," people said. " It is no longer willing to accept forms and formulæ only on account of their age. It has set out on a voyage of inquiry, and, finding some things which are doubtful, others which are insufficient, is searching for forms of experience more in harmony with the realities of life and of knowledge. . . ."

Youth was, in fact, at it again.

" Girls are so wild in these days," Vicky cheerfully complained. " Nancy and Imogen both go on in a way we'd *never* have dared to do. Nancy dances all night (of course, chaperons are a back number now) and comes home alone, or with some wild, arty young men and women, or, worse still, with one wild, arty young man, at five o'clock in the morning, and lets herself in with a bang and a rush, and often lets the arty young people in too. No, Nancy, I say to her, you don't let your friends in to my house before breakfast, and that's that. Not several of them at once, nor one by herself or himself. If they don't want to go home to their own beds, they must just go and carouse in any hotel that will receive them, for in my house they shall *not* carouse. *Nor* sit on the dining-room sofa and smoke, and carry on conversations in tones that I suppose you all think are hushed. It shall not be done, I said, so that is settled. But is it settled ? Not a bit of it. Nancy merely changes the subject, and Charles and I are woken by the hushed voices again next morning. Edwardian manners, people tell me : well, I'm a Victorian, and I don't care if it *is* 1907."

" You were doing much the same in 1880, my dear," Rome interpolated.

" Oh, well, I've forgotten . . . were we ? . . . Well,

anyhow, you can't say I was behaving like Imogen.
She doesn't care for dancing much, and she's such a
baby still that cocktails make her tipsy and cigarettes
sick ; she prefers raspberry syrup and chocolate cigars,
which is really more indecent at her age. At nineteen,
I was thinking of proper young-ladyish things, like
young men, and getting engaged ; but Imogen seems
never to have heard of either—I mean, not of young
men in their proper uses. She plays childish games,
and dashes about on her bicycle, and makes ridiculous
lists of all the ships in the navy and how much they
weigh and how many horses they're equal to, and slips
off to Portsmouth all by herself to see them launched,
without a word to any one, and, of course, makes herself ill. I said to her one day, ' I suppose you'll go
and marry into the navy some day, Jennie ; nothing
else will satisfy you.' But she opened her eyes and
said, ' *Marry* the navy ? Oh, no. I couldn't do that.
I should be too jealous of him. You see, I want to be
in the navy myself, and I know I should hate his being
in it when I couldn't. It would only rub it in. I
want to do nice things myself, not to marry people
who do them. I believe, mother, I'm perhaps too
selfish to marry ; it's *my* life I want to enjoy, not any
one else's. Besides, there might be babies, and they
would so get in the way, little sillies.' They wouldn't
get in your way, I told her (only, of course, it isn't
true, because they always do, the wretches), if only
you'd behave like other grown girls, and not be for
ever climbing about and playing silly games. You're
such a baby yourself, that's what's the matter. What
on earth the child's book will be like that's she's so
busy with I can't imagine. *She* knows nothing
about life, bless her. There's Phyllis married, and
running her home so capably, and Nancy at least
carrying on like a girl, not like a child in the

nursery—but Imogen! I lose my patience with her
sometimes."

And even as her mother spoke, Imogen was in
Hamley's in Regent Street, looking at toy pistols and
blushing. She was blushing because she had just
been deceitful, and was afraid that the lady attending
on her guessed. " For what aged child is it ? " this
helpful lady had asked. " Would caps or blank
cartridges be what he'd want ? I mean, if he's *very*
young. . . ."

" Oh, no," Imogen mumbled, " he's not awfully
young. Blank cartridges, he likes. . . ."

She bent her abashed face over the weapons, fingering
them. A sordid fib : was she seen through ? She
chose her pistol quickly, paid for it, and hurried out
of the shop. When she got well away, she extracted
the weapon from its cardboard box and tucked it,
with a guilty look round, into the side pocket of her
skirt.

She strode along with a new reckless gallantry.

" Patrick slipped among the crowd ; that queer,
cosmopolitan, rather sinister crowd that is to be found
around the Marseilles docks. Was he followed ? His
hand strayed to his hip pocket. His keen, veiled eyes
took in the passers-by without seeming to look. If he
could get through the next hour without mishap, he
would be aboard and a-sail. But could he ? Prob'ly
not. . . ."

While Imogen thus walked in foreign ports or track-
less forests, a happy, dreaming spinster, a reckless
adventurer armed to the teeth, many of her contemporaries and elders walked in suffragist processions,
adventurers too, and no less absorbed than she. Stanley,
disgusted now by the increasingly reasonless methods
of the militants, had definitely turned her back on them
and joined the constitutionals. These arranged orderly

and ladylike processions, headed at times by Lady Carlisle.

"There can be no doubt," wrote the more dignified press, after one such procession, "that many of these lady suffragettes are absolutely in earnest, and honestly believe that the cause for which they are contending is a just and sane one. But the fact remains that they are in the minority : that the sex, *qua* sex, is still content, and proud to be content, to accept the symbol of petticoat. . . ." (How indecent," cried Vicky, " to gossip about our underwear in a leader by a man ! ") . . . "the symbol of petticoat as the badge of disenfranchisement." Women, the article continued, are of low mental calibre, and will never understand politics, and if they did it would interfere with their only duty, the propagation of the race.

"I love journalists," said Rome, reading this to her papa at their Sunday breakfast. "They always write as if women did that job single-handed. They are so modest about men's share in it, which is really quite as important as ours. They even kindly call us the fount of life. Dear, generous, self-effacing creatures. . . ."

But papa was shaking his head, gravely.

"You make a joke of it, my dear. But this low mental equipment on the part of the writers on our leading papers is really a tragedy. The guiders of public opinion. . . . The blind leading the blind. . . . How can we avoid the ditch ? "

"Indeed, we certainly don't avoid the ditch. We are all in it, up to the neck. But if one is to be sad on account of the low mental equipment of writers or others, there will be very little joy left. For my part, I find a considerable part of my joy in it ; it assists in providing the cheering spectacle of human absurdity.'

"Pass me the paper, my dear. I want to read about . . . I want to see it."

Rome smiled behind the screen of paper which papa put up between him and her. Well she knew what papa wanted to see in it. He was looking for news of Mr. R. J. Campbell and his New Theology, searching for tidings of Pantheism and the Divine Immanence. And, sure enough, he found them. There was a Saying of the Week. Among the eminent persons who had said other things, such as Dr. Clifford, who had remarked, a little meiosistically, " It is not necessary to burn a man who is seeking the truth," and the Lord Chief Justice, who had observed, more topically, " One of the greatest errors that motorists can make is to believe that upon their blowing their horns everybody should clear out of the way," and Prince Fushimi from Japan, who had said, " I do not wish to object to the *Mikado*, as I am sure its writers did not intend to hurt the feelings of a great nation, but I shall, of course, be glad if it is not performed," and two doctors, one of whom had said, " Kissing consists in depositing some saliva on the lips or cheeks of another person," and the other, " Those who do not like milk will get cancer "— among all these utterers of truth came Mr. R. J. Campbell, remarking brightly, not for the first time nor for the last, " The New Theology is the gospel of the humanity of God and of the divinity of man."

" True," said papa, within himself. " Very true. Very proper and intelligent indeed."

He sighed gently behind the newspaper. He had had, of late, his doubts as to Higher Thought ; as to whether it was very intelligent, very proper, or very true. It was strange in so many ways ; high, doubtless, but perhaps for earth too high. And there were strange tales going about concerning the Gurus who led in prayer and in thought. And the leg of that unfortunate young man . . . how could people believe such nonsense ? The element of folly in all human creeds was becoming, in the case of Higher Thought, painfully evident to papa.

This New Theology, now—this young man Campbell —he seemed, somehow, nearer to solid earth than did the Higher Thinkers. He might talk of the Divinity of Man, but he did not, as papa, having read his book on the subject, knew, mean anything silly by it, only what all the mystics have meant—the divine spark in the human heart. As to the humanity of God—well, he probably meant no harm by that either. He was but an anthropomorphist, like the rest of us.

The theologians had been hard upon that book of his. It was not, of course, the book of a scholar; all it said had been said much better by Loisy and other Catholic modernists, whom Mr. Campbell palely reflected. But it gave a good, peptonised version, suitable for the unscholarly mind. And its reviewers had been unkind. They had nearly all attacked it. Dr. Robertson Nicoll in the *British Weekly* had snubbed it at considerable length. The *Church Times* had said, " The book is one long offence against good taste," and the *Methodist Recorder*, " Frankly, we do not think this book worth reading, and to price it at six shillings is enough to make us join in the Book War." Theological reviewers were not always fair, as papa, since he had published his own mighty and erudite work on *Comparative Religions*, had known. For himself, he had liked Mr. Campbell's book, even though it was rather bright than scholarly, more an appeal to the man in the City Temple than to the student or the theologian. Papa, besides being a student and a theologian, had of late been also on Sundays a man in the City Temple. He had said nothing of it yet to any one; he was trying it. He liked it; there was nothing in it to bewilder or offend. The Divine Immanence: call it Pantheism who chose, it was a beautiful idea. It was in no degree incompatible with the Divine Transcendence; why should it be, since there was also the Divine Ubiquity?

Brooding on these matters, papa finished breakfast somewhat silently, and lit his pipe.

"A beautiful day," said Rome, smoking her cigarette at the open window. "I shall be out for lunch and tea, papa. I am joining a party of pleasure; we are going to explore, in our cars, to Newlands Corner, where we shall have trials of skill and of speed. You won't come with me, I suppose?"

"No thank you, dear, I think not. I'm too old for trials of skill and speed; too old, even, for exploring."

Precisely, thought Rome, glancing at him with her indulgent smile, what papa was not and never would be. He would very surely go exploring this morning, searching the riches of the spiritual kingdoms. Much more exciting than Newlands Corner. . . . To papa at seventy-seven, as to Mr. R. J. Campbell at whatever age he might be, theology could still seem new. Rome wondered whether it was an advantage or a misfortune that to her, at forty-eight, all theologies, as most other of the world's businesses, seemed so very old. The only things that seemed new to her in 1907 were taximeter cabs.

"Well, good-bye, dear, and good luck," Rome wished her papa.

Of 1907 there is not very much more to record. Two or three items of news may perhaps be mentioned. Maurice's son, Roger, aged twenty-four, now attached, at his own urgent desire, to the literary side of his father's paper (He can't do much harm there, I suppose," Maurice said, "though he'll not do any good either; he hasn't the brains ") published a novel. It was a long novel, and it was about a youth not unlike what Roger conceived himself to be, only his home was different, for his father was a churchwarden and bore the bag in church, and bullied and beat and prayed over his children ; fathers in fiction must be like this, not heretical and intelligent journalists. The book conducted the youth from the nursery through his private and public schools (house matches, school politics, vice, expulsions, and so on), through Cambridge (the Union, the river, tobacconists' assistants, tripos) to journalistic, social and literary London, where it left him, at twenty-four, having just published his first novel, which was a great success.

" God, what tripe," Maurice commented, but to himself, as he turned the pages. " Exactly what the boy *would* write, of course. No better, and no worse. Well, poor lad, he's pleased with it enough. And it will probably be handsomely reviewed. It's the stuff to give the public all right." His thoughts strayed to a familiar, rather bitter point. If he had been given (by Amy : how fantastic a thought !) a son with brains ; a son with a hard, clear head or an original imagination ; a son who, if he wrote at all, wouldn't produce the stuff to give the public, a son who, like himself, would see the public damned first. . . .

Roger was, as his father had predicted, handsomely reviewed, for the Edwardians rather liked the biography-of-a-young-man type of novel, and loved details of school life. Roger had his feet well on the ladder of successful fiction-writing. Roger would be all right. Meanwhile, his head swelled even larger than before. His father perceived that the innocent youth really believed his reviewers, and conceived himself to be a writer and a clever young man.

The other items I record of the year 1907 I quote from the diary of Imogen for the 16th of March.

" *Indomitable* launched, Glasgow. Largest and quickest cruiser in the world. 17,250 tons. 41,000 h.p. 25 knots. *Invincible* and *Inflexible*, same type, building. Finished book, began to type it. Got guinea prize from *Saturday Westminster* for poem."

21

WHITHER ?

AND so to the last years of Edwardianism. In them that gay, eager, cultivated period listed gently to the political left. The Socialist budget, as it was called by its opponents, " the end of all things," as Lord Rosebery a little optimistically called it, agitated the country. Old Age Pensions were at last established, to the disgust of Tories, who had, however, when members of Parliament, to be careful how they expressed their disgust, for fear of their needy constituents. " Whither are we drifting ? " inquired the Conservative Press, in anger and fear. " Here is Socialism unabashed : the thin end of the wedge which shall at last undermine the integrity and liberty of our Constitution." Here were sixty millions a year, not insurance, but a free dole, squandered on supporting old persons who might just as well be supported in workhouses. What would that come to in Dreadnoughts ? Anyhow, we had got to lay down six or seven Dreadnoughts a year for the present, if we were to be to Germany in the ratio of two keels to one, which was assuredly essential. " They are ringing their bells ; they will soon be wringing their hands," said the Tory leaders. The radical element in the government strengthened ; Sir Henry Campbell Bannerman died, and in Mr. Asquith's ministry Mr. Lloyd

George was Chancellor of the Exchequer. But it remained, on the whole, a Liberal-Imperialist government, and left most of the radicalism to Labour, whose parliamentary strength was increasing and unifying. Wherever we were drifting, it was not towards extreme radicalism.

As to Ireland, a bill was passed to reduce her docks, thistles, and noxious weeds : no other bill.

Parliamentary affairs and party politics were no more exciting and no more tedious (for that last is impossible) than usual. Of more interest were the first flying machines that really flew, the drawings of Mr. Augustus John, exhibited at the New English Art Club and condemned by critics (except those who liked the kind of thing) as essays in a savage and childish archaism, and deliberate insults to our intelligence (whither, indeed, art was drifting, when such drawings could be praised ?), and the establishment of the White City at Shepherd's Bush, with the Franco-British Exhibition (sadly dull), and flip-flaps, switchbacks, wiggle-woggles, and scenic railways (most exciting, and an insidious snare for pocket-money ; you could get rid there in one evening of the careful hoardings of weeks ; also, if you were as weak in the stomach as Imogen, you felt repentant after a few goes). Thither President Fallières, on a visit to King Edward was taken, to enjoy the Franco-British exhibition and cement the *entente cordiale*, which, however, needed it less then than now, for the Edwardians were on the whole most enthusiastic about this international understanding. "There is no longer a Channel," they said, publicly and politely ; but in their hearts, for they were no more foolish than we, they still gave thanks for this useful, if unpleasing, strip of sea.

To forge faster the other link in the Triple *Entente*, that only possible guarantee for a world peace, King

Edward visited the Tsar of all the Russias, at Reval.
So there we were, grasping these two great military
powers firmly by the hand, ready to face any emergency. We had got ahead of Germany in this matter
of Russia. For all the European Powers, discreetly
averting their eyes from the chronic bloodstains on
the bear's savage claws, were courting her for her
legions. To have the bear at their beck and call—
that was what every one wanted, against the emergencies
which might arise. And never was a time when emergencies seemed more imminent, more dangerous,
more frequent, such a state of simmering unrest was
Europe's in the days of Edward the Peacemaker.
Of the Kaiser Wilhelm and his Uncle Bertie it has been
said that their relations " lapsed into comparative
calm only when they were apart from one another."
Their subjects feared and hated each other ; the press
in each country stirred up terror of invasion by
the other ; " the German invasion," " the English
invasion "—these phrases were bandied about in two
jealous, frightened empires. The German spy scare,
the British spy scare, these fevers were worked up in
the jingo press of two countries. " You English are
mad, mad, mad," said William. " I strive without
ceasing to improve relations and you retort that I am
your arch-enemy. You make it very hard for me."

For that matter, nations always make it hard for
one another ; it is their function. We did make it
hard for Germany, but Germany made it harder for
us, and France made it hardest for every one.

Anyhow, here was the Triple *Entente*, full-armed, to
meet the Triple Alliance, and some one or other would
see to it that they did meet before long.

The chief European emergency which arose at the
moment was an attack of megalomania on the part of
Servia, in 1909. The Serbs had the madness to dream

of a greater Servia, which should unite the scattered peoples of their race—" a dream," said the English press, " as hopeless as that of Poland *rediviva*. Greater Servia will either be realised under the sceptre of the Hapsburgs, or will not be realised at all." The awkwardness of the situation, so far as we are concerned, was that Russia was, as usual, backing her mad little militant friend, and had to be dissuaded with great tact from upsetting the apple cart. However, a joint note to Servia from the Powers quieted her for the time being, and the lid was shut down temporarily on the seething European kettle of fish.

Other intriguing matters of this year were the building, in British dockyards, of three huge battleships for Brazil, which disgusted others than young Imogen Carrington ; the Olympic games in July ; the publication of various not unamusing books ; and the deaths of two old men, Algernon Swinburne and George Meredith. Our two greatest Grand Old Men had departed from us, and no more would pilgrims alight at the Pines, Putney, or go exploring to Box Hill. The office of our literary G.O.M. was filled now only by Mr. Thomas Hardy, for Mr. Henry James was still an American. Sometimes one speculates, aghast, what would happen should we ever be left with no candidates for that honourable post—that is to say, with no celebrated literary man or woman (for there might, though improbably, be a G.O.W. some day) over seventy years of age, no Master for the younger writers to greet on the festival of his birth. It would be an undignified state of affairs indeed, and one need not anticipate it at present, for behind Mr. Hardy there looms more than one candidate of respectable claims.

The closing years of this reign were brightened further by Commander Peary and Dr. Cook, who both maintained that they had discovered the North Pole. It was ultimately decided that only the Commander had done so, as the doctor had had the misfortune to mislay his papers in Greenland ; but his was a sporting venture, and deserving of all applause, and he had a good run for his money.

And so an end to Edwardianism. The new Georgianism dawned on a nervous, gay, absorbed nation, experimenting in new but cautious legislation, alive on the whole, to new literature and new art, alive wholly to whatever enjoyment it could find, and thoroughly tied up in Continental politics, so that when that mine was fired we should go up with it sky-high.

PART IV
GEORGIAN

FIRST PERIOD: CIRCUS

I

THE HAPPY GEORGIANS

THE first Georgian years, the years between 1910 and 1914, are now commonly thought of as gay, as very happy, hectic, whirling, butterfly years, punctuated, indeed, by the too exciting doings of dock and transport strikers, Ulstermen, suffragists, the *Titanic*, and Mr. Lloyd George, but, all the same, gay years. Like other generalisations about periods, this is a delusion. Those years only seem especially gay to us because, since July, 1914, the years have not been gay at all. Really they were quite ordinary years. In fact, it is folly to speak of these insensate seasonal periods as happy or the reverse. It is only animate creatures which can be that, and it is unlikely that all, or the majority, of animate creatures should be visited by circumstances making for pleasurable emotion or the reverse at the same time as one another, except in the case of some great public event. Some early Georgians were gay, some sad, some bored, some tepid and indifferent, as at any other time.

Nevertheless, it so happened that the persons in this so-called narrative were all quite sufficiently happy during this period. They were all having, in their several ways, a fairly good time.

2

PAPA

MR. GARDEN'S way was, it need scarcely be said, a spiritual way. He was now over eighty, and his was the garnered fruit of a long life of spiritual adventure. He had believed so much, he had believed so often, he had fought with doubt so ardently and with such repeated success, he had explored every avenue of faith with such adventurous zeal, that he had at last reached a table-land from whence he could survey all creeds with loving, impartial pleasure. Even Mr. Campbell's New Theology had not enmeshed him for long ; he passed through it and out of it, and it took its place among the ranks of Creeds I Have Believed.

And now, in some strange, transcendent manner, he believed them all. Nothing is true but thinking makes it so ; papa thought all these faiths, and for him they were all true. What, after all, is truth ? An unanswerable riddle, to which papa replied, " The truth for each soul is that faith by which it holds." So truth, for papa, was many-splendoured, many-faced. God must exist, he knew, or he could not have believed in Him so often and so much. The sunset of life was to papa very lovely, as he journeyed westward into it, murmuring, " I believe . . . I believe. . . ." Catholicism (Roman and Anglo), Evangelicism, Ethicism, Unitarianism, Latitudinarian Anglicism, Seventh-Day Adventism, Christian Science, Irvingitism, even poor Flossie and her chat, he did very happily and earnestly believe. He believed in a mighty sacramental Church that was the voice of God and the store-house of grace ; he believed that he was saved through private intercourse and contract with his Lord ; he believed in the

Church established in this country, and that it should be infinitely adaptable to the new knowledge and demands of men ; he believed that the world was (very likely) to be ended in a short time by the second coming of Christ ; he believed that God was love, and evil a monstrous illusion ; he believed that God permitted the veil between this world and the next to be rent by the meanest and most trivial of His creatures, if they had the knack. Indeed, papa might be said to have learnt the art of believing anything.

Irving said it was pleasant to find that papa was once again an Irvingite. Indeed, the creeds after which he had named his children now all flourished in papa's soul. No longer did he shake his head when he remembered in what spiritual moods he had named Una, or Rome, or sigh after that lost exultation of the soul commemorated in Vicky. Had another child been given to him now he would have named it Verity, in acknowledgement of the fact that nearly everything was true.

What wonder, then, that papa was a happy Georgian ?

3

VICKY

VICKY, dashing full-sail through her fifties, was a happy Georgian too. She was handsome in her maturity, and merry. People she loved, and parties, and gossip, and bridge, and her husband and children, and the infants of her daughter Phyllis, and food and drink and clothes, and Ascot, and going abroad, and new novels from Mudie's, and theatres and concerts and meetings and causes, and talk, talk, talk. Life, she held, is good as you get on in it ; a broad, sunny

and amusing stream, having its tiresome worries, no doubt, but, in the main, certainly a comedy. Vicky as an early Georgian was a generously fashioned matron, broader and fuller than of old, with her fair skin little damaged by time, and not much gray in her chestnut hair, which she wore piled in a mass of waves and curls, in the manner of early Georgian matrons. A delightful woman, with an unfailing zest for life. You couldn't exactly discuss things with her, but she could and did discuss them with you. She would tell you what she thought about the world and its ways in a flow of merry comment, skimming from one topic to another with an agile irrelevance that grew with the years. A merry, skimming matron ; certainly a happy Georgian.

4

MAURICE

MAURICE had not, since he married Amy, been a happy Victorian or Edwardian, and he did not become an exactly happy Georgian, but he was happier than before. In his fifties he was no nearer accepting the world as he found it than he had ever been. It still appeared to him to be a hell of a place. He was, in his fifties, a lean, small, bitter man, his light hair graying on the temples and receding from the forehead, his sensitive mouth and long jaw sardonically, cynically set. He was popular in London, for all his bitter tongue and pen ; he and his paper were by now an institution, known for their brilliance, clarity, hard, unsentimental intolerance, and honesty. You might disagree with Maurice Garden ; you might even think that he had an evil temper and a habit of mild intoxication ; but you had to respect two things about him, his intelligence and his sincerity. Tosh and slush he would not stand, whether it might be about the Empire, about the poor suffragists in prison who would not eat, about White Slaves (whom his paper called, briefly and precisely, prostitutes, holding that the colour of their skins was an irrelevant point to raise when considering the amelioration of their lot), about the poor tax-robbed upper classes, or the poor labour-ground lower. He would print no correspondence couched in sentimental terms ; if people desired to write about the sufferings, say, of birds deprived of their feathers for hats, they had to put it in a few concise words, and to say precisely what steps they wished to see taken about it. No superfluous wailings or tears were permitted, on any topic, to the writers in the *Gadfly*. The editor had a good deal of trouble with the literary side of his paper, which inclined, in his opinion, to roll logs, to be slavishly in the fashion in the matter of admiring the right people, to accept weak articles and rubbishy poems from people with budding or full-blown reputations, and, generally, to be like most literary papers. His son, Roger, he did not for long permit to adorn the literary staff : to do so would have been, in view of the calibre of Roger's intelligence, gross nepotism. Roger had to get another literary job on a less fastidious paper ; meanwhile, to his father's disgust, he continued to produce novels, and even began on verse, so that he appeared in current anthologies of contemporary poetry. Also, he got married. So did his sister, Iris. That settled, and his children well off his hands, Maurice felt that his only and dubious link with family life was snapped, and that he was free to go his own way. He left his wife, offering to provide her with any material she preferred for a divorce, from a mistress to a black eye. Amy accepted the offer, and these two victims of a singularly unfortunate entanglement found rest from one another at last. It was, Amy complained, too late for her to marry again ; of course, Maurice, selfish pig, had waited till it was too late for her but not for him. But Maurice had no inclination to re-marry ; he had had more than enough of that business. The only woman he had ever seriously loved had married ten years ago, ending deliberately an unhappy, pas-sionate and fruitless relationship. Maurice's thoughts were not now woman-ward ; he lived for his job, and for interest in the bitter comedy of affairs that the world played before him. His silly, common, nagging wife, his silly, ordinary, disappointing children, no more oppressed him ; they could, for him, now go their own silly ways. He was free.

5

ROME

ROME was a happy Georgian. For her the comedy of the world was too amusing to be bitter. She, in her splendid idle fifties, was known in London as a lady of wits, of charm, of humour ; a gentlewoman of parts, the worldly, idle, do-nothing, care-nothing sister of the busy and useful Mrs. Croft, contributing nothing to the world beyond an attractive presence, good dinner table talk, a graceful zest for gambling, an intelligent, cynical, running commentary on life, and a tolerant, observing smile. Life was a good show to her ; it arranged itself well, and she was clever at picking out the best scenes. When, for instance, she had an inclination to visit the House of Commons, she would discover first on which afternoon the Labour members, or the Irish, were going to have a good row, or Mr. Lloyd George was going to talk like an excited street preacher, or Sir Edward Carson like an Orangeman, or any other star performer do his special turn, and she would select that afternoon and have her reward. Our legislators were to her just that—circus turns, some good, some poor, but none of them with any serious relation to life as lived (if, indeed, any relation with that absurd business could be called serious, which was doubtful).

So the cheerful spectacle of a world of fools brightened Rome's afternoon years. Before long, the folly was to become too desperate, too disastrous, too wrecking a business to be a comic show even to the most amused eyes ; the circus was, all too soon, to go smash, and the folly of the clowns who had helped to smash it became a bitterness, and the idiot's tale held too much of sound and fury to be borne. But these first Georgian years were, to Rome, twinkling with bland absurdity. She cheered up Maurice in the matter of that prose and verse by means of which his son made of himself a foolish show, reminding him that we all make of ourselves foolish shows in one way or another, and the printed word was one of the less harmful ways of doing this. It was no worse, she maintained, to be a novelist and poet than any other kind of a fool, and one kind or another we all are. After all, he might be instead a swindling company promoter. . . .

" No," said Maurice. " He hasn't the wits. And, you know, I don't share your philosophy. I still believe, in the teeth of enormous odds, that it is possible to make something of this life—that one kind of achievement is more admirable—or less idiotic, if you like—than another. I still think bad, shallow, shoddy work like Roger's damnable, however unimportant it may be. It's a mark on the wrong side, the side of stupidity.

You don't believe in sides, but I do. And I'm glad
I do, so don't try to infect me with your poisonous
indifference. I am a man of faith, I tell you; I have
a soul. You are merely a cynic, the basest of God's
creatures. You disbelieve in everything. I disbelieve
in nearly everything, but not quite. So I shall be
saved and you will not. Have a cocktail, Gallio."

6

STANLEY

STANLEY'S son was at Oxford, reading for a pass, for
it was no manner of use, they said, his reading for
anything more. He was a nice boy, but not yet clever.
"Not yet," Stanley had said of him all through his
schooldays, meaning that Billy was late in developing.
"Not yet," she still said, meaning that he was so late
that he would not have developed properly until his
last year at Oxford, or possibly after that. Not that
Billy was stupid; he was quite intelligent about a
number of things, but not, on the whole, about the
things in books, which made it awkward about examina-
tions. Nor was he intelligent about politics; in fact,
politics bored him a good deal. However, he was
destined for a political career. Stanley's cousin, Sir
Giles Humphries, a Liberal member of Parliament, had
promised Stanley to take Billy as a junior secretary
when he left Oxford, if he should show any capacity
for learning the job. Billy's Liberal political career
would thus be well begun. Meanwhile, Billy was an
affectionate, companionable boy, who hid his boredom
and his ignorance from his mother as well as might be,
and very nicely refrained from making mock of militant
suffragists in her presence, for, though Stanley had

ceased to be a militant, many of her friends were, in these years, in and out of prison.

Molly wouldn't go to college. No one, indeed, but her mother suggested that she should. She was obviously not suited, by either inclination or capacities, for the extension of her education. Stanley would have been glad to have Molly at home with her when she left school, for Molly had the heart-breaking charm of her father, even down to his narrow, laughing eyes, and odd, short face. Stanley adored Molly. Molly was tepid and casual about votes, and had no head for books, and not the most rudimentary grasp on public affairs, and she was worse at meetings and causes than any girl in the world. She didn't even pretend, like Billy. She would laugh in Stanley's face, with her incomparable impudence, when Stanley was talking, and say, " Mumsie, darling, stop committing. Oh, mumsie, not before your chee-ild," and flutter a butter-fly kiss on Stanley's cheek to change the subject. And she wanted to go on the stage. She wanted to go, and went, to a dramatic school, to learn to act. Well, better that than nothing, Stanley sighed. If she *does* learn to act, it will be all right. If she doesn't, she's learning something. If it doesn't make her affected and stupid, like actresses, I don't mind. And surely nothing can make Molly less than entrancing. But, whatever comes of it, Molly has a right to choose her own life ; it's no business of mine what the children decide to do. In her conscious reaction from the one-time parental tyranny over daughters, Stanley forgot that there might also be parental tyranny over sons, and that Billy, too, had a right to choose his own life. It is creditable to Billy that she could forget it. Billy was the best of sons.

Meanwhile, Stanley was fighting (constitutionally) for votes, women's trade unions, the welfare of factory girls, continuation schools, penal reform, clean milk, and the decrease of prostitution. It may be imagined that all these things together kept her pretty busy; unlike Rome, she had no time to visit Parliament on its best days; she only went there when one of the topics in which she was interested was going to be raised. She got thus, Rome told her, all the dry bread and none of the jam. However, Stanley preferred the dry bread days, though they were invariably stupid and disappointing.

Though only a very little of all she had at heart got done, Stanley was happy. She laboured under the delusion that the constitution and social condition of her country were, on the whole, faintly on the upward plane. That was because she was unfairly biased towards the Liberal party in the State, and too apt to approve of the measures they passed. She approved of Old Age Pensions; she even approved, on the whole, of Mr. Lloyd George's Insurance Act; and she approved of the People's Budget very much.

7

IRVING

IRVING was nearly always cheerful, except when he was cross. Irving was like that. He had been a cheerful Victorian and a cheerful Edwardian, and was now, in his late forties, a cheerful Georgian. He had a beautiful and charming wife, creditable children, a house in Devonshire and a house in London, a great deal of money (though the super-tax robbed him of much of it), two motor-cars, good fishing, shooting and stag hunting, and an excellent digestion. He had his troubles. The People's Budget troubled him a good deal, and the land taxes, and all the unfair, socialist legislation to which he was subject. He sometimes threatened to go and live abroad, to escape it. But he did not go and live abroad. He was, for all his troubles, a happy Englishman.

8

UNA

UNA, too, was cheerful. She was unaffected by reigns and periods. She was a very unconscious Georgian. Not like Stanley, who said, " We are now Georgians. Georgian England must be much better than any England before it," nor like Roger, who would murmur, " We Georgians face facts . . ." nor like Vicky, who cried, " I will *not* be called a Georgian ; not while that little Welsh horror rules over us." Una hardly knew she was a Georgian, and, indeed, she was not, in any but a strictly technical sense. Her mind was unstirred by what used, long ago, to be called the Zeitgeist. She was happy ; she enjoyed good health ; her daughters were like polished corners and her sons like young plants ; her husband's acres flourished and his corn and wine and oil increased (as a matter of fact, his wine, always a trifle too much, had of late years decreased ; Ted was a soberer man than of old) ; Katie, their handsome eldest, had married well ; and Una found in the countryside the profound, unconscious content that animals find. Riding, walking, gardening, driving about the level Essex lands, she, attuned to the soil on which she lived, was happy and serene.

9

IMOGEN

THE younger generation of Georgians were happy enough.
They were married, engaged, painting, writing, dancing,
at the bar, at the universities, at school. They were
behaving in the several manners suitable to their
temperaments and years. Their lives were full of
interests, artistic, literary, athletic, and social. Vicky's
Nancy was learning to paint futuristically ; she had
now a little studio in Chelsea, where she could be as
Bohemian as she liked, and have her friends all night
without disturbing any one. Night clubs, too, had of
late come in, and were a great convenience. Phyllis
was bringing up her children. Hugh, eating dinners
in the Temple, read of torts and morts, but dreamed of
machinery, and drew diagrams in court of pistons and
valves, and jotted down algebraic formulæ when he
should have been jotting down legal notes. Hugh was
really a mechanician, and his heart was not in law,
though he liked it well enough. His brother Tony
had gone from Cambridge to the Foreign Office, and,
when not writing drafts, was a merry youth about
town.

Imogen was happy. She felt her life to be pleasure-
soaked ; a lovely, an elegant orgie of joy. And pleasure,
orgies of dissipation even, did not absorb her, but were
ministrants to the clear, springing life of the imagination. Imagination brimmed the cup of her spirit like
golden wine. She felt happy and good, like a child in
an orchard, ripe apples and pears tumbling in soft
grass about her, the silver boat of the moon riding in a
green sky. For her birds sang, sweet bells chimed and
clashed, the stars made a queer, thin, tinkling song on

still and moonless nights. The people hurrying about the city streets and squares were kind and merry and good, like brownies; the city itself was a great, gay booth, decked and lit. Dawn came on a golden tide of peace; noon drove a flaming chariot behind the horses of the sun; evening spread soft wings, tender and blue and green; night was sweet as a dream of apple-blossoms by running water. When she wrote, whether by day or by night, her brain felt clear and lit, as by a still, bright taper burning steadily. Her thoughts, her words, rose up in her swiftly, like silver fishes in a springing rock pool; round and round they swam, and she caught them and landed them before they got away. While she wrote, nothing mattered but to seize and land what she saw thus springing up, to reach down her net and catch it while she might. Verse she wrote, and prose, with growing fastidiousness as to form and words. When she had first begun publishing what she wrote, she had been too young; she had fumbled after style like a blind puppy; she had been, like nearly all very young writers, superfluous of phrase, redundant. She read with fastidious disgust in her first book of stories such meaningless phrases as, "He lifted the child bodily over the rail and dropped it into the sea." Bodily; as if the victim might, on the other hand, have been only caught up in the spirit, like St. Paul. What did I mean, she asked, across the years, of that bungling child, knowing that she had indeed meant nothing. But now style, the stark, bare structure of language, was to her a fetish. It was good to be getting on in life—twenty-three twenty-four, twenty-five—so that one's head was clearer, if not yet very clear. The very young, thought Imogen, are muddled; they love cant and shun truth; they adopt and use imitative phrases; they are sentimental and easy idealists behind their masks of cheerful, slangy hardness. Undergraduates, male and female, and their non-collegiate contemporaries, are the most obscurantist of reactionaries ; facts annoy them and they pretend they do not see them, preferring to walk muffled through life, until life forcibly, year by year, tears the bandages from their eyes. The later Georgian, the post-war very young, were to be even more sentimental, muffled and imitative than their predecessors, because of the demoralising war, which was to give them false standards in the schoolroom. But the pre-war adolescents were sentimental enough.

The sharp, clear and bitter truth—that was the thing to aim at, thought Imogen, in her twenty-fifth year, knowing she was still far, but not knowing how far, from that. That courageous realism which should see things as they were, she desired, knowing herself to be still a false seer, blinded and dazzled by her personal circumstances, warped and circumscribed in her vision by the circle of her life. Perhaps she was too comfortable, too happy. . . . Or perhaps, like most people, too emotionally alive, strung too sharply to every vibration, for the clear, detached intellectuality she craved.

I feel things too much, she thought, smiling to be thinking what so many people thought, what too many even said, of themselves.

I don't feel things much. I am not easily moved by life. . . . Why did people so seldom say that, and so much more seldom think it ? No doubt because every one feels things terrifically, is quite horribly moved by this most moving business, life. No one believes him or herself to be insensitive, for no one is insensitive, life not being an affair it is possible to be insensitive to.

In a deeper layer of consciousness, where herself watched herself, Imogen thought that, though she might

believe herself to be sensitive to life, she at any rate
knew why she believed it, knew why every one believed
it of themselves, and that redeemed her from the
commonplace boast, and gave her over the people who
say " I *feel* too much, that's where it is," the advantage
that the conscious must always have over the unconscious, the advantage, if it be one, that is perhaps
the main difference between sophisticated and primitive
forms of life.

Meanwhile Imogen, like her cousin Roger, wrote and
published verse and prose. After all, it didn't matter
what one wrote. People wrote and wrote, and nearly
every kind of thing got written by some one or other,
well or ill, usually ill, and never so well as to touch more
than the very outside edge of the beauty and adventure
which was life. Written words opened the door, that
was all. Beyond the door lay the adventure, bright
and still and eerily clear, like a dream. Strange seas,
purple with racing currents in the open, but under the
eaves of coral islands green and clear like jade ; white
beaches of those same islands, hot in the sunshine under
the spreading leaves of bread-fruit trees ; yams and
cocoa-nuts and pineapples dropping with nutty noises
on to emerald-green grass ; a little boat moored at the
edge of lapping, creamy waves ; witty monkeys and
brilliant parrots chattering in the jungle ; a little fire
at night outside the tent, and a gun ready to one's
hand. Great fishes and small fishes swimming deeply in
the jade rock pools, sailing and sailing with unshut eye ;
the little boat sailing too, pushing off into the wide
seas dotted with islands, white wings pricking sky-
ward like faun's ears. Or deep orchards adrift with
blossom, rosy-white ; jolly colts in paddocks, dragging
with soft lips and hard gums at their mother's milk ;
the winds of April hurtling the cloud shadows across
the grass. Long lanes running between deep hedges

in the evening, and the rustle of the sea not far, and the velvet dusk waiting for the moonrise, and queer, startled noises in the hedges, and quiet munching noises in the fields, and the cold, mocking stars looking down. And painted carts of gipsies, and roadside fires, and wood-smoke and ripe apples. And hills silver and black with olives and cypresses, and steep roads spiralling up them to little walled towns, and hoarse, chanted songs lilting among vineyards, and the jingling of the bells of oxen. And the streets and squares of rainbow-coloured towns, noisy *cafés*, and lemon trees in tubs, beautiful men noble with the feathers of cocks, beautiful women in coloured headkerchiefs, incense drifting out of churches into piazzas, coffee roasting in deep streets. To swim, to sail, to run naked on hot sands, to lie eating and eating in deep scented woods, and then to sleep; to wake and slip into clear, brown pools in sunshine, to spin out words as a spider his silvery web; to wear a scarlet silk jacket like a monkey's and little white trousers, and, for best, a little scarlet crinoline over them, sticking out, very wide and short and jaunty, and a scarlet sunshade lined with white, and on one's shoulder a tiny, flame-red cockatoo, and at one's heels two little black slaves, shining and black as ebony, with ivory teeth a-glisten and banjos tucked beneath their arms. To clap one's hands, twice, thrice, and presto! an elegant meal— mushrooms, cider and pêche melba, and mangoes and pineapple to end it, and then, when it was ended, a three-coloured ice. What joy! Dear God, what a world! What adventure, what loveliness, what dreams! Beauty without end, amen.

Then why write of what should, instead, be lived? Wasn't the marvellous heritage, the brilliant joke, the ghostly dream, of life enough? Nevertheless, one did write, and was, inexplicably, praised for it. Black marks on paper, scribbled and niggled and scrawled, and here and there the splendour and the joke and the dream broke through them, like sunshine flashing through prison bars, like music breaking through the written notes.

While she gave to the fashioning of the written word all the fastidious, meticulous austerity of devotion that she knew, Imogen in her personal life was not austere or fastidious or devoted at all. She idled ; she lounged about ; she was slovenly ; she bought and sucked toffee ; she read omnivorously, including much trash ; she was a prey to shoddy, facile emotions and moods, none of which had power to impel her to any action, because a deep, innate scepticism underlay them all ; she was a sentimental cynic. She loved too lightly and too slightly ; she was idle, greedy, foolish, childish, impatient and vain, sliding out of difficulties like a tramp who fears a job of work. She did not care for great causes ; public affairs were to her only an intriguing and entertaining show. She was a selfish girl, a shallow girl, a shoddy girl, enmeshed in egotism, happy in her own circus, caring little whether or no others had bread. Happy in her circus, and yet often wretched too, for life is like that—exquisite and agonising. She wanted to go to the Pacific Islands and bathe from coral reefs ; wanted money and fame ; wanted to be delivered for ever from meetings and tea-parties, foolish talkers and bores ; wanted to save a life, watched by cheering crowds ; wanted a motor bicycle ; wanted to be a Christian ; wanted to be a young man. But not now a naval man ; she had seen through the monotony and routine of that life. She wanted in these days to be a journalist, a newspaper correspondent, sent abroad on exciting jobs, to report wars, and eruptions of Vesuvius, and earthquakes, and Cretan excavations, and revolutions in South America, and international conferences.

10

ON PUBLISHING BOOKS

From time to time Imogen, in common with many others, brought out books, large and small. They would arrive in a parcel of six, and lie on the breakfast table, looking silly, in clownish wrappers with irrelevant pictures on them. Imogen would examine them with mild distaste. How common they looked, to be sure, now that they were bound! As common as most books, as the books by others. Dull, too. What if all the reviews said so? One couldn't help caring what reviews said, however hard one tried not to. It was petty and trivial to be cast up and cast down by the opinions of one's fellows, no wiser than oneself, expressed in print, but so it was. Why? Chiefly because they *were* expressed in print, to be read by all. One's disgrace, if it were a disgrace, was so public. People who didn't know that reviewers were just ordinary people, with no more authority or judgment than they had themselves, believed them. If people read in a review, " It cannot be said that Miss Carrington has been successful in her new book of stories," they thought that it really could not, not knowing that almost anything can, as a matter of fact, be said, and often is. And if a reviewer said (as was more usual, for reviewers are, taking them all in all, a kindly race), " This is a good book," people who didn't know any better really thought that it was so. Then the author was pleased. Particularly as the book wasn't really good in the least.

" I can't say I am much concerned about my reviews, one way or another," Roger had once said to Imogen. But he *was* concerned, all the same. Did he, did all the people who said they didn't mind things, know that they really did ? Or were they indeed deluded ? People were surely often deluded ; they said such odd things. " It's not that I mind a bit for myself, it's the principle of the thing," they would say. Or, " I don't care a damn what any one says of me," or " It isn't that I'd mind taking the risk, but one has to think of other people." And the people who said, " I know you won't mind my saying . . ." when they knew you would, or " I don't want to spread gossip, but . . ." when that was just what they did want, or " You mustn't think I'm vexed with you, dear," when they left you nothing else to think.

Did these lie ? Or were they deceived ? Imogen, pondering these apparently so confused minds in her own, which was more approximately accurate (for she would deceive others, but could not easily deceive herself) could not decide.

II

ON SUNDAY WALKS

On Sundays the early Georgians used to go from London in trains, getting out somewhere in Surrey, Sussex, Bucks or Herts, to walk in muddy lanes or over blown downs, or through dim, green-gray beechwoods or fragrant forests of pine. It is pleasanter to walk alone, or with one companion, or even two, but sometimes, unfortunately, one walks (and so did the early Georgians) in large groups, or parties of pleasure. Imogen found that she occasionally did this, for it was among the minor bad habits of her set. It did not greatly matter, and these strange processions could not really spoil the country, even though they did very greatly talk. How they talked! Books, politics, personal gossip, good jokes and bad, acrostics, stories, discussions—with these the paths and fields they traversed echoed. But Imogen, like a lower animal, felt stupid and happy and alone, and rooted about the ditches for violets and the hedges for nests, and smelt at the moss in the woods, and broke off branches to carry home. To herself she would hum a little tune, some phrase of music over and over again, and sometimes words would be born in her and sing together like stars of the morning. But for the most part, she only rooted about like a cheerful puppy, alive with sensuous joy. Her companions she loved and admired, but could not emulate, for they were wise about things she knew not of. Even about the flora and fauna of the countryside they really knew more than she, who could only take in them an ignorant and animal pleasure. She had long since guessed herself to be an imbecile, and, with the imbecile's cunning, tried to hide it from others. What if suddenly every one were to find out, discover that she was an imbecile, with a quite vacant, unhinged mind? If these informed, educated, sophisticated people should discover that, they would dismiss her from their ken; she would no more be their friend. She would be cast out, left to root about alone in the ditches, like a shameless, naked, heathen savage.

As she thought about this, some one would come and walk by her side and talk, and she would pull herself together and pretend to be passably intelligent, albeit she was really drunk with the soft spring wind and the earthy smell of the wood.

12

ON MARRIAGE

IMOGEN loved lightly and slightly, her heart not being much in that business. Life was full of stimulating contacts. She admired readily, and liked, was interested, charmed and entertained. Men and women passed to and fro on her stage, delightful, witty, graceful, brilliant, even good, and found favour in her eyes. Poets, politicians and priests, journalists and jesters, artists and writers, scholars and social reformers, lovely matrons, witty maids, and cheerful military men, toilers, spinsters, and lilies of the field—a pleasant, various crowd, they walked and worked and talked. So many people were alluring, so many tedious, so many tiresome. One could, unless one was careless, evade the tedious and the tiresome. But supposing that one had been very careless, and had married one of them? What a shocking entanglement life might then become! How monstrously jarring and fatiguing would be the home!

"Whether one marries or remains celibate," Imogen reflected, in her pedantic, deliberating way, "that is immaterial. Both have advantages. But to marry one of the right people, if at all, is of the greatest consequence for a happy life. People do not always think intelligently enough on this important subject. Too often they appear to act on impulse, or from some inadequate motive. And the results are as we see." For she was seeing at the moment several ill-mated couples of her acquaintance, some of whom made the best of it, others the worst. Many sought and found affinities elsewhere, for affinities they must (or so they believed) have. Others, renouncing affinity as a baseless dream, wisely accepted less of life than that, and lived in disillusioned amenity with their spouses.

An amazing number of marriages came, on the other hand, off, and these were a pleasant sight to see. To come home every evening to the companion you preferred and who preferred you—that would be all right. (Only there might be babies, and that would be all wrong, because they would want bathing or something just when you were busy with something else.) Or to come home to no one ; or (better still) not to come home at all. So many habits of life were enjoyable, but not that of perpetual unsuitable companionship.

Thus Imogen reflected and philosophised on this great topic of marriage and of love, which did not, however, really interest her so much as most other topics, for she regarded it as a little primitive, a little elementary, lacking in the more entertaining complexities of thought. Metaphysics, poetry, psychology and geography made to her a stronger intellectual appeal ; the non-emotional functionings of the dwellers on this planet she found more amusing, and the face of the planet itself more beautiful.

Nevertheless, to be a little in love is fun, and makes enchantment of the days. A little in love, a little taste of that hot, blinding cup—but only enough to stimulate, not to blind. One is so often a little in love. . . .

13

BILLY

BILLY left Oxford with his pass. His Liberal cousin accepted him, having it on the authority of Stanley, whom he greatly regarded, that Billy had the makings of a good secretary. Billy denied this, and said he would prefer to be a veterinary surgeon, or else to farm in a colony. But his mother had decided that he was to be political. Political. He thought he saw himself. . . . And anyhow, where was the sense of politics ? A jolly old mess the politicians made of things, and always had. . . . Somehow politics didn't seem a real thing, like vetting or farming. There was so much poppycock mixed up with it. . . .

But there it was. His mother must have her way. He supposed it would be a shame to disappoint her. Molly wouldn't look at politics, and one of them must. So in October he was to begin looking at them. One thing was, Giles Humphries probably wouldn't keep him long ; he'd soon see through him. . . .

" Doesn't make much odds, anyhow," he reflected, gloomily. " One damn silly job or another. Mother'll never let me do what I want. 'Tisn't good enough for her. I wish people wouldn't *want* things for one : wish they'd let one alone. Being let alone . . . that's the thing."

Rome said to Stanley, " You'll never make a politician of that boy. Why try ? "

" He's too young to say that about yet, Rome. I *should* like to see him doing some work for his country. . . ."

" They don't do that, my dear. You've been misinformed. I thought you went to the House sometimes. . . . Really, Stan, I can't imagine why you should try to turn Billy, who'd be some use in the world as an animals' doctor, or a tiller of the soil, or, I dare say, as a number of other things, into anything so futile and so useless and so singularly unsuited both to his talents and to his honest nature as a politician. I suppose you'll make him stand for Parliament eventually. Well, he'll quite likely get in. People will elect any one. But he'd only be bored and stupid and wretched there. He's got no gift of the gab, for one thing. You let the child do what he wants."

" I'm not forcing him. He knows he is free."

" He knows nothing of the sort. He knows you've set your heart on this, and he doesn't want to vex you. Really, you mothers. . . ."

So Billy, in the autumn of 1913, became the inefficient secretary of his kind, inefficient, Liberal cousin, who was, however, no more inefficient than his fellow-members of Parliament.

14

EXIT PAPA

THOSE were inefficient years; silly years, full of sound and fury, signifying nothing. They were not much sillier than usual, but there was rather more sound and fury than had been customary of late. It was made by militant suffragists, who smashed public property and burned private houses with an ever more ardent abandon; by Welsh churchmen, who marched through London declaring that on no account would they have their Church either disestablished or disendowed; by dock and transport strikers, who had a great outbreak of indomitability and determination in 1911, and another in 1912; by Mr. Lloyd George's Insurance Act, which caused much gnashing of teeth, foaming of mouths and flashing of eyes; by Liberals and Conservatives, who, for some reason, suddenly for a time abandoned that sporting good humour which has always made English political life what it is, a thing some like and others scorn, and took on to dislike each other, even leaving dinner parties to which members of the opposition party had been carelessly

invited ; and by the men of Ulster, who, being con-
vinced in their consciences that Home Rule would
be disastrous to the material well-being of Ulster,
covenanted to defeat the present conspiracy to set up
a Home Rule Parliament in Ireland, and, to this end,
got a quite good conspiracy going themselves. There
was also, it need hardly be said, plenty of sound and
fury on the Continent, particularly in the Balkans.

They make, these years, a noisy, silly, rowdy, but on
the whole cheery chapter of the idiot's tale. Howbeit,
they were less noisy and less silly, and far more cheery,
than the chapter which was to follow.

Just before this chapter began, papa died. Afterwards they said, it is a mercy papa is dead ; that he
died before the smash that would so have shattered
him. Papa, gentle and sensitive and eighty-four,
could scarcely have endured the great war. Down
what fresh avenues of faith it would have sent his
still adventurous soul exploring, seeking strength and
refuge from the nightmare, would never be known.
He died in May, 1914. He died as he had lived, a great
and wide believer, still murmuring, " I believe . . . I
believe . . . I believe . . ." a credulous, faithful,
comprehensive, happy Georgian. He had moments
when agnosticism or scepticism was the dominant
creed in his soul, but they were only moments ; soon
the tide of his many faiths would surge over him again,
and in all these he died.

" Dear papa," said Vicky, weeping. " To think that
he is with mamma at last ! And to think that now he
knows what is true. . . . Oh dear, how will he ever
get on without all those speculations and new beliefs ?
One knows, of course, that he is happy, darling papa
. . . but will he find it at all *same ?* "

Rome said, " Why ? Taking your hypothesis, that
there is another life, why should it be supposed to be a

revelation of the truth about the universe, or about God? Why should not papa go on speculating and guessing at truth, trying new faiths? You people who believe in what you call heaven seem to have no justification for making it out such an informed place."

" Oh, my dear; aren't we told that all shadows shall flee away, and that we shall *know*? I'm sure we are, somewhere, only you won't read the Bible ever."

" On the contrary, I read the Bible a good deal. I find it enormously interesting. But the one thing we can be quite sure about all those who wrote it is that they had no information at all as to what would occur to them after their deaths. That is among the very large quantity of information that no one alive has ever yet had. So, if you think of papa in heaven, why not think of him in the state in which he would certainly be happiest and most himself—still exploring for truth? Why should death bring a sudden knowledge of all the secrets of the universe? You believers make so many and such large and such unwarrantable assumptions."

" My dear, we must make assumptions, or how get through life at all? "

" Very true. How indeed? One must make a million unwarrantable assumptions, such as that the sun will rise to-morrow, and that the attraction of the earth for our feet will for a time persist, and that if we do certain things to our bodies they will cease to function, and that if we get into a train it will probably carry us along, and so forth. One must assume these things just enough to take action on them, or, as you say, we couldn't get through life at all. But those are hypothetical, pragmatical assumptions, for the purposes of action ; there is no call actually to believe them, intellectually. And still less call to increase their number, and carry assumption into spheres where it doesn't help us to action at all. For my part, I assume practically a great deal, intellectually nothing."

Vicky was going through her engagement book, seeing what she would have to cancel because of papa's death, and all she answered was, absently, " Dear papa ! "

SECOND PERIOD: SMASH

I

SOUND AND FURY

THE so bitter, so recent, so familiar, so agonising tale of the four years and a quarter between August, 1914, and November, 1918, has been told and re-told too often, and will not be told in detail here. It is enough, if not too much, to say that there was a great and dreadful war in Europe, and that nightmare and chaos and the abomination of desolation held sway for four horrid years. All there was of civilisation—whatever we mean by that unsatisfactory, undefined, relative word —suffered irretrievable damage. All there was of greed, of cruelty, of barbarism, of folly, incompetence, meanness, valour, heroism, selfishness, littleness, self-sacrifice and hate, rose to the call in each belligerent country and showed itself for what it was. Men and women acted blindly, according to their kind. They used the torments of others as stepping stones to prosperity or fame; they endured torments themselves, with complaining, with courage, or with both; they did work they held to be useful, and got out of it what credit and profit they could; or work they knew was folly, and still got out of it what they could. They went to the war, they stayed at home, they scrambled for jobs among the chaos, they got rich, they got poor, they died, were maimed, medalled, frost-bitten, tortured, imprisoned, bored, embittered, enthusiastic, cheerful, hopeless, patient, or matter-of-fact, according to circumstances and temperament. Many people said a great deal, others very little. There were all manner of different attitudes and ways of procedure with regard to the war. To some it was a necessary or unnecessary hell, to some a painful and tedious affair enough, but with interests and alleviations and a good goal in sight ; to some an adventure ; to some (at home) a satisfactory sphere for work they enjoyed ; to some a holy war ; to others a devil's dance in which they would take no part, or which they wearily did what they could to alleviate, or in which they joined with cynical and conscious resolve not to be left out of whatever profits might accrue.

But to the majority in each country it was merely a catastrophe, like an earthquake, to be gone through blindly, until better might be.

2

THE FAMILY AT WAR

OF the Garden family, Vicky was horrified but enthusiastically pro-war. Her two sons got commissions early, and she helped the war by organising bazaars and by doing whatever it was that one did (in the early stages, for in the later more of violence had to be done) to Belgian refugees. Maurice and his paper were violently pacificist, and became a byword. Rome saw the war and what had led up to it as the very crown and sum of human folly, and helped, very capably and neatly, to pack up and send off food and clothes to British prisoners. Stanley was caught in the tide of war fervour. She worked in a canteen, and served on committees for all kinds of good objects, and behaved with great competence and energy, her heart wrung day and night with fear for Billy. In 1917 she caught peace fever, joined the peace party and the Women's International League, signed petitions and manifestos in support of Lord Lansdowne, and spoke on platforms about it, which Billy thought tiresome of her.

Irving lent a car to an ambulance, and his services to the Ministry of Munitions, and became a special constable. Una sent cakes to her sons and farm-hands at the front, and employed land-girls on the farm. She took the war as all in the day's work; there had been wars before in history, and there would be wars again. It was awfully sad, all the poor boys being taken like that; but it sent up the price of corn and milk, and that pleased Ted, for all his anxiety for his sons.

The younger generation acted and reacted much as might be expected of them. Vicky's Hugh, who joined the gunners, was interested in the business and came tolerably well through it, only sustaining a lame leg. Tony, his younger brother, was killed in 1916. Maurice's Roger, whose class was B2, served in France for a year, and wrote a good deal of trench poetry. He was then invalided out, and entered the Ministry of Information, where he continued, in the intervals of compiling propaganda intended to interest the Green-land Esquimaux in the cause of the Allies, to publish trench poetry, full of smells, shells, corpses, mud and blood.

" I simply can't read the poetry you write in these days, Roger," his mother Amy complained. " It's become too terribly beastly and nasty and corpsey. I can't think what you want to write it for, I'm sure."

" Unfortunately, mother," Roger explained, kindly, " war *is* rather beastly and nasty, you know. And a bit corpsey, too."

" My dear boy, I know that; I'm not an idiot.

Don't, for goodness' sake, talk to me in that superior way, it reminds me of your father. All I say is, why *write* about the corpses ? There've always been plenty of them, people who've died in their beds of diseases. You never used to write about *them*."

" I suppose one's object is to destroy the false glamour of war. There's no glamour about disease."

" Glamour, indeed ! There you go again with that terrible nonsense. I don't meet any of these people you talk about who think there's glamour in war. I'm sure *I* never saw any glamour in it, with all you boys in the trenches and all of us at home slaving ourselves to death and starving on a slice of bread and margarine a day. Glamour, indeed. I'll tell you what it is, a set of you young men have invented that glamour theory, just so as to have an excuse for what you call destroying it, with your nasty talk. Like you've invented those awful Old Men you go on about, who like the war. I'm sick of your Old Men and your corpses."

" I'm sick of them myself," said Roger gloomily, and changed the subject, for you could not argue with Amy. But he went on writing war poetry, and gained a good deal of reputation as one of our soldier poets. On the whole, he was more successful as a poet than as a propagandist to the Esquimaux, a phlegmatic people, who remained a little detached about the war.

Stanley's Billy hailed the outbreak of hostilities with some pleasure, and was among the first civilians to enlist. Here, he felt, was a job more in his line than being secretary to his Liberal cousin, which he had found more and more tedious as time passed. He fought in France, in Flanders, in Gallipoli, and in Mesopotamia, was wounded three times, and recovered each time to fight again. He was a cheerful, ordinary, unemotional young soldier, a good deal bored, after a bit, with the war. On one of his leaves, in 1916, he married a young lady from the Vaudeville Theatre, whom Stanley could not care about.

"I know mother wanted me to marry a highbrow girl," he confided to Molly. "Some girl who's been to college or something. But I haven't much to say to that sort ever, nor they to me. Now Dot . . ."

But even Molly had her misgivings about Dot. She was not sure that Dot would prove quite monogamous enough. And, as it turned out, Dot did not prove monogamous at all, but rather the contrary.

Molly herself had become an ambulance driver in France. She frankly enjoyed the war. She became engaged to officers, successively and simultaneously. She acted at canteen entertainments, and gained a charming reputation as a comedienne. At the end of the war she received the O.B.E. for her distinguished services.

Her mother knew about some of the engagements, and thought them too many, but did not know that Molly had for a time been more than engaged. She never would know that, for Molly kept her own counsel. Molly knew that to Stanley, with her idealistic view of life and her profound belief in the enduring seriousness of personal relations, it would have seemed incredibly trivial, light and loose to be a lover and pass on, to commit oneself so deeply and yet not count it deep at all, but emerge free and untrammelled for the next adventure. It had seemed incredible to Stanley in her husband; it would seem more incredible in her daughter.

"Mother's so different," thought Molly. "She'd never understand. . . . Aunt Rome's different too, but she'd understand about me; she always understands things, even if she despises them. She *would* despise this, but she wouldn't be surprised. . . .

Mother would be hurt to death. She must never, never guess."

As to Vicky's daughters, Phyllis was useful in some competent, part-time, married way that may be imagined. Nancy turned violently anti-war and became engaged to a Hungarian artist, who was subsequently removed from his studio in Chelsea and interned. Imogen was everything by turns and nothing long. The war very greatly discomposed her. It seemed to her a very shocking outrage both that there should be a war, and that, since there was a war, she should be found, owing to a mere fluke of sex, among the non-combatants. The affair was a horrid nightmare, which she had to stand and watch. People of her age simply weren't non-combatants ; that was how she felt about it. Strong, active people in the twenties ; it seemed a disgrace to her, who had never before so completely realised that she was not, in point of fact, a young man. War was ghastly and beastly ; but if it was there, people like her ought to be in it. However, since this was obviously impossible, she sulkily and simultaneously joined a pacificist league and became a V.A.D., in the hope of getting out to France. She was an infinitely incapable V.A.D., did everything with remarkable incompetence, and fainted or was sick when her senses and nerves were more displeased than usual by what they encountered, which was often. She was soon told that she had no gifts for nursing and had better stick to cleaning the wards. This she did, with relief, for some time, until her friends said, why not get a job in a government office, which was much more lucrative and amusing. Sick of hospitals, she did so. She was under no delusions as to the usefulness of any work she was likely to do in an office ; but still, one had to do something. She could not write ; her jarred, unhappy nerves sought and found a certain degree of oblivion in the routine, the cameraderie, the demoralising absurdity, of office work, which was like being at school again. Also, it was paid, and, as she could not write, she must earn money somehow.

So, indolent, greedy, unbalanced, trivial and demoralised, Imogen, like many others, drifted through the great war. Two deaths occurred to her—the death of her brother and companion, Tony, which blackened life and made the war seem to her more than ever a hell of futile devilry ; and the death of Neville, a young naval officer, to whom she had become engaged in 1915, and who was killed in 1916. It was a queer affair, born of the emotionalism and sensation-seeking that beset many people at that time. She had not known him long ; she did not know him well. She was aware that it was ignominious of her to encourage him, merely on the general love she bore to the navy, a little flattered excitement, and a desire, new-born, to experience the sensation of engagement. They had few thoughts in common, but they could joke together, and talk of ships, and of how they loved one another, and about him was the glamour of the navy, and she felt, when he kissed her, that stimulation of the emotions and senses that passes for love. When they talked about things in general, and not about their love, she heard within her that cold voice that never lied saying, " You cannot live with this nice young naval man. You will tire each other." Worse, they sometimes shocked one another. Could it be—disastrous thought—that she had outgrown the navy ?

" You're a rum kid, darling," he said to her. " You and I disagree about nearly everything, it seems to me. We shall have a lively married life. . . . But I don't care. . . ."

But he did care a little, all the same. Imogen sometimes suspected that, like herself, he had begun to think they had made a mistake. But then he would take her in his arms, and when they embraced neither of them felt that they had made a mistake.

However, one is not embracing all the time, and Imogen slowly came to the point, between one leave and another, of deciding to end the affair. The navy and she had grown away from each other ; there was no doubt about that.

But before they could discuss this point, Neville was killed at Jutland.

Imogen wept for him, and believed for a time that she loved him profoundly and missed him horribly. But the small, cold voice within her that never lied whispered, " You are only sorry that he is dead for his sake, because he loved being alive and ought to be alive. You sometimes miss his kisses and his love, but you are glad that you are free."

She spent an unhappy week-end with his parents in the country. These did not very greatly care for her, only for Neville's sake. Neville's father was a rector, very simple and village, his mother a rector's wife, very parochial and busy. With them, Imogen felt leggy and abrupt, and the wrong kind of girl. She couldn't be articulate with them, or show them how bitterly she felt Neville's death before he had properly lived. They were unhappy but not bitter ; they said, " It was God's will," and she could not tell them that, in her view, they spoke inaccurately and blasphemed. Yet their hearts were (to use the foolish phrase) broken, and hers by no means. She caught Neville's mother looking at her speculatively from behind her glasses, and wondered if she were wondering how much this gauche young woman had loved her boy. She wanted to beg her pardon and dash for the next train. They could not want her with them ; to have her was a duty they thought they owed to Neville. " I've no right here," she cried to herself. " They loved him. I was only in love with his love for me. Their lives are spoilt, mine isn't."

She did not visit them again. That was over. Neville took his place in her memory, not as a personal loss, but as a gay, heartbreaking figure, a tragic symbol of murdered, outraged youth.

But when Tony was killed, the world's foundations shook. He was her darling brother, her beloved companion in adventure, scrapes and enterprises from their childhood up. She could by no means recover from the cruel death of Tony, which shattered the life of his home.

But daily work in an office, so cheerful, so fruitless, so absurd, was an anodyne. Offices were full of people who did not mind the war, who, some of them, rather enjoyed the war. There are no places more cynical than the offices of governments. Not parliaments in session, not statesmen in council, not cardinals in conclave, not even journalists emitting their folly in the dead of the night. Encased in an armour of this easy cynicism against the savage darts of the most horrid war, Imogen and many others drifted through its last years to the war's cynical culmination, the horrid but welcome peace.

THIRD PERIOD: DÉBRIS

I

PEACE

A HORRID peace it was and is. It is the fashion to say so, and, unlike most fashionable sayings, it is true. But at first the fact that it *was* peace, that people were not killing each other (in such large numbers and for such small reasons) any more, was enough, and made every one happy. A poor peace enough: but the fact remains that the worst peace is heaven compared with the best war. It was like the first return of chocolate éclairs. "They're rather funny ones," people said, "not quite like the old kind; but still, they *are* éclairs." So peace. It was indeed a rather funny one, not quite like the old kind; but still, it was peace. And what, if you come to that, was the old kind, that any other should be compared unfavourably with it? The trouble is, perhaps, rather that this new variety *is* like it.

The Peace Treaty has been called all kinds of names —patchwork, violent, militarist, manufactured, makeshift, frail, silly, uneconomic, unstatesmanlike; and all the names except the last may be true. (Unstatesmanlike the treaty was certainly not; very few treaties drawn up by statesmen unfortunately are that; and, in fact, this word unstatesmanlike seems often to be curiously and thoughtlessly used, in a sense directly contrary to that which it should bear.) Well, even if nearly all these opprobrious names were true, it seems

a pity to be always discontented. Wiser were those
who encouraged the infant, patted it on the back,
and greeted the unseen with a cheer. Like beer, like
shoe leather, it seemed costly and poor. But who were
we, that we could afford to be particular ? " We've
got," said the resigned citizen, " to put up with these
poor, nasty-looking things, that last no time at all.
Beer it's not, and shoe leather it's not, and peace it
won't be, properly speaking. A kind of substitute
they all are, like margarine. But what I say is, we're
lucky to get them." So we were.

Idealists, such as Stanley Croft, though they did not
admire the Treaty of Versailles, saw it as the material
out of which the living temple of peace might yet be
built, on that great corner-stone, the League of Nations.
The League of Nations was to the peace-wishers as
his creed is to the Christian ; it bound them to believe
in a number of difficult, happy, unlikely and highly
incompatible things, such as lasting peace, the freedom
of small nations, arbitration between large ones, and
so forth. They joined the League of Nations Union,
full of hope and faith. Stanley did so, at its inception,
and became, in fact, a speaker on platforms in the
cause.

2

THE LAST HOPE

STANLEY, in her late fifties, looked and spoke well on
platforms ; she looked both nice and important. Her
blue eyes, under their thick, level brows, were as starry
as ever, her voice as deep and full and good, her mind
young and alert. A clever, high-minded, balanced,
vigorous, educated matron of close on sixty ; that was

what Stanley was. She was the kind of matron to whom younger women gave their confidence. Her son and daughter did not give her their whole confidence, but that was not her fault.

Billy was demobilised. A seamed scar cut across his cheek, and his eyes were queer and sulky and brooding. He disliked by now his wife Dot. She reciprocated the feeling, and very soon left him for another, so he divorced her. Stanley could not help being glad, Dot had been such a mistake. She was not the kind of wife to help her husband in his parliamentary career. She was more the kind who succeeds him in it, but even that Stanley could not know in 1919, and she regarded Dot, as, from every point of view, a wash-out.

" Look here, mother," Billy said to her, with nervous, sulky decision, " I can't go back to that secretary job. Nor any other job of that kind. Sitting jobs and writing jobs bore me stiff. I've done too much sitting, in those beastly trenches. And politics anyhow seem to me plain rot. I want to train for a vet. I'm awfully sorry if you're sick about it, but there it is. Why don't you make Molly take on a secretary-to-a-Liberal job ? She couldn't be worse than I was, anyhow."

"A vet, Billy ! Darling boy, why a vet ? Why not a human doctor, if you must be something of that sort ? "

" Want to be a vet," said Billy, and was.

As to Molly, she became secretary to no Liberal, for she married, in 1919, a flight commander, and his politics, if any, were Coalition-Unionist.

So much for Stanley's hopes for political careers for her children. She sighed, and accepted the inevitable, and put her hope more than ever in the League of Nations. If that could not save the world, nothing could. . . .

Certainly nothing could, said Rome. Nothing ever had yet. At least, what did people mean, precisely, by save? Words, words, words. They signified, as commonly and lightly used, so very little.

3

THE CHARABANC

THE post-war period swung and jolted along, like a crazy, broken-down charabanc full of persons of varying degrees of mental weakness, all out on an asylum treat. Every now and then the charabanc stopped for a picnic, or conference, at some nice Continental or English watering-place, and there were very cosy, chatty, happy, expensive little times, enjoyed by all, and really not doing very much more harm to Europe than any other form of treat would have done, since they had, as a rule (the amusing reconstruction of the map of Europe once effected), practically no effects of any kind, beyond, of course, strengthening the already perfect harmony prevalent among the victorious allied nations.

Reparations was the great topic at these chats; but it was and is such a very difficult topic that no one there (no one there being very clever) made much of it, and it has not really been decided about even now.

International politics were, in fact, in the years following the great war, even more greatly confused than is usual. Only one great international principle remained, as ever, admirably lucid—that principle so simply explained by M. Anatole France's Penguin peasant to the Porpoise philosopher.

" Vous n'aimez pas les Marsouins? "

" Nous les haïssons."

" Pour quelle raison les haïssez-vous ? "

" Vous le demandez ? Les Marsouins ne sont-ils pas les voisins des Pingouins ? "

" Sans doute."

" Eh bien, c'est pour cela que les Pingouins haïssent les Marsouins."

" Est-ce une raison ? "

" Certainement. Qui dit voisins dit ennemis. . . . Vous ne savez donc pas ce que c'est que le patriotisme ? "

There was no confusion here.

Home politics, in each country, seemed to lack even this dominant *motif*, and confusion reigned unrelieved. In Great Britain a Coalition Government was in power. The usual view about this government is that it was worse and more incompetent than other governments ; but it seems bold to go as far as this. "The nation wants a return to a frank party government," non-coalition Liberals and Conservatives began saying, and said without intermission until they got it, in 1923. They sometimes explained why they preferred a frank party government, but none of their reasons seemed very good reasons ; the real reason was that they, very properly and naturally, wished their own party to be in power. The Die-Hards and the Wee Frees came to be regarded as valiant, incorruptible little bands, daring to stand alone ; Co-Liberals and Co-Unionists were understood, somehow, to have compromised with Satan for reward. There is a good deal of unkindness in political life.

4

SETTLING DOWN

MEANWHILE, the people settled down, were demobilised from the army, and from the various valuable services which they had been rendering to their country, and began to fall back into the old grooves, began to recover, at least partially, from the war. But the war had left its heritage, of poverty, of wealth, of disease, of misery, of discontent, of feverish unrest.

"Now to write again," said Imogen, and did so, but found it difficult, for the nervous strain of the years past, and the silliness of the avocations she had pursued through them, had paralysed initiative, and given her, in common with many others, an inclination to sally forth after breakfast and catch a train or a bus, seeking such employment as might be created for her, instead of creating her own. The helpless industry of the slave had become hers, and to regain that of the independent and self-propelled worker was a slow business.

Further, she was absorbed, shaken and disturbed by a confusing and mystifying love into which she had fallen, blind and unaware, even before peace had descended. All values were to her subverted ; she fumbled blindly at a world grown strange, a world as to whose meaning and whose laws she groped in the dark, and emotion drowned her like a flood.

There revived in force about this time the curious old legend about the young. The post-war young, they were now called, and once more people began to believe and to say that one young person closely resembles other young persons, and many more things about them.

" The war," they said, " has caused a hiatus, and
thought has broken with tradition. Thus youth is no
longer willing to accept forms and formulæ only on
account of their age. It has set out on a voyage of
inquiry, and, finding some things which are doubtful
and others which are insufficient, is searching for
forms of expression more in harmony with the realities
of life and knowledge."

Many novels were written about the New Young,
half in reprobation, half in applause ; famous literary
men praised them in speeches ; they were much spoken
of in newspapers. All the things were said of them
that have been said of the young at all times, only now
their newness, their special quality, was attributed to
the European war, in which they were too young to
have actively participated, but which had, it was
believed, exercised upon them some mystic and trans-
muting influence. Once more the legend flourished
that the number of years lived constitutes some kind
of temperamental bond, so that people of the same
age are many minds with but a single thought, bearing
one to another a close resemblance. The young were
commented on as if they were some new and just
discovered species of animal life, with special qualities
and habits which repaid investigation. " Will these
qualities wear off ? " precise-minded and puzzled
inquirers asked, " when the present young are thirty
and middle-aged, will they still possess them ? Do the
qualities depend upon their age, or upon the period of
the world's history in which they happen to be that
age ? " But no precise or satisfactory reply was ever
given. It never is. Inquirers into the exact meaning
of popular theories and phrases are of all persons the
least and the worst answered. You may, for instance,
inquire of a popular preacher, or any one else, who
denounces his countrymen as " pagan " (as speakers,

and even Bishops, at religious gatherings have been known to do) what, exactly, he means by this word, and you will find that he means irreligious, and is apparently oblivious of the fact that pagans were and are, in their village simplicity, the most religious persons who have ever flourished, having more gods to the square mile than the Christian or any other Church has ever possessed or desired, and paying these gods more devout and more earnest devotion than you will meet even among Anglo-Catholics in congress. To be pagan may not be very intelligent; it is rustic and superstitious, but it is at least religious. Yet you will hear the word " pagan " flung loosely about for " irreligious," or sometimes as meaning joyous, material and comfort-loving, whereas the simple pagans walked the earth full of what is called holy awe and that mystic faith in unseen powers which is the antithesis of materialism, and gloomy with apprehension of the visitations of their horrid and vindictive gods; and, though no doubt, like all men, they loved comfort, they only obtained, just as we do, as much of that as they could afford. And, whatever Bishops mean by pagan, as applied to modern Englishmen, it is almost certain that they do not mean all this.

Never, perhaps, was thinking, writing and talking looser, vaguer, and more sentimental than in the years following the European war. It was as if that disaster had torn great holes in the human intelligence, which it could ill afford. There was much writing, both of verse and prose, much public and private speaking, much looking for employment and not finding it, much chat about the building of new houses, much foolish legislation, much murder and suicide, much amazement on the part of the press. Newspapers are always easily amazed, but since the war weakened even their intelligence there could not be so much as a little extra departure from railway stations on a Bank Holiday (surely most natural, if one thinks it out) without the ingenuous press placarding London with "Amazing scenes." The press was even amazed if a married couple sought divorce, or if it thundered, or was at all warm. "Scenes," they would say, "scenes;" and the eager reader, searching their columns for these, could find none worthy of the name. One pictures newspaper reporters going about, struck dumb with amazement at every smallest incident in this amazing life we lead, hurrying iack to their offices and communicating their emotion to editors, news editors and leader writers, so that the whole staff gapes, round-eyed, at the astonishing world on which they have to comment. An ingenuous race; but they make the mistake of forgetting that many of their readers are so very experienced thay they are seldom surprised at anything.

During these years, the sex disability as regards the suffrage being now removed, women stood freely for Parliament, but the electorate, being mostly of the male sex, showed that the only women they desired to have in Parliament were the wives of former members who had ceased to function as such, through death, peerage, or personal habits. Many women, including Stanley Croft, who, of course, stood herself, found this very disheartening. It seemed that the only chance for a woman who desired a political career was to marry a member and then put him out of action. Such women as were political in their own persons, who were educated and informed on one or more public topics, had small chance. "We don't want to be ruled by the ladies," the electorate firmly maintained. "It's not their job. Their place is, etc."

The world had not changed much since the reign of Queen Victoria.

And so, with the French firmly and happily settled
in the Ruhr, their hearts full of furious fancies, declaring
that it would not be French to stamp on a beaten foe,
but that their just debts they would have, with Germany
rapidly breaking to pieces, drifting towards the rocks
of anarchy or monarchy, and working day and night
at the industry of printing million-mark notes, with
Russia damned, as usual, beyond any conceivable
recovery, with Italy suffering from a violent attack of
Fascismo, with Austria counted quite out, with a set
of horrid, noisy and self-conscious little war-born
States in the heart of Europe, all neighbours and all
feeling and acting as such, with Turkey making of herself as much of an all-round nuisance as usual, with
Great Britain anxiously, perspiringly endeavouring
both to arrest the progressive wreckage of Europe and
to keep on terms with her late allies, and with Ireland
enjoying at last the peace and blessings of Home Rule,
Europe entered on her fifth year since the Armistice.

5

A NOTE ON MAURICE

In this year Maurice's paper perished, having long
ceased to pay its way, and, in fact, like so many papers,
suffering loss on each copy that was bought. This is
as natural a state of affairs for papers as living on over-
drafts is for private persons, but neither state, unfortunately, can last for ever. The money behind the
Gadfly at last gave out, and the *Gadfly* ceased to be.
Maurice, at the age of sixty-five, was deprived of his
job and his salary, and became a free-lance, but no
less fiery and stubborn, journalist. There were more
things to oppose, in his view, than ever before, and he

opposed them at large, in the hospitable pages of many
a friendly periodical. His opposition had no effect
on the affairs of the world, but, in combination with an
adequate supply of alcoholic nourishment and his
blessed emancipation from married life, it caused him
to remain self-respecting and fit, kept senility at bay,
and assisted him to bear up against the repeated shocks
of Roger's published works.

6

A NOTE ON IMOGEN

THE P. & O. liner hooted its way down Southampton
Water. The land, the Solent, the open sea, were
veiled in February mist. Imogen, leaning on the rail
and straining her eyes shoreward, could only see it
dimly, darkly, looming like a ghost through fog. That
was England, and life in England ; a mist-bound
world wherein one blindly groped. A mist-bound
and yet radiant world, holding all one valued, all that
gave life meaning, all that one was leaving behind.

For Imogen was going, for a year, to the Pacific
Islands. Hugh, too, was going there, to make maps
and plans for the government. Imogen was going
with him, exploring, wandering about at leisure from
island to island. The perfect life, she had once believed
this to be. And still the thought of coral islands, of
palm and yam and bread-fruit trees, with the fruits
thereof dropping ripely on emerald grass, with monkeys
and gay parrakeets screaming in the branches, and
great turtles flopping in blue seas, with beachcombers
drinking palm-toddy on white beaches, the crystal-
clear lagoon in which to swim, and, beyond, the blue,
island-dotted open sea,—even now these things tugged

at Imogen's heartstrings and made her feel again at
moments the adventurous little girl she had once
been, dreaming romantic dreams.

But more often this bright, still world beyond the
mists seemed like the paradise of a hymn, a far, un-
natural, brilliant, alien place, which would make one
sick for home.

Yet she had chosen to go, and no remonstrances,
repentances and waverings had quite undone that
choice. In that far, bright, clear, alien place, beyond
the drifting mists, perhaps thought, too, was lucid and
unconfused, not the desperate, mist-bound, storm-
driven, helpless business it was in London. In London
all values and all meanings were fluid, were as windy
clouds, drifting and dissolving into strange shapes.
Life bore too intense, too passionate, an emotional
significance ; personal relationships were too tangled ;
clear thought was drowned in desire. One could not
see life whole, only a flame, a burning star, at its heart.

Through years and years this could not go on ; the
entanglement of circumstance, the enmeshing of soul
and will, was too close for any unravelling ; it could
only be cut. Under the knife that cut it—and yet
was it cut at all, or only hacked all in vain ?—Imogen's
soul seemed to bleed to death, to bleed and swoon
quite away.

What had she done, and why ? All reasons seemed
to reel from sight as they churned for open sea between
those mist-blind shores. Parrakeets ? Bread-fruit ?
Lagoons and coral reefs ? Oh, God, she cared for none
of them. She had been mad, mad, mad.

" *To leave me for so long . . . you can't mean to do
it. . . .*"

Above the turning, churning screws the hurt voice
spoke, how truly, and stabbed her through once more.
Can't mean to do it . . . can't do it . . . can't. . . .

Oh, how very true indeed. And yet she must do it and would. It was no use; it would solve nothing, settle nothing; merely for a year she would be sick for home among the alien yams.

But, at the thought of the yams, and the bread-fruit, and the grass and parrakeets more green than any imagining, and of the very blue lagoons, a little comfort stole into her heavy heart. A merry beach-comber on a white beach—that was a thing to be, even if nothing could be a really happy arrangement but to be two merry beachcombers together. At the thought of the two merry beachcombers who might have been so very happy, the tears brimmed and blinded Imogen's eyes.

What a mess, what a mess, what a bitter, bemusing muddle, life was! One renounced its best gifts, those things in it which seemed finest, most ennobling, most enriching, holding most of beauty and of good; these things one renounced, and filled the dreadful gap with turtles, with a little palm-toddy, with a few foolish parrakeets.

What an irony!

Through the blinding mist, above the rushing sound of foaming waters, the voice cried to her, "*Imogen, Imogen . . . come back. . . .*"

Imogen wept.

Alas for the happy vagabond, fallen into such sad state.

7

FINAL

ROME saw Stanley off to Geneva. Stanley had obtained employment in the Labour department of the League of Nations. She was pleased, and keen, and full of hope. The League would save the world yet. . . .

"It's going to be the most interesting work of my life, so far," said Stanley, leaning out of the train. "To find one's best job at sixty-two—that's rather nice, I think. Life's so full of *hope*, Rome. Oh, I do feel happy about it."

"Good," said Rome, and "Good-bye, my dear," for the train began to move.

"Good-bye, Romie. . . . Take care of yourself: you're looking tired lately."

"I'm very old, you see," Rome said, after the retreating train, and a passer-by, turning to glance at the slight, erect, gray-haired lady, thought that she did not look very old at all.

But she was very old, for she would soon be sixty-four, and, further, she was very tired, for she had cancer coming on, inherited from mamma. She had not mentioned it to any one yet, beyond the doctor, who had told her that, unless she had operations, she would die within a year. Operations nothing, Rome had said; such a bore, and only to prolong the agony; if she had to die, she would die as quickly as might be. She further decided that, before the pain should become acute or the illness overwhelming, she would save trouble to herself and others by an apparently careless overdose of veronal. Meanwhile, she had a few months to live.

The thought that it would only, probably, be a few months, set her considering, as she drove herself home in her car, her practised hands steady on the wheel, life, its scope, its meaning, and its end. Life was well enough, she thought; well enough, and a gay enough business for those who had the means to make it so and the temperament to find it so. Life was no great matter, and nor, certainly, was death; but it was well enough. We come and we go; we are born, we live, and we die; this poor ball, thought Rome, serves us for all that; and, on the whole, we make

too much complaint of it, expect, one way and another,
too much of it. It is, after all, but a turning ball,
which has burst, for some reason unknown to science,
into a curious, interesting and rather unwholesome
form of animal and vegetable life. Indeed, thought
Rome, I think it is a rather remarkable ball. But of
course it can be but of the slightest importance, from
the point of view of the philosopher who considers the
very great extent and variety of the universe and the
extremely long stretching of the ages. Its inhabitants
tend to overrate its importance in the scheme of things.
Human beings surely tend to overrate their own importance. Funny, hustling, strutting, vain, eager little
creatures that we are, so clever and so excited about
the business of living, so absorbed and intent about it
all, so proud of our achievements, so tragically deploring
our disasters, so prone to talk about the wreckage of
civilisation, as if it mattered much, as if civilisations had
not been wrecked and wrecked all down human history,
and it all came to the same thing in the end. Nevertheless, thought Rome, we are really rather wonderful
little spurts of life. The brief pageant, the tiny, squalid
story of human life upon this earth, has been lit, among
the squalor and the greed, by amazing flashes of intelligence, of valour, of beauty, of sacrifice, of love. A
silly story if you will, but a somewhat remarkable
one. Told by an idiot, and not a very nice idiot at
that, but an idiot with gleams of genius and of fineness.
The valiant dust that builds on dust—how valiant,
after all, it is. No achievement can matter, and all
things done are vanity, and the fight for success and
the world's applause is contemptible and absurd, like
a game children play, building their sand castles which
shall so soon one and all collapse ; but the queer, enduring spirit of enterprise which animates the dust we
are is not contemptible nor absurd.

Rome mused, running leisurely across Hyde Park, of herself, her parents, and sisters and brothers, of how variously they had all taken life. Her papa had made of it a great spiritual adventure. Her mamma —what had mamma made of life ? She had, anyhow, accepted papa and his spiritual adventure, and accepted all her children and their lives. And yet, always and always, mamma had remained delicately apart, detached, too gentle to be called cynical, too practical to be called a philosopher, too shrewd to be deceived by life. Dear mamma. Rome very often missed her still. As to Vicky, she had skimmed gracefully over life's surface like a swallow, dipping her pretty wings in the shallows and splashing them about, or like a bee, sipping and tasting each flower. She had plunged frequently, ardently, and yet lightly, into life. Maurice had not plunged into life ; he had fought it, opposed it, treated it as an enemy in a battle ; he had made no terms with it. Stanley had, on the other hand, embraced it like a lover, or like a succession of lovers, to each of which she gave the best of her heart and soul and mind before she passed on to the next. Stanley believed in life, that it was or could be splendid and divine. Irving and Una both accepted it calmly, cheerfully, without speculation, as a good enough thing, Irving with more of enterprise and more of progressive desire, Una placidly, statically, eating the meal set before her and wishing nothing more, nothing less. Both these accepted.

And Rome herself had rejected. Without opposition and without heat, she had refused to be made an active participant in the business, but had watched it from her seat in the stalls as a curious and entertaining show. That was, and must always, in any circumstances, have been her way. Had she married, or had she gone away, long ago, with Mr. Jayne, would she then have been forced into some closer, some more intimate spiritual relationship with the show? Possibly. Or possibly not. Life is infinitely compelling, but the spirit remains infinitely itself.

Anyhow, it mattered not at all. Life, whatever it had, whatever it might have, meant to her, was in its last brief lap.

> *And all our yesterdays have lighted fools*
> *The way to dusty death. . . ."*

Her little drift of dust was so soon to return and subside whence it came, dust to dust.

She thought that she would miss the queer, absurd show, which would go on with its antics without her, down who knew what æons. Perhaps not very many after all; perhaps all life was before long dustily to subside, leaving the ball, like a great revolving tomb, to spin its way through space. Or perhaps the ball itself would dash suddenly from its routine spinning, would fly, would rush like a moth for a lamp, to some great, bright sun and there burst into flame, till its last drift of ashes should be consumed and no more seen.

A drift of dust, a drift of storming dust. It settles, and the little stir it has made is over and forgotten. The winds will storm on among the bright and barren stars.

Rome smiled, as she neatly swung out at the Grosvenor Gate.

EMILIE ROSE MACAULAY

(1881-1958) was born at Rugby, Warwickshire; her father was an assistant master at Rugby School. Due to her mother's ill health the family moved, in 1887, to a small Italian town, Varazze, where they lived for seven years. She was then educated at Oxford High School for Girls, and Somerville College, Oxford, where she read Modern History.

While living with her family in Wales, Rose Macaulay wrote her first novel, *Abbots Verney* (1906), published after they had moved to Great Shelford, near Cambridge. It was here that Rose become an ardent Anglo-Catholic. Here, too, her childhood friendship with Rupert Brooke matured and through him she was introduced to London literary society: Walter de la Mare, Hugh Walpole, John Middleton Murry and Naomi Royde-Smith in particular. She moved to London and in 1914 published her first book of poetry, *The Two Blind Countries*.

During the First World War she worked at the War Office where, in 1918, she met the novelist and former Catholic priest Gerald O'Donovan, the married man with whom she was to have an affair lasting until his death from cancer in 1942. Throughout these years Rose was to become a voluntary exile from the church, her reconciliation only being effected in her seventieth year. Before and between the Wars Rose Macaulay wrote at least one novel every two years, as well as essays, poetry and criticism. This flow, however, was dramatically interrupted by the advent of the Second World War, seeing the destruction of her flat and loss of her entire library.

A traveler all her life, Rose Macaulay went to Trebizond in 1954. This inspired her last and most famous novel, *The Towers of Trebizond* (1956), which was awarded a James Tait Black Memorial prize and became a bestseller in America. She was created a Dame Commander of the British Empire in the 1958 New Year's Honours, but seven months later, having started a new novel, Rose Macaulay suffered a heart attack and died at her home.